Books by B. V. Larson:

## Undying Mercenaries Series:
*Steel World*
*Dust World*
*Tech World*
*Machine World*
*Death World*
*Home World*
*Rogue World*
*Blood World*
*Dark World*
*Storm World*
*Armor World*
*Clone World*
*Glass World*
*Edge World*
*Green World*
*Ice World*
*City World*
*Sky World*
*Jungle World*
*Crystal World*
*Throne World*

Visit BVLarson.com for more information.

# Throne World

(Undying Mercenaries Series #21)
by
B. V. Larson

Copyright © 2024 by Iron Tower Press.

This book is a work of fiction. Names, characters, places and incidents are either products of the author's imagination or used fictitiously. Any resemblance to actual events, locales or persons, living or dead, is entirely coincidental. All rights reserved. No part of this publication can be reproduced or transmitted in any form or by any means, without permission in writing from the author.

ISBN-13: 979-8324588571
BISAC:    Fiction / Science Fiction / Military

*"Let them hate, so long as they fear."*
— Emperor Caligula, 38 AD

## -1-

A few months back, Etta and Derrick had gotten married. They'd tied the knot almost in secret—which made sense to me. Any girl who was marrying a hog *should* feel ashamed. Anyways, at least this twist of fate was over and done with.

Or so I thought.

My momma wasn't happy. She wanted a *real* wedding, and she kept carrying on about it for weeks. Finally, Etta relented, and they started planning.

I was long in the face by April, I don't mind telling you. By then, they'd managed to stretch out a simple one-and-done ceremony into a giant shindig. In addition to my humiliation over being the father of a hog-bride, I was going to have to shell out big-time for a full-blown spring wedding.

Naturally, the women were dead set on doing the deed in the backyard. I dutifully pointed out that outdoor weddings were always a gamble. I was against it—hell, I'd been against Etta getting married in the first place—but what young bride ever listened to her daddy when she was planning her big day?

In the end, we got lucky. The weather was perfect, a nice roll of the dice for an April afternoon in southern Georgia Sector. Saturday morning dawned clear and bright, with a breeze whispering through the blossoming dogwoods. The temperature was comfortable, too. A storm had just ripped through on Thursday, but there was no hint of it left in the blue skies above us today.

By noontime, the sun cast its warm embrace over the backwoods and the boglands beyond. The winds were even on our side, blowing in fresh, stink-free air from the east.

As to the venue itself, my tottering momma and all her church-friends had done a bang-up job turning our ratty scrap of land into a private garden. The backyard had been transformed after a great deal of work—much of which consisted of my dad and I dragging rusty farm equipment back around behind the sheds so you couldn't see it. My dad, grumbling and daunted by the workload, had even rented one of those new-fangled gardening machines that trimmed all the hoary old bushes and saplings automatically. Hell, even the grass in front of my shack was cropped short and plucked weed-free.

Rows of white chairs were neatly aligned on the newly manicured back lawn. Each chair was adorned with a shiny pink ribbon that fluttered softly in the breeze. At the end of the aisle, one of those flower-arch things stood tall and proud. It was intricately decorated with a cascade of white and pink flowers. A whole henhouse worth of church-ladies had come up with that contraption—but it looked real nice after all the fuss was over and done with.

Carlos arrived a few hours before the ceremony. He was the only guest I'd asked to attend. Della was here too, of course. She was Etta's momma, after all. She stood among the bustling women who were putting the final touches on the plastic dining tables where the reception was to be held after the ceremony. She looked even more lost and confused than I did.

Something bumped my hand—something cold. It was an icy brew.

"Drink up, big guy," Carlos said.

I didn't need any urging. I upended the bottle and drained half of it, wiping my mouth with my sleeve. I grimaced after that. The rented monkey-suit Etta had put me into now had a stain on the sleeve. I shrugged, uncaring. It would probably soak in and disappear by the time the guests arrived, anyways.

"I can't even believe they're doing this," I said.

"What?" Carlos asked, looking at me sharply. "Setting up so much junk for a one-hour ceremony?"

"No… I mean like… the whole thing…"

Carlos walked around, narrowing his eyes as he gazed up at me, studying my face. "You don't like this wedding at all, do you? You don't approve. Why not?"

"Uh… nothing. It's fine. Etta's old enough. It's about time she settled down."

Carlos was still squinting and trying to figure things out. I was already regretful that I'd said anything negative at all.

He unwrapped one finger from his brew and pointed with it. "That's the trouble, isn't it?"

I followed his gesture. He was pointing toward Derek, who had just arrived with his best man and a couple of ushers. They were all dressed up like penguins.

"Nah…" I lied. "The kid's all right."

Frowning, Carlos lifted his arm and began tapping on it. He took a shot of Derek and ran a scan.

"Ah, come on," I said, feeling a sinking sensation in my gut. Why had I let Carlos in on my misgivings?

"What the fuck?" Carlos exclaimed. His eyes sprang wide. "Derek Jensen, Security Specialist, first class…. He's a frigging hog, McGill! Did you know about this?"

I heaved a sigh. I shouldn't have invited Carlos. I should have left well-enough alone.

"I get it all, now…" Carlos said, staring at Derek and his friends. "That's why you invited me down here for this, isn't it? I thought you were just being generous, giving me a fair crack at those bridesmaids in frilly dresses—but no. You brought me down here with work to do."

"Huh?"

He lowered his voice to a near whisper. "How do you want me to do it? Before or after the ceremony? Do you even have a plan?"

"What the hell are you are talking about, Carlos?"

"I'm talking about taking out your embarrassment. It's obvious you couldn't do this yourself. You need to be standing around in plain sight, so no one can blame you."

"Carlos, I don't want you to kill the kid."

He squinted at me. "Are you serious? You're telling me, right here, right now, that you're okay with some active-duty hog clapping cheeks with your daughter? You know what he's doing, right? You know the depravity—"

I reached down with a big arm. There was a big hand on the end of it, which laid heavily on Carlos' shoulder. "Listen to me. I don't want you to kill him. I don't want you to kill anyone. Just shut up and drink your beer. You're a guest here—that's all."

Carlos grumbled and eyed me in disbelief now and then, but he did stand down. I watched him, but he made no move, surreptitious or otherwise, to nail Derek. Finally, he decided to chase the bridesmaids and every other available-looking lady in the crowd.

I was glad to see that. After a time, I relaxed again and was able to enjoy the day as more guests arrived.

I was enjoying things, that is, until Della decided to pester me.

"I've never been to an Earther wedding before..." she said. "Are these costumes and behaviors all normal?"

"Yep. This is how we do it—unless it's raining, then we go inside a church for the festivities."

"Most odd... James?"

"Huh?"

"Have you... researched Etta's choice of mates?"

I eyed her. She was looking good. Her face was a year or two older than her best, as we hadn't died lately. Not since we'd blown up the space cannon on Crystal World. That had been last year...

"Uh..." I said. "Researched Derek? What are you talking about?"

"He's Hegemony, James. You never mentioned that before. Neither did Etta."

*Damnation...*

Did everyone have to spy on each other with their tappers these days? It was almost diabolical. A man couldn't hide anything about himself... no matter how shameful.

I sighed. "Yeah, he's a hog."

"You *knew* about this? And you're still allowing this farce to continue?"

"What am I supposed to do about it? The girl is free to make her own choices, you know."

Della's lower jaw jutted out. She was pissed off, and it wasn't a good look for her. "It's just like everyone says. The parent goes soft when they spend too much time doting on a single child. Don't concern yourself. I'll think of something..."

That's when I saw the blade in her hand. It flashed up at me, reflecting a glint of Georgia sunshine. She'd pulled it out from her blouse—fishing it from between her finely tanned breasts—then slid it into her tiny wedding-outfit purse.

Again, my oversized hands had to take action. I reached out and plucked the purse from her.

She squawked and squared off with me.

All of this consternation hadn't gone completely unnoticed. My momma was hurrying across the yard with a determined look in her eye. She wasn't going to tolerate any shenanigans on this special day.

"Now, James," the old lady said. "You give that lovely lady her purse back. You hear?"

"Yes, Momma..." I said with an appropriately sheepish look.

I didn't cooperate immediately, however. Instead, I brought my knee up and crashed it into the purse. There was a snapping sound.

Then I handed the purse back to Della. She looked confused. She opened it and pulled out a busted-off handle.

"You broke my blade? That weapon was forged on Dust World, I'll have you know!"

"Yeah, well... leave the next one at home."

She left my side in a huff.

My left hand was dripping blood, so I wrapped it in a napkin until it stopped. The napkin was one of those fancy cloth ones you have to wash—the type they have at swanky restaurants. Not wanting to leave a guest with nothing to wipe their mouth on, I returned it to the table, bloody side down, and stepped quickly away.

By the time the wedding ceremony finally kicked off, I figured I'd saved Derek's life a half-dozen times. No one who was remotely associated with Legion Varus wanted to see one of our own permanently hooked to a hog.

That long list included me, actually. If I'd had my druthers, I'd have stuffed Derek into a recycling chute somewhere and lost his file... but that would have made Etta very unhappy. I knew that, so I pretended things were all good.

When it came time, I solemnly walked Etta down the aisle and passed her off to Derek. I didn't grin at the couple—it just wasn't in me—but I did manage a wintery smile.

This public humiliation was just one of those things, I figured.

Later on, someone kicked me awake.

"At least pretend to be interested, James," Della hissed at my side.

I snorted up in my seat, where I'd been sprawling and lolling my head. The praying and the proclaiming was coming to a conclusion at last. Why did officiants always feel the need to talk a man's ear off at weddings?

A minute or so later, the preacher-fella announced that it was finally over and done with. Derek lifted the veil and kissed his bride.

Dear Lord, that was a painful moment for both me and Della to suffer through. She was digging her nails into my left wrist, but that wasn't the only thing that was upsetting me.

My little girl was finally growing up. She was twenty-five physically—or thereabouts—and going on forty in the mind.

Despite that, it all seemed too soon...

## -2-

After making sure that no one murdered Derek while I wasn't looking, I drove the two newlyweds all the way down to Orlando. There were plenty of cruise ships leaving the port—it seemed like one left every hour on the hour.

These ships were different than the old ones from the previous century. Instead of being wallowing, deep-water vessels, they were larger, flatter, and they operated by hovering over the water rather than sinking down into it. Instead of being built of heavy steel, they were all shaped polymers with titanium bones where they needed some strong points.

Once the two kids were safely aboard the hovercraft, I watched it buzz out over the ocean. I felt safe to leave them behind and steered my parents' tram northward. I turned on the autopilot, and I relaxed on the long drive back home to Waycross.

I honestly hoped the two kids would have a good time. They were slated to spend a week in the Caribbean, enjoying the sun on countless beaches, plus some good food. They really did serve good food aboard cruise ships. In fact, just thinking about cruise ship buffets made my mouth water a bit.

I wondered why I'd never taken Galina on a cruise. Maybe it'd be a good idea... I considered calling her up and discussing the concept, but I never did. Instead, I fell asleep.

It was pretty late by the time I crossed the border into Georgia Sector. I let the tram buzz along, clanking and shuddering over the old roads. When the vehicle sensed the driver wasn't awake or paying any attention at all, it always went into safety-mode and slowed down.

This was irritating, but at least you didn't have to drive or guide it in any way. But it was frigging *slow*. It was like being driven home by your grandma—worse than that, even.

Somewhere around 9 p.m. my forearm started tickling and brought me awake. Someone was calling me on my tapper. They'd managed to wake me up, through sheer repetition and determination.

Now, since it had been a wedding day and essentially part of my kid's honeymoon send-off, I'd naturally turned off all forms of messages and direct calls. That'd work for ninety-nine percent of the usual garbage I got every day on my tapper—but not with this caller.

"James? Damn it, James! Are you asleep?"

"I sure as hell am, Galina," I mumbled, stretching in my seat. "Say, what'd you think of my idea?"

"What idea?" she asked.

"Oh… wait a minute… I don't think I even asked you yet, did I?"

"What's wrong with you? Are you drunk as well as sleeping?"

"No, not a drop, I swear."

She gazed at me sternly and suspiciously.

I forced my mind to wake up. "What are you calling me about anyway, girl?"

"First, I want to know what idea you were thinking of asking me about."

"It was nothing at all," I said. "I was in a stupor. Just dreaming, probably."

Her face softened. "You're dreaming about me?"

"Of course, I am," I lied. "I do it all the time. Just look down here," I said, lowering the viewpoint of my tapper a notch or two. "Here's the evidence."

"That's disgusting, McGill. You still haven't told me what idea you were talking about."

"Well… I was putting the kids on one of those hovercraft ships, you know, the ones that drive up on all the best beaches all around the Caribbean? They let you get off and play in the water."

"Yes, that sounds nice. But I've heard they're very bad for the environment."

"I'm sure they are," I said, not caring at all. "But anyways, I was thinking that you and I could take a trip like that sometime."

To my surprise, her face brightened. "You want to take a trip with me?"

"I sure as hell do. I haven't had a proper date in a month."

"Hmm... That's very sweet, James... but I have something to discuss. Something that's far more important. Critical, even."

"How's that?"

"Do you remember the last time I asked you to go find something for me, and you found it, but you saw no solution?"

"Huh?" I said, totally baffled as to what she was talking about.

She sighed. "James, do you recall there is a person—or rather, um, excuse me, a *nonperson*—who you and I aren't supposed to mention under any circumstances?"

I frowned, my eyebrows knitting together in a mix of confusion and hard thinking. I could think of a number of individuals we weren't supposed to bring up—but then I had it. I knew who she must be talking about.

"Drusus?" I said. "That's it! You're talking about—"

"No! I'm not, you idiot!" she exclaimed. "That name isn't one I would ever dare to speak. And you should never utter it, either!"

"Well then, what the hell are we talking about?"

"Shut up. Just shut up, James. I don't know why I try to have phone calls with you. It's a near impossibility. You don't have a secretive bone in your body."

"I'll take that as a compliment," I said.

"So..." she said, "what about it?"

"Uh... what about what?"

"What about the disposition of the nonperson which you were searching for? ...the nonperson we aren't talking about right now?"

15

"Uh... Oh! Oh... you mean—"

"Yes, dammit!" she said, losing what little cool she had left. "Where the hell is Drusus, you idiot?"

"I already told you about that. He's down there in the bottom of Central in that evil chamber—"

"Shut up!" she insisted, cutting me off. "Just shut up and listen. I want you to find out if there's some way we can extract him from his current state."

I thought that over, squinting a bit. Drusus was locked up in the Vault of the Forgotten, a place where lost souls were sent to languish. There, through a devilish process, their fleshly bodies were stripped away. They were left with only their bare intellect. Essentially, the prisoners were floating brains and ganglia, just a mass of nerves and gray matter. Sometimes they had eyeballs—but sometimes they didn't.

It made me shudder just to think about it. Non-persons were left in a timeless condition, half-aware, half-dreaming, unable to escape or really live until some bureaucratic official among the Intel boys at Central decided it was time to pull the plug.

"You're right..." I said, rubbing my chin and frowning some more, "it really is unfair what they did to him. Maybe I can find a way to help... But why do you want to free him now, though? Before, you didn't seem to care much."

Galina looked furtive. This was a natural state of mind and appearance for her. She always had motivations that were easy to see for an outsider—but then she also had her secondary motivations as well. Ugly ideas that squatted inside that pretty head of hers, ideas she hid from everyone.

"There are changes being discussed at the top at Central..." she said. "Let's just say that it would be to my advantage if Drusus were—dammit—I mean to say, that this non-person in question were back to a normal state of being again."

"Uh... okay. I guess I can look into it."

"Be gentle and discreet in your investigations, James. The Intel people are still angry about last time."

"Can I count on your father's protection in this matter?" I asked her.

She pursed her lips and looked evasive. "You've got *my* protection," she said. "That's even better."

"Uh... No, it's not."

"Well, it will have to do," she snapped.

I crossed my arms and squinted at her. I shook my head. "Sorry. Not good enough."

"James," she sputtered. "I could order you—"

"Nope. You can't. This isn't a normal assignment. You can't just assign it to me like I'm some grunt in Legion Varus. You could tell me to shoot some alien, sure. You could tell me to flush a recruit out of the legions. No problem. But this? This isn't in the regs book."

"I would consider it to be..." Galina said quietly, "a personal favor."

"Oh yeah? A personal favor? What kind of favor am I getting in return?"

"That's a very rude suggestion," she said.

"How so?"

"I've already done a lot for you," she said. "I erased all official reports of your having murdered Intel agents, for instance. My father let you slide after having destroyed a space cannon at Crystal World—a fantastic value to Earth."

"Yeah, yeah..." I said, still unimpressed. Those were things which I had negotiated and gotten many months ago. To my mind, this is an entirely new situation.

Galina glared up out of my tapper at me. "I find your lack of gratitude disturbing, James."

I rubbed my fingers together in front of the pickup. "What's in it for me?"

She sighed. "How about this? How about you and I take a nice, entertaining hovercraft ride? Just as you suggested not five minutes ago."

"What?" I said, "a honeymoon cruise?"

"I'm not proposing marriage, James, but—"

"Whoa," I said, "a honeymoon without having to get hitched? I've got to admit, that sounds pretty good."

She looked down and seemed somewhat evasive, but I could tell that was exactly what she had in mind.

"Who's paying?" I asked.

I wasn't exactly short of cash, but I had just put on a serious wedding and paid for two young fools to go touring around the Caribbean. I didn't really want to purchase another pair of tickets like that so soon after the last two.

"I'll pay," Galina said.

I nodded. To her, money was of little consequence. She'd always been a rich kid with an incredibly rich daddy who was also powerful in a political sense.

"All right," I said, "you got yourself a deal. I'll set up some reservations, and I'll send them to you for payment. And then—"

"Hold on," Galina said, "we're not making any travel plans until you've completed your mission for me."

"Uh, what mission was that again?"

"Up at Central, James. Remember?"

"Oh yeah..." I said, "you want me to go deal with Dickson and the Vault—and all those people." I sighed and shook my head. It was a tall order. "All right, all right," I said, "I'll do what I can. No promises, but you know, Drusus deserves some help. I've got to at least try."

"That's very honorable of you," she assured me, and she signed off.

I studied the Georgia night outside the windows of my tram. I was getting pretty close to home, now.

Reluctantly, I reached up a big lumpy hand, doubting my own sanity. I activated the tram's navigational system and redirected it to the Atlanta sky-train station. The vehicle found a new route, exited onto another interstate, and I was clanking along in a new direction.

I watched the stars out the driver's side window until I fell asleep again.

Sometime after midnight, I reached Atlanta. I sent my parents' tram rattling away into the night, and I knew I would miss home.

All talks of vacations were phantoms of the distant future for now. I was working again, but not in a defendable, official way.

I bought a red-eye ticket up to Central City and boarded the flight.

## -3-

Early the next morning, I was yawning, scratching, and wandering around the Central City sky-train station, looking for ground transport. I wasn't heading for Central itself, not yet at least. I needed a few items first.

Taking a robo-taxi into the Gray Zone sector, I shopped around in various disreputable junk stores.

Finally, I found a bin of the devices that I was looking for. Essentially, these were conical wraps that looked almost like casts for one's forearm and wrist. They would slide over the arm, strap down, and cover your tapper. The shielded interior prevented signals from entering or exiting your body.

These questionable items were usually bought by cheating spouses. If you wanted to disappear and pretend it was just a network glitch, these things were gold. You could prevent your significant other from locating you. Without such a protective device, anyone could track you and match-up your activity with individuals who were in close proximity.

Putting on one of these tight-fitting sheaths took a man off the grid for a while. During those precious hours, you could lose yourself among the populace at large. It was almost like wearing a stealth suit.

So here I was, digging in a bargain bin, trying to find a cheap device I could use to hide myself from the prying eyes of the world. I didn't want to buy one new—and I didn't want a fancy unit with bells and whistles. Buying such a thing left traces in databases that might flip up some red flags.

I examined and discarded dozens of units. Today, I wanted to hide from even worse snoops than Galina. I wanted to hide from the Intel boys at Central. I wanted the ability to drop off their radar at will.

The bargain bins were disappointing in this regard. The trouble with these primitive, rather straightforward devices was that although they weren't expensive, they weren't always as effective as you'd want them to be.

In my own case, I was dealing with a unique problem: I happened to have a gigantic forearm.

My entire life, I'd found that most articles of clothing were unavailable in my size. Even when I bought items that used nanotechnology to stretch, like smart cloth, there were difficulties. Things simply weren't designed for someone of my girth.

At two meters in height, I was extremely rare, beyond the one percent line of humanity. Manufacturing companies didn't like to make things for the one percent in any target audience. So, they cheated.

I'd always found that when I stretched an article of clothing out to be big enough to fit me, it tended to get so thin that the material wasn't able to perform its true purpose. In other words, I sometimes put on shirts, and although they did balloon enough to cover my broad back, they would oftentimes become so thin, so sheer, they'd rip down the middle whenever I moved.

In the case of a tapper inhibitor, this sort of thing was unacceptable. The material had to stay thick enough to actually prevent leaked radio waves and ward off probing emissions from scanners. That was the whole point—and making the sheath thinner didn't help at all.

So here I was, digging through bins, stuffing one conical device after another over my arm. I let each one clamp down and squeeze me like some kind of demented blood pressure cuff. Then I tested the emissions with a handheld device designed for that purpose.

They failed. Every time. I quickly pushed the release button and tossed away each device in disgust.

After I'd gone through them all, much to the annoyance of the shopkeeper lady that ran the place, I finally gave up. I was going to have to do this the half-assed way.

I selected one that at least fit me, even though it leaked data. Then I moseyed on to another aisle and bought a big roll of silvery tape. I bought the kind that had real metal in it, the kind used for HVAC systems.

By the time I reached the shopkeeper lady, she was frowning, and she had her hands on her hips in disgust. It was an ugly look. The place was so cheap they didn't even have a robot scanner to buy from, and I considered mentioning that—but I wisely passed on tossing out this insult.

Buying my odd items, I exited the store. Once outside, I left the Gray Zone and headed for Central proper. Naturally, I didn't put on any of the stuff I'd purchased before I entered the building—hell no!

No one was going to get past security with a tapper that didn't read. No, that wouldn't do at all. I stuffed these items in the bottom of my bag and went through security as normal.

I played the usual game of admitting that I hadn't been formally recalled to Central for a legion mission—but pointing out that I had done many clandestine operations for various departments of Central in the past.

I knew this factoid was marked in my file. There were no details, of course, nothing about being tele-cast out into deep space to perform various acts of skullduggery and sabotage. No, there was just a subtle mark or two in the data core indicating I'd performed work as an operative for people inside this building in the past.

As usual, this allowed me to enter without any serious questions being asked.

Once inside, I headed straight for the bathrooms. I slammed myself into a stall and tore off a bit of the thick tape I'd bought in Gray Sector. I used this to tape over the video pickup that was about nose-high in the front door of the stall.

Yes, our Intel bastards had even bugged the bathroom stalls with cameras, as rude as that might seem. No doubt some of them spent their long, dull days getting their jollies out of measuring wangs and the like.

21

I disabled the camera surreptitiously, pretending I was merely hanging my jacket. As if by accident, I scraped a bit of tape off my thumb over the precise pinprick hole where the camera was lurking.

Once that was done, I opened up my little kit and got to work. First, I slid the sheath over my hand and began to work it down my wrist. Damn, it was a tight fit! The tape would go on last.

"McGill, what are you doing at Central?"

It was Winslade, talking out of my tapper at me.

*Goddamn it!*

His face was frowning up from my arm, which was, of course, aimed in my direction as I was in the midst of covering it up.

Winslade must have placed an alert upon my whereabouts. Once I'd entered Central proper, he'd immediately been informed and decided to phone me.

As he was my superior, the same as Imperator Galina Turov, he was able to override all of my precautions, including simply not answering the phone call. He was able to force the call through and pop up with his rat-like face staring up into my nostrils.

I wanted to curse. I wanted to stab my tapper with my knife—but I held my cool.

I considered simply sliding the blocking sheath over his face and wrapping it with tape as fast as I could. It would seem to Winslade as if I'd walked into those bathrooms and simply vanished from the Earth…

"McGill?"

I forced a smile. "Hello, Tribune Winslade," I said. "What can I do you for?"

As I spoke, I gently peeled away the overly thin polymer sheath that I had been about to put on top of my tapper and stuffed it into a pocket.

"I asked you a question, McGill," he said. "What are you doing here?"

"Well, sir…" I said, "I just happened to be in town doing a little shopping, see. I know a few ladies in these parts, and seeing as it's springtime... I thought I'd drop in and make a few conjugal visits, if you know what I mean."

Winslade pursed his lips so hard it looked like he'd sucked the guts out of a lemon. "I don't believe what you're telling me, McGill. Not a single word of it."

"Uh..." I said.

"That's right, I'm not the fool that you seem to take me for. You know about the critical meeting being held here today at Central. You know something about the unusual nature of the contract we're attempting to secure for Legion Varus. Who sent you here to spy upon these business dealings?"

"Huh?"

"You can tell your masters, McGill, that I won't have it!"

"Have what, sir?" I asked, utterly confused.

Winslade rolled his eyes. "All right, fine," he said. "Since you're here and you're a member of the legion, I'm not going to have you arrested. Not this time."

"That's mighty kind of you, sir." I had no earthly idea what he was talking about, but not being arrested was almost always a good thing.

"What I'm going to do instead..." he continued, "is contain this before it expands and gets out of control."

I was back to squinting in confusion again.

"I know who you work for," he said. "I know who makes private deposits in your bank account."

"Uh... you mean, like, when the Central lab people experiment on me like a bunny rabbit?"

"No, I'm not talking about that nonsense. I'm talking about a much bigger score. You've been working for the Turovs! You've been one of their operatives for years."

He said this like it was one of the worst accusations he could possibly make. I did understand to some degree why he would be so angry if he believed I was working for the Turovs. They had, after all, engineered a number of inexplicable mass-murdering events. There had been the small matter of dropping a huge piece of space debris into the Eastern Mediterranean and slaughtering tens of millions of hapless citizens, for instance...

Most people bought the propaganda on every news outlet, or they looked the other way. There were those, however, like me and Winslade, who remembered such devastating events and knew who had been responsible.

I gave myself a scratch. "Just what exactly are you wanting me to do, sir?"

"Listen... I want you to work for me for a change," he said. "Work for Legion Varus. That should be your first concern. You owe us loyalty more than any other entity."

"Not so," I said. "There's my family, and then the Lord—"

He made a disgusted sound. "I mean in a professional capacity."

"Well... yeah, okay. You got a point there."

"I can't pay you as the Turovs can," Winslade said, seemingly under the impression that I was swimming in billions of credits, which I truly wasn't.

Usually, Galina bought me cheap. Just look at the current situation. I was up here working for her in order to get myself a week-long cruise and some special favors from her during our shared vacation. That was damn near free compared to the kind of thing Winslade was talking about.

"No pay, huh?" I asked, sounding disappointed.

"None whatsoever."

"Well..."

"I'm appealing to your sense of duty, McGill," Winslade said earnestly. "If I allow you to come up here, if I let you join this meeting, will you swear to me on your honor as a centurion of Legion Varus that your loyalties will first go to the legion itself, and only secondly to your paymasters?"

I thought that over. My mouth went slack for a moment. Finally, I nodded. "Sure thing, Tribune," I told him. "You know me. Money doesn't mean all that much to a McGill."

He squinted at me. Finally, he nodded. "That is true. You live in a shack in a stinking swamp. Such an individual cannot be easily persuaded by gratuitous amounts of cash... All right. I'm going to trust you, Centurion. Come up to my offices immediately."

And that was that. Sadly, I stuffed away my shiny tape and my overly thin tapper wrap. I straightened my uniform and walked out of the stall. I headed upstairs, taking a long, long elevator ride to the upper reaches of Central.

It did occur to me as I did so that I was going in a precisely opposite direction from where Drusus was imprisoned in the very depths of the Earth below my feet. But there was nothing for it. Sometimes, a man's true objectives were delayed. And sometimes, if he followed other wandering paths, he found a new route to his ultimate goal, one that would never have occurred to him before he followed an odd twist of fate to see where it might lead.

## -4-

When I finally arrived at Winslade's office door, I was surprised to see him burst out through the doors before I could even open them. In his wake were two more primus-level officers, his simps known as Primus Gilbert and Primus Collins. Both of them served me a dirty look as they approached.

I could tell right off that neither was happy to see me. This was a little annoying because, to my mind, they both owed me a great deal. In fact, Primus Collins had been close to frigid before my more experienced hands had opened her floodgates. You'd think the woman would be grateful for that, but nooo…

She was probably still butthurt about the fact I hadn't talked to her lately and had taken up with any number of other women since our brief affair.

I mentally shrugged. There was no doubting the ancient wisdom that went something like, 'if a man spends his whole life waiting for gratitude, he's in for a big disappointment.'

"Come, come McGill," Winslade said. "You're late, as usual. One would think that when crashing a meeting that you weren't even invited to, you could at least show up in a timely manner."

Whatever you might say about Winslade, those skinny shanks of his could move pretty fast when they wanted to. The group hurried after him—except for me, who brought up the rear. That was due to the giraffe-like nature of all my limbs. I found I was able to easily keep up with my sweeping, thumping footsteps.

"Hey… uh… Tribune? Just where exactly are we headed? I thought this meeting was at your place."

"My offices are much too small and shabby for the likes of the people who are attending today," Winslade told me without even turning his head.

"It would be best, McGill," the undertaker-looking dude known as Primus Gilbert said, "that you stare straight ahead. At no point should you speak your mind during these proceedings."

Collins snorted at that. She knew me better. "I don't know why McGill is even here. Tribune, do we really need a thuggish bodyguard for a routine negotiation meeting?"

"Probably not," Winslade snapped back, "but in any case, that's not why he's coming along. McGill does have certain… shall we say… shared history with the client we're meeting with today."

"Oh Lord," I said, "that can't be good. Most aliens don't like me too much after I wreck one of their planets."

"Oddly enough, this particular patron *does* have a positive view of you. There's no accounting for taste, I guess."

He would say no more. We followed him to the elevators, at which point we were whisked away up into and beyond the clouds themselves. Near the top of the vast building, we finally halted. We got off and looked around.

"We've got to be damn near the roof," I exclaimed, looking out the windows at the puffy white clouds that obscured the streets far below.

Winslade again set off down another long corridor. Right about when we reached the terminus of it, I finally caught on.

I knew this hallway. I recognized the twin rows of hogs that stood on each side of it, too. The hog color guard all stared ahead. Their chin straps tightly clamped their helmets onto their heads, and their rifles were gripped in motionless hands. They looked like a roomful of statues to me.

"Holy crap," I said, "are we going to the consul's office?"

"Of course, McGill. That should have been painfully obvious by now," Winslade snapped at me.

He led the three of us to the door at the end of the two rows of hogs, and we were allowed inside.

Huffy staffers ushered us through the high-ceilinged lobby. They squabbled about us being late for the meeting.

I glanced at the clock, and I saw that it was indeed displaying 09:02 am.

Two minutes late? Go figure.

Old Consul Wurtenberger was the highest ranked officer on Earth, and he was a man who liked his trains to run on time. Being two minutes late was a sin. The sort of stain that might never wash off.

We entered the main office, which was large and sumptuous. To one side, there was a full library of old-world European flavor. There was a fireplace and books—real paper books! The other side was festooned with hanging velvet curtains and golden ropes. I'd felt-up those ropes before—they were made with real spun metal. It was weird.

In the center of the large room was an outsized conference table around which several men sat.

I immediately corrected myself mentally. One of them was not a man at all—he was a Nairb. What's more, I recognized him on sight.

Sure, he looked like just about every other Nairb that had ever lived: he was a green, loose bag of snot with semi-translucent skin and a bad fishy stink that clung to him everywhere he went. But it had to be the particular Nairb known as Seven.

Earth had risen in stature so greatly over recent years that our planet now needed professional representation among the Galactics. Seven had somehow cozied himself up to our consul, and like accountants in most board meetings, he had become a haunting ghost that couldn't be shaken.

I for one didn't mind the alien's presence. Sure, Seven was a bureaucrat of the most officious type, but he was also a drinking man. He and I had shared plenty of interesting moments in the past. If I could possibly call any alien a friend, it would probably be this one.

I considered shouting a greeting to him across the table, but I refrained. Even my dull brain was able to surmise that this group was so stuffy any loud, boisterous comments from me would be unappreciated.

We continued shuffling closer to the consul and his gigantic conference table. I frowned at the massive table as we drew near to it. The technological wonder wasn't just any flat surface made of fake wood with rounded corners. No sir.

It glowed, alive with holograms. Maps and data floated above it, responding to anyone's touch or airy gesture. During strategic planning sessions, officers gathered around, their fingers dancing over the holographic surface, plotting the course of interstellar maneuvers for fleets and troops alike.

To me, an experienced but imprecise witness, it appeared the conference table itself was both larger and more ornate than the one that Drusus had set up for himself in this same location. That was a bit of a shocker. I'd never seen a table as ostentatious as the one Drusus had used—not until today. He'd been outclassed by this monster.

Apparently, to put his mark on his new office, the consul had decided to outspend his predecessor in a lavish display. I whistled as I walked up to the device and ran my fingers over the glowing icons with a loving, appreciative gesture.

"Cease and desist, human," Seven said. "Your input isn't approved of."

My hand jerked back, but now the other two officers who were seated near the consul looked disgusted.

"In fact…" said the man known as Tribune Kraus from Legion Victrix. He eyed me with narrow slits. "I don't approve of your presence at all. This is unacceptable, Winslade. This is a tribune-level meeting. What were you thinking?"

The other guy, who's name I couldn't place was head of Germanica. He gave us a fresh sneer. "It's true. No one instructed you to bring an army of sycophants in your wake. Shoo them out. They can wait in the lobby."

Alarmed, Primus Gilbert and Primus Collins did a U-turn and stepped quickly and smartly away. They didn't say a word as they retreated.

I, on the other hand, didn't budge. I stood tall. After all, Winslade hadn't ordered me out. These snoots could damn well screw themselves.

Primus Collins reached out a delicate hand as she walked by me. She put this hand on my right wrist, and she tugged.

I pretended not to notice. In truth, I barely felt her touch.

Instead, I looked expectantly toward Winslade. He was my direct commanding officer. The decision was up to him.

Winslade glanced toward me and then at the rest of them nervously. He fluttered his fingers in the air. "Well, I guess if we aren't supposed to bring these others, I'll send them out. I wasn't informed about this detail."

"Halt," Wurtenberger said.

Speaking for the first time, the consul stood up and his belly rubbed unpleasantly against the table as he rose to his full height—which wasn't much. "You are Centurion McGill, no? Hmm. There is a possible reason why you should remain in attendance. These other two, I agree with you, Kraus, they are superfluous."

He gave a sweeping gesture with his fingers towards Primuses Gilbert and Collins, and they hurried away, looking even more sour than before.

At the door, as Collins exited, she gave me one final venomous glance of hate.

I decided to take her poor sportsmanship in the best possible light. She was probably just feeling a mite jealous. I tapped a few fingers against my forehead as if she'd given me a hearty salute.

After the door shut behind Winslade's simps, Winslade and I took our seats at the grand table and waited for the meeting to begin.

"Our agenda item," the Nairb said primly, "deals with the matter of contract distribution."

Winslade perked up immediately. He looked like a hound dog when someone starts cooking bacon in the kitchen.

The leaders of Victrix and Germanica also appeared to be interested, and everyone looked at the Nairb expectantly.

"We have a new contract offer," Seven said. "This is unusual, as it is from a brand-new client. This client is unusual in several respects."

Naturally, I already wanted to shout out, "Who is it?" loud and clear. But I managed to refrain from doing so.

*Self-control!* I told myself. It was all about self-control in important meetings like this one.

The Nairb then proceeded to drone on for a while, describing the general terms of service, but not getting to the important part.

Who was hiring us? Where were they? And what the hell was the mission about? That was all I cared about.

After he'd talked about damned near everything else, the sort of stuff that I tended to tune out, a gasp went up from everyone there.

Dammit.

All of a sudden everyone seemed surprised. Even Wurtenberger. His high-capacity mouth was hanging open.

Winslade's hands were up, and I'll be damned if they weren't rubbing together like a raccoon scrubbing a slug.

And the two prissy tribunes from Germanica and Victrix, hell, they were practically making O-faces.

What had I missed?

"Can that amount be right?" asked the Germanica puke.

"Legion Victrix accepts the offer," announced Tribune Kraus, jumping the gun.

Damn! The offered stack of credits must have been high. He didn't even seem to care what the hell he was going to have to do to get it.

"Your statement is premature," the Nairb said. "As you've not yet been offered the contract, you cannot accept it."

"Well…" Kraus said, shrugging and spreading his hands, "as the commander of the most accomplished, famous, and sought-after legion represented here, I can only assume that if I were to accept, my legion would be selected. The others represented here are, as any knowledgeable client must comprehend, little more than obnoxious rabble."

Both Winslade and the tribune of Germanica rankled at this. The Germanica guy seemed even more outraged than Winslade, to tell the truth.

"What utter nonsense!" he complained.

Kraus was right about Legion Varus. We were highly disreputable—bordering on criminality. In appearance and reputation, we were downright shabby. Rather than saying we were famous, I would rather say we were *infamous*.

But to place Germanica in the same bucket as Varus, well, that was plainly unfair. Germanica was, along with the Iron Eagles, behind only Victrix in fame and glory.

When the squabbling had died down, the Nairb spoke again. "Gentlemen, let me finish, please. The mission also has a couple of other positive and negative factoids you may be interested in before you begin bidding for it so vociferously."

All of the tribunes backed down, but they were all eyeing one another, seething beneath the surface. Among the legions of Earth, everyone needed contracts to maintain their status, and their wealth. We needed credits to pay our backers, buy gear, make payroll—all that sort of thing.

Alien money wasn't the only way this could be done, but it was the easiest. Sometimes, there were government contracts foisted upon us from Central without our consent. Under those circumstances, the payments were nominal and thin.

Apparently, whatever number of credits had been offered in this case, it had to be astronomical. Despite the fact I was cudgeling my mind, trying to remember what had been said by the Nairb earlier while I was dozing and daydreaming, I couldn't recall the precise figure.

But whatever it was, it obviously had been high enough to grab the attention of all three of these greedy men, probably double or triple anything we'd get from the government of Earth. They were therefore in tight competition to secure the deal.

"On the positive side," the Nairb continued, "the nature of the mission itself is favorable. It is essentially a nobility escort task. You are to serve in the capacity of protecting and serving the whims of a small alien oligarchy."

If it was possible, all three of the tribunes looked even more excited. It sounded like a cushy deal. Usually, we were deployed to solve serious disputes like civil wars or an alien invasion—but not this time. This sounded more like the task of performing the services of a color guard. Even on a violent, unpleasant planet such contracts were always sought after.

Winslade's fingers, although he had folded his hands, were now squirming over one another in greed. "And what, pray tell," he said, "would be the bad news?"

"The distance to the actual destination planet," the Nairb continued, "would probably be considered a detriment. The destination world is in the Mid-Zone."

We all gasped again at that—even me, this time. The Mid-Zone was a nearly unexplored region of space, thousands of light years from Earth. It was more or less halfway to the galactic center, where the Galactics, like the Mogwa themselves, reigned supreme.

Taking on a contract from there… well, the positives would include probable relative safety. Unlike going the other direction toward the frontier, the Mid-Zone was relatively civilized and more peaceful than wild places like Crystal World had been.

On the negative side, however, was the sheer distance to the destination. It would probably take months, perhaps seasons, to reach the planet in question. That meant the deployment was bound to be a long one.

Winslade nodded, thinking that over. "Legion Varus is interested," he announced. "In fact, we are the only legion here who has ever served in the Mid-Zone."

"Lies!" the Victrix man, Kraus, shouted. "Victrix was also there. We served at City World, just as you did. This Germanica fop here is the man out, the man without regional experience. I've long heard your men lack the gumption required to venture outside of Province 921."

The Germanica tribune glowered at the two of us. Angrily, he opened his mouth to make yet more objections, but Wurtenberger finally spoke then, and his voice cut through everyone's grumblings.

"I'm pleased to see such hot eagerness for this contract," he said. "Certainly, the amount is large, and the duties, from our current perspective, seem relatively light. However, are you all certain that you're interested in this wild adventure into the Mid-Zone? This will be only the second time Earth has dared to venture so far from the confines of Province 921."

Kraus reached out a hand and slapped the table. "I'm still in. Victrix accepts the contract. And there's no one else here of superior quality."

He broke off as the Germanica man leaned forward, not to be outdone. "Germanica also accepts the contract," he said. "What's more, we will accept a ten percent discount to the contractual price."

There was another gasp around the table. He was lowering his price already. Hell, we hadn't even heard all the details yet. These guys must be hard up for money. Again, I wondered just how much had been offered.

Finally, it was Winslade's turn to speak. Capping off the other two, he placed both his hands on the table, and he stood up.

"Legion Varus," he said, "will accept this contract with a twenty-five percent reduction in payment."

There were open-mouth stares, which turned into snarls when the other two tribunes realized they'd been heavily undercut. They looked wounded and angry.

I nodded appreciatively. I was kind of enjoying the entire experience. I'd never been around during contract negotiations before. It reminded me of farmers bidding on livestock and used trams at a Sunday auction in Waycross.

## -5-

I've got to tell you, I was pretty damn excited to learn we were finally getting a solid shot at one of those sweet, sweet escort missions. Ever since I joined the legions, and even before, I'd heard about such gigs. Our most elite legions, stuffy prissy prigs like Germanica and Victrix, the guys who were right here in the room with me, always got the most cush deals like the one we'd landed today. That was because the rich aliens who wanted to show off liked to pay for the best. If your planet was in a bad way, you didn't have the extra cash laying around to showboat. That was when you hired a blood-and-guts crew like Legion Varus.

But not today! We were finally going to get to see how the other half lived.

The situation was all the sweeter since Victrix was involved. Kraus and his peacocks were famous for flying out to the stars in comfort and style. They polished their armor on some rock for a year or so, playing color guard to a tyrant, and then cashed a big check. They rarely had to do so much as fire a gun. No wonder their kits always look so good.

I was all grins. We had a good shot at this deal. What alien in his right mind would pay twenty-five percent more for spit and polish? Not many, I figured.

Of course, the big discount did weigh on my mind a bit… that move seemed insane on the face of it, but to have an easy mission for once—that seemed worth it.

"Are there any further discounts in the offing?" Wurtenberger asked.

Kraus and the Germanica asshole were both red-faced. They glowered. They glanced evilly at Winslade. They hated being undercut, but then again, they also hated undercutting their own prices.

"Given the circumstances," Tribune Kraus said tersely, "I will concede the low bid to Winslade and Legion Varus. However, I claim the right to plead my case directly to the client. Our services are obviously superior to any ham-handed fiasco the Varus troops are likely to deliver. He might well take my offer instead."

The Germanica guy made a face, scrunching up his lips, thinking it over. "I too," he said, "will pass on matching or exceeding Legion Varus's drastic price cuts. However, we've agreed to a ten percent reduction already. I will make my case, offering a first-class legion for a middling price. I, too, would like to make my case to the client directly. Germanica will provide a balance between cost and performance. Parsimony should insist upon them choosing us."

Wurtenberger nodded sagely in agreement.

Winslade still looked pretty happy. He figured we had this in the bag. Most customers were, after all, always interested in saving billions of credits if it was possible to do so.

But it wasn't certain. Sometimes, aliens had their minds set on the fame and glory of Earth's so-called finest coming to serve them. Only meeting the client would tell.

"Very well then," Wurtenberger said. "The private pre-meeting is over. Let us now introduce you to our clients."

He signaled his sidekick Nairb. Seven humped away and left the room. He was gone for some time, but at last, he returned with a shuffling group of aliens. I turned in my seat, as did Winslade.

When we faced the group approaching the conference table, we almost lost control of ourselves. As it was, I gasped aloud.

Following the Nairb were three odd individuals. All of them were strange to look at. The one in the middle—at least I knew his shape. He was a Mogwa.

After a moment, I recognized him. It was none other than Grand Admiral Sateekas, the single Mogwa in the universe best known to me. His spidery body was upright, almost perky, with a jaunty arrogance in the positioning of his eye-groups.

He studied us all as he approached. His six foot-hand things churned with a wobbly gait as he reached the conference table.

Getting over my initial shock, I smiled and waved in recognition. But then, after my eyes had slid from the familiar appearance of Sateekas to his companions, my grin faded. In fact, my mouth began to droop at the corners.

"What the holy hell are those things?" I asked aloud.

"Those alien beings," Seven said, answering my rude question, "are known as Nebrans."

"Nebrans? They look more like… I don't know… big-ass monkeys, or raccoons or something."

They were in fact definitely mammalian in appearance. They stood about a meter tall, and they had two hands and two feet each. Their bodies were furred in a pattern that reminded me of a skunk, but sort of in reverse. In other words, there was more white fur on their pelts than black.

But whatever the case, their faces had quivering noses and dark, beady eyes that implied a primitive alertness. They studied us even as we studied them.

Their furred hands were empty, but they worked the air, clutching at nothing as if reflexively. They wore no clothing, except for a single item—a belt around their middles. The belts were metal, and they looked to me like they wouldn't be easy to remove. Cinched-up tight against their bellies, I saw them occasionally reaching down to them, touching them gingerly and adjusting the belts as if pained by them.

Sateekas proudly approached the conference table. He mounted the largest chair opposite Wurtenberger. As was his custom, he stood upon the chair rather than squatted in it as an attempt to look a little more imposing.

The two Nebrans squatted on either side of his chair, not taking up seats of their own. Their beady eyes, puffs of white hair, and those dark noses poked up over the top of the table, and they examined us with an inquisitive intelligence. You could tell just by looking at them that they were thinking—probably about something dirty.

"These are my servants," the Mogwa said. "Please excuse their manners. They are in training. They have not yet been fully tamed."

The humans glanced around at one another. All of us were probably thinking something along the lines of *what the fuck?* But no one said it.

Why the hell had he brought two alien skunk-monkeys with him? He'd said they weren't entirely tame, either. It was rude by any measure.

But no one asked any questions. Here at Central, we held to the time-honored tradition of salespeople everywhere: *the customer was always right.*

"Welcome to my chambers, Grand Admiral," Wurtenberger said. "Allow me to introduce—" He began gesturing towards the tribunes, but the Mogwa cut him off.

"I'm working with a tight schedule," Sateekas said. "Have the negotiations been concluded?"

"In a sense they have, sir," Wurtenberger said. He turned toward Seven and nodded. "My attaché will explain."

Grand Admiral Sateekas eyed the Nairb. He seemed to be full of distaste. It occurred to me that probably the only thing worse than a Nairb serving a Mogwa was the one that was serving another empire. Seven had to be the lowest of the low in Sateekas' eyes.

He offered no objections, however, and just listened. The Nairb went over the numbers, and the suggested ranking of the legions, and our force descriptions.

Sateekas listened politely. He gave no sign during the presentations by all three of the tribunes as to which he felt was the best choice to make. When the entire presentation was over and done with he did, however, flick a single appendage in my direction.

"Why is the McGill here?" he asked. "Is his presence the harbinger of some unexpected misfortune?"

"Not at all, Grand Admiral," Winslade responded, fluttering his hands in a calming gesture. "But if you wish to have him removed, I will do so immediately."

Sateekas considered. "No, that will not be necessary. But now that you have made your cases, I wish to introduce you to these two. They are principles in this arrangement."

So saying, he stepped away from his throne-like chair and climbed upon a secondary table. The two odd beings he'd brought with him followed him and crouched under the table. One of the Nebrans provided a velvet-lavender pillow from somewhere, which the Mogwa squatted upon.

I glanced over at Wurtenberger, and I realized that it had been stolen from one of his couches. He frowned briefly, but said nothing. Perhaps he was a little bit upset that one of his best upholstered items had been pressed into service as an ass-cushion for the Mogwa without asking.

"Approach," the Mogwa said.

All of us looked at one another, uncertain as to what we should do. Finally, taking initiative, Winslade stood up. He walked around to where the Mogwa and the two nose-twitching Nebrans were, and he stood before them.

I was impressed. Winslade was normally not a brave soul, but in this instance, when so much money and possibly a nice jolt of prestige was at stake, he had decided to seize the day.

"What can I do for you, Grand Admiral?" he asked.

"I had expected the Victrix man to be first," Sateekas said, "but so be it. Nebrans?"

The two aliens stepped forward, noses twitching harder. They craned their long necks.

Sateekas gestured impatiently toward Winslade. "Extend an appendage," he said. "Come, come!"

Suddenly, old Winslade had a new expression on his face—he looked like he wished he hadn't chosen to go first.

But as he was in front of everyone, Winslade went with the flow. He extended an arm, bending forward slightly at the waist, and he allowed the two Nebrans to sniff him.

They used their small, strange hands to trace the veins on his wrists, and the hairs on his knuckles. One of them even licked a finger.

Winslade flinched, but to his credit, he did not strike at them or yank his hand back and yelp in fear. He was uncomfortable, mind you, but he stuck it out.

Finally, the two Nebrans seemed satisfied by this strange ceremony, and they stepped back to either side of Sateekas' perch.

The Mogwa gave no sign as to how Winslade's performance had been received, and neither did the Nebrans.

"Next!" The Mogwa shouted. "Come, come!" He slapped his limbs around impatiently.

Winslade returned to the seat next to me, and he gave me a wide-eyed, bewildered look, but he said nothing.

Both Kraus and the Germanica stooge seemed perplexed, but it was the Germanica tribune who took the next step.

He scooted back his chair and stood up. He approached the three, with Sateekas perched on his pillow and his two freakish aliens to either side of him.

Again, as before, they made a ceremony of sniffing and examining the hands of the Germanica tribune. He could not hide his disgust, curling back a lip. He lifted it enough to show teeth. His nose was wrinkled, and his eyes were squinched tight—but he managed to say nothing.

This time, however, I noted that the twitchy Nebrans were more intrusive—even invasive. One of them reached out and grasped the kneecap of the distressed tribune. The other fiddled around with the snaps on his military boots. I got the feeling that, were they allowed to, they would prod, finger, and sniff every inch of the man.

Was this perhaps how they liked to greet people? Was it some kind of religious ceremony? I didn't see any way in which they could be judging the military quality of an officer through such a bizarre process—but then again, I was no alien.

At last, the examination was complete, and the Germanica man was allowed to return to his seat.

Without being prompted, Kraus stood crisply. The Victrix tribune marched toward the Mogwa and stood at attention. Without a moment's hesitation, he extended a hand, one to each of the two Nebrans.

I realized then the wisdom of his behavioral pattern. He was attempting to gain brownie points, even now, even in this small way.

He had waited to go last. Why? Because he had gained knowledge. He'd watched the process and examined the patterns in this strange ritual. By doing so, he was able to execute it flawlessly, more confident than those who had preceded him.

It was a small hedge, but I thought it was a wise one. I nodded my head. Whatever else you could say about this upright, arrogant prick of a man, you had to admit he knew what the hell he was doing when it came to schmoozing aliens.

This time, the third time, the Nebrans were even more thorough in their examination than before. One of them even dared to reach up to the tribune's waist. He dared to unsnap the strap that held the tribune's holstered service pistol in place on his hip.

"Ah, ah!" Kraus said, smiling and reaching a hand down to snap the pistol in place again. He had the air of a man scolding small children.

But when he went to re-secure his weapon, we all noticed that it was gone. One of the two Nebrans—the bastard on the left—had the weapon in his strange hands. He held it up like he meant business.

Before anyone could do much more than gasp, the furry asshole fired the weapon. A power bolt tore through the tribune's chest. He was wearing a dress uniform and nothing in the way of armor. No protection at all.

The Nebran saw fit to hold down the trigger and pump another six bolts into Kraus' body before he flopped down on the deck with a shocked look on his face.

Tribune Kraus was steaming and twitching on the floor. He was dead, of course.

The reaction from around the room was predictable. Everyone gasped. They threw their eyes wide. As we were military men, most of us began to rise and reach for our own weapons.

I, however, was cut from a different cloth than most of them. I'd seen too much action. I'd died too many times. My actions over time had become much more decisive than your typical brass-wearing fop that wandered the halls of Old Central on Earth.

My weapon was already out. In fact, as soon as the Nebran had fingered Tribune Kraus' pistol, I'd unsnapped my own holster and put my hand upon the grip of my gun.

Quick-drawing the weapon, I didn't bother to stand up. I just braced myself on the table, both elbows down, pistol up, aiming carefully.

Zap, zap!

Two power bolts flew. Both the Nebrans were nailed in the head. Due to the small size of their skulls, their heads were blown completely away from their long sinewy necks.

Then, without hesitation, I trained my weapon on the third alien in the room. This was the Mogwa known as Sateekas.

I was taking no chances. All of my actions were automatic, but before I could pop off another shot, a delicate, fine-boned hand laid over my own crusty mitts.

The hand was owned by Winslade.

"I think that's enough, McGill," he said.

"What is this?" Wurtenberger shouted. "Assassination?"

He was demanding this of Grand Admiral Sateekas, who was watching everyone in the room.

"A pity…" Sateekas said, reaching out a long appendage to kick at the two smoking corpses of his Nebrans. "We've been training these two for quite a while, but again, they have failed me. I'd hoped at the mere sight of dangerous aliens such as yourselves—but no, we have yet to beat the inquisitiveness and the rebellious nature out of these creatures."

"You knew they were going to attack?" Wurtenberger complained. "Why didn't you warn us?"

"That would have removed all value from this test of your skills." The Mogwa pointed a waggling limb in my direction. "The McGill-creature demonstrated the correct response. Decisive action was taken. I have videoed this entire event, and I am transmitting it to all the Nebrans aboard my battlecruiser. The lesson might sink in."

Everyone was pissed, as one might expect. The Mogwa drew himself up after listening to various complaints. He didn't seem to care much about our squawking and carrying on.

"Very well," he said, "I've made my decision. I choose Legion Varus. They alone have shown both the appropriate behavior patterns and the lowest price. How could I possibly come to any other decision?"

With that, Sateekas exited the chambers. He left behind a lot of slack-jawed humans in his wake.

Wurtenberger called for bio people to come in and take the Nebran's bodies away. The air conditioning system was able to suck away most of the vile fumes from the alien dead laying on the floor.

Once the room was calm and relatively stench-free, he addressed the group. He turned toward Germanica first.

"The client has made a decision. You have a second opportunity to alter your bid. Possibly if you were to match the price set by Legion Varus—"

"No!" the tribune of Germanica said loudly and firmly. He shook his head. "I have not reconsidered my choices. With everything now made clear, I believe this task is best left to the excellent Varus." He made a generous gesture toward Tribune Winslade.

To my mind, I thought I saw a smirk playing around the corners of his mouth. Had Winslade truly bought himself a pig in the poke?

Winslade looked a bit sweaty, and I thought perhaps he was having similar fears.

"Very well then," Wurtenberger said. He glanced toward the body of Tribune Kraus from Victrix, which had yet to be removed. "In the interest of saving time, I will assume that Victrix is not interested in altering their offer in any way. I hereby declare the contract to have been bid and accepted. Congratulations, Tribune Winslade. Legion Varus will serve upon a star that is now newly under the control of Segin."

"Newly under the control?" Winslade asked.

"Yes, of course. Why did you think Sateekas wants to hire a legion? Has your mind failed to gather the details? The Mogwa at Segin have recently gone on a burst of conquering, invading their neighboring planets. Those bizarre twitchy creatures, the Nebrans, are from a star system not too far from City World. They've been conquered only a few months prior. Sateekas wishes for you to help him garrison his new possession, and through force of arms, subdue these problematic natives."

Again, he gestured toward the spot where the two furry-looking, raccoon-monkey-things had both died horribly on his carpet.

"Now, I'm calling this meeting adjourned. Please leave so I can bring in an appropriate cleanup crew. These carpets will have to be scrubbed, and all the air filters will have to be changed. Seven, make a note of it."

The Nairb did so dutifully.

Winslade got up, and I walked after him. Both of us felt somewhat stunned.

"Uh…" I said, "Tribune Winslade, sir? What the hell just happened?"

"The technical term for that process, McGill," he told me, "was a con-job. And we were the chief marks."

"Oh…" I said, "that's pretty much what I thought."

## -6-

After the endless meeting finally broke up, I automatically headed for the exit in the elevator without even pausing for any after-meeting conversations with the other participants. "McGill, where are you going?"

*Damn it…*

Primus Cherish Collins was on my tail. She was like a bloodhound when it came to detecting a man who was trying to escape pointless yapping.

I turned around on one heel and put on a smile. I let her catch up to me and stare up into my fool face.

We stood there in the midst of that line of weird, expressionless hogs. I was almost willing to believe that they were robots or something. A few of them had missed a spot or two when they'd shaved, though. That was the only way I could tell the difference.

"What can I do you for, Primus?" I asked in a cheery tone.

"I'd like to get your perspective on what just happened in the meeting."

"The one you just missed?"

She showed me some teeth. It wasn't a pretty look. "What other meeting might I be referring to, McGill?"

"Uh…"

I could tell she was pissed off because I'd been in there with Winslade while she'd been kicked to the curb. It was therefore time for some tact.

"Ah, don't worry yourself none," I said. "You didn't miss much. The good news is: we got the contract!"

She blinked at me twice. "We did?"

"Yep. Old Winslade, I'm sure he's over there talking to Wurtenberger about it right now."

Cherish looked nervously toward the big doors that led into the even bigger office. I knew that she wanted to go in there, and she wanted to be part of the brass-filled yakking session. She wanted to find out everything that had happened. She hated missing a single fart in the woods. But, despite her burning curiosity, she didn't quite dare to interrupt her betters.

Seeing as she was distracted, I took this opportunity to step away again.

She clamped onto my wrist, however. I faced her again with that fake grin.

"Come over here," she said, and she led me away like I was a bad kid in school. Around me, the hog guards were still doing that staring thing. I tried to get a reaction from them, making faces and pointing a waggling finger at the back of Cherish's angry little head.

But none of that worked. They were stone cold, these guys. I was vaguely impressed.

When we were close to the elevators and out of earshot from the hog-statues, Cherish stopped dragging me and peppered me with hissy questions.

"So, we really got the deal?"

"I swear it on my momma's—"

"What kind of a deal is it?"

I told her very briefly about how it had been sold as an escort mission, but had turned out to involve some rather rebellious raccoon-monkey-skunk bastards.

She frowned at that, especially when I got to the part about the twenty-five percent discount.

"Twenty-five percent? That's insane. Our operating costs alone... What was Winslade thinking?"

I shrugged, as I didn't much care.

"That wasn't your idea, was it McGill?"

"Hell no. I barely talked. All I did was shoot those furry reverse-skunk-striped weasels when the time came."

"I bet you enjoyed that, didn't you?" she asked.

"Uh... yeah, pretty much."

After that, Cherish let go of my hand. She stood there, teeth clenched, brain working hard. She wasn't even looking at me, really. She was just sliding her eyes around, mumbling to herself and cursing a bit under her breath.

"Hey... how about you and I go to get something to eat?" I suggested. "My stomach's an empty pit right now, and it's way past lunchtime."

Cherish finally glanced back up at me as if startled by the idea. She was in a fog of thoughts. She was an ambitious little lady, and it sometimes caused her to forget about her normal bodily functions—like eating.

She took in her breath, and I could tell she was actually considering the idea.

That was another good sign. I'd found over the years that if you have a woman who's pissed off and jealous, the best thing you can do is ask her on a date. That settles them right down most of the time.

Finally, she shook her head. "No... no... There are too many preparations. Too many balls I have to get rolling. The legion isn't prepared for deployment. We'll send out warnings and get ready to muster out. We'll have to put out the call to all the officers, first."

"Oh..." I said, disappointed. She was right. I was going to have to dig into all that bullshit myself.

"There isn't even a budget yet. No arrangements for travel money—nothing. This is a nightmare. Do you have any idea how long we've got before they want us to ship out?"

I shrugged. I had no idea at all. Of course, they'd probably discussed such issues during the overly long meeting, but I'd naturally blanked out all that boring stuff. Even the things I hadn't ignored, I was quickly forgetting about just as I stood here yakking with this girl.

"No... not really..."

"You're useless," she said, shaking her head.

"Oh, now that's not true," I said. "I'm useful for several things."

I put up my hand and began counting off big fingers with it. "Number one, I shot down those two aliens on the spot. That impressed Sateekas right there."

She rolled her eyes and crossed her arms.

"Number two, I'm hilarious. Just take me on a date to see. Get a couple of beers in me and some good food and—"

She shook her head again. "That's not happening, McGill. Not tonight."

"Not tonight?" That was suggestive. I almost asked her, *what about tomorrow, then?* but thought the better of it.

"You've got one more finger up," she pointed out. "What's the third thing?"

I smiled. In fact, I grinned. "I think you know what the third thing is."

She stared at me for a moment, pursing her lips tightly. "That's inappropriate talk, Centurion."

"Aw, come on!" I laughed, and I waved over my shoulder as I walked away.

With vast relief I managed to get into the elevator at last and I let it whisk me away.

Down, down, down I plunged through Central.

During that overly long trip, I had to privately account myself as a near wizard, having escaped Cherish like that. It hadn't been an accident that I'd managed to do so quickly—far from it.

The key move was when I'd propositioned her in an offhanded manner. That move had put her on the spot. She could've either gone on a date with me right then and there, or she could bail out. If she'd kept pestering me, that would have made her look interested—so she'd bailed.

In my opinion, that was one of the best moves a trapped man had available to him to avoid long, pointless discussions. I'd cut right to the chase. Did she want a date or not?

Over the years, I'd often faced women who wanted to talk my ear off. But asking for a date usually fixed the situation immediately.

What was doubly good about it was the move sometimes worked, and you got yourself a date. If it didn't, you usually escaped from all the yakking. Either way, it was a win-win.

Now, my mind turned to the next thing on my internal list—which was finding food.

As I was way, way up in the upper stratosphere of Central, I was able to worm my way into an officer's mess that I'd normally not be allowed access to. Because I was already here, and I had just attended a high-level meeting, I was able to sneak into a primus-only cafeteria.

It was a sumptuous affair. Three burgers, two loads of fries, and a couple of apples later, I was full.

Well... almost full. I looked around for alcohol but found they didn't serve anything like that, at least not here, until well into the evening hours. Snapping my fingers in disappointment, I headed back to the elevators again.

My mind wandered to new ideas. I thought about heading out into the streets next. There were some ladies in this town I could chase—but then, I had a nagging thought.

There was something else I was supposed to be doing. What was the original reason I'd come up to this town in the first place?

Oh yeah... *Galina*.

Galina had given me a private mission to perform. She'd asked me to check on Drusus, to actually see him in his tank, and to find out if there was anything I could do to spring him.

Of course, that seemed damn near hopeless to me, but I shrugged. I might as well give it a try. Right now was the best time, as my tapper still had a couple of hours of high access codes available to it.

The way Central worked involved tappers and access codes, all of which had expiration dates. If you got into a high-level meeting, especially one with the freaking consul himself, you were automatically awarded access to a lot of places that a near grunt-level Varus man like myself was normally not allowed.

Still though, hmm, I was fairly certain I didn't possess the codes necessary to get all the way down to the holiest of holies beneath Central. The Vault of the Forgotten was supposed to be exactly like it sounded: Forgotten.

I racked my brain and even knocked my knuckles on my thick skull for a moment or two, trying to come up with a plan.

At last, I thought I had one. I left the elevators that went upstairs into the guts of the pyramid-like structure of Central, and instead headed over to the second, dimmer-lit lobby in the back.

These elevators were much more rarely used. They led down into the depths.

Stepping aboard the first one that came available, all the while under the scrutiny of a suspicious hog, I tapped at the buttons without even looking at them.

To my relief, I was allowed to travel down to the detention levels, then past that to the war rooms. Next up was the Intel zone. That's where the worst creeps in the building resided.

What level had Agent Dickson said his office was on?

106... I was pretty sure that's what he'd said.

I tapped the number in, and I waited for several long seconds.

The elevator car didn't budge. In fact, the metal box didn't do anything at all.

Knowing this was a time to be patient, I just sat there, humming tunelessly.

This was unusual. Normally, any elevator doors like to open themselves when you were sitting still at a given floor.

Now, if access was officially denied, I should have been informed of the fact. The elevator system would tell you to go to hell straight away. When I'd tried accessing places where I wasn't wanted in the past, the system had spit me out wherever it thought I belonged instead.

But today was a different day. The elevator car wasn't doing a damn thing.

Finally, there was a buzzing sound. It was the intercom. A voice began talking—there was no face, the screen was dark.

"Centurion McGill?" it said. "Why are you attempting to access floor 106?"

The voice didn't identify itself, but I figured under the circumstances, it didn't have to.

"I'm heading down there to meet an old friend," I said.

That was absorbed without any response for a moment. "You are mistaken. You've got no friends on floor 106, McGill."

"No, I'm not. His name is Dickson. Agent Dickson—at least that's the code name he went under when I was his best buddy."

The voice went quiet again. I strained my ear-flaps, but heard nothing but the muted rumble of elevators going by in the shafts nearby. My own elevator was deathly still.

Experimentally, I rattled the open-door button.

Nothing. It didn't even change the light color. It was as if I wasn't touching it at all.

I thought about ramming my combat blade in between the crack in the doors and trying to pry it open—but I told myself to just relax and to go with the flow. After all, I'd started this confrontation. It was best to bluff it through to the end.

Finally, the voice came back, except this time it had shifted somewhat. It was a little bit higher in tone.

I knew that voice in an instant. It was Agent Dickson.

"McGill?" he said. "What the hell are you doing? Irritating me again?"

"Don't worry, I'm not here to sell you any cookies," I said. "Today, I'm here to confess."

"Confess what?"

"All my sins."

It was quiet for a moment. "What the hell are you talking about, McGill? If this is some kind of practical joke—"

"I tell you it's not, sir. It is *not*. Let me come on down to your office and we'll sort this out together."

For about thirty more seconds, nothing spoke to me. The elevator was motionless, quiet, and so was the voice in the wall. Even when I hammered on the doors and shouted, there was no response.

Finally, without any further word from the strange voice, the elevator began to move again. It was moving downward.

I watched the numbers flash by. Eventually, it stopped on floor 106, and the door swished open.

I wore a big grin. My hands were wide open and spread to my sides. I looked like I was about to hug my Aunt Sally on Christmas Day.

A stern team faced me. Dickson was there with a weapon in his hands, a neural pistol, it looked like. Two others with spear-length shock rods stood to either side of them. I thought I knew the name of the guy on the left...

"Brinkley?" I said. "And Dickson? Who's this fellow over here?" I pointed at the third, scowling hog.

"Never mind him," Dickson said.

All three of them were glaring at me. You have to understand that the Intel boys and I had never quite seen eye-to-eye. That was probably my fault, as I'd killed a number of them over the years. On the other hand, they'd tortured me to death a few times as well.

Today, I wanted to move past all that bad blood. I was trying to convince them that I was harmless—but I wasn't sure I could pull it off. My main tactic in such situations was to simply lie my ass off—but these guys were really good at detecting that sort of thing.

"I repeat, McGill, what the hell do you want?"

"To confess, Dickson. To show you some things—stuff you've never seen before."

He blinked a couple of times. Brinkley laughed. "Yeah, right... This yokel knows nothing, Dickson. Let's shock him into a fetal ball and leave him in the elevator. I'll ship him back upstairs with an apple in his mouth."

"Better yet, we could send him to detention," the other, hog-like character said. "Let those boys have some fun with him after we're done."

Dickson didn't even look at either one of them. He didn't seem to be listening to them, either.

Instead, he locked eyes with me. Sighing, he waved the other two away. He stepped aboard the elevator at my side.

He still had his small, slim neural pistol in his hands. It was the kind of thing that was meant to project a nerve shutting-down effect. At close range, it could make you go limp as if you were paralyzed. The only trouble with that kind of weapon was if you shot a guy with it too much, his heart would stop pumping, and his lungs would stop breathing. I doubt any of these guys cared about that, however.

"What are you doing, sir?" Brinkley asked.

"Shut up. I'll deal with this myself. Go back to your offices."

The elevator door began closing. The two guys with the shock sticks—shock spears really, looked stunned and befuddled. I gave them a little wave as the doors slid shut.

"All right, McGill," Dickson said. "You've had your fun at my expense too many times. Is this all a big prank, or have you got something to say?"

"I surely do! In fact, I've got something to *show* you. That's much better than talking about it."

He eyed me warily. I could tell he half expected me to spring at him and try to beat him down. That had happened before, and it might happen again. But today that wasn't really my plan. I needed Dickson because I needed to use his high-level clearance.

"We're gonna take a little trip *down*," I said, pointing at the floor with a big finger.

When we finally got to floor minus 500, we switched over to another set of elevators. These went down farther—down to about minus 525, or thereabouts. It was hard to tell because the numbers weren't even displayed at this point.

Dickson began to get kind of nervous. "Where the hell are you taking me?"

"Never been down here, huh?" I asked.

"No, and you shouldn't have been, either. This is insane. Are you taking me down to some level that's all dirt and drills? Maybe with bots scooping out more earth? That's a hell of a lot of work just to try to perm a man, McGill."

I could see he was completely distrusting me and mistaking my motives for the worst. I laughed. "Don't worry about that. I'm taking you down to see the Vault of the Forgotten."

He stared at me, and he opened his mouth a bit wider than before. Some would call it a gape. "The Vault of the Forgotten? No one wants to see that place."

"But there are interesting people inside. That's what I want to show you. There's somebody there I want you to talk to."

He was beginning to sweat. Now, far be it for me to judge a man's metabolism, as it *was* getting hotter down here. If you go down far enough into the earth, you know, it actually does get hot.

But I didn't think that was a problem. Not in this case.

Dickson was scared. In fact, he was damned close to wetting his pants by the time the elevator dinged for the last time.

We were let out into a lonely, echoing passageway that seemed to lead to nowhere. No one was in sight, and the halls echoed our every footfall.

## -7-

Of course, the reason I'd brought Dickson down here had nothing to do with him. He wasn't worth jack squat to me—except for his security clearance.

He had the access codes to get all the way down to the darkest dungeons. As a senior Intel officer, he pretty much had the run of the place.

Dickson was like a private company cop. He'd been hired to snoop around in a very large building. That meant he had to have access to every chamber in the entire place. If not him, then who?

Just looking at him, I knew he was nervous, however. He knew there were areas where even he shouldn't venture.

He worked for the largest world government that Earth had ever seen. In fact, I believe at this point that Hegemony was the most extensive and nefarious government in all of Province 921.

Hell, I'd even put our government up against some of the worst organizations I'd seen out along the frontier. The governments of Rigel, the Squids, the Saurians—none of them could hold a candle to Old Earth. There were so many secrets down here, so much sheer deviltry, it didn't even bear thinking about.

Even the security procedures were weird down here. The floors didn't have numbers anymore. Instead, they were defined by "zones". Like Zone Echo or Zone Bravo. At least that's what all the signs said.

The air pressure felt strange, too. It was heavy and thick. I had to wonder just how far down we were. Way below sea level, that was for sure.

The chambers in Bravo Zone were icy cold, but not in Echo. It was hot in Echo Zone. To me, it felt like you could sense Earth's mantle. It seemed these puffcrete walls were holding back secrets—maybe lava crawled restlessly, not too far below from the soles of my boots.

At last, we reached the steamy gates of the Vault of the Forgotten.

"This has got to be the sketchiest place I've ever been, McGill," Dickson said nervously. "How in the hell do you even know about it?"

"Just put your hand on this here plate."

Dickson looked at it like it was going to bite him or something, but he did it anyway. Both of us were scanned excessively by the automated security system. There was no staff down here, just machines.

Finally, a section of the wall slid away, a big slab of rock that moved with a slight grating noise. A dark maw yawned wide.

I walked right in like I owned the place, leaving Dickson in the doorway. He lingered there, looking like a lost little boy at the supermarket.

I ignored him and his questions. As far as I was concerned, he'd already done me the service that I'd needed. If he turned around right now and ran out of the place screaming, that'd be fine with me.

Unfortunately, I wasn't so lucky. He eventually followed me inside.

The vault was just as strange as I remembered. The blue lights, the gurgling, bubbling tanks, the brains with scraps of flesh left attached to them. They swayed and drifted in their tanks.

I had to wonder if these prisoners looked different from one to the next because they'd been here so long. Maybe over the last century or two they'd used different techniques to remove the unnecessary body parts. Or, maybe there was some purpose to their various levels of dismemberment.

A few had a lock of hair growing out of the back, despite lacking proper skulls or scalps. Others had eyeballs that either could move or couldn't. These drooping eyes—usually blind—dangled on their optic nerves and stared at the bottom of their tanks.

Some of them even had scraps of skulls and skin. All of it was positively creepy.

Could it be that during the process of reanimation, some of these things had been grown further along than was necessary? Could a revival machine simply be programmed not to regrow the entire body, but instead to only grow the parts some ghoulish operator heartlessly selected?

It was absolutely freaky, and the place almost gave me the willies enough to make me shudder.

I ran a finger along the nameplates looking for Drusus. The tanks weren't laid down in alphabetical order. It didn't even seem like there was a chronological organization to how they were sorted.

My old granny, back when she'd put preserves away in the cellar, was very meticulous about dates and times. She always marked down the nature of the preserve, and she even wrote notes on the jars. Like, "prunes from a good year" or "sweet as apple pie," stuff like that.

The system here seemed to be quite a bit more vague. It was definitely ad-hoc—like a parking lot. If there was enough room on a shelf, and a few working plug-ins for oxygen and nutrient fluids, a new jar was stuffed into the slot and installed.

There were no guards here, no wardens. I'm sure someone came through to mind the place, but you didn't have to worry about anyone escaping. Nobody had any hands, arms, or even a finger to lift that could benefit themselves.

A few of the strange, drifting remnants had working sensory organs. These tracked me as I wandered by—but none of them spoke until finally, one warbling voice came out of a hidden speaker.

"I know you…" it said.

I whirled, the hackles standing up on the back of my neck. It was the voice of a ghost. All of them had voices like that.

It wasn't Drusus. I could tell by the voice. Sure, it was a simulated female voice, faked by AI, but it probably sounded more or less like the original.

"Uh... and who might you be, ma'am?" I asked.

"For fuck's sake, McGill," Dickson interrupted from behind me. He'd crept near without me noticing. "You're going to talk to these things?"

"I sure as hell am," I said. "That's why I came down here."

Dickson looked positively freaked out. His eyes were bulging almost as much as these brains were.

"Don't wet your pants," I told him. "Just listen." I turned back to the creatures in the vault. One of them was looking at me with a single, alert eyeball.

"How do you know me, ma'am?" I asked the brain in the tank.

"Know you...? That's right... I do... It was so long ago—or maybe it was only last week. Don't you remember? You were the one who unplugged me."

I had to blink at that. The fact was, her words had made my blood run cold.

It was true. Once, about a decade ago during the Green World campaign, I'd come down here with Floramel. We'd been planning to make certain inquiries about advanced cloning techniques.

I'd met a lady brain on that fateful day, and I'd felt sorry for her. I racked my own malfunctioning organ, trying to remember what she had been named.

Finally, I had it, snapping my fingers.

"Elizabeth?"

"Yes!" she said. "That's my name. I'm so glad you uttered it. I couldn't remember it until just now when you said it aloud."

This kind of talk freaked me out. How the hell had she recognized one James McGill while she couldn't remember her own name?

I shrugged. I supposed spending a century floating in a tank would probably have negative effects on anyone.

"They brought you back?"

"Apparently," she agreed. "I can remember when the water leaked out, my vital fluids spilling all over the deck. I realized that I'd been exposed, and I was about to die."

"Um... sorry about that."

"Don't be. Dying was a relief, you know. Oh, I panicked at first. I cursed you and yours. But then, before it was over, I relaxed. I realized it was all for the best. In fact, I felt gratitude as I passed away. Imagine my horror to find myself back in this tank again an unknown time later."

"Huh..." I said. "They must've regrown you from some DNA files somewhere."

"I have surmised the same," she said.

"But why the hell would they do that? What do you know that's so valuable to them after all this time?"

"I cannot say," she said, "but I'm sure it has to do with my participation in the resistance against the Unification."

"Whoa!" Dickson said, suddenly throwing up both his hands in alarm. "I don't want to hear any of this. McGill, you shouldn't listen, either. I'd have to report it."

I turned on him. "Report what?" I said. "You're the one who brought me down here. Isn't talking to this nice brain-lady the reason why you did it?"

"*I* brought you?" Dickson said. "You were the one who told me we needed to come down."

I cut him off and jabbed his skinny chest with a thick finger. "Listen, Dickson, you know how this game works. You're in this now—you're in this deep. You'd best just shut up and go along to get along. We'll be out of here in a few minutes. You don't want anyone knowing about how you led me down here to talk to some rebel brain, do you?"

He sputtered a bit, but I cut him off again.

"I bet you're not even supposed to be down here. Not without special papers signed by some hog hall-monitor."

Maybe it was just the blue light, but to me, Dickson looked a little sick. He narrowed his eyes, squinted at me, and brought up a sharp finger of his own.

"You're not going to intimidate me, McGill," he said. "I know people. I know *important* people."

"Shut up and keep your panties on. We'll be out of here in a minute."

"I'm the one with the clearances, you cretin!"

"That's right," I told him, smiling. "There's no way I could get down here without you. How's that going to sound during inquiry? Even if they halfway believe your story, they're going to realize you showed poor judgment. It'll be a black mark on your record forever."

"Threats? You're actually threatening me?"

"Look… we're all friends here. What you need to do now is wait till I'm done talking to this nice brain-lady, then escort my ass out and forget this ever happened."

Dickson shut up, but he also showed me lots of teeth. They gleamed yellow with a black light effect. It made him appear strange and alien in nature. It was almost as if a skull was grinning at me out of the dark.

I turned back to the lady-brain. "Elizabeth?" I said to her, "sorry to ask you, I don't want to impose, but since I once did you a nice turn… maybe you could do something for me?"

"I know what it is you want, McGill," she said.

"Uh… how's that?"

"There's only one thing that I could give—information."

"Yep, that's right."

"You cause me to feel sadness, McGill, with this request."

"Why's that, exactly?"

"Well… you have to know that I've suffered countless interrogation techniques over a century or more, right?"

"Yeah, I figured…" I told her.

"I'm just now realizing this must be one more such technique. A last clever ruse generated by the fiends who operate this bastion of vast, thoughtless evil."

"Whoa, whoa! Hold on!" I said. "I'm not going to ask you to give away any of your comrades. In fact, I'm not going to ask you to tell me anything you don't want to talk about."

She hesitated for a moment. A single bubble rolled up from the back of her. I didn't want to even know where that had escaped from. She was all wrinkly gray-matter. There shouldn't be any bubbles…

"When I came down here, I wasn't looking for you," I said. "In fact, I thought you were dead."

"That does make sense…"

"I came down looking for another prisoner. I just want to know where he is. I can't find him."

"Give me the name," she said.

"Drusus," I said, "an officer of Hegemony, once a tribune of Legion Varus."

"Drusus…?" she said. "Yes, there was one here by that name, but he's gone now."

"He's gone?" I said, looking around wildly. "Where'd he go?"

She made a weird bubbly sound. I think it was a laugh. "Pardon me if I'm unable to give such detailed information. All I know is that the various minds here can converse, those of us who are still capable of it. Some of us rave, some of us insist on making all kinds of delusional plans to escape. Drusus was a mind of reason and thoughtful logic. I enjoyed his company, even if he was what I would consider one of the enemy."

"That's right," I said. "Drusus is one of the good ones, a true believer. He doesn't really serve Hegemony. He serves Earth overall."

"I hope that you're right. I also hope he still exists, and he hasn't been expunged completely."

All this time, Dickson was watching this conversation. His eyes were flashing back and forth between me and the brain. The fact that I was bringing up Drusus, another non-person, another someone of importance that was supposed to be forgotten, I don't think that was setting his mind at ease at all. Not one little bit.

"I've heard enough of this, McGill," Dickson finally said. "I was a fool to come down here with you, but I'm going to fix that." He turned around and walked out.

I looked after him. Already, my mind downshifted to thoughts of murder. It was a weakness in my character.

"I fear that one's up to no good, McGill," the lady-brain told me. "Don't turn your back on him."

"Don't you worry," I told her. "I think I've got him thoroughly bamboozled."

But then—I heard something.

It was a siren, an alarm going off. There were flashing lights out in the main passage.

*Goddamn it!* Had Dickson set something off?

"Tell me!" I begged the lady-brain. "Just tell me where Drusus is!"

"He'll overhear…"

I turned slowly back toward the entrance. There Dickson stood, silhouetted in the doorway of the vault. He had his neural pistol in his hand again. That double-crossing snake.

"Who's that in there?" Dickson shouted, as if he had just discovered me. "Identify yourself, intruder!"

He shined a bright light on me. I knew right away what he was doing. All of a sudden, he'd turned his body cams on, and he was recording this encounter.

"There you are, Dickson!" I boomed. "Come over here and help me with this tank." I made a show of reaching up and fooling with Elizabeth's enclosure. The liquid sloshed. "This is the one you wanted, right? I think we can unplug it from the wall, no problem."

"Get away from that, McGill," Dickson shouted.

"What?" I said, gaping at him. I looked as dumb as a bag of hammers. "But this is the one you wanted, isn't it? That's why you brought me down here, to carry this big old gurgling tank—right?"

Dickson had heard enough. He knew I was screwing up his arrest video. The cover story he'd pulled together in his nasty little mind was being destroyed by my antics.

"You country fuck," he growled—and then he fired.

I took the first one in the side, right near the kidney. The second hit me in the arm. That bicep flopped. I had half a mind to yank Elizabeth's tank out again and smash her brain to pieces. That would probably kill her. Maybe this time—just maybe—they wouldn't revive her and put her back on her shelf again.

I hesitated too long. Dickson had grown tired of my special brand of nonsense. He began blazing away with that neural gun, firing beam after beam into me.

I felt weak and sick. Then I took one in the neck, and that did it.

I went sliding down onto the deck as if every bone in my body had turned to rubber. My spinal cord could no longer instruct my limbs. I was still conscious—but crippled.

Dickson ran off then, shouting and sounding alarms. I heard him on his tapper, breathlessly demanding backup. He was a good actor. Sooner or later, a pack of hogs would come running.

I lay gasping like a fish on the deck of a boat, and I realized I was having trouble breathing. My heart was still pumping, mind you, but breathing…? That was the problem. I took in air in gasps.

"McGill?" Elizabeth said. "Are you still there?"

"Yes, ma'am," I croaked out, barely able to utter the words.

"You tried to do it again, didn't you? You tried to help me. In fact, you came down here just for that singular purpose. Why is that?"

"Don't know…" I said. I could barely force my numb face to form the words.

"I know why you came to rescue me from this purgatory. There can only be one answer. I used to be quite attractive—as you clearly know. You found pictures of me from the distant past, didn't you? Images of my full-bodied youth. That's so sweet."

"You got me…" I croaked out.

By this time, I could hardly even open my eyes. All I could see was blue glimmers. I couldn't move my head at all. My jaws, my tongue, they were all losing functionality.

"So sweet," Elizabeth said. "I'm going to reward you with something, just in case you're ever able to walk and talk again."

I made a grunting sound. It wasn't a yes, it wasn't a no, it wasn't even really a question mark. It was the best noise I could make with my dying lungs.

"I'm going to tell you where Drusus went," she said.

And then, she told me.

Ninety seconds later, I was dead.

## -8-

"Well, well, well," said a voice—I didn't like the sound of it from the very beginning. The voice was male and sounded amused. "What have we got here? Centurion McGill? How the hell did he die?"

"Don't even look it up," another, softer voice said. A young woman.

The feminine voice was familiar, but I couldn't quite place her. My ears perked up, even though my eyes weren't open. Actually, there wasn't much perking to do, because my ears were just as weak and unresponsive as the rest of me. I could hear at this point, but that was about it.

"What do you mean, 'Don't look it up?'" the first guy said.

"I know James McGill. He dies often—and it's safer not to know why."

I *knew* that voice. It had been years, but I was sure about it. I mumbled, trying to get out the name, "Dawn?"

"Hey, he's trying to talk. That's a good sign. Do we have a score yet for this clown?"

"He's not a clown," Dawn said sweetly, defensively.

That was so nice. Why had I left this girl?

Oh yeah. I remembered now. She wasn't part of Legion Varus. Our brief fling had flourished during the Edge World campaign.

Drifting thoughts left me curious about what had happened to Dawn. After all, due to my interference in intergalactic politics, a big Skay came along and tried to steal Earth's moon.

The problem was, Dawn had been working on the Moon at the time…

"Oh, I get it," the swaggering bio said, "you're letting me know I've got some competition, here."

Dawn made a pffing noise. I got the feeling that she had little regard for him. That was a good thing. I almost smiled, my rubbery lips forming a curve that was vague in nature.

"Dawn?" I managed to croak out.

"Ah, shit," the bio-boy said, "he recognizes you, too? Now, I'm getting curious. I'm looking him up."

"Don't," Dawn said, but he didn't listen to her.

I heard his fingers tapping on keys. He was consulting the computer in the revival chamber. "Centurion James McGill, revivals: unknown. That's weird. We usually keep a strict count. I think by law, we have to, don't we?"

"I told you not to look," Dawn said.

He pressed ahead, ignoring her sage advice. "Apgar scores for revivals—lots of revivals all over the cosmos—and those are just the ones we know about. Mysterious disappearances, months being dead. Two years, once. Wow. This guy was either having a great vacation, or... Oh, shit!"

"What?"

"Did you see his estimated chronological age? This fossil is a senior citizen, technically. Did you know your boyfriend is probably older than your grandpa? Maybe you like it freaky, is that it?"

Dawn pouted. "He doesn't look that old…" she said, and I felt her delicate touch running over my right arm. Sure, she was probably just looking for a spot to attach a probe to take a measurement—but she didn't have to run her fingers all along the length of my arm to do that.

It was a sweet touch. Just the sort of thing I remembered from Dawn.

I cracked open one eye. Two blurs hovered over me. "Who's the clown?" I managed to squeeze out of my throat, flicking a finger at the bigger of the two.

"He's no one…" she said, then she leaned close and lowered her voice. "James? Don't get riled."

"Riled?" the bio said, overhearing her. "I'll have you know, McGill, this is *my* revival chamber. You're *nobody* here. You're just a lump of meat that I managed to breathe life into."

This big-talker wasn't improving my mood any. He seemed like a smug prick.

I considered murdering him before I left the room, but Dawn's gentle touch was back. Her fingers touched my brow, and she stole away the heat that was overcoming my mind.

Did she know what I was thinking about? She probably did.

I forced my rubbery lips into a wide smile. I managed to prop myself up on my elbows. "I need a shower."

"I'll second that," laughing-boy agreed.

I rose like Frankenstein's monster, swinging my legs off the gurney. I slid onto the deck and stood up on wobbly legs.

Dawn made an effort to steady me with her light grip, but I almost urged her not to. If I slipped and went down, well, I didn't want her to get hurt in the process.

The smart-ass bio with the big mouth kept yapping. "Well, McGill, at least you broke up the tedium for us. First revive of the day. Time to recharge the plasma tanks and reload the bonemeal hopper."

I didn't say anything. I couldn't trust myself to be civil, and I didn't want to blow things with Dawn. Instead, I stumbled over to the showering booth, slid inside, and let the light sprays of water and mist wash away the amniotic fluid and cleanse my newly reborn body.

I had to force myself to think. Right now, my situation looked good. *Really* good.

I'd expected to be permed, or at least awakened by the likes of Dickson. In that case, I'd have been revived in Central's detention center, waiting for an interrogation. Next up would have been a quick auto-trial, followed by possible incarceration…

But none of that had happened. Instead, I was on a ship, or at least in orbit somewhere.

"Where am I?" I said.

"Don't you know your own ship, McGill? Maybe your brains *are* addled. I'm going to take a point off this Apgar score, lowering it to a seven."

"You're on *Scorpio*, James," Dawn answered my question.

"Uh… anyone know what happened?" I asked, pretending to be in the dark about my criminal demise.

"I don't know why you died," Dawn said. "There's no reference in the records... Just a name."

"What name?" I toweled off, put on my uniform, adjusting my cap to the exact, precise angle that I liked it.

"Imperator Galina Turov…" Dawn said in a small voice.

There was a bit of coolness in her words. I could tell that she still didn't like Galina.

It'd been a lot of years, but Galina had once made a point of kicking her out of my presence. She'd gotten her transferred or something. I couldn't even remember the details.

"Huh. That's weird," I said, as if I was aware of no earthly reason why Galina might have done such a thing.

But that, of course, was a lie of omission. I knew exactly why Galina had had me quietly revived aboard *Scorpio*. She'd assigned me a clandestine mission. She probably knew where I died, down in the Vault of the Forgotten—a place I wasn't supposed to be.

Therefore, she must suspect that I'd completed my mission, and I had the information she sought.

The funny part was I did know where Drusus had ended up. That brain-lady Elizabeth had told me. She'd said he'd been transferred to the Turov estate.

That gave me a shudder even now, lightyears away. I didn't want to think about the grim nature of Drusus' predicament. One would think that when you were reduced to a brain floating in a tank, well sir, things had gone as deeply down the road to Hell as was possible.

But… in this case, I suspected Drusus might be in an even worse place now. Maybe they'd built him a new body and started torturing him or something. Who knew?

In any case, Galina had known she wasn't going to learn anything from me if I wasn't breathing, so she'd arranged for my files to be transferred out to *Scorpio* and instructed my betters to give me a quiet revive. I guess it was the least she could do.

It all made sense, and I was happy I'd had someone pulling strings for me on the outside of Central. I've always said that if you're going to perform a crime, it was best to do it for someone powerful, someone who had your back.

Once I was fully kitted out, I turned around and faced Dawn. She was eyeing me curiously.

The moment our eyes met, she cast them down again. Was she still upset about the fact that Galina Turov's name was on my revival order? Probably so.

"Hey! Listen," I said, "are you actually part of Legion Varus now?"

She nodded.

"Oh, that's gotta be quite a story. I'd love to hear the details."

Dawn's eyes flicked up to meet mine then dropped again.

"How about tonight?" I asked, popping the question straight out on the floor between us. "After your shift. I'll buy you dinner down on Lavender Deck. You can tell me all about it."

Dawn's eyes did that up-down thing again. The term "Lavender Deck" seemed to pique her interest.

Normally, crewmembers weren't allowed down there. The food was better. The company better. *Everything* was better down there.

But the fine people who hung out on Lavender Deck generally didn't want to see crewmen and legionnaires dirtying up the place.

Dawn gave a little shrug. She was still butthurt, I could tell.

"I don't know..." she said, "maybe."

"Great!" I said, as if she'd written the date down on granite with blood for ink. "I'm gonna be holding you to that, girl. See you at five."

Then, before she could weasel, I gave her a big grin and a small shoulder squeeze with my overly large hands. I made sure to be very delicate as she wasn't a large girl.

That's when a rude snort erupted from across the room. I didn't even bother to look at that other bio-weenie. He was irritated by this development, I'm sure—but I didn't care in the slightest.

I marched out of the revival chamber then, passing over the familiar decks of *Scorpio*. As my tapper wasn't full of commands and demands for my presence from all my superior officers, I decided just to blend in as if nothing strange had happened.

Rather than making calls and inquiries and checking on officer scheduling, I walked straight for my unit's module. When I entered, unannounced and unexpected, there were quite a number of surprised-looking adjuncts, noncoms, and enlisted men.

Everybody was flabbergasted to see me. I found Harris and demanded all the troops fall in and prepare for an inspection.

"Uh…" he said, "that's all good, sir… but there's a little bit of a problem."

"How's that?"

"Well, sir… uh… you know about our new centurion, don't you?"

My eyes flashed to his. I could tell he was being serious, not just making a joke to piss me off.

I sighed. "Who is it?"

"Centurion Leeza," said a voice behind me.

I turned slowly, and there, lo and behold, was another woman I knew all too well. The last I'd seen of her, she'd been working in the tech group, and she'd lost her rank of centurion. Clearly, there had been a few changes recently.

"Hey, Leeza," I said, "great to see you!"

I walked up, threw her a half-hearted salute, and held out a hand. She shook it firmly, but there wasn't a gleam of delight in her eyes—far from it.

"There seems to be some sort of misunderstanding, McGill."

"There sure as hell is," I agreed. "But I wanted to thank you personally for holding down my little fort here at 3rd Unit. I just can't thank you enough for filling in. I'm sure it was an imposition. Once we get this all straightened out, I'm going to transfer an extra month's pay out of my personal accounts to yours."

"Hold on, McGill," Leeza said. "I don't think you grasp the situation. You've been replaced. Permanently."

I blinked a couple of times. "Well now, I'll have to see about that, old friend."

Leeza looked sour. I could tell there was no sugar to be had here, no matter what kind of history we had.

Hell, you'd think she'd be more grateful toward me. I'd once saved her skinny butt after she'd committed outright treason against Earth. But no, here she was, giving me a hard time and trying to oust me from my chair at 3$^{rd}$ Unit.

I turned to Harris with twisted-up lips. "Where the hell are Leeson and Clane?"

"Leeson's probably hiding somewhere, wetting himself in the back," Harris said, "but Clane... I think you've been out of touch for a long time, sir."

I looked at him sharply. "How's that?"

"Adjunct Clane transferred out," Leeza answered.

"What? What'd you do, woman?" I demanded in what might have been misconstrued as an accusatory tone. "Did you give him a hard time or something?"

She shook her head. "No, I think when he got the summons to return to Legion Varus and learned the deployment was all the way out to the Mid-Zone... well, he resigned his commission."

"That's right," Harris said. "He was always a bit too soft to be a Varus man. He did some good tours with us, he did some good work. I'll give him that. But he just didn't have the grit to stick with this outfit for decades."

"Huh..." I said, thinking that over and shaking my head. "Too bad. He was a good officer."

Clane had ditched us. Go figure. It wasn't the first time, and I'm sure it wouldn't be the last. Such things happened at Legion Varus with some regularity.

People grew tired of the lifestyle after a decade or two. Sure, there were benefits. You didn't age, because you were constantly dying and being brought back to life out of a tank of slime. That was a nice perk.

But then there were long deployments which frequently lasted more than a year. And there was the dying... Lots of dying. Some people just weren't cut out for it.

"Well, who's the new third adjunct, then?" I asked Leeza.

"That's hardly any concern of yours... but the position is open. If you're interested in the job, I might possibly—"

I laughed, cutting her off. "No thanks! I'm not going to take a demotion like that. You can stop worrying your little head about it. I'm going to get all this straightened out."

Leeza looked tense and upset, but she let me walk out of the module without further comment.

With long strides, my horse-like legs carried me all the way up to Gold Deck. I needed to talk to my commanders. The kind of talking I was going to do was best done in person, not with a tiny screen on your forearm.

The first man I met up with was none other than Primus Graves.

"Fancy seeing you here, McGill," he said, as I walked into his office. "I didn't think you'd be joining us on this campaign."

"I wouldn't miss this for the world! I was actually in the meeting where the contract was hammered out with Sateekas."

He squinted and blinked a couple of times. Then, he shook his head. "You never did know your place."

"On the contrary, sir, I know my place. It's right downstairs in the 3rd Unit, 3rd Cohort of Legion Varus."

Primus Graves shook his head slowly. "You've been replaced," he said. "The length of time you spent AWOL... it was simply unacceptable."

"I wasn't AWOL, sir. I was dead."

"That's no excuse. I was left with a hole in my roster on this mission. You do realize it's been two and a half months since we left Earth, right?"

It was my turn to blink in surprise. *Two and a half months?* Holy shit, that was alarming... Galina had sure taken her sweet time getting me out of purgatory.

"Be that as it may, sir—" I began.

Graves waved me off. "Not interested," he said. "I made the call and Winslade, our tribune, approved it. Maybe you can find a position somewhere among his staffers. If someone isn't court-martialing you for your disappearance, that is. Either way, it's not my problem now."

71

I stood up. "Thank you kindly, Primus. I'll take that referral up to the next link in the chain."

Graves looked annoyed, but according to the appeals process on demotions and reassignments, I did have the right to talk to the man who'd actually given the order and approved it—which would be Tribune Winslade himself.

I didn't even have to punch any hogs to get myself into Winslade's office a few minutes later. But, once inside the dinky lobby, I was left cooling my heels in the waiting area. After fifteen long, dull minutes, during which I did my best to annoy his best-looking secretary, I learned some hard truths.

It had indeed been two and a half months since I'd drawn breath. One hundred and ten days, to be exact. Months of non-existence. That wasn't my longest spell of death—not even my second longest. Still, though, it was disquieting…

When Winslade finally found a slot in his schedule to meet with me, he was less than cordial.

The rooster-like man didn't even look up from his desk when I came in and stood at attention. Finally, with a sigh, he waved at me as he finished scribbling something on his computer desktop.

"What is it, McGill?"

"I've got a serious problem, sir."

He looked even more annoyed. "I'd say you *are* a serious problem. Isn't it enough that you've been allowed to breathe again, against all odds and all logic?"

"No sir," I said, "I'm afraid it isn't. I have no current assignment. Unless you were thinking of having me come up here and play office-boy again…"

"Absolutely not! We'll have no repeat of that nonsense."

He was, of course, remembering a day when I, along with Raash, had terrorized his office staff. The rare combination of my incompetence and Raash's vile habits had brought work to a standstill.

I spread my big hands wide. "I'd like to ask just exactly how Centurion Leeza came to be in charge of my unit, sir."

He shrugged. "We needed a replacement. Leeson didn't want the job—not even on a temporary basis. So, I looked at the rosters and found that Leeza had once served as a combat centurion. With Legion Germanica, no less."

I bit back some harsh words. Leeza had been a centurion with Germanica, but then she'd gone and abandoned that post in a treasonous fashion. She'd gone off first with Armel, then with Claver. The girl was far from reliable.

I could have dumped on Leeza, but I decided I wouldn't immediately besmirch her reputation—not unless I had to.

"That's all very good, sir... but last I heard, she was only an adjunct."

He frowned thoughtfully. "That is true... but given that she was previously a centurion..."

"Sir," I said, "she was demoted for good reasons, which I won't go into now. What I would like to say is I can offer you an excellent and quick solution to this entire dilemma."

He pursed his lips and stared up at me. "I highly doubt that."

"Just hear me out. My adjunct, Clane, has decided to quit the legion."

"Oh... that's true, isn't it?"

"That leaves 3$^{rd}$ Unit short an officer anyways. How about this, sir? How about I return to my post as the centurion of the 3$^{rd}$, and Leeza becomes my new adjunct?"

"Hmm...."

"The music stops, and everybody has a chair. Problem solved!"

"Not so fast, McGill," Winslade said. "Leeza has, it's true, been problematic according to her record. However, you apparently were involved in some kind of apprehension and deadly arrest in the very bowels of Central. Are those reports correct?"

I gasped. "Is that what you heard? It was nothing like that, Tribune. I swear it! All I did was go down to the Intel zone and crash their officer's mess. I might've had a few beverages, you understand... and Dickson might've taken exception to my brash manner. But the rest of that nonsense about me and vaults and labs and whatnot, that's all bullshit, sir. All of it."

Winslade frowned at me. I could tell he didn't believe me, but then again, he didn't know quite how bad my crimes had been. Dickson had once served in Legion Varus, and he wasn't well liked by anyone who'd met him back then. Any report coming from his office was viewed with almost as much suspicion as my excuses were.

Winslade was therefore left with a dilemma. Finally, he sighed. "Well… I guess I could demote you to adjunct for the unapproved leave of absence. And then—"

"Oh, come on, sir. You can't seriously believe Centurion Leeza will do a better job running 3rd Unit than I have!"

Winslade pursed his mouth. He hemmed and hawed. He piddled around on his desktop with a finger and a few icons.

Finally, he grunted. "Very well. It shall be as you say. It's the easiest solution, as it only pisses off one officer who I have little regard for in any case. Go on, go on. Run back to your module and gleefully deliver the news to her. Crush her heart and her ambitions."

"Uh… hold on a second, sir. I've got one more request."

"Seriously? I've got a request as well: get out of my office!"

"I'm reading that vibe, sir. I surely am. But do you think you could find it in your heart to send her the note and pretend it had nothing to do with me?"

Winslade stared at me in a combination of disbelief and disgust. "Why would I go to such a special effort?"

"Sir, just think about it. She's already going to be hating on me for this. But if it's clear you made the decision—which you just did, sir, to be fair—she's going to hate me a smidge less. Otherwise, this is going to create a morale problem in my unit right from the get-go."

He pondered that. Finally, he nodded. "I suppose you're correct in this matter. Two times in a row—will wonders never cease? I will compose the order into a letter, and I will fire it down to Leeza before I leave the office today."

"Excellent, sir. Thank you, sir." I spun on my boot heel, but I didn't make it to the door.

"One more thing, Centurion," Winslade said.

"Yes, sir?"

"Don't be late tomorrow."

"Tomorrow, sir…?"

"Yes. We're having an exercise, don't you know?"

Naturally, I had no clue there were scheduled events, but it made perfect sense. We were halfway through a long voyage. The legion had likely conducted a couple of major exercises by now.

I sighed inwardly. I was going to have to lead a unit into battle immediately after we'd been torn apart, with the upper officers struggling for control. That wasn't a good way to kick things off.

"My men will be sharp and ready to go," I told him.

Winslade finally let me out of his office and off Gold Deck entirely.

I was vastly relieved. I'd re-secured my position in 3rd Unit, and the only downside was a single pissed-off subordinate officer.

Shrugging, I went immediately to the next critical item on my internal to-do list: It was time to hunt down Dawn and get her to go on that date with me.

## -9-

In the end, I was successful with Dawn. I was able to get her to go on a date, and after she pouted a bit, she spent the night with me. I guess she was tired of that arrogant prick of a sidekick she'd been working with in the revival chamber.

I kicked things off with a sure-fire win, sneaking her down to Lavender Deck. I had this process down to a science by now. The key to it was that the Lavender Deck restaurants wanted to keep out riffraff like me—but they needed customers. Since this was a long-ass trip all the way out to the Mid-Zone, there weren't enough VIPs aboard on any given night to keep the place in business.

They'd developed a cunning work-around. They allowed scum like me to enter until five-thirty, at which point only VIPs were allowed into the doors. The solution was painfully simple. I showed up with Dawn in tow at about five-twenty-five, and was seated by unhappy, grunting staffers.

The trick was then to drag things out as long as possible. We went to the bar first, had a few, then went to the restrooms before taking a table in the back. Scowling waiters served us, not caring about their tip—which was mighty thin after this treatment—as they knew it was already 6 pm and the important people were filing in. We weren't even supposed to be there, but we were, so they were cornered.

"This feels awkward, James," Dawn whispered. She was fielding some cold stares and getting uncomfortable.

"How's that?"

"People are staring. Haven't you noticed?"

I made a show of gawking around. "By damn... you're right. This never happens! I know what it must be: You're so freaking pretty, these high-level officers can't keep their eyes off you."

This gained me a smile. She relaxed enough to enjoy the meal, which was as fine as could be had on *Scorpio*.

We still caught a few dirty looks from various primus characters. These mostly came from people like Primus Gilbert. He was a sallow fellow who looked like he'd had all the blood drained out of him at birth.

Gilbert hadn't said a word to me since we'd been at that meeting with Consul Wurtenberger and the rest, and I was glad he didn't change that vow of silence tonight. All he did was shuffle his chair around so that his ass was aimed in my direction. This prevented his eyes from being offended by something so lowbrow as a mid-ranked officer in his immediate presence.

I ignored him and did my best to woo Dawn. She was a fine creature.

During dinner, Dawn told me her story of woe. How her moon base had been destroyed, she'd gone from job to job afterward, unable to secure anything solid and permanent until she found the legions. I made sympathetic noises as I chewed. At no point did I mention the undeniable truth that I'd had a hand in the destruction of her former post on Luna.

"I was a trained bio who specialized in revivals...? What was I supposed to do?"

Nodding, I made a grunt and swallowed. "I get it. The legions always need people like that—and Legion Varus needs them most of all."

"It was the signing bonus in the end," she told me. "That's what really got me."

I nodded, sucking on a rib bone and trying not to make too many slurping sounds while I did it.

"They dangled the biggest signing bonus of every interested outfit... and I hadn't worked for months. That's how they got me to sign. Now, here I am being shipped to distant stars on a warship. I've never been on a real deployment before. Nothing like this, James. What's it going to be like?"

I put down the last bone solemnly, wiped my hands on one of those cloth napkins, and then wiped my mouth with the other side of it. Damn, these fancy napkins never absorbed much of anything, especially not when you're having ribs for dinner.

"Dawn," I said, "I'm not going to lie. It's going to be rough. You'll probably end up churning out bodies on Blue Deck like you've never seen before."

She heaved a sigh. I watched her perfectly formed boobs go up and down as she did so.

That sight made me want to kick myself. How in the nine hells that Raash believed in had I ever lost track of this girl? It was just like Galina had said, she was *enchanting*.

Of course, Galina hadn't meant that comment in the most friendly manner—but it was true, nonetheless.

Dinner dragged on until we were able to escape, and I took her back to her place—not to my own unit. Why not slide her into my own bunk, you might ask? Because I knew what was going on back there.

Leeza was probably throwing a hissy-fit after she got a rude text from Winslade. If I'd been on hand at that moment, no matter what I did or said, she'd blame me. She'd claim—quite unfairly, as she had no evidence—that I'd somehow engineered her demotion and demise.

Leeza was doomed to serve under my leadership rather than the other way around. She'd never been a forgiving woman, and I suspected this situation was going to stick in her craw. But there was no way I was willing to work under her. Not after she'd just come swaggering in and stole my unit from me. Hell, by most measures, she was still a traitor.

Some people are truly grabby, I'll tell you.

After dallying for the night with the soft caresses of Dawn, during which we managed a rekindlement of our past romance, I crept away at something like three a.m. I reached my own bunk at last and collapsed upon it.

I was snoring within 30 seconds. My plan was to sleep-in just a bit—possibly all the way to 0700.

But alas, a much-deserved rest was not on the cards for old McGill. Klaxons went off a few hours after my head hit the pillow. Emergency sirens and flashers were going crazy.

These alarms were the bad kind, too, the ones that indicated something serious had gone wrong aboard the ship.

"What in the hell…?" I grunted, struggling out of bed. I fumbled with my boots and cursed up a blue streak.

My door popped open, and a panicked-looking Harris shoved his head in. "They're loose!" he said. "They're all over the fucking ship!"

"What's loose, Adjunct?"

"The robots! Those fucking robots!"

He ran away, shouting for everyone to gather their arms, suit-up, and prepare for battle.

*Robots?* I thought to myself. What in the hell was that about? I'd only spent two months in limbo, but everything seemed to be going to shit.

Sure, there'd been tons of reports delivered onto my weary tapper since I'd been revived. I'd been charged with reading them all, but I'd chased Dawn instead. There were memos, announcements and schedules—all kinds of stuff like that. A lot of these documents were glowing red and even purple on my left arm this morning. But there was no time to read any of that nonsense now.

I stuck my head out of my cabin before I'd even gotten my belt to cinch itself up.

"To arms! To arms!" someone was shouting—it sounded like Sargon. He was thumping around in the barracks, rousting the light troops and heavy troops alike out of their beds.

Men were streaming from the upper decks of the module. They were half-dressed, guns snapping as power-packs were rammed into slots, and safeties were released.

I got out a morph-rifle myself, set it for close assault combat mode, and stepped out onto the deck. I still had no idea what the hell was going on, but everybody aboard *Scorpio* seemed to be going nuts.

Then, Harris shouted something that cut through the general confusion.

"Shut up! Shut up, everybody! Just shut up and *listen*!"

Harris always had had a good ear—especially when something dangerous was around. I recalled one time back on Dark World where he'd heard the slow grinding sound of Vulbites boring their way through the skin of the great orbital factory...

He'd been right about that noise then, and I suspected he was probably right now.

I waved my arms and shushed everyone around me. At last, with our eyes searching the ceiling and the walls, we all listened in the relative quiet.

Then, we could hear it. The sound of heavy, tramping feet. The marching sound was odd, however, as it was more of a metallic clanking noise than the thump of boots on decks.

When humans walked down the passageways of *Scorpio*, they made a very familiar sound. We all wore boots of the same style, made with identical materials. But this tramping noise, although it was definitely a sound of marching—was different. As if the army on the move they had a different kind of shoe...

"What the hell is that?" I said.

"Robots!" Leeson shouted suddenly.

He was at the porthole in the module doorway. We only had one window that let a man look out of the module into the passageway beyond.

We shared that adjoining passageway with nine other identical modules. Altogether, with two support modules, the big ship housed our entire cohort on this deck. The modules were essentially cubes in which groups of soldiers lived. We lived with our own isolated units, with about 120 men in each.

Although it might seem rather pointless and even claustrophobic to be crammed in with so many others and sealed off from the rest of the ship, it was actually a functional protective mechanism. The modules could be jettisoned into space under critical circumstances, such as an abandonment of ship. Since each module was hermetically sealed, if one was compromised with gas or a bio agent, those deadly fumes wouldn't spread to the others—at least, not easily.

Each module had its own independent and separately functional ventilation system. It was safer that way.

The tramping feet—if they even were feet—halted. They didn't stop at our door, fortunately—but they were somewhere near. We wouldn't have been able to hear them otherwise.

A new sound split the air. It was a metallic screeching noise, as if heavy metal was grinding against more heavy metal. A ripping, groaning sound indicated something big had been torn apart.

Next, a massive volley of gunfire broke out. There were distant shouts, and more of those strange, tramping feet. Screams began echoing down the passageway moments later.

"They're at Module Five," Leeson said, straining his eyeballs to gaze down the passageway. "Looks like they're killing everybody."

I grabbed onto Leeson's collar and yanked him from the window. "*Who's* killing everybody?"

"The fucking robots," he shouted at me. "That's who. You got the briefing about this exercise today, didn't you?"

My mouth gaped like a fish. "I thought that was going to happen on Green Deck or something…"

Leeson laughed. "Nope, not this time. We're supposed to play hide and go seek with an army of those damned robots. And let me tell you, those fuckers aren't playing around."

We all checked our weapons, adjusted our kits, polished our gear, and sweated. We could hear each other breathe, we were listening so hard.

There were shouts, there were screams, more gunfire. Eventually, it began to die down.

"They're killing them! They're killing them all!" Harris said. There were a couple of beads of sweat on his forehead. They glistened there, and suddenly I came to a decision.

If there was one thing that didn't sit well with me, it was playing with my dick in this tin can, waiting around to be slaughtered. If we were going to die today against these robots, then we were going to do it standing on our own two feet, blazing away—and hopefully catch them in a crossfire.

"Okay men, we're getting into this," I shouted. "Heavies, line up right here. Harris, you're leading the first wave."

"Say what?"

"You heard me. Move down that passageway and hit those robots in the ass before they can finish off 7th Unit. They'll just come down here next if we don't act now."

Harris complained. He cursed. He showed me his teeth, and he made very crude comments about my heritage—but he also gathered up his men.

We opened the big door, which slid aside with a grinding sound. Harris led the way with three dozen armored men at his back. They moved to battle without roaring battle cries. Legion Varus men preferred to strike silently in the manner of wolves, rather than bay and bark like a pack of excited hounds.

I organized Leeson's men next, gathering up his weaponeers. I personally shouldered one of the spare belchers they had in their lockers.

"What's that for?" Leeson said, pointing at my weapon.

"Sometimes, robots are hard to kill."

He didn't ask any more questions. With Sargon and me in the lead, a squad of weaponeers followed Harris. There was already a huge hullabaloo going on out in the passageway, and things were about to get a lot louder.

## -10-

It was a hard struggle, and most of us died by the end of it. I'd fought machines like these before. Skinny stacks of metal tubing with a lot of circuitry inside. They had good AI, and about a thousand finely tuned electric muscles.

My light troopers couldn't do shit. Snap-rifle rounds just bounced right off the chassis of these robots, leaving only a ding or a dent. My heavies in their armor with their morph-rifles did better. They scored up the robots, and the robots scored them up as well.

But our most effective weapons were the belchers. We ended up using the heavy troops as decoy targets to engage the robots' attention. Then we sighted carefully over their shoulders, between their legs—sometimes right through their flailing limbs if we had to. The moment we were on target, even if it might injure a comrade—we took the shot. We nailed those robots with powerful, narrowly focused blasts.

The enemy did notice this after a while, I have to give the programmers credit. They adjusted their tactics, and began to focus on the weaponeers. After they'd nailed a few of us in return, however, a giant voice rolled out over the entire ship.

"3rd Unit, 3rd Cohort, cease fire. You are in violation of the rules. Cease all action. You're ordered to stand down and return to your home module. For you, this exercise has ended."

The robots lowered their weapons, and so we did as well. After a couple of parting shots, we retreated to our own module and gave each other a lot of back slaps and hearty guffaws of joy.

Somehow, Harris had managed to survive the battle. "We kicked their *asses*," he kept saying.

Despite taking point, I figured he'd escaped death by making a single, cunning adjustment to my orders. He'd led the way to Module 5, sure, just as I'd told him to. But then when he got into the busted-in doors, he'd stepped to one side and ushered the rest of his men to charge through ahead of him.

That simple expedient had allowed him to lead his men to the door, but not get nailed in the initial assault. I decided not to scold him for his slick move. We'd won in the end. If he'd gone in first, it wouldn't have made any difference, anyway.

Back inside our own module, I was greeted home by a skinny woman named Leeza. She stood with her hands on her hips.

As I'd judged our light troops to be useless against the robots, I'd left her behind. Still, she had this look on her face as if she was about to scold me for stealing cookies.

"Hey, Adjunct," I said, marching forward and giving her a hearty wave. "Did you see that action? We kicked their titanium tubes! We smeared them!"

She nodded, but she seemed unimpressed.

I frowned a bit and walked closer, lowering my voice so the others, who were all cheering and breaking out beers all around us, wouldn't overhear.

"Pardon me if I say this, Adjunct," I whispered, "but it looks to me like you got a bug up your butt. What's the matter?"

Now, in my own mind, I knew exactly what the problem was. She'd just been demoted from centurion to adjunct, and nobody—especially not a woman like her—could take that easily.

But she shook her head as if marveling at me. "You broke the rules, McGill," she said. "They told me you were going to pull shit like this, but I didn't know it was going to be this bad."

I frowned more deeply, not quite knowing what she was talking about. Hadn't Graves said something similar when he'd ended our local battle? "Uh… broke what rules? Are we still talking about your demotion?"

"No," she snapped. "And I'd appreciate it if you didn't bring that up again."

"Sure thing…"

"I'm talking about the published memo describing this training exercise. Our orders were to stay within our isolated modules. Every unit was to remain in place. The moment the fighting broke out, you raced down the hall and attacked our adversary, ruining the entire test."

My mouth was gaping. I had known none of this. Of course, I hadn't made the slightest effort to read anything about the nature of this exercise...

"Oh…" I said, thinking it over. "Maybe that's why Graves told us to stand down, huh?"

"That's exactly right. You wrecked a lot of robots using belchers, too, I understand? Belchers were outlawed in this struggle."

"Uh…" I said, suddenly understanding. "Um… was there anything in that announcement about why they outlawed belchers?"

"Because they can damage the walls of modules. This action wasn't fought inside the main Green Deck zone, which has thicker walls and can take a light artillery strike. From what I understand, there are big fist-sized—even head-sized holes punched all over inside Module 5."

"Um… I guess that's so…"

"On top of that, the robots themselves weren't similarly equipped with belchers. I bet you didn't notice that, either?"

"Well, now that you mention it…" I said, scratching one foot on the deck. I was feeling a little bit itchy. "I guess I did notice. I just felt that was done to make things fair. After all, they're robots and all…"

Leeza smiled grimly. "Well, I've got a little bit more information for you. Graves has contacted me privately. At first, he was blaming me for this monumental fuck-up and the breaking of all the game rules. But after I informed him that you had taken command of 3$^{rd}$ Unit in my stead, he wants to talk to you."

She lifted her tapper and flicked an unhappy face from her tiny screen to mine. I realized then that Graves was online and was listening to our talk.

I winced. Leeza was stiffing me. That much was obvious. None of this could be an accident. She was twisting the knife in and thoroughly enjoying my difficulties with our chain of command.

My thoughts were unhappy ones. Maybe I'd made a mistake by bringing her aboard as my adjunct. I'd cozied up to a viper and hugged it against my chest. Mark me down as being as dumb as old Queen Cleopatra herself.

"Hey, Primus Graves," I said. "Did you see that fight? We trashed those robots!"

He cut me off and gave me the verbal thrashing that I'd been expecting. I gaped and gawked and made excuses. He wasn't interested. In fact, much to my chagrin, he demanded that I attend a meeting up on Gold Deck immediately.

"A meeting regarding what, sir?"

"The exercise has concluded all across the ship. A certain Director Cunningham wants to discuss this with you."

"Director Cunningham...?" I said, searching my memory. That name did indeed sound familiar...

Suddenly, an image came to me. Yes, I had it. Bald, fat, glasses... There'd once been a Director Cunningham aboard ship, and that guy had been in charge of the robots we'd faced previously.

With a little bit of help from Alexander Turov, I'd gotten his funding cut and had him shipped right out of Legion Varus, and hopefully out of Hegemony entirely. Apparently, I had failed in this final regard. Director Cunningham was back, and he was back with redesigned robots, too.

I could attest to having faced these machines twice, and I had to admit, they were much tougher this time around.

Eventually, Graves got tired of chewing on me. With a sigh, I lowered my tapper.

"Adjunct Leeza!" I shouted. She turned around on one heel, and she did so sharply. At least she wasn't openly disregarding my orders. She was still giving me the attention and respect I deserved.

"Yes, Centurion?" she asked.

"You take your lights to Green Deck right now, and you drill the hell out of them."

She looked a bit confused. "But what about—"

"The rest of the unit? Our specialists, weaponeers, and most of all, our heavies have to recover. They did all the fighting and dying today. Your group didn't do jack squat. I want to see your troops do well on the field tomorrow, and I don't want to see anybody taking a break until sundown today."

She nodded, rousted up her lights, and marched them out the door. She didn't give me one more word of protest.

I thought to myself that might not be a good thing. It was better to have a woman who was openly bitching and complaining at you than one that was secretly conniving and seeking your demise through nefarious means. I'd rather deal with a snake right in front of my boots, hissing and striking, than one who was hiding in your pack ready to bite your ass.

But I'd have to take care of that problem later. Right now, I was on my way to Gold Deck.

I told Harris to authorize an extra ration of alcohol from our supplies to congratulate the men who were returning from revival chambers. I gave one more hearty congratulations to Leeson, Harris, and the surviving heavies and weaponeers, then I began marching up to Gold Deck once again.

To amuse myself along the way, I contacted Dawn to ask her for another date for the evening.

"I'm sorry, James," she said. Her face was sweating. Her hair was down across both eyes in wet locks. "Today is a double-down day for me. I'm probably going to be working until midnight reviving all these dead troops."

I thought about that, and I realized it made sense. We'd just had a massive exercise all across the ship. Robots had gone to dozens of modules and killed hundreds—possibly thousands—of men. That sort of thing really got the protoplasm and the bone meal flowing in the revival chambers.

Even though it hadn't been a *real* battle, the carnage was still dramatic. They were recycling and churning out fresh troops every twenty minutes in each revival chamber we had on Blue Deck.

"All right," I said. "Never mind. Good luck."

"Hey," she said. "I'm glad to see you made it."

She gave me a little smile, and I gave her one back. She still liked me. This could turn into something good for old McGill, and I really hoped it would.

Dawn helped my mood tremendously. I arrived on Gold Deck in good cheer and went to meet Graves and Director Cunningham. Whistling, smiling, and throwing out salutes every which way, I took a seat at the conference table and waited for the discussion to begin.

Director Cunningham was the last to arrive. He brought with him a burned robot carcass of blackened metal and twisted, exposed wires.

"Whoa," I said. "Get that thing out of here, Cunningham. It stinks!"

He glared at me in instant recognition. He leveled a stiff finger in my direction.

"There he is," he said. "I should have known. What special hatred do you hold in your heart for me, McGill?"

"Uh…" I said, thinking that over seriously. "Well sir, I don't much like robots, and I don't like wasting government money, either."

His face, if it were possible, turned a bit redder. It was now closer to a shade of purple. He seemed really pissed, but he was containing it with a great deal of effort.

I had to wonder if the man's blood pressure was spiking. He looked like he could use a tad more exercise.

"Director," I told him, "maybe you should get out from behind your desk more often and work off some of that paunch in the exercise room."

He showed me teeth then, and that was as ugly as it sounded.

"There," he said, turning to Graves. "You see that? Unrepentant mocking. He wrecked million credits worth of government hardware by breaking all the laws that we've given him. I'm demanding a retest!"

"A retest?" Graves said. He honestly didn't seem to be all that sympathetic toward Director Cunningham. He never had been. He didn't like robots any more than the rest of us did. Still, he a primus and a stickler for regulations. I'd broken the game, so here we were. He was never one who was going to run around sweeping up messes I'd made or publicly cheer them on.

"That's what I said, Primus Graves."

"What kind of exercise would you suggest?" Graves asked. "We have enough data on your robots' performance up against my men."

"Let's do something different, then," I suggested loudly.

Both men looked at me.

"What would you suggest, McGill?"

"He shouldn't be suggesting anything," Director Cunningham snapped, but Graves waved for him to shut up.

"I got it!" I said, snapping my fingers. "We just had a good old-fashioned slap-down with regular weaponry. How about we fight it out with different weapons this time?"

"Like what?" Graves said, waving for me to hurry up. I could tell he was bored with this entire thing already.

"Stun-sticks!" I said. "One touch makes your limb freeze up and become useless. Hitting the head or the torso—that's a kill-shot."

Cunningham frowned. I don't think he liked the idea. "What's the point of this? It sounds like you just want to avoid another death."

I shrugged. "Okay, let's make headshots or two hits to the body a kill. Would that make you happy?"

Cunningham looked thoughtful. "I still don't see the value—"

"Look, we'll be testing your abominations in a new way. The playing field will be leveled. We'll take the same results from injuries. Right now, your robots have tougher bodies than humans do—let's see how they make out when that doesn't matter."

Director Cunningham thought it over. "I doubt that these stun-sticks you're talking about would have much of an effect on my robots. They're heavily insulated against EMPs and electrical charges. Their outer carapaces are all polymers now, rather than metal."

"Don't sell your own engineers short," I said. "I'm sure you can rig something up. Just have them set their limbs to go numb if we hit them. Then they could hop around on one foot, or whatever. That's what my men will do if your robots get a hit on them."

Cunningham worked on his tapper for a moment, and then he finally looked up. "I think we can do it... There will be some software to edit... But actually, I think the results of such a test might be valuable. I like the idea—"

"Great," I said, slamming my hands together with a loud, popping sound.

Director Cunningham winced.

"That's a deal, then," I said. "As soon as all my men are revived, we'll face you on Green Deck."

"And when will that be?"

Graves did a little tapping on his desk. His fist came up, and he leaned on it, burying it in his left cheek. He seemed bored. "Probably 48 hours," he said at last.

"Unworkable!" Cunningham said. "That's too late. I plan to pack up and go back through the gateway posts before that. I want to do this by tomorrow morning. I've got to move on to other legions, other ships—"

"Yes, all right, whatever," Graves said. "I'll put in a request to accelerate the revival rate of McGill's troops. McGill? Can you be ready by, let's say, 0900?"

"Make it an hour later, and you've got yourself a bargain."

Graves shrugged. "Good enough. I'll clear Green Deck from ten until noon—but don't wreck the place."

"Wouldn't dream of it, Primus."

Graves checked the Green Deck event scheduling, he blocked out the hours, kicking out the people who wanted to use it for regular physical training and target practice. It was moments like this when you really needed the highest-ranked primus in the legion behind you.

Cunningham wasn't quite done yet. He wanted to berate me, report me and show all kinds of boring-ass still-shots of wrecked robots. He had price tags on every image, detailing repair estimates. It was going to take many millions of credits to rebuild them all.

But neither Graves nor I gave a shit. As soon as he was able, Graves declared the meeting adjourned, and I hustled my way off Gold Deck.

I had some work to do in preparation for tomorrow…

## -11-

A grudge-match battle began on the Green Deck the following day at ten on the dot. Many of the troops in my unit were grumbling about having to face death again at the hands of robots. They felt they'd taken enough abuse only the day before by these same machines—but they still formed up ranks behind me.

We marched through Portal 17 onto *Scorpio*'s amazing Green Deck. Somewhere opposite us, across the vast expanse of the cylindrical-shaped exercise room and nature preserve, an equal number of robots entered the grand chamber. I had to wonder what tactics and plans their artificial minds were hatching against us. Only time would tell.

"This is bullshit!" Harris kept saying over and over again. "Absolute bullshit!"

"Somehow," Centurion Leeza remarked, "I find these complaints amongst the officer ranks even more irritating than I did when I was your commander."

The two of them scowled at one another. I could tell that no love was lost, but all things considered, Harris seemed to be in a good mood. He was pretty happy, in my estimation, that I'd retaken command of 3rd Unit.

"What are your orders, Centurion?" Leeza asked. There was a flat tone to her voice.

That was faked, I could tell. She was bitter underneath that forced, level tone. While she accepted my leadership over her, she was by no means happy about it. She was at least resentful—if not outright rebellious.

"Your team of lights will take point," I told her. "Fan out. We need to know where these robots are before we can kick their butts."

She nodded, and her platoon broke up into squads, then teams. They sprinted away, disappearing into the green gloom ahead of us.

"Where are we going to set up?" Harris asked me. "Are we heading for the lagoon? Maybe we can short circuit these guys in the water, the way we did last time."

"There's no way," Leeson said, "Director Cunningham wouldn't bring his bots back here again without having made them waterproof."

Thinking it over, I nodded. "Yes," I said. "That trick won't work twice on those bots. And I know from experience that shock rods actually function underwater. Sometimes, they might actually do more damage due to the connectivity of water."

"Where then?" Harris demanded.

I pointed off to our left, indicating the thickest carpet of jungle and brush on Green Deck. "Down there," I said, "in the thicket."

"Oh yeah..." Harris said, eyeballing the dense forest. "That's where those dumbasses built shields and stuff. They hid from us all day until the end of that King of the Hill battle."

"That's right," I said.

Harris laughed, and he began talking about what jackasses the unit commanders had been who'd faced us on that day.

I ignored the chatter. I was playing it cool—but I was already worried.

A key to victory in any tactical engagement was to spot your enemy first. I had my two techs, Natasha and Kivi, scanning with everything we had—which wasn't much.

My eyes were constantly roving over the lush landscape, looking for robots. I didn't know how fast they could move through this admittedly rugged terrain. I expected they would be faster than humans, though.

For all I knew, they'd already spotted us. What if they were already charging toward our position right now? The thought haunted my mind. I couldn't shake it.

I started shouting orders, clapping my hands. I got my unit moving at a trot. We reached the thick jungle, and it was about then that I heard a warning call of "Contact!" from Leeza's light troops. It almost came too late.

There were shouts of alarm and cries of pain coming from the tallest grass to our left. Two of Leeza's light troops came racing out, wide-eyed.

One was limping. The other's left arm hung limply, flopping around. They'd obviously been touched by the numbing, paralytic effect of shock rods.

"That's your baby, Harris," I said. "Charge and engage."

He turned and waved for a squad of his heavies to follow. He sprinted toward the action.

I was kind of freaked out. How had the enemy gotten across this huge chamber so fast? They must be able to run faster than any human in history.

Fortunately, this wasn't a full-on army of robots. It was only an advance party of scouts. They'd already put down several members of Leeza's 2nd Squad. Deciding to back Harris up, I committed more heavies—and myself as well.

We dove into the fight right at the edge of the tall grass in chest-high foliage. We traded blows back and forth. One of Harris's heavies went down, struck in the head, but then, as we outnumbered them by better than two to one, we were able to put down all the robots.

Still, when I counted back the damage, I found that a total of seven troops of mine were either incapacitated or outright marked as dead.

"Looks like the enemy sent out scouts, same as we did," Harris said, breathing hard.

"Right…"

I made a call over my tapper, ordering Leeza to pull back her probing squadrons of light troops. I doubted they could outrun the robots anyway, and they certainly couldn't face them all that well.

Light troopers were our least experienced men. A lot of them were fresh recruits, so while they had lighter gear and were accustomed to doing something like running around fast and swinging sticks at an enemy, they were vastly less experienced than our heavy troopers. My regulars and veterans had fought and died in dozens of campaigns.

"That's the right decision, Centurion," Harris said. His eyes were rolling around in his head, trying to look every which way at once. "They've already found us. We can't allow them to hit us with greater numbers the way we just hit them. Hell, they're already winning."

I nodded, trying to come up with a plan. Right now, the way I calculated it, if a hundred of these robots rolled in against a hundred humans, we were toast. Even in this thick, dense foliage, which I'd hoped might confuse their sensors, I got the feeling we'd lose.

We might take down half—maybe more than that, but then we'd be overwhelmed. A straight-on mass fight was therefore hopeless.

There was another worry, too. The factor of fear and morale. In combat, humans didn't always make a simple calculation and do whatever was the best for their team. We tended to think of ourselves as well. It was a natural instinct.

After you've taken a few harsh, painful blows, possibly losing the use of a hand or a foot—or something worse, humans tended to worry about their own well-being. They simply want to get the hell away from the enemy.

The way I figured it, robots wouldn't suffer from any similar morale problems. They'd most likely just stand and fight to the death, unless recalled by a commander. That meant that in order for us to win, we'd have to beat them down until their last metal finger would no longer function.

"Natasha?" I shouted. "Kivi? To me!"

The two tech girls hustled to my location. They squatted, puffing, looking around.

"You've got to give me a map," I told them. "You've got to give me something. Where are the enemy?"

Natasha shook her head. "We don't have much. We've had a few contacts, but not many yet."

Kivi looked even less happy. She was monitoring losses. "We've lost three more light troops in the last two minutes, sir."

"Damn it…"

I was beginning to regret all my decisions. I shouldn't have challenged Director Cunningham to this contest. I shouldn't have chosen these particular weapons.

All of us were wearing nothing but light gear. We didn't have any armor. We were all essentially in light trooper pajamas, nothing thicker than a spacesuit. On top of that, we'd given up a lot of our technological advantages.

These weaknesses, of course, affected the robots as well as my unit. But when we were down to our skivvies and had no ranged fire capabilities—well, humans were inferior to these damn robots. I didn't like to think about that, but there it was, a stark reality staring me in the face.

Natasha was saying something, but I didn't quite get it at first. She showed me a map at last. She'd come up with a vague graphic. Based on contact, she'd projected declarations from a half dozen squad-sized groups in our troops.

"The robots are forming a semicircle."

"Surrounding us?" I asked, my head twisting this way and that.

"Not exactly. It's more of a crescent-shaped formation. But they're definitely herding us in, gathering us all together."

I could tell right off what that meant. They were going to get us all rounded up and into one spot and then crush us.

My lower jaw jutted out as I studied the data.

"I'm sorry, James," Natasha said. She understood just as I did how perilous our tactical situation was. "If we'd had buzzers or something, I could have spotted them a lot earlier. We might not have fallen for this."

Here we were, stuck in a thick tangle of jungle and underbrush—and the enemy robots knew it. They were stalking us, herding us together—and setting us up for a slaughter.

## -12-

"We're going to play for time," I said, coming to a fast decision. "Leeza? How many squads you got left?"

"Two…" she said. "Two and a half."

I cursed a bit. "How many veterans do you have?"

"I'm down to two."

"Okay. Organize your remaining troops into three groups. You'll be leading the third one personally. You're going to play rabbit."

"How's that again, sir?"

"What? Is this your first day in the legions? You're commanding light troops in a tight battle. One of the best uses for your soldiers is to operate as decoys. I want to send your troops, two at a time, running away from this forested region we're huddling in. Have them circle back, back toward the entrance where we came in. Their mission is to try to get the robots to break ranks to chase them."

It was a desperate play, but it was all I could think of doing. Leeza sounded like she didn't really believe in the plan, but I didn't really care what she thought.

Within a few minutes, my orders were being executed and troops were sprinting away in pairs. It didn't take long for the robots to take the bait. They were by nature somewhat simplistic-minded when they saw groups of troops breaking formation, running away, essentially evading their trap. They felt compelled to act. Groups of four—exactly four—followed each pair of human troops they spotted, running after them into the brush.

I smiled to myself. This was exactly what I'd wanted.

"Send more!" I yelled at Leeza. "Send them all in pairs!"

Again, the enemy dispatched four robots to chase after each set of two light troops that Leeza sent out as decoys.

It made perfect sense. After all, with odds of two to one, the robots were certain of success. But each time they dispatched four of their number for a sure kill against our worst troops, they simultaneously weakened their primary force. That main group was still lying in wait. They were in a thinning line in front of my platoon of heavies.

Once I determined that the enemy had been reduced in strength by at least half, I ordered my best troops to advance and make contact with the robots.

We crept forward at first, then charged through the heavy brush when we spotted them. Behind us, our fleeing light troopers were getting caught, sometimes putting down a robot, but always being slaughtered in the end—but they were doing so far from the main fight.

Harris, Sargon—all of my best fighters—we raced into hand-to-hand. These men were powerful and highly experienced. We engaged the core of the robot force.

In a moment of inspiration, I grabbed up a big wad of greenery with my left hand. This bouquet was nothing more than some lengthy palm fronds and a big jungle leaf I'd ripped loose from plants in the underbrush.

But when I led with my bundle of greenery, charging at the robot I'd chosen for close combat, the thing recoiled from the big, blocky, flapping mass that was coming at it. Perhaps its sensors were not able to identify and codify the level of threat they represented.

This gave me a fraction of a second to get in close, to get in past those flickering limbs. My first touch landed on its right forearm, the limb that carried its own shock rod.

The robot dropped the weapon. The arm went limp at its side.

But then the thing seemed to recover and realize that the foliage I'd shoved into its cameras was harmless. It knelt with startling speed, snatching up the dropped shock rod almost before it touched the jungle floor and swept it up toward me.

Reaching out, it nicked me. It slipped the crackling stick underneath my left arm and got me in the ribs.

There was an explosion of pain and numbness. It was a weird, tingling mixture of two discordant sensations. How could one feel pain and simultaneously feel a lack of functional nerves? I don't know, but whoever had designed these damn things had come up with the perfect formula for such a terrifying result.

Experience paid off for me again, however. I whipped my own weapon up and touched the robot lightly on the bulbous head.

A kill shot. The robot dropped dead at my feet. Or at least it was marked in some database somewhere as dead.

Roaring, I then raced off to engage another.

In the end, we put down all the robots that had been left behind, but we lost a startling number of our own troops.

"Too many down," Harris said, breathing hard. "Too many." One of his feet was limp and flopping at the end of his ankle. He walked on it anyway, probably grinding bones, tearing ligaments. He didn't seem to care, so I didn't bring it up.

"Kivi's gone," Sargon said. "Damn it, that last frigging machine. It raced right past me, and it got to her. She's down and out."

Sargon himself didn't look too good. One arm hung useless from the shoulder down.

"What are we going to do, sir?" he asked.

"What are your orders, Centurion?" Harris asked.

Everyone was looking at me.

I was breathing hard. I looked around, trying to take stock of things. Too many were gone. Moller was gone. Carlos was gone. Even Leeson, for all of his experience, hadn't lived through the battle.

"Natasha," I said, calling on my last and best tech. ""How many robots are left? You're watching communications. You're monitoring all this. Give me an estimate."

She worked her tapper. She looked deflated, and she shook her head. "Leeza's lights… They're pretty much gone. Groups of four robots ran them down and butchered them. I have to guess there are between forty to fifty robots. They're soon going to return to this spot to finish this off, James."

All my troops looked at me. They were all breathing hard, sweating. Most were injured and winded. They weren't exhausted—not yet. They weren't terrified, either—but everyone knew we were in some deep shit.

Adjunct Leeza lifted her hand. "The decoy move worked before. Let's do it again. Give me your bios, your techs—your most worthless fighters. Keep just your heavies and your weaponeers. I'll try to lead off everyone I can while you smash the ones that struggle in from tracing my lights."

It wasn't a bad plan, but I felt I needed better. I turned to Natasha, who was actively tugging at my sleeve. "What is it, girl?" I said.

She was frowning at her tapper. She had been allowed to keep it—mostly because it was attached to her. She also had a pack with a larger computer inside. That provided us with some analytical software and a repeater for our comms.

That was all she'd been issued, however. We had no buzzers, no drones, no mines—nothing like that. But she did have her superior computer and networking capabilities, plus her natural know-how.

She was frowning down at her forearm. "James… I'm getting some signals I don't understand."

I frowned. "Toss it to me."

She flicked at her forearm, and my own screen lit up. I examined her data, trying to figure out what the hell I was looking at. We only had a minute or two of time to think before those robots that were straggling back toward us would find us and probably kill us all.

I looked at a whole bunch of blobs superimposed on a map of the Green Deck's park-like outlines. There was the central lagoon, the big pile of boulders that sat at one side, and the waterfall at the other. Acres of varied grasslands and miniature forests, some thick and some thin, spread out from this end to the other.

"See, look at these lines," she said, pointing a finger between my dumb face and my forearm.

I frowned, trying to figure out what the hell she was talking about. "Tell this to me like I'm four years old, Natasha," I said, "and make it fast."

"There are signals, James... Some kind of radio traffic is going on between that spot right there and these robots."

I blinked at that, trying to grasp what she was telling me. "Okay, what's there? What's at your mystery spot?" I said, tapping a blunt finger on the region she was indicating.

"That's door twelve. The door the robots came in through. These signals are coming from right there."

I reached up a single fingernail and scratched at my itchy, sweating head. "So the hell what?"

She shook her head. "They're not supposed to have anything there. Unless they left a reserve force of robots, maybe one broke down right there—but with this level of traffic, that doesn't make sense."

"What do you think's happening?" I asked.

I could now hear some clanking. The robots were definitely returning.

"If I'm going to play decoy again, sir," Adjunct Leeza said, "it's got to be now."

"All right," I said, "go on. Take everybody but Natasha."

The bios complained, some of them even whimpered, but it didn't matter. Anyone who could walk or even crawl that wasn't a frontline combat troop was sent in random directions to lead the returning robots astray.

Again, the robots split up to pursue the runners. If there was one advantage we had over these robots, I thought to myself, it was their utter predictability.

"James?" Natasha said, "James, I think I know what it is."

"Talk to me, girl."

"That spot at door twelve. That's where these robots are getting their directions from."

"Huh?" I said.

"I don't think they're strategizing, James. I think there are some operators—human operators—right there. They walked in those doors, they set up camp and they are gleefully watching, recording and maybe instructing, but they're definitely monitoring all their robots."

A feral grin sprouted across my face. My eyes lit up, and it wasn't a pleasant expression.

We were going down. We were losing this fight. But maybe, just maybe, we were going to get some payback.

"Sargon, you come with me. We've got a new mission, and it's going to be fun."

The two of us ran off into the jungle, heading in a beeline directly for the source of those mysterious signals. I left Harris behind alone, to marshal his heavies and to manage his last stand.

Hopefully, by decoying off more robots, he would at least have superior numbers each time he faced the enemy. The key to success in many battles was to force to weakness, to outnumber the enemy wherever you faced them. So, even if a force was outnumbered, they may be able to use careful maneuvering to apply what strength they had to smaller, detached groups of the enemy.

Normally, such tactics worked best when the enemy wasn't sure what they were facing. After taking losses and hearing reports of defeats, they could misinterpret that as facing a greater army.

Fear would then take hold in the human heart, and an army would often break in the face of a well-led, hard-fighting, force. History told of dramatic battles where high-quality commanders achieved victory against all the odds.

Look at armies led by men such as Julius Caesar, who battled hundreds of thousands of Gauls with just a few thousand hard legionnaires, Charles the Great, the Berserker King of Sweden—or Napoleon facing Royal troops in the streets of Paris. In all these cases, small, well-organized, competently led armies had broken enemy forces five times larger than their own.

I left Harris to attempt to apply those exact tactics as best he could. But in the meantime, Sargon and I went on a private mission of vengeance.

I took Natasha's coordinates, which were easy enough to follow. They were marked clearly on my tapper's map. We made a beeline for the spot. We didn't bother with any subterfuge. We ignored struggling men and robots. We ignored the dead at our feet. We pushed past bloody leaves, even a few squalling wounded who'd been left in the jungle to either die or be found and butchered by more robots.

None of that mattered anymore. This was our final act, our last hurrah.

We moved fast—not at a dead run—but at a steady, ground-eating pace. We had to get there fast before my own unit was completely defeated. If all my men were marked dead, the exercise would likely be called off, and we would be declared the losers.

I wanted to reach these characters hiding in front of Portal 12 before the game was up.

When we did reach them, we burst out of the brush. They were utterly surprised.

There were four operators, each squatting over a backpack. Small, parabolic antennas poked out of each of these packs.

It was a typical gang of tech-nerds. I bet none of them had done a pushup in the last decade.

We didn't release a battle cry. We didn't scream and whoop. We just charged into their midst and began cracking heads.

We wanted *kills*, quick, hard, immediate kills.

The shock rods, however, with their neural-paralytic effect, were designed to stun and cause pain more than they were to butcher people. Still, we gave it our best try.

The operators climbed awkwardly to their feet, squalling, but were quickly put down again. We applied the shock-rods vigorously, the weapons buzzing and snapping as we repeatedly struck skulls, ears, noses… When they still squirmed and howled, we moved on to more sensitive locations like elbows, kneecaps, balls, and guts.

Grunting like savages, we worked them over. We were angry, I don't mind admitting it. These losers had tormented my men, hunting them down with terrifying machines and abusing them. It was hard to stop getting even.

Oh, sure. They shouted for us to cease our abuse. They claimed to be noncombatants. They said we were violating some rule or another.

All their bleating fell on deaf ears. We were beyond mercy.

They weren't supposed to be here. They were the ones violating the rules of this engagement. Anyone who dared to step onto Green Deck during an exercise like this… well, their lives weren't worth spit.

Sargon, in fact, hawked a big one and spat upon the last shivering form he'd run down in the shrubbery and given a savage beating.

That was when another figure emerged from the forest. He was zipping up his pants, and he looked stunned.

"What the hell is this?" It was Director Cunningham. He'd apparently been off in the jungle somewhere, taking a piss.

"Hey, Director," I said, giving him a crooked smile.

Somewhere along the line, during the day's fighting, my jaw had become slightly dislocated and swollen on one side. The eye above this swelling could barely open.

I walked toward Cunningham, giving him a deathly smile.

"McGill?" he said, as if horrified and disgusted all at once.

"The one and only," I told him. "We discovered your little watch party here, sir," I said, "and we felt the need to break in on it. Just in case you guys were doing some cheating."

"We're not cheating," he insisted. "We're simply observing in order to get good data from our robots. We have to measure their performance, you barbaric fool!"

"Okay, I get it, Mr. Director."

This entire time I was walking toward him.

He was angry. His hands were on his fatty hips. He shook a finger at me, pointing at each of his collapsed operators, some of whom were still squirming around.

Sargon was looking kind of crazy. His gaze slid back and forth, and it caught mine. He gave me a little up-down with the eyebrows, but I gave him a tiny shake of my head.

I didn't want him to draw his weapon or otherwise abuse Director Cunningham. Not right now.

"You do realize, Director," I said, "that you are essentially the primary commander of the robot force?"

"Yeah? So what?"

"So, now that we've captured you, you have the ability to turn off all of your robots, to make them stand down. We demand that your army surrenders to us."

Director Cunningham snorted. He looked shocked by my suggestion. Finally, he laughed and shook his head. "I get it now. All this is nonsense. That's not going to happen, McGill. You'll be lucky if I don't have you up on charges for abusing these men. There's absolutely no way we're going to surrender and give you a cheesy victory."

That was it for me. I'd heard enough.

I lunged forward and began to methodically beat him down.

I started with the kneecaps. He squalled as he fell, stunned and keening, onto his extremely portly ass.

"Don't you want to hit him in the head, Centurion?" Sargon asked me.

"I'm working my way up to it."

More blows rained down. The stick in my hand crackled so much it started to get hot and smelled of burnt hair.

His elbows were useless. His shoulders slumped next. Numb all over, he flopped onto his face in the muck of the jungle-filled chamber. Face down in a small mudpuddle, he gurgled and blew bubbles.

On Green Deck, there were scheduled rainstorms. These usually came in the early mornings, before the artificial dawns. As it wasn't noon, this puddle hadn't completely dried up yet.

A couple more deft taps was all it took. I paralyzed his neck, and that did the trick.

He snuffled, he gargled, he wriggled somewhat, but he had so many numb points, so many paralyzed limbs and muscles, he couldn't even turn his head.

And then, in that tiny mud puddle, he at last inhaled. He gargled in the churned-up muddy rainwater. He drowned in what was no more than a cereal bowl's worth of liquid and died at my feet.

"Seems to me, Centurion," Sargon said, "that Director Cunningham would have done better to give up."

"Agreed, Veteran. Agreed," I said. "Some people are just too damn stubborn for their own good."

Walking around to the various operator stations, I studied the devices they were carrying. With a shrug, I turned them all off.

Within a minute or so after that, a voice came rolling out across Green Deck. It was that of Primus Graves. I knew that we had many observers today, among them Graves and Tribune Winslade.

"All right," he said, "it looks like all the robots are now disabled. I count six human survivors. This exercise is at an end. The humans win. Please evacuate Green Deck. The cleanup crews will be coming in shortly. Anyone found wounded and unable to exit the exercise chamber under their own power will be recycled. Graves out."

After a quick glance at one another, Sargon and I hustled to the nearest exit. We left Green Deck to the evil work of the bio crews coming up from Blue Deck.

We wanted nothing to do with them. Hell, to my mind, those ghouls were worse than the robots we'd just fought to a standstill.

That made me turn my mind to the sweetness of Dawn, the one and only bio I knew who didn't fit into the category of vast evil where I firmly placed the rest of her kind. No, she was different from the others, and I was determined to have dinner with her tonight.

## -13-

Director Cunningham was revived up on Gold Deck. He bitched, naturally enough, but he got no sympathy from the legion brass. Eventually, he packed up his robots and his sullen techs and went back to Earth.

To most soldiers aboard, I was something of a hero. They were still buying me drinks and clapping me on the back whenever they saw me. Word had spread that I'd single-handedly chased Cunningham and his hated robots off the decks of *Scorpio* for good.

I hoped it was a permanent thing, but I doubted Cunningham's sort of evil could ever be completely stamped out. If the robots were cheaper than real men, the bean-counters down at Central were going to keep pushing for their inclusion in our rosters.

Ah well, such problems were for another day.

Things were pretty dull for the next few weeks. We were flying all the way out to the Mid-Zone, after all. That meant zipping along in hyperspace for thousands of lightyears. Even with our latest, fastest ship it took a long time to get out there.

During this long flight, a new regimen was announced by the staffers up on Gold Deck. They wanted us to clean up our kits.

At first, we were bewildered. With great regularity, we made sure that every weapon was serviceable. Every piece of armor fit and was adjusted to maximum comfort and functionality. There was never a slit or a crease so deep that it would endanger our lives.

But that wasn't what they were talking about. That wasn't what they were talking about at all. They wanted us to *polish* our armor, to shine it up, and to bang out the dents. They even discussed the idea of chrome-dipping certain surfaces so that they would gleam under the light of the alien sun we were going to serve under.

"I can't believe this bullshit," Harris complained. "If we go around polishing up all of our kits, they're just going to get scarred and need to be polished all over again."

Leeson wagged a finger at him. "You're missing the point, Harris. I can tell you've never been on one of these kinds of missions before."

"Neither have you!"

"Yeah, well… I've seen the other prissy legions marching and sparkling. This is all about looking good. It's all about spit and polish."

"I understand the spit part," Harris said, "but I don't get the point of the polishing. A gun fires just the same with paint on it or without."

"You should be happy, it means we aren't flying into a meat-grinder."

The two of them went on like that, but I soon ignored them.

A few more dull weeks went by, and it seemed like Primus Gilbert had forgotten about the house arrest he placed me under. My weaseling had worked. Accordingly, I started sneaking out of my module to pester Dawn.

Tonight, I'd dared to take Dawn all the way down to Lavender Deck again. I'd bribed and cajoling my way back into our favorite eatery, the Blind Fish.

"What in the hell is that?" Dawn whispered, leaning toward me.

"Huh?" I said, glancing both directions.

I hadn't seen anything amiss, but I began looking for Primus Gilbert. We weren't supposed to be down here, after all.

Dawn was having a sumptuous meal of sea bass while I was digging into one of those big Jungle World turtles that I was so fond of. Cooked in its original shell and served up as a meaty stew, it was excellent. Imported food of this quality was rare and every bite was worth savoring.

Gaping around like an owl with a broken beak, I spun my head but saw nothing amiss. Then, I noticed Dawn was looking over my shoulder. Something or someone was on my six.

I turned around in my chair, craning my neck—and then I saw him.

Dawn wasn't pointing Primus Gilbert. Far from it. Instead, a large, blue-scaled lizard stood out in the passageway. Raash was just outside the restaurant's main entrance. He was arguing in his usual irritable manner with the wait staff.

"I'll be damned..." I said. "That's Raash!"

"You know that alien?" Dawn asked, stunned.

She was relatively new to the orbit of James McGill. The truth was, I knew lots of aliens. I frequently got them and myself into all kinds of trouble.

"What the hell is he doing here...?" I asked myself aloud.

I got up and approached Raash. He caught sight of me and pointed a nasty, scaly arm in my direction.

"There he is! That's the one. The most disreputable ape-descendant to ever draw breath. Why do you protect him?"

The waiters were highly alarmed. They were probably one step from calling security. I could tell they didn't want to let this big, stinky alien into their fine establishment—and I couldn't blame them for that. When I walked up, they turned in my direction.

"Centurion McGill? Do you know this alien, sir?"

"I sure as heck do," I said, extending a hand for a hearty shake toward Raash.

He ignored this friendly gesture. He didn't even look at my hand. He stared intently at me instead.

A thick, weird, gray-colored tongue slipped out from between his countless teeth and then disappeared again. It was a giant version of the strange tongues parrots always seemed to have. On its way back into his mouth, it made a raspy, leathery sound passing over his curved fangs.

"The McGill..." he said. "I have found you at last."

"That you have, Raash. That you have."

The waiters threw up their wimpy hands and beat a hasty retreat. They'd decided this overgrown reptile was my problem now.

They were correct in this assumption. Raash had always been my problem. It seemed like the lizard liked to follow me through the cosmos.

"Come on in," I said, knowing he wasn't going to be easily dissuaded from doing so.

I guided him through numerous chairs and tables. People yelped and exclaimed as his scaly tail banged into their knees and his clawed feet uncaringly trod upon their toes.

Raash didn't care about any of this. He followed me and squatted on a chair next to Dawn. We'd taken a spot over by the big aquarium that was full of exotic alien fish.

One of the fish came near to investigate the newcomer. The football-sized creature looked like a cross between a jellyfish and a hermit crab.

Tendril-like tentacles dangled down from the shell, but when it examined Raash, it seemed to not like what it saw. It sucked all of its numerous limbs into its shell and promptly dropped to the bottom of the tank, which was covered with colorful gravel.

"Oh, you scared it," Dawn said.

"Who is this female?" Raash demanded, pointing rudely at Dawn. "Could it be you have yet another mating toy? They seem innumerable, McGill."

"Uh… Raash, this is Dawn. She's a bio from Blue Deck."

Raash regarded her, and she regarded him. Right about then, Dawn wrinkled up her nose. Her nostrils narrowed in disgust. Her hand went to her mouth and her nose, trying to cover them both at once.

I knew what the problem was without asking. See, Raash was a true predator. Like most meat-eating animals, he wasn't too tidy with the things he ate and later excreted. He had a distinctly unpleasant, pungent odor which had wafted in her direction.

"Hey, buddy," I said, picking up the menu and tapping on it. "How about I order you a couple of specialty items I know you're gonna like?"

"You offer me sustenance?" Raash asked. "All attempts at bribery and befriendment will be unsuccessful, McGill. I'm here on official business."

I ordered some food anyway and then set aside the menu. No matter what Raash said about his aloofness and dedication to any given mission, I knew he was easily swayed and usually hungry. Even the simplest of gifts could work miracles.

"And what might your mission here be, my reptilian friend?"

"Do not name me friend. That is yet another attempt to cast scat upon my reputation." He turned to Dawn suddenly. "You should be made aware, female," he said, "that you are mating with a criminal member of your species. Not only is he promiscuous and a liar in the extreme, but he—"

"Hey, hey, hey!" I protested. "Settle down, Raash, old buddy. I invited you to this table, and you're being rude."

Raash grumbled. His parrot-like tongue slipped out again, rasping nastily on his teeth. That was a new habit, and I wasn't too fond of it.

"Can you just talk and be friendly, or what?"

Dawn had stopped eating, and she looked like she was about to lose what she had already consumed of this fine dinner. I was beginning to regret having brought Raash over to my table. Maybe I should have tried to have the waitstaff evict him after all. Even if he *had* killed them in a fit of rage, well, he at least wouldn't have freaked out my girlfriend so badly.

But here I was, allowing my natural good nature to come between myself and success once again. Sometimes, I was just too damned agreeable for my own good.

"I am here to investigate various anomalies," Raash said.

"I see... why were you looking for me?"

"Experience and deductive logic. When something suspicious happens aboard this ship, I know who is most likely to be involved."

"Uh..." I said, trying to piece together the lizard's puzzling words.

"He means you're a troublemaker, James," Dawn said, helpfully.

"Oh…" I said, "yeah, that's right. But I'm not up to anything today—nothing that I'm not usually up to, that is."

Raash aimed his slitty eyes at me. He didn't blink often, which I found disconcerting.

I noticed Dawn was quietly and gently scooting her chair closer to me and farther away from Raash. The longer the conversation went on, this was likely to continue.

Oftentimes, when people got near Raash, they felt an urge to get away from him and go pee or something. Seeing as he was a cold-blooded predator from another planet and easily twice as large as your average human male, I knew that eventually, Dawn's butt was likely to end up on my lap as she sought my protection.

"So," I said, "you're here on business, not pleasure?"

This wasn't any kind of a surprise to me. Raash always worked as a spy or a mercenary of some type. The thing was, he was extremely bad at not standing out. He could infiltrate organizations, but everyone who laid eyes, ears, or nostrils on him knew right off that something was wrong.

"I've already said as much, human. Confirmation should be unnecessary."

"Well… why don't we have some food first?" I suggested. "That's a human tradition."

"Your traditions are foolish," Raash told me. But, perhaps in order to make a rare effort to blend in, he agreed.

"What the heck are you doing?" Dawn whispered to me.

Raash had become distracted by the fish tanks near us. He stood and approached the bubbling aquarium nearest to our table.

The tentacled thing in its shell on the bottom had dared to creep out into the open once again. Raash opened a panel and reached his arm over the top and inside. He was clawing up the gravel, splashing water on the floor and apparently trying to catch his dinner.

"These morsels do indeed look tasty," he said. "I rarely go in for seafood, but—"

Dawn gave a little shriek as Raash captured something with a sudden lunge and dragged it out with his claw-like fingers. Fish blood and silver scales dribbled everywhere. Raash shoved his catch into his grinding maw. He chewed it up and exclaimed about the flavors.

"This is indeed a flavorful repast. At last, you humans have grasped the joys of consuming the living. I've never understood how you could eat dead things all the time. Your diet is disgusting and lacks proper nutrition."

Dawn's shriek caught the attention of the waitstaff. They hurried toward us in a swarm. Raash made ready to fight with them, but I managed to talk him down, and we left the restaurant as a group.

"...and don't come back anytime soon, sir," the maître d' told me in a cold voice.

I shook my head sourly. I knew I was in for a five or possibly six-figure tip the next time I dared show my nose in this fine establishment.

Dawn made up an excuse, and she managed to escape the two of us. Her little butt looked good as she hurried away.

"Damn it, Raash," I said, watching her go. "You chased off my date."

"Ah," he said. "So, you admit she is your mate?"

"Not exactly..."

"Tell me," he said. "How many of your young has she borne?"

"None!"

Raash snorted, causing something slimy to hit the deck in front of us. I did a little hop to step over the mess.

"Then she is without value," he told me. "Do not lament her escape."

I decided to switch the topic, as I knew that we were never going to understand each other on this point. I'd always gotten the feeling that among Saurians, mating wasn't the most pleasurable experience—especially for the females.

"Okay," I said, "now that we're alone, just tell me why the hell you're here, so you can get off my ship and out of my life."

"Not so fast, human," he said. "I have questions for you."

"And who's behind these questions? Alexander Turov?"

Raash pretended to be shocked by my statement. "Again, you profess a belief in fantasies," he said. "I have never—and I will never—work for any human."

"Raash, you told me you were working for Turov the last time we met."

"Nonsense," he said. "And you can never prove that."

"Okay, okay. Whatever. Just tell me what you want."

"There was an individual aboard this ship. A human official known as the Director."

"You mean Cunningham?" I asked, frowning.

"Yes. Yes. That is the moniker."

"Ah, I get it. You're here because Cunningham ran off to Hegemony and ratted on me."

"He said you were destructive and obstinate."

"I'm both of those things…" I admitted, "but I'm a legionnaire in Legion Varus, and it's in the job description. I'm expected to be ornery."

Raash nodded as if I'd imparted a great piece of wisdom. "You are therefore guilty of destroying government property with regularity and an utter disregard for cost."

"I admit to nothing," I told him.

Raash lifted up his own tapper, which was embedded in his arm. He tapped at it with his talons. "It is too late for retractions. I have recorded your confession. This gesture is most excellent of you, but I cannot guarantee you will be granted any special leniency as a result."

"I wouldn't expect any."

"There is another matter," he said, "but I do not believe you are capable of enlightening me in this area."

I found my interest slightly piqued. "Just try me. I know lots of things."

"No," Raash said, "I shall proceed with my original plan."

"Which is to do what?"

"To perform an audit."

"An audit? An audit of what?"

"My subjects will be certain individuals on Gold Deck. As I said, the matter does not concern you, McGill. I will report what you have offered to my superiors. I make no promises. You may or may not experience merciful results."

"Whatever, Raash," I said, and I parted ways with him.

As he'd indicated, he rode all the way to the top of the ship in the elevator. He was actually going up to Gold Deck.

I thought about following him, but then decided I didn't really care enough to bother. I was more interested in hunting for Dawn.

Stepping off at Blue Deck, I went searching for her. She demanded that I shower, saying I smelled like Raash. It took me better than an hour to smooth all her feathers back into place.

In the end, she stopped fussing, and we spent a nice night together.

## -14-

By the following morning, I'd forgotten about Raash. Dawn had driven all thoughts of that stinky lizard out of my mind.

I yawned, I stretched, and I put on my uniform. Then I ran around the module, kicking tails with my size thirteen boots.

The troops were soon up and hopping down to the cafeteria for breakfast. This was followed by an overly long session of armor-polishing. There were lots of eyeballs rolled during this last activity, let me tell you.

Harris brought me a brand-new complaint, with Sargon in tow behind him. Sargon had our old 3rd Unit battle flags in his hands. Harris grabbed one from Sargon and shook it in my face.

"Tell me what's wrong with these, sir," he asked. He seemed truly upset.

Sargon stood to one side, looking annoyed as well.

"What about them?" I said, taking one of the banners from Harris and unfurling it. There was the wolf's head, red and black on a field of yellowy gold. They looked okay to me.

"What's wrong with this flag?" Harris demanded. "Why can't we use these same banners—the ones we've always used?"

"Uh…" I said, "I don't see any reason why you can't. They look okay to me."

"Because they've been shoving new ones at us. Redesigned turds."

He then proceeded to get out a fresh carton, which he tore open with a combat knife, nearly slashing the tips off all the banners that were stored inside.

There was a new, simpler design. It was a little more stylish. To me, they didn't look that bad, but they definitely weren't our old venerable, original banners.

I scratched my head. "Where'd you get those from?"

"From upstairs," he pointed sharply at the roof of the module.

I knew he meant Gold Deck. "Huh…" I said.

"They say our old ones are too ratty. They've got to be replaced."

"Not only that, but they replaced them," Sargon complained, "with this goofy new design."

I eyeballed all this, frowning a bit. Sure, these old banners were a little bit frayed and tattered. They had, after all, snapped in the wind on dozens of planets over decades of time. Still, they had a lot of sentimental value to people like Harris and Sargon, in particular.

Originally, when I'd first joined this unit, Harris had been our most senior veteran. Later on, when he moved up to adjunct, Sargon had become our most senior non-commissioned officer. As was tradition in every unit, the most senior noncom was responsible for these rarely used banners and other regalia.

"I've died under this banner," Harris griped. "What? Thirty or forty times?"

"More like a hundred," Sargon said.

Harris glanced at him with a frown. He didn't like to be reminded of how many times he'd died. He didn't like to even think about that. "The point is, I've shed a lot of blood underneath these banners. All of us have." Harris shook the old banner under my nose. "I don't like having to put something new on just to fancy it up for some alien prince."

I put my hands on my hips, and then I huffed.

"Okay," I said at last, "I'll tell you what, just for you two boys' sake, I'm going to go upstairs, and I'm going to ask about this. Give me one of each."

They then carefully and reverently rolled up an old banner that was, to be fair, ripped and torn in a few spots. It had even been repaired through careful nanite needlework at some point or other.

They handed this to me, folded in the precise manner they'd been taught decades earlier. Then, they took one of the new banners, pulled it out of the bag, and shoved it at me in a wad.

I took the two banners and marched out of the place. I could tell by their looks, they were highly satisfied with my response. As soon as I'd gone down the passageway far enough, I glanced over my shoulder. I saw no one was following me, so I took an immediate turn toward the nearest officer's watering hole.

It wasn't open yet—not for alcohol—but I was able to get a nice sandwich in there with something tasty on the side. Naturally, I had absolutely no intention of going to Gold Deck to complain about these banners. But the appearance that I'd done so would buy me points with my two top subordinate leaders. It would pay off good dividends later on, so, I was willing to put on a show for them.

Spotting me in a chair at a table by myself, another centurion walked over. He slammed a big hand on my back, which made me grunt as it landed with significant force. I turned and was unsurprised to see Manfred.

He was one of my best friends in the legion and in life itself. He commanded the 7$^{th}$ Unit, and he grinned down at me.

"Mind if I join you, mate?" he asked. He had a Manchester accent and an attitude to match.

I waved for him to sit, and he slammed down a tray of slop beside me. He eyeballed the two banners, which I'd left on a third chair nearby. I didn't want them too close, as I knew I was liable to give them extra stains. And since I was eating a lot of ketchup today, it might be hard even for the nanites to take out those marks.

"I see you've got yourself there a couple of those new banners that Turov designed," Manfred said.

I grunted and turned to stare. "Turov?"

"Yeah, sure. I'd think you'd have been the first to know Galina Turov was aboard the ship."

I frowned. I hadn't known that at all. "When did she show up?"

"Last night, late—with a whole entourage of suck-ups from Central," he shook his head. "She came in with this new design, and all these flags. Her dwarves carried them behind her. It was like she was a princess, and they were dragging her train."

"So… what's she here for?" I asked, "other than redesigning our regalia."

"What?" Manfred said, leaning back. "You don't even know about the briefing? Turn your forearm up, man."

I did so, somewhat reluctantly, and he tapped at it a few times. There, in glaring red print, I was presented with a memo demanding that I deliver my recalcitrant ass to a meeting up on Gold Deck with all the other centurion-level officers in less than an hour's time.

"Oh…" I said, staring at the unmistakably clear words.

Manfred had moved on from my tapper to poking at my gauntlets and my epaulets. "These don't look mint. It's not all rubbish, sure," he said, "but where's chrome and polish? You'd best get sorted."

I grunted. He was right. Of course, my unit had been slow to respond to these demands for a new, improved appearance. But now Galina that was aboard and planning some kind of assembly with us—that changed things a bit.

As military men throughout time had learned, inspections were the key to enforcing discipline. It was one thing to stipulate a long list of slovenly habits to avoid. It was quite another to publicly examine and possibly humiliate those who failed to meet these standards.

"Crap…" I said.

I dug into my food, and Manfred did the same. He made many jokes at my expense, but I ignored them.

I had to eat fast and then touch up my gear. It was going to be hard to get up to Gold Deck in time after that.

"See you there, mate," Manfred said, standing up and stumping away. He was a man who was as broad as I was tall.

Both of us were unusual in our own way, but in personality, we got along extremely well.

I returned to my unit, tossing the extra flags aside. I immediately called upon Adjunct Leeza.

"I need your help, right now," I told her.

"Help with what?"

"With my armor. It looks like shit."

She looked me over, frowning. Her armor was probably the only kit with a mirror-like shine to it in the entire unit. This was partly because she hadn't served in Legion Varus very long, but also because she had been in Germanica for so many decades prior. When it came to spit and polish, that outfit knew how to do things right.

"Are you kidding me?" she asked. "You want me to scrub your kit for you? Why can't you get a specialist or a regular to do that sort of thing?"

"Because you know how to do it right," I told her, "and I need to be heading up to Gold Deck real soon..." I told her about the meeting with the other centurions. She was aghast.

"We don't have much time…" she said.

Without complaining any further, she actually did help me. I had to give her that much. She helped out without producing a continuous litany of complaints.

She got out her polishing kit, and we both went to work together.

There were many whispers and comments when people saw this—especially from Carlos. He made obscene gestures behind Leeza's back and gave me questioning up-down flashes of his eyebrows.

I ignored him and his insinuations. No, I was not visiting Leeza in the night. I was still very definitely with Dawn—which was already highly complicated now that Galina was aboard the ship. I could have denied everything, but I knew loud denials would only make Carlos more likely to spread rumors to the contrary. Besides, I simply didn't have time to deal with him right now.

Fifteen long minutes later, we had my armor in the best shape it had ever been. It still was nowhere near what a man from Victrix was accustomed to, but it would have to do.

Harris then approached me, looking from me to the armor and then at the two flags.

"Well, how'd it go?" he asked.

"How'd what go?"

He picked up the new banner that he hated and shook it in front of me. "How did this go? Did you get rid of these frigging things or not?"

"Haven't met with her yet," I admitted, "but I'm going up there now to do so."

"Ah," Harris said, as if suddenly getting everything at once. "I understand! You want to look good before you meet with her. I get it. Sly-boots, McGill! Who am I to tell the biggest tomcat in Legion Varus how to play it with a woman like Turov?"

He threw his hands high and backed away, smiling.

Leeza studied me in confusion after he left. "What's all that about?"

"I don't know," I said. "I think Harris has been hitting the hooch early today."

Leeza frowned at that, but she was already frowning at my back because I was marching for the exit. Gold Deck and the meeting of the centurions was only a few minutes away.

As it turned out, I rode up with a dozen men such as myself. We all shared an elevator.

They chattered, they complained, and everybody gleamed so much it was giving me an eye-ache.

We shuffled into the largest meeting chamber on Gold Deck, which was a small amphitheater. About a hundred and twenty centurions attended.

The primus-level officers were already there. Most of them were in the front row along with staffers and support-personnel for Tribune Winslade and his ilk.

Up at the front of the room was Primus Collins. I smiled a bit, happy to see her on the stage. It could have just as easily been that sour drink of water known as Primus Gilbert or, even worse, the lumpy, scowling, and grizzled Primus Graves.

But no, at least there was going to be something to look at today. Primus Collins was fairly attractive, and I happened to know personally she could be pretty fiery in bed when the mood struck her.

Collins's eyes slid around the room, looking at the crowd and seemingly doing a count. She paused briefly upon me and Manfred. I lifted a hand and waved at her. She ignored this and slid her eyes away from me again.

Manfred, sitting next to me, laughed, guffawed, slapped his knee, and nudged his shoulder into me.

"You still got an eye for that one, too?" he asked. "Looks to me like she's not interested."

I shrugged. "If a man doesn't shoot his gun now and then," I said, "there's going to be no rabbits in his bag when he returns home at night."

"Yeah, sure," Manfred said. "But if he pops off at every rabbit in the forest, he's likely to run out of ammo."

I shook my head seriously. "I never run out of ammo."

Manfred laughed again, and then the meeting was called to order.

Finally, at long last, the leader of this entire affair made her grand entrance. Imperator Galina Turov had one of the new flags with her, and her armor looked brand-spanking new. Not only that, but it had clearly been dipped in chrome from helmet to boots.

She'd also added some golden accents. Her belt buckle, her epaulettes, and the rims of her goggles, which she had slid up onto her head, were gilded.

"Hey mate," Manfred said next to me, "you think that's real gold?"

I looked at Galina. I squinted and then nodded. "I'm fairly certain of it," I told him.

"Crazy woman…"

"All right, officers," Galina said, "it is my privilege to address the brave men and women of Legion Varus. I suppose you've all been wondering why you were called here today."

"If I have to start wearing golden underwear," Manfred half-whispered next to me, muttering under his breath, "I'm going to shoot myself."

This sent me into a rumbling laugh of my own.

Galina caught this, and her eyes flashed hotly in my direction. All this time, she hadn't bothered to look directly at me—but the moment I was doing something that might possibly disrupt her speech, she zeroed in on me instantly. I therefore knew she was keenly aware of my presence, and my exact location in the crowd.

I just smiled at her mildly and listened. I wasn't in the mood to make any more loud, disruptive noises. At least not yet.

Galina relaxed a fraction and let her eyes drift over the crowd again. "As you might've surmised," she said, "we are getting close to our destination planet. We can now reveal the details of this world and our mission."

Now, that did perk me up. Manfred and I both shifted in our seats, leaning forward a notch or two. Maybe this wasn't a grand meeting about flags, regalia, and gold-rimmed glasses. Maybe this was going to be more important than we thought.

"Collins?" Galina said, nodding to Primus Collins, who was playing the role of her butt-monkey today.

Collins briskly tossed images at the grand screen that was behind Galina. She began making sweeping motions with her hands and fluttering fingers.

The screen, of course, was also the back wall of the conference room. It was a very large surface, something like five meters high and twenty wide. Not only that, but it had the capability of projecting in a three-dimensional manner, right into the room itself.

A vast swirling collage of stars, well known to all of us, came to life. It was the spiral galaxy known as the Milky Way.

"Our knowledge of the shape and the configuration of our galaxy has been growing steadily," Galina said. "We know there are only two major arms, like most galaxies have—over ninety percent of them. The other so-called arms are simply swirls of stars, clusters, and the like, which we believe now were once independent dwarf galaxies, and which were consumed by the Milky Way long ago. None of that matters today, however."

I stifled a yawn and forced myself to listen.

At this point, Primus Collins had managed to spin the galaxy around with her fingers to a point where Earth was now a single, shining blue-green dot among millions of white ones.

"This is Sol," she said, "our home star. As you can see, we're something like two-thirds of the way out from the center of the galaxy, at the very rim of the Galactic Empire itself. This ship has been traveling toward the center for several months, but we haven't even made it halfway yet."

Here, a line appeared to represent *Scorpio's* course. It stretched from the blue-green dot representing Earth halfway to the Galactic Core. The center of this storm of stars we called our galaxy looked like a giant cotton ball to me. There, the Galactics resided. Theirs were the oldest and most powerful of civilizations.

"We have traveled out of the Frontier Provinces and into the region known as the Mid-Zone. The Mid-Zone is actually quite large and, in fact, consists of more stars than the entirety of the Frontier Zone."

Bands of colored light began to glow. The Frontier was blue. The Mid-Zone was green. Then, Primus Collins tilted the entire galactic picture on its side. Instead of a disc, it now appeared to be a huge circle.

On the outer edge, about the last third away from the center of the galaxy, it was all rust-red. Stars at that distance were largely unexplored. At least thirty percent of the star systems in the galaxy had never been visited by the Galactics.

I stopped listening and reflected upon the entirety of the Empire. It had grown and grown until it had run out of gas and begun to collapse inward. It was experiencing decay to this very day. The outer areas beyond the Frontier Zone were essentially a wilderness. Millions of star systems that were inhabited by unknown, dangerous civilizations. The Silicoids with their crystal drones had been a prime example. We'd fought against them the year before.

But today, Galina wasn't talking about the fringes of the galaxy, she was talking about the Mid-Zone, which was lit up with a sickly green glow. This thick band completely encircled the golden sphere in the center.

"This, then, is the Mid-Zone," she said. "Earthlings have only been this far from home once before to visit a star system known as Segin."

Here, another planet lit up, this time in a bright red. It was known to us as City World, or Segin. City World was full of ungrateful Mogwa, a splinter colony of the Galactics. Forlorn and forgotten, far from the Core, the Mogwa there were outcasts. They could only dream of the grandeur of the Imperial halls.

"Segin has been very busy since we last visited the Mid-Zone," she continued. "The Mogwa here, whatever you might say about them, are industrious. They're led by our ex-governess known as Nox and Grand Admiral Sateekas. They've been busily building and militarizing for years now."

*Hmm,* I thought to myself, frowning a bit. This briefing wasn't quite what I'd been expecting. Talk of building up, militarization—that didn't sound as calm and ceremonial as I'd hoped this mission would be.

"In fact," Galina said, "they built up a large defensive army—which soon became offensive. They've now conquered several worlds in the immediate vicinity of Segin."

There was a *pop-pop-pop* sound. More star systems now glowed pink, all surrounding Segin in a seemingly random pattern.

My mouth opened as I began to grasp the situation. Grand Admiral Sateekas had gone on an aggressive campaign of conquering his neighbors.

I didn't like the sound of that. If there was one thing that Sateekas wasn't good at, it was any serious military campaign. He was okay when he was just parading his fleet around, impressing local yokels—but actual combat? Invasion and conquest? Nope.

In my estimation, those were things beyond his capacities. But apparently, he didn't agree with me on this.

Galina was now tapping another planet. This one lit up purple.

"This is Nebra," she said. "The most recent and the most impressive of the Mogwa conquests. It's a green world, somewhat Earth-like. It's a little larger than Earth, with big leafy forests covering most of it."

That made me smile. At least this new planet wasn't some wasteland.

"The solitary local sun," she said, "is yellow—a bit more yellow than our home system. It's a K-class dwarf, quite friendly and stable. An excellent, reliable source of light and heat. Predictably, on the fourth planet from the sun, life has indeed flourished."

A green world spun on the screens. It looked nice—but looks could be deceiving.

"The creatures living on Nebra are of a medium technological level. They're dangerously intelligent—and definitely duplicitous in their nature."

Here, the image of the planet faded away, and what appeared in its place was something that I knew all too well. It was one of those damned, raccoon-skunk-monkey aliens.

I stood up then, unable to contain myself. I pointed a long arm, at the end of which was a long finger, toward the image that dominated the screen.

"I know those skunk-guys," I shouted. "They're serious assholes!"

A ripple of laughter went through the crowd.

## -15-

The rest of the briefing went off the way such things normally did, and I soon began to pay less and less attention. I'd already met with these skunk-creatures personally and taken their measure—and that's why I was now referring to them as skunks.

Sure, they had more white fur on them than black, but to me, they still looked and acted like skunks. Skunks with hands that walked upright. *Tricky* skunks. Creatures you couldn't trust under any circumstances.

Galina explained at great length that we were going to serve on Nebra as a color guard, and to support the Mogwa troops. The Mogwa forces had come from Segin to garrison this planet that had been recently conquered by Sateekas.

The more I listened to the briefing, the bigger my frown grew. Then my arms came up and crossed themselves. I was no longer buying her official story. None of it added up in my mind.

The Mogwa marines that I'd met, while not outright cowardly, were never the troops assigned to do low-level grunt-work. They were, in fact, exactly the kind of soldiers that would work well as a color guard.

They liked to march around in little one-man tanks. They didn't like to get dirty—and they especially didn't like to risk their own lives.

On the other hand, here we were, a bunch of humans from the frontier planets. We were barbarians at best in the minds of any Galactic. Grunting savages who'd been hired to help out.

Did it make sense then that we'd be working as the shiny, elite troops there to impress the skunks? Nope.

Maybe… I thought. Maybe the Mogwa troops from Segin had grown tired of Sateekas' ambitions. Maybe they'd decided to return home to Segin. That could be why he needed a garrison force.

It was either that, or things were a lot worse on Nebra than anyone was letting on. I wouldn't be surprised to learn there was a full-blown rebellion going on.

Whatever the case, I was suspicious.

For the rest of the presentation, I no longer listened to either Primus Collins or Galina Turov. Instead, I watched their two small shapely forms as they moved around, making the wall screen behind them do tricks.

They displayed videos showing various aspects of life on Segin. The Mogwa colonists there had now expanded out beyond their city dome. I looked at the growing fleet that they'd built under Sateekas and Nox's leadership. It was impressive.

While I stared at the women and admired them offhandedly, my mind kept on working on the central problem. My radar was up, and I was disbelieving in this mission, at least as it had been presented to me so far.

Eventually, the presentation came to an end. People began to shuffle out, but I stayed in my seat.

"Come on, mate," Manfred said, slapping me with a silvery armored gauntlet. "You can wake up, now. Meeting's over."

"I'll be along in a minute," I said, and I remained in my chair.

Shrugging, Manfred stumped away. Soon, the rest of the conference room emptied out.

There was no one left but Galina and her simps—plus me, the lone man in the audience.

I didn't say anything. I didn't raise a hand. I didn't get up and walk toward the stage. I just sat there.

Galina pretended not to notice me. She ordered her underlings around, and they scurried like mice at her slightest whim. They made scooping motions to gather in holographic images. They shut down computers, and even carted away a number of boxes full of the new legion banners that had so offended my comrades down in the modules.

But I didn't care about any of that. Not now.

Finally, at long last, Galina turned and looked at me. Her eyes were squinty. Her mouth was pursed tightly.

"Dammit, McGill. What do you want? Don't pretend that you just fell asleep. I've been watching you, and you've been watching me. I know you're trying to pull something."

"Not at all, Imperator," I said. "Nothing nefarious is going on, sir. I was just wondering if… well… maybe we could have a private word?"

Galina folded up her lips in disgust. Her hands moved up to rest on her shapely hips.

Primus Collins was no less disgusted. She'd been my girlfriend at times, at least briefly. Like every woman in the James McGill ex-girlfriend zone, she'd always hated my long-standing relationship with Galina Turov. If I even talked to Galina, she thought it was ill-advised, illegitimate, and somewhat insulting.

Galina slid her eyes toward Primus Collins. "Cherish," she said. "Please return to your regular post."

Cherish dared to pretend to be surprised. She put a spreading web of fingers over her chest. "Me, sir?"

"Out! All of you, out!"

The rest of the underlings in the room grabbed up their cartons full of flags and their snack trays. They bustled out of the room without so much as a glance back at me or Galina.

Primus Collins was the last one out. She was walking angrily, and I watched as her little butt exited at last.

When she was gone, Galina and I were alone in the room.

"All right, then," she said. "What is this? Don't try to pretend you just want a date. You wouldn't make such an effort just to spend some time with me. I'm sure you have a dozen women waiting down in the modules to give you the attention you crave, anyway."

*Wow.* That sounded like a bitter speech. Had she heard about Dawn?

I smiled and made no attempt to defend myself. I spread my hands wide. "Galina," I said, getting up at last and approaching the stage in a slow swagger. "It's really good to see you, and I mean that."

"Don't," she said as I approached.

She'd thought perhaps I was going to go for a hug, but I didn't. I stopped short.

"So sour!" I said. "Has it been too long since—?"

She glared at me. "McGill, if you've got something to say, say it. I'm quite busy. I've got to organize this entire mess, and we're arriving at Nebra very soon."

That made my eyebrows raise up. Possibly, she'd mentioned this important fact during a presentation, and I'd simply dozed through it. Either that, or our arrival date was classified information. Either way, it was definitely big news.

Hell, within a week, my men could be dropping on Nebra and doing something more important than polishing our guns.

"I wanted to talk to you," I said, "about a certain tidbit of information you asked me for a few weeks ago."

Galina's eyes slid left, then right. "We can't discuss that here."

"What would you suggest then, sir?"

She turned, spinning on one heel, and walked out. I followed her, enjoying the view. Damn, the girl still had it. Her hindquarters hadn't aged a day, not as far as my highly trained eyes could detect.

She led me to her private office, which also doubled as her quarters. I was surprised she wasn't staying on Lavender Deck, but up here on Gold Deck instead.

I moved immediately to her tiny bar and began mixing myself a drink. When I attempted to offer her one, she demurred, putting a hand up to stop the glass from touching her fingers.

"Tell me what you learned."

"Uh…" I said, "you mean about Drusus, right?"

She appeared to suffer a conniption upon the utterance of this single, unmentionable name. She squawked, fluttered her hands, and urged me not to speak that word again, as if Drusus's mere name was a curse.

Perhaps, these days, it was.

"This isn't going to work," she said hotly. "Not this time. You're not going to weasel any favors out of me—or get any more free drinks. I'm not going to tolerate such nonsense. Not today."

"Okay, okay," I said. "I'll tell you the story plain and straight. Drusus has been moved to Eastern Europe, to Moldavia, to be precise."

Galina winced when she heard that forbidden name again, but then, as the meaning of my words sunk into her skull, she froze. She stared at me for a long moment, not speaking. Slowly, her small mouth opened. "You don't mean—?"

"Yep," I said. "It looks like your daddy's the one who sprung 'you know who', or rather transferred him to the private Turov dungeons."

"How do you know this?" she asked.

I shrugged. "I got my sources—an eyewitness, so to speak."

I was thinking, of course, of Elizabeth. Sure, she was just another lady-brain floating in a tank down in the Vault of the Forgotten. But she'd been there when they'd hauled Drusus away.

Galina immediately began strutting around the room while I watched her, intrigued. She was talking to herself.

"My own father did this," she said. "First, he moved him down there, stripped his body away, left him floating in a tank. And now you're telling me that he's taken an even more direct interest in Drusus? That he's moved that poor man into his personal collection?"

Those words perked me up. I'd never heard about this "personal collection". I had to wonder if everyone in that collection was dead, or near-dead, like Drusus himself.

"I told you that you weren't going to like it."

"No," she said, "I don't like it. I don't like it at all. He's never said a word about this change. Never even a hint. *Damn.* What is my father thinking?"

"Well," I said, "look at it this way. At least you aren't in a jar. You're yourself—and you look great. If anybody's head is next on the chopping block, it's got to be Wurtenberger's, not yours."

"Yes, yes," she said, "but it's still too close. It's all too close and too frightening."

I didn't quite know what she was talking about. I mean, after all, it was her own daddy who was doing these things. If anybody in heaven and earth was fairly safe from the wrath of Alexander Turov, it had to be Galina, his oldest daughter... didn't it?

Galina heaved a sigh. She heaved several of them. She was almost hyperventilating. I could tell.

"Hey," I said, pouring myself another drink. I brought one to her as well. This time, when I put it into her hand, she took it. "Relax, girl, you're going to be okay."

She gulped the drink. I made her another, and she gulped that, too.

Finally, it seemed like she could breathe again. She'd been having some kind of anxiety attack.

Damn. I'd never met anybody in my whole lifetime who was as scared of her own daddy as this girl was. That seemed wrong just on the face of it. I began to feel sorry for her.

"James," she said finally. Her voice was quieter, with a different tone.

"What?"

"I don't want to know what's happening back on Earth. I don't like it, and I'm scared."

I walked up behind her then. She was leaning over a desk with her hands resting upon it. Her fingers were splayed.

She was watching videos, videos that appeared to be from the Turov estate. There were pictures there, pictures of two young girls.

I figured it had to be Galina and her sister. They were playing in the grass and in the leafy gardens. I squinted. Some of the objects I saw in the background, things moving around, what were those?

Cars? Old-fashioned cars? They weren't aircars. They weren't trams. No. They had headlights. They had rubber tires.

Could that be real? No one put rubber on the feet of their vehicles. Not anymore.

Just how old was Galina?

I touched her gently on the shoulder with a single hand. She reached up her hand, and she clasped mine. She dug her nails in.

"I'm scared, James," she said. "I'm worried."

"It's all right," I said lamely. "I'm right here."

She turned around slowly, and she had a single tear on her cheek.

"I'm not gonna let anything happen to you," I told her.

I leaned down, and I gave her a nice kiss on the head, but that wasn't enough for her. She reached back up. She grasped onto me hotly, and we began to make out.

I was a bit stiff at first, surprised. I hadn't expected things would go this way, although given our history, I should have.

I thought about Dawn. I really did, and those thoughts made me stand there, unresponsive, for something like ten or fifteen seconds.

But Galina was hot and vital. She was very familiar, pressing herself against me, kissing me. I could taste her tears.

We made love then, and it was a weird, passionate thing. It had been a long time since we'd touched one another, but it felt like we'd never been apart.

## -16-

Dawn was sweet—but she wasn't dumb.

The next morning, she figured out two very simple things. One, that Galina Turov had returned to *Scorpio*. Two, I'd ghosted her that very evening.

Dawn had put those two things together with a big plus sign, and she'd come up with the obvious conclusion. Any female who knew James McGill well could do that math.

She didn't even call me to break up. She just sent me a text, which I discovered in the morning when I was climbing out of bed with Galina next to me.

We were in her quarters, and we'd had a pretty fun time, but now it was time to pay the piper.

"Ah, hell…" I said, reading an angry, overly long breakup note from Dawn.

"What's the matter?" Galina said.

Was there an odd, lilting note in her voice? It made me think that possibly, just possibly, she knew what I was complaining about.

"I had this girlfriend, see… Well, I guess it doesn't matter now."

"Oh," she said, "I'm so sorry to hear that."

The thing was, she didn't sound sorry at all. Not even a smidge.

"What's the text say?" she asked. She was curious—and maybe slightly amused.

I frowned, swept it all aside, deleting it. This caused the next text in line to pop up on my forearm. It was from Raash.

"More trouble," I complained. "Raash wants to meet with me today."

"What?" Galina said, spinning around and staring at me. Her entire demeanor had shifted. "Did you say Raash?"

"I sure did. That big, stinky lizard with the long tail and the blue scales. You know him rather well."

"I certainly do," she said. "Are you telling me that alien is aboard this ship?"

"Uh… yeah... didn't you know?"

"Of course, I didn't know! And you didn't tell me. Why didn't you tell me?"

"Uh…"

Galina began running around the cabin all of a sudden. She pulled on her clothes in a madcap fashion. She ran fingers through her hair, but added no product and applied no brush. She hardly ever moved this fast. Not even when we were in a combat zone.

"What's the matter?" I asked.

"You're an idiot, James! A fool!" she said. "This place is probably bugged. This cabin—everything is bugged!"

"What are you talking about?"

Galina whirled on me. "James, do you remember what we were discussing just yesterday in this very room?"

"Uh… sure I do," I said, "like when I put my hands on your hips and—"

"No, no, no!" she said. "I'm talking about the information that I arranged for you to find at Central."

I thought hard for a second. Then I threw a finger up. "Oh yeah. The Vault of the Forgotten, Drusus, all that stuff..."

She went near-berserk. She whipped a hand up to my face and slapped her palm over my mouth.

Her fingers were rasping up against my teeth and my lips hurt a bit—but I was so stunned I didn't even grab her hand to push her away. The girl had gone crazy.

Breathing hard, she leaned forward and whispered into my right ear. "McGill, you can't possibly be this stupid."

She took her hand away from my mouth for a moment. I assured her that I was indeed just as big of a dumbass as she was suggesting. I had no earthly idea what she was talking about.

"Let me spell it out for you," she whispered. "Raash works for my father. You know that, right?"

I nodded slowly. I did remember something to that effect, but I figured that by now the lizard had moved on to some other job. He oftentimes worked as a mercenary in many capacities all over the cosmos. I don't know how the hell he kept getting his jobs, but he always seemed to pop up when you least wanted him to.

"How long has he been aboard *Scorpio*?" she asked.

I shrugged, thinking that over, counting off the days. "I don't know, not that long. He came in right before you arrived."

"He's obviously been preparing for my arrival. Tell me everything."

I told her about the day down at the Blind Fish when he'd first surprised Dawn and me while we were at dinner.

She paced around the room while I related these tales. Every time she spoke to me, she did so in a whisper with her hand cupped over her mouth, putting it up to my ear.

It was kind of odd to have her hot breath blowing into my big right ear, but I decided not to complain about it. I wondered if her cabin really was bugged.

"Come on," she said at last. "Let's go."

We exited the room and marched through the passageways. She led me into a side passage that opened up into an intermediate deck that was between Gold Deck and Blue Deck.

There was no one down here except a few service robots and maintenance crew. They looked at us in surprise, but then shook their heads, figuring we were probably a couple of officer lovers looking for a secret place to express our passions for one another.

That gave me ideas, and I did attempt to paw at Galina now and then, but she was having none of it. She shook me off every time.

She led me inside a small janitor's closet. We had a tense conversation in the dim lit space. There were motors thumping nearby, along with noisy ventilation systems and gurgling pumps. Altogether, there was lots of cover noise—not to mention the fact that we were on a deck that I'm pretty sure Raash didn't even know existed.

Finally, she felt able to talk openly with me. She did so with occasional hard slaps to my face and belly. Fortunately, she never went for my groin—but I knew she was thinking about it.

"Why didn't you tell me?" she hissed. "Raash obviously knew I was coming!"

"I don't know about that..." I said lamely.

Another slap landed. My left ear rang a little.

"Can't you put two and two together? Raash came here right before I did. He immediately questioned you, then ran up to Gold Deck to prepare for my arrival."

"Well... I thought he was investigating all that stuff with Director Cunningham. You know, about all his robots."

"Of course, he had a cover story! That doesn't prove shit—in fact, it proves the opposite. He's almost as ham-handed of an operator as you are!"

She was breathing hard now, and staring at the deck, snarling and working her fingers in the air like a crazy-lady.

For my own part, I was half bored. I wasn't scared of Raash. I wasn't all that scared of Alexander Turov either—even though I probably should be.

"Okay, okay," I said. "So Raash is spying on us. So what? You said it yourself, he's obvious and lame."

"James, it matters because he probably has evidence against me now. I'm convinced he bugged my cabin."

"How's that?"

"When I first arrived on this accursed ship, I was guided directly to that chamber. I was told it was the nicest VIP cabin aboard *Scorpio*."

"And you know what?" I said. "I think it is... except maybe for some of those apartments down on Lavender Deck..."

She put a finger in my face. "Yes, exactly. Why would I be put on Gold Deck? I'm no longer an official member of this legion or this crew. I should have been quartered down on Lavender Deck. That's where all the VIPs go."

I thought that over, gave myself a scratch, and nodded. "Yeah. Okay. That's a little bit funny…"

"It's a *lot* funny. Worse, it's not funny at all!"

She wasn't making any sense now, and she went back to pacing.

I watched her absently, wishing this whole panic-attack was over already. I looked for a place to sit, but there wasn't much. I flipped over a bucket, threw the mop on the floor that had been standing in it, and sat upon the bucket glumly.

I could already tell, with a high degree of certainty, that I wasn't getting any more sugar from Galina. Worse, Dawn's sweetness had dried up, too. I pushed a fist up into my cheek and lamented my recent choices in life.

Galina treated me to a long and sordid tale about how her father had been spying on her for quite a long time now. Ever since she'd managed to evade him and his quest to make her the consul of all Earth, she'd never really felt safe since that time.

As I'd recently seen Drusus, or rather the lack of him, down there in the Vault of the Forgotten, I had to admit she had good reasons to feel this way.

"Is your dad, like, planning anything big these days?" I asked her.

She finally stopped pacing around talking to herself and gesticulating wildly in the air with her fingers. She turned to face me. She put her hands on her knees and bent low. Our heads were on an even level when she stared into my eyes.

"What do you think, James?" she asked.

I shrugged. "I don't know. He seems about the same as he's ever been. Bossy, old… kind of prissy…"

"He's different. You might not have noticed—but he is."

"What's different?"

"My father has been running the show on Earth from behind the scenes for a long time. Now, he's coming out into the open, more and more. He's like a spider that no longer fears the light."

"Oh... I get it. You know, sometimes critters from our bog grow so big and so bold, they come out into the daylight. It's like they no longer care who sees them, because they're not afraid of the birds anymore—or the snakes."

"Yes!" she exclaimed. "I think you've got it. The fact he's coming out into the open more often, that he's no longer hiding himself—that's the part that scares me."

I only half knew what she was on about, and I was getting bored again. I wanted to get out of this noisy, steamy, in-between level of *Scorpio*. I had a unit to run—and apparently, a new girlfriend to scare up.

"You're leaving this ship, aren't you?" I asked her.

"Oh, hell yes. I'm getting off *Scorpio* before I'm trapped here somehow."

"Where are you going to go? Back home?"

She shook her head violently. Her hair flew. "No, that's not safe. I'm going to find somewhere else to go, somewhere no one can find me for a while. I'll take a sudden leave. Or fake an illness—I'll think of something."

"Uh... so... do you want me to kill you again, or anything?"

"No, James..." she said, closing her eyes. "Let me try to explain. You realize that Drusus was running our entire planet a couple of years ago?"

"Yeah..."

"And now he's a specimen in a collection underneath my father's castle? A plaything, a prisoner for all eternity? That's worse than being permed."

She did have a point there. Drusus had been most foully treated.

"How are we going to get him out of that jar, by the way?" I asked her.

"What?" she said, as if the idea had never occurred to her.

"Come on," I said. "We owe Drusus, you and I both. Besides, we can't just keep running. We need to get our lives back."

For some reason, these words perked her up. She stared at me for a time, and her expression shifted. "What are you suggesting...?"

"Huh? I'm not really suggesting anything."

"Oh yes, you are," she said. "You've played the part of the assassin before. Do you have a plan?"

I was blank, dumbfounded. My jaw hung low. I barely knew what the hell she was talking about.

But then, it came to me.

Was Galina suggesting that I should attempt to kill her father? What a terrible thing! That the girl could even entertain such thoughts…

I wasn't sure that I could kill my own daddy, no matter how big of a criminal he was. It made me feel a bit sorry for Galina. For all their faults, at least my own family members weren't evil.

She stared at me, like she was a cat with her tail swishing. Her eyes bored into me as if I was some great puzzle.

"If you do *something*," she said at last, "I was never part of it. I never agreed to anything. Remember that."

"Uh… okay…" I had a thought then, and I asked her about it immediately. "What about our vacation?"

"What?"

"We're supposed to go on a cruise, remember? You promised me."

She appeared to be astonished. "You've got to be kidding."

"I held up my part of the bargain. I found out where Drusus is."

"You're about to land on a new unknown world in the Mid-Zone. Raash, my father's gargoyle, is tagging me across the cosmos—and all you can think about is some sex-filled vacation?"

"That's right," I said. "That's exactly what I'm telling you."

Galina made a sound of exasperation and disbelief. Then, she leaned close to me. She gave me a kiss and smiled. "I'm getting off this ship, now. I know you can't come with me, or I'd take you along. If you're still unpermed at the end of this campaign, I'll go on that cruise with you, okay?"

"I guess so…" I mumbled, knowing it was probably the best offer I was going to get.

Then she skipped out of the place, slamming the rattling door behind her. When I followed her out into the passageway, I was surprised to see she was gone.

That girl could really move her hindquarters when she was afraid for her own skin.

## -17-

Some of the things Galina had said the day before had left me feeling paranoid. Sure, the idea that Raash was some kind of a super-genius spy who was putting bugs everywhere was plumb crazy—but I couldn't rule it out entirely.

The whole idea annoyed me. At the very least, it had already cost me two girlfriends in the span of twenty-four hours. To my mind, that meant something had to be done, even if this whole crisis was imaginary. Accordingly, I went to visit the person I knew who was the very best at tech stuff like this, Specialist Natasha Elkin.

We were supposed to go down to Green Deck for some exercise or other, and Natasha looked alarmed when she saw me coming.

"I'm sorry, Centurion," she said, "but I'm not quite packed up yet."

Her kit was indeed all over the place. She always liked to over pack and carry too much junk with her. She was like one of those women who brought six different hairbrushes for a weekend trip when just one would suffice.

But with Natasha, it wasn't hairbrushes. It was all kinds of extra tools and gizmos and detection devices. Way more buzzers than was reasonable, too. I didn't know how the girl could walk under all that garbage she'd shoved into her ruck, but it wasn't my business to complain about that—not unless she couldn't keep up.

"Glad to see you're preparing. You look good. Everything looks good," I told her, putting her at ease. That's when I lowered my voice. "But, there's a problem…"

"Oh…?" She lowered hers and stepped closer. "What's going on?"

"I need you to do a little special work for me."

She blinked a couple of times. She glanced down at the deck and then she looked up again.

"Hacking, right? What is it? Do you want to see where we're going to land on Nebra? Where the drop-pods are targeted? I suppose, I could…"

"No, no, that's not it," I said, "not this time. Listen up. Do you know if it's possible to put a tracer on someone's tapper—someone who doesn't want a tracer on their tapper? And to do it in a sneaky way, so that someone doesn't even know you're tracing them?"

She stared at me uncomprehendingly for a few seconds. Then, all of a sudden, her face changed. She began to twist-up her lips in an ugly fashion. Slowly, her hands rose until they planted themselves on her hips. Within a matter of seconds she'd gone from a concerned subordinate soldier to a full-on Karen about to give me a scolding.

"James," she said, "I'm not going to put a stalker app on some poor girl's tapper just because you want to—"

"Whoa, whoa, whoa," I said, throwing my hands up. "Nothing like that! Well… actually… exactly like that, but it's not for any girl."

Then I explained the situation with Raash. I made no mention of Galina or anything of that kind. In my version of events, he was stalking me because Central was interested in my whereabouts.

She seemed a little confused. "Why don't you just try to protect yourself?" she said.

"How's that?"

"There are a lot of different ways a man can shield his tapper from being traced by an unauthorized source. Sure, if it's Hegemony or something, there's pretty much nothing you can do—but some clown like Raash? He is not legally permitted to track anyone who's not in his chain of command,

and since we're in Legion Varus and he's not, no one can allow him to do this."

"Yeah, well…" I said, looking around. A lot of the people in my unit were noticing that Natasha and I were having a whispered conversation. Already, the gossip had begun to fly.

*Damnation.* Sometimes my unit was like a bunch of birds on a wire.

"Listen," I said, "can you do it or not?"

"Yeah… I can do it. Of course, I can do it," she said, "but for Raash? That's weird."

"*Will* you do it? For me?"

She looked down at the deck. She shrugged. "Yeah, of course. Why not? I can't get into any trouble. He's not even operating in an official capacity. Hell, I didn't even know he was aboard *Scorpio*."

"He's here to follow me around," I told her. "To keep an eye on me and others."

"Well, all right. I don't know why you don't just go to Tribune Winslade or Captain Merton and get him kicked off our ship—but it's your business."

"That's right, it is. When you've got it done, throw me the app—and thanks a lot, girl."

I turned around and left. Natasha went back to stuffing too much crap into her ruck.

But I knew she would work hard on this side-project every free moment she had. She'd probably fuss with it while she was standing in line to go down to Nebra in a drop-pod.

She was like that. I'd probably made her day by giving her a little side mission to mess with.

A few days later, we made planetfall over Nebra. It was a vibrantly green world. The ice caps, at both the north and south of the globe, were somewhat smaller than they were back home. There were plenty of seas and lakes, but not as much water as there was on old Earth.

It was the kind of world where, instead of looking at the shapes of the continents, you looked at the shapes of the seas in the middle of one giant continent. The oceans and lakes came in various sizes and levels of salinity. Probably the largest of them was the one up to the north, a sea that looked like a big bald patch on the dome of the world, with a white ice cap floating in the middle of it. That was simply known as the North Ocean. The next largest one was down near the equator. It didn't have much of a special recognizable shape to it, reminding me perhaps of a puzzle piece with round, bulbous lobes angling out here and there. It was probably the size of a continent like Africa back home, but with a much more varied shape to it.

But the forests! Those big, deep forests—most of the planet seemed to be covered by trees. There weren't many deserts, either. Almost the whole planet was green.

"What a jewel of a world," I said, marveling at the screens in our module.

"Looks hot to me," Leeson complained. "Better break out the AC units for all of our suits."

"Yeah, you got that right," Harris seconded the motion, "hotter than Hell."

Of all my adjuncts, only Leeza came to stand next to me. She was marveling at the world, too.

"A brand-new planet," she said. "You're the only one who's met the aliens that we're going to be dealing with. What do you think of them?"

I glanced down at her. "Those guys weren't very encouraging. They're kind of… well… kind of tricksy."

"How do you mean?" she asked.

I explained my one single encounter with the skunk-aliens back at Central. She frowned as I described their behavior.

"How technological are they?" she asked.

"I don't know. I attended that briefing, but it was boring."

"Of course, it was…"

"They're smart enough to know what a gun can do. They've got roads, they've got vehicles, they've got cities. They're not total primitives."

"Well, that's good. At least," she said.

I grunted noncommittally. Then I decided to brighten things up a little bit with a smile. "Everything's going to be fine. This is going to be the best gig Legion Varus ever had. You'll see."

I was obviously lying now, but it seemed to be working on Leeza—she was new.

"You think so...?" she asked.

"Yep. I'm sure of it. I mean, just think about it. We've rolled the dice so many times, isn't it about time we got a lucky roll? You know, all sixes at once?"

She was frowning again for some reason. Maybe I'd gone too far with my pep-speech bullshit.

"I thought these aliens were savages."

"Yeah... But so what? They're little guys, almost harmless. This is going to be great."

We turned and eyed the new world again. Leeza traced the shape of the big ocean near the equator.

"Such an odd formation," she said. "I wonder what kind of tectonic shifts could have created this?"

I eyed her. She wasn't anywhere near as pretty as Galina. She wasn't anywhere near as sweet as Dawn, either. But she had a shape to her that was attractive enough for a man who was in need.

What's more, we had a history. I couldn't look at her without thinking about some of those times, and some of the special moves she'd surprised me with long ago. I had to wonder if she was still into that kind of thing...

In fact, I was just about to ask her out to dinner—even though that was more or less against regs, seeing as I was her direct superior. At least we were both officers, so it would be just frowned upon, not a straight out policy violation.

But then, before I could pop the question, we were interrupted by a message from Tribune Winslade.

He erased the wall image of the alien globe we'd been studying. In fact, his vast nasty visage consumed the entirety of the largest wall of the module.

Winslade was *way* too big. Some people's faces simply aren't meant to be stretched out to their limits and beyond. With nostrils bigger than dinner plates and narrowed eyes like canoes, he looked down upon us like some kind of prissy elder god.

"Legion Varus," he began, and even his voice was boomingly loud, "there's been a slight change of plan. Admiral Sateekas has requested us to arrive early—tonight in fact."

"Aw, shit..." I heard Harris complain behind me. No changes of plan ever made him happy.

"We will be staying in warp under sharp acceleration until we get quite close to Nebra. At that point, we'll emerge from warp and perform a dramatic landing at the planet's capital."

Here, his face melted away, and the world map was back—but bigger this time. Blinking icons indicated where and when we were supposed to drop.

"In order to make it seem like we have more troops in the Legion than we truly do, we'll launch every lifter and drop every individual soldier separately."

I frowned at that. That wasn't our normal approach. In fact, it sounded dangerous.

Situationally, we had various invasion methods. We could teleport in commandos—but that seemed to be off the table this time.

Otherwise, we pack our men into lifters, which were large landing vehicles designed for invasions like this. Each of these ships could hold an entire cohort, over a thousand men and their equipment.

Lastly, if we were able to get really close to a planet, right down near the atmosphere itself, drop-pods were oftentimes used. If the enemy was putting up a lot of flak, it was cheaper to lose a few thousand soldiers in pods than it was to let them score a hit on a lifter.

But, in any case, we never used both the drop-pods and the lifters—certainly not at the same damned time. That meant we were presenting more targets and giving the enemy more opportunities to hurt us. It just didn't make any sense.

"Is he saying we're going to launch lifters that are empty?" Leeza asked, aghast.

"I think so," Leeson said, coming up behind to us.

"What's the frigging point of that?" Harris demanded angrily. "It's a whole lot of risk. That's what it is—just to be showy. Winslade's gone crazy."

All of us were somewhat baffled and disturbed, but I figured it was my job to settle some nerves.

"It makes perfect sense," I lied loudly, "remember, this is a different kind of mission. This campaign is low danger with high pay. Looking tough is the whole point. In other words, we're going to scare the bejeezus out of these aliens, rather than shoot them. That's the whole damn point!"

I wasn't entirely bullshitting. As I understood it, this was exactly how Victrix and Germanica usually made their paychecks. They weren't really paid to fight much, they were paid to frighten. It was all about impressing the peasants.

Something like seven hours after Tribune Winslade announced our little change of plans, every legionnaire on the ship was preparing to disembark. All of our heavy equipment—our revival machines, our pig-drones, our star-falls. All the big stuff was loaded up in the lifters.

The invasion ships launched away from Red Deck one at a time. Each launch made *Scorpio* shudder a bit under our boots.

Then the battleship moved into lower orbit, surrounded by the smaller lifters. The lifters began to descend toward a spot that was on the Western shoreline of that large, puzzle piece-looking ocean down near the equator—dammit, Leeson had been right. It was going to be hot down there.

Every individual soldier aboard was then ordered to report to Red Deck. Every passageway on *Scorpio* lit up with instructions to follow.

We were ready, and we didn't hesitate. We'd spent the day putting together our gear, packing everything on the lifters and shipping them out.

Now came the scary part: the landing itself.

I was commanding a goodly number of splats. In other words, it was the first time in a drop-pod for a number of my recruits. Ah, sure, we'd done drills and simulations—but that was never the same thing as falling out of space at ten thousand kilometers an hour.

I lined up Sargon, Moller, and our other noncoms to make sure none of the light troopers chickened. Then I had a few of my regulars demonstrate walking out into open space over a dilating hole in the floor. They were sucked down with violent force toward a pair of huge, slamming robot arms. Resembling giant metal robots that were clapping for all they were worth, the arms enclosed each troop in a tomb-like drop-pod. The pods were then spun around, aimed, and fired at the planet below.

Leeza's light troopers—especially the greenest ones—looked like they were going to shit in their spacer suits.

The key to this sort of situation was to keep shouting, keep shoving, and keep them moving along. We never gave them a second to think.

Every few seconds, another individual stepped out into the void and was sucked down to disappear into the deck. The hatchway then scissored closed.

There was a blasting rumble, what with the rushing gases and explosions beneath, vibrating our boots. Then the top hatch opened again, and the next recruit was shoved into the middle of it and swallowed whole.

Now and then, one of them almost didn't make it. A few fingers strayed out to their sides—they were supposed to cross their arms over their chests.

Sometimes, they hesitated a little too long, or they weren't quite centered in the middle of the chute. There were, in fact, a thousand ways a trooper could die during this kind of exercise. Over the decades, noob splats like these guys had discovered damn near all of them.

I kept the line moving. I was standing up near the hatch, shouting, hurrying people along through all the noise and terror by slamming my hands together.

I did glance down the shaft a few times and spotted some red smears. Places where broken plastics, wadded-up metal and bits of hair and bone could be seen.

Yep. Someone had bought it. Fortunately, no one had actually witnessed the helmet being crushed with the skull inside turned to pulp. That was good, as such sights could be bad for morale.

It was our first confirmed splat of the day, but I wasn't going to acknowledge that. I just kept them moving.

Sargon caught my eye, and I gave a little shake of the head. So, he ignored the telltale signs as well.

"Come on, come on, let's go, go, go," he shouted.

We grabbed each recruit, placing our hands on their shoulders for a moment, until that floor opened up. Then we pretty much shoved them out there—not hard enough to ragdoll them out of position, but hard enough to make it impossible for them to hesitate on the rim of that trash-compactor. That was the best way to handle green troops.

After all the lights had gone down the ship's gullet, the heavies stepped up. These guys didn't need any urging. No one had to force them to take their medicine.

Like robots, they stepped into open space with perfect timing. It was a real pleasure to watch. Like seeing Olympic gymnasts execute moves they'd practiced a thousand times before.

Once they were gone, the officers began to go, and then the specialists. I went with the specialists' platoon, which was led by Leeson.

While we were stepping along in line, heading for the big hole in the deck, Natasha poked me in the back.

"What is it, girl?" I demanded, craning my neck back around to look at her.

"I finished it!"

"Huh?"

"Raash, remember? The tracker app?"

I gaped for a second, uncomprehending. Then, I had it. "Oh, oh—that's great! Thanks a lot, Specialist!"

That was all the time we were allotted to shout at one another. I turned back toward the chute ahead. It was my turn at last.

As always, I got a brief thrill in my guts when I stepped out into nothingness. Everything went black as I was sucked downward. The pod slammed together around me a split-second later. That massive *clang* was like the hammer of doom.

This noise always made a man wince, like the sound of an unexpected gunshot going off near your skull. You couldn't help but feel a jolt of adrenaline.

Automatically, I bent my knees as the pod spun around, positioned itself, and fired down toward the planet in a screaming arc.

I was now flying headfirst toward the atmosphere, which was not far below. Fortunately, there were a few screens with numbers and visuals to keep the mind busy. Watching the planet come flying at you while you're going headfirst toward it—that wasn't the most relaxing sight.

But the numbers helped. Green indicators showed the pod's integrity was good, the oxygen levels were high, my speed was within limits, and the angle of the entrance into the atmosphere was appropriate. All of that data served to smooth-over frayed nerves.

For several long minutes, I flew toward Nebra. I was able to admire the greenery and the slate-blue oceans.

I punched through the clouds, and a few seconds later, my pod spun around and began firing braking jets to slow my rate of descent. Although there wasn't supposed to be any defensive fire coming up from the planet—and I saw none—the pods were programmed to behave the same way every time.

Every pod's purpose was to get the payload down to the target planet as quickly as possible. Drop-pods were more likely to survive any defensive fire from the enemy on the ground if it got there quickly, rather than slowly.

So, there was only one speed at which a drop-pods flew—which was as fast as they could go without burning up due to friction in the atmosphere. It was always a nightmarish death-ride to the ground for the occupant.

About six minutes after it had all begun, the fun was over. My pod had dug a small, smoking black hole into the dirt.

I found myself lying on my side next to a tree my pod had struck with great heat and force. I was a bit sore in the kneecaps, and my elbows had been banged around as I shot through and splintered the trunk of a mighty jungle tree.

I shook off a stunned feeling and yanked the emergency pulls that fired off explosive bolts all over my tiny capsule. The hatch sprung away and landed several meters off in the jungle.

I climbed out, feeling a bit sore, but tried to hide it. As a centurion, it was always good to look like you were enjoying a nice walk in the park rather than limping and cursing your way onto a new planet.

So, I climbed out, gathered my kit, and began scanning the data that flooded my internal helmet HUD. I was looking for the dead and injured from the drop.

The final tally wasn't too bad. The grand total was two dead. Both of them had gotten their tickets punched during the very early stages of the drop.

Two splats, not bad. A few others were reporting injuries—none of them incapacitating. That was good, as I would have been required to execute any soldier who couldn't walk straight. A quick trip through the revival machine was always the quickest way to make any soldier hale and healthy again.

"Good work, everybody. Good work," I shouted.

Looking up, I saw thousands of black pods with white plumes of exhaust trailing above them, leading back up into space. The drop was well underway.

We dragged all our troops out of their pods and formed up at various rally points. My officers and noncoms split everyone into squads and took cover—just in case.

We'd all been dropped within a few hundred meters of one another—which was a very tight formation. It was dangerously tight, in fact. The pods might have struck one another, or a pod might have come down on top of a walking man.

Apparently, no one up on *Scorpio* really cared about that sort of thing. They wanted to be impressive, fast, and scary. If a few of us died in order to achieve these goals, well, that was just how things went.

Who was it that said you had to break a few eggs to make an omelet? I couldn't remember, but it was definitely the attitude on display here today as we made our impressive first entrance onto the stage known as Nebra.

For the first time since I'd made the drop, I checked my tapper for incoming vital messages. One of them was from Natasha.

Frowning, I opened it. Something began to install itself. The app only took a few seconds—then it was implanted and glowing.

Curious, I tapped on it with one gloved finger. The app opened.

I saw a radar graphic. An arrow pointed off to the north. A number appeared: 1237 meters, it said.

Then, I gazed off northward. Raash had landed with us? He was only about a kilometer away? That was weird…

Then, the number of meters began to decrease. He was moving in my direction.

What the hell was all that about?

## -18-

It took us a few minutes to get our act together, but when the call came to stand and march, we were ready. All of the 3rd Cohort was in this area, in between what looked like a large plantation and a well-groomed dirt road. The road ran off in either direction from the open area where the plantation was, into a deep, thick jungle on either end. There was maybe a few square kilometers of open land in between. We'd chosen to land here for obvious reasons. There were some trees, but not a thick, dense undergrowth that would be difficult to land in for drop-pods.

"All right, 3rd Cohort," Graves said, "form up in a column on the road, four abreast. 1st Unit takes point. 10th Unit takes the rear. You don't have to jog, but I don't want any laggers, either. We're supposed to set up camp in a fortified area outside of their capital city before dark. So, shake a leg, troops. Let's move!"

Graves cut the signal, and I began slamming my hands together, as did all my other officers and noncoms. We got our people onto their feet, got their gear organized, and headed for the road.

As we were 3rd Unit, it took a few minutes for the long column to sort itself out. While we were waiting for our turn, we met up with a group of the local natives.

"Oh, how cute they are!" Natasha exclaimed.

"They are adorable!" Kivi agreed. "Centurion, how could you call these beautiful people skunks?"

"Don't let them paw your guns," I suggested.

The women ignored me.

I stared toward the aliens with squinting eyes. Now, it was true, these looked like smaller, possibly younger versions than the ones I had seen back at Central. Could they be children—or cubs? I wasn't sure, so I didn't stop Kivi and the other girls as they walked up and tried to make friends with the locals. Theirs was a reasonable instinct to have—but I was in a less than trustful mood.

Harris watched me closely. "You don't trust these furry little bastards, do you?"

"Nope."

"They don't look like much…" he said thoughtfully, "but I guess they could bite a man's dick off if he had no armor. They look like they got lots of sharp teeth inside those mouths."

I frowned at him. "I wasn't thinking along those lines, Harris."

While we formed up on the roadway, a dozen or so of the locals—all children and females by the look of it—began handing out large blue flowers. Most of my men rejected these gifts, but our women accepted them enthusiastically.

We were walking without our helmets on at the moment, as it was quite warm, and the air was very breathable—oxygen-rich even.

Natasha attached her blue blossom to her arm. That was a little odd… I noticed these thick-petalled blooms came with ropey vines dangling down. I assumed these were roots of some kind, but they still seemed to be alive.

The green tendrils wrapped around whatever they came into contact with. Dripping sap, they adhered quickly to Natasha's shoulder. She quite liked the look of it.

Kivi went a step further. She put her gift on top of her head.

There was a brief rustling as the green shoots spread and turned into a webwork of vines on top of Kivi's noggin.

I watched with interest. I half expected the plants to drive a spike into one of her eyeballs, something like that—but no such nastiness occurred. Instead, the flower sat on top of her head like a tiara. Kivi proudly marched out onto the roadway, showing it off to anyone who might take an interest.

After a few minutes, the cohort was fully assembled on the roadway, and we began to march. The dirt was orangey-brown, a sharp contrast with the vibrant green grasses. As we followed the road into the forest, we were soon swallowed up in a green gloom.

Overhead were endless trees, all leaves and branches and vines. Thick underbrush had replaced the grasses on the sides of the road. Even the sounds shifted as we marched into the jungle. The winds vanished, and instead, we were met with the buzzing of insects and the dripping of water from the distant leaves above.

Somewhere far overhead, it began to rain. Small drops condensed into larger and larger ones as they rolled off leaves. At last, they splashed down onto our heads as we marched.

"There's gotta be something like a mosquito in this jungle," Harris complained. "Just you wait and see. There's always something that drinks your blood in these kinds of places."

His words made me scoff, but they also worried me a little bit, too. I began to slap at myself reflexively whenever a bug buzzed near.

We marched a kilometer into the jungle, then two. The road was alternately muddy and then dry. Now and then, you could see a hut where some local was working in the forest. There wasn't anything as dramatic as a village to be seen anywhere.

But then, as we came to an area of thinner foliage. We saw and heard the movement of massive beasts.

"Whoa," Sargon shouted, pointing. "That's a dinosaur! That's a friggin' dinosaur, sir!"

I craned my neck, and I had to agree with him. The beast in question wasn't anything threatening, not like the raptors of Steel World.

No, these creatures were much larger, the size of a bus at least. They swung their heads around on long necks. They were kind of like a brontosaurus but with a heavier, thicker build. The head was bigger, and the shoulders and neck were bulkier.

Positioned on their broad backs were platforms. These were strapped on and looked like a collection of sticks and leather. Workers squatted up there—white and black-furred skunk-men.

"They're logging," called out Natasha, coming to me excitedly. She was taking pictures with her tapper as if we were on some kind of jungle safari. "They're knocking down these trees, cutting them up, and moving them out of the forest. That's gotta be it."

I looked, and I did have to agree. That did seem to be what they were doing.

Carlos was excited as well. "Look at these amazing specimens. These skunks have got good nature preservation skills," he said. "They taught me about this back when I was in bio school. Environmentalism, you know? All that stuff?"

"Yeah?" I said, barely interested.

"We usually just blow natural sites like this all to hell and back, but that's not how everybody lives." Carlos went on like that, excitedly ranting about living in natural harmony and such-like. He was saying something about the skunks being a people that never took too much from the forest, and it never took too much out of them.

As we walked along, the beasts would stop now and then. They'd swing their big pendulous, dumbass-looking heads around and eye us curiously.

As we marched further into the trees, there were more and more of these dino-loggers.

The road ahead of us began to weave and go up and down through hills. We lost sight of the unit ahead and the unit behind as we went down into a lower section in between two hills, crossing a stream that had no bridge. We just slogged through a foot or two of flowing water and kept on going.

That was when I heard my first scream.

The whole unit halted as I threw my fist high. There was some shouting up ahead. A moment later, ripping gunfire broke out.

"All right," I shouted, "this could be an ambush. Heavies forward, lights go out and flank!"

My men immediately launched themselves into motion at my command. They advanced rapidly, spreading out into the jungle.

All eyes were looking toward whatever was over the next rise ahead of us. We could see the flashing of gunfire, the constant rattle and ripple of accelerated slugs slamming into the leaves overhead.

Our distraction was such that we barely noticed the cow-like dinosaurs were randomly shuffling closer and closer on our flanks. They looked at us as if intrigued. I supposed these big dumb-asses had never seen a human before, so their curiosity wasn't all that unusual.

They seemed quite tame at first—but then something went terribly wrong.

One of those long, long necks dipped with a big head on the end of it. It dipped down toward, of all people, Kivi. It reached down, and in one massive flex of its jaws, it snapped her head clean from her body. She staggered one more step and fell, decapitated.

"Holy shit," Harris said. "It's these damn dinosaurs. They're attacking! Light them up!"

It was true. After that one odd attack, it seemed like all the dinosaurs had come to life. They were, in fact, surging forward from both flanks.

There were dozens of them now, with more coming out of the trees farther back. They'd dropped their burdens, and their riders were gone from the platforms on their backs. They weren't interested in carrying logs any longer. Instead, they now seemed intent on charging into our midst.

We turned our guns on them, and we opened up. Some fell, gouting dark blood. They flopped onto the road, crushing individuals. One of those killed was Moller, another was my best scout, Cooper.

Most of the lighter troops were able to dance away, but not all of them. They did more damage with those massive, tree-sized, thundering legs than they did with their bites, but one did manage to get in close enough and pluck the right arm off Natasha.

That's when I knew what was happening.

"It's the damn flowers!" I shouted, roaring it over my tactical chat channel, overriding all the other screams, confusion, and swear words. "If you're wearing one of those blue flowers, throw them away! Rip them off! Get rid of them!"

A dozen of my troops all around me hastened to obey. They ripped at the flowers, tore at them—but the blooms had quietly sunken into skin, clothing, hair—whatever they could grasp onto.

Those strange, weeping roots had entwined themselves, latching onto us. That made it difficult to rip loose these strange gifts we'd received from the local population.

Some of the girls, Leeza among them, tore at their flowers, ripping the petals from them, tearing at the lumpy, clinging vines at the base. When they finally managed to pull them loose, there was blood as well as sap running freely and dribbling to the mud at our feet.

A dozen of my troops—mostly female—were killed. Some were decapitated, like Kivi. Others were trampled or dismembered by the snapping jaws of the idiot dinosaurs.

When all of us had gotten rid of every vestige of flower that we'd accepted, the attack slowed and finally stopped.

I reported the attack to Graves, who told me rudely that he already knew. "Don't your people know any better than to take gifts from rebels?" he demanded.

"I think the girls were just trying to be friendly, sir…"

Graves made a sound as if he was spitting and disconnected.

With a dozen dead and another dozen injured, we gathered up all the gear dropped by the dead and the wounded. I had to shoot a few wincing troops who couldn't walk.

Harris fell in line with me after that. Once we were all marching along, the mood was much bleaker than it had been.

Nebra had seemed friendly, even cheerful, at first. But now everyone was beginning to realize it was anything but that. It was a rebel planet, and these skunk men… well… they were damned tricky.

"That's what you meant, isn't it?" Harris said. "That's what you were talking about. Bullshit like this…"

"How's that, Harris?"

"You warned us. You warned everybody about these fucking skunks—and yeah, I'm going there. That's what they are. These aliens are skunks. They're not raccoons or monkeys or nothing cute like that. They're stinky, conniving, vicious skunks!"

I nodded, as I couldn't disagree.

"They planned this," he said, marveling and putting things together. "They had some cute little kids come up, give us some flowers—and you know what? I bet they feed these flowers to those big dumb-fuck dinosaurs every day. I bet you they're like sugar cubes to a horse."

"Yep. I bet you're right."

"So… they roared onto the road and wrecked us. What? Did they lose ten or fifteen of their dinosaurs? Well, hell, maybe they don't care about that. Not if they could kill some of us. What bastards…"

"I think you've got the idea now, Adjunct."

It was at this point that I made a dumb-ass mistake.

I'll be the first to admit it—I'm not the sharpest knife in any drawer. But this one… even I should have seen it coming.

When we were gathering stuff up to move out, I picked up some scraps. Big blue flowers—just petals mind you—and some lumps from their cores

I wanted to take them to camp and have them studied by our bio people. I even had some fantasies—I'll admit it right now—of presenting these specimens to Evelyn. She was a bio-centurion who loves new alien biology, especially something weird like these plants.

Maybe she'd figure out they were releasing a pheromone. Or that the color had driven the dinos crazy. I knew she'd want to study how the heck they grew those little roots into people so fast and latched onto them.

So, I picked up a few scraps of dino-bait. I thought they were probably less interested in shredded bits, and anyways, we'd trashed so many of their dino buddies.

One last dinosaur wandered near. He charged suddenly, like the rest, and this time luck was with him, not me. He charged on my six, coming out of a dense section of forest. You couldn't even see anything but that head poking out for a few seconds—then he went for it.

On the good side, my men knew this thing was dangerous by now. They understood instantly that this wasn't just a friendly cow-type creature that was going to nuzzle us and walk away. No, this leathery monstrosity was deadly.

So, when it reared up and threw a few trashcan-sized footpads in the air, ready to stomp down on yours truly, they all let loose.

A rippling barrage of fire tore through the jungles. They shot the neck, mostly—and the head. The head came off in a splash of blood and gore.

One might think that when a crazy-big dinosaur had its head blown off it would die instantly. And in this case, you'd be absolutely right.

Unfortunately, it was already rearing up and looming over me.

Even as I turned, dropping all the scraps of alien flowers I'd stupidly gathered, it was already too late.

I cranked my head way back to look as the monstrosity was looming over me. It was a good four meters up to the point where the head had been blown off the neck.

Then it came toppling down. I wasn't able to dive out of the way in time, and the beast smashed the living shit out of me.

I can half-remember lying in utter pain after that, crushed beneath a couple of tons of dead dinosaur meat, trying to draw a breath. But then my body gave out, and I died for my first time on Nebra.

Somehow, I knew it wouldn't be my last.

## -19-

"MCGILL!" It was Graves, and he was angry.

"Primus, sir? I have to ask that you leave until our patient has completely recovered."

"Bullshit! I don't need any sawbones to tell me when a man's ready to pick up his rifle again. Get out of my way! McGill? Get your lazy ass up off that table and stop goldbricking!"

I released a groan, and it was a real one.

Some hard hands tried to push me off the table. A pair of hand-flapping bios complained about this. For once, they were playing the part of the protector, rather than the ghoul.

They bitched at Graves about protocols and procedures but without much success. Nobody dared to get into his face.

Graves had a bad rep when it came to dying unexpectedly. Any officer in Legion Varus had the right to shoot an underling they didn't like, and Graves took that privilege to the extreme. Just about everybody in the legion knew it.

So, I slipped onto the floor, and no one helped me up. I was flop-dick naked and a bit sticky.

We were in some kind of tent. I could tell that already. The walls were plastic, and you could feel the gravelly ground right through the floor.

The revival chamber was hot, way too hot. This had to be a deployed setup, not even on one of the lifters.

That was just great. I was catching a ghetto-revive already, and we'd only just landed on this shit-streak of a planet.

Struggling to my feet, I pulled on my uniform. I was allowed no comforting shower, no medical evaluation by the bio-people—none of that.

Instead, I pressed myself into my clothes, half-blind and grumbling. I followed Graves using the glare of his suit lights to show me which way he'd gone. The dark jungle felt like a hot, humid nightmare to my freshly printed skin.

"It's nighttime already, huh?" I asked.

"Of course, it is. You've been napping for six whole hours."

"Uh…" I said. "Is there any special reason for this this unusual level of urgency, sir? I mean… I thought this Nebra gig was supposed to be a walk in the park."

"Oh, sure. It's going to be lobsters and champagne every night, McGill. You can wear your best dress and stick one of those blue flowers in your hair, if you want to."

I was groggy, half-blind, and a little bit dumb, but it seemed to me that Graves was being sarcastic.

"I'm overseeing your long-overdue revive personally," he told me, "because I've discovered there's another species of alien here on this planet that's not supposed to be among us."

"Huh?"

"You heard me. I want to know your side of the story before I do any arrests or executions."

I stuck a big finger in my ear and waggled it. Some nasty stuff flew out. I thought hard about what he'd said—but I was completely baffled. I didn't think that was due to being dead a few minutes ago, either.

"Can you give me a bigger hint, sir?" I asked.

"I'm talking about Raash," he said, "that damn lizard is here on this planet, and I think he might have had something to do with putting the aliens up to the blue flower trick that killed damn near twenty percent of my cohort."

"Twenty percent? That's crazy!"

"Yeah… you died early. Before we got out of that jungle, there was a dozen other attacks. Different types of dinosaurs, too. Not just those big brontosaurus-looking bastards. The worst of them look like an allosaurus, they tell me. Whatever the fuck that is."

"Something with big teeth that likes to eat men?"

"That's right."

"Huh… well, uh… did you mention Raash, sir?"

He stopped and whirled around. His chest-lights were blindingly bright. "Don't play dumb with me. I don't like that game."

Graves was not one for enjoying my poor relationship with the truth. He wasn't much of a man for jokes, either. So, I believed him.

"What about Raash, sir? How could he even be here?"

He pushed an unforgiving finger into my breastbone. "Because you brought him here."

"What? Sir, I did nothing of the kind!"

"Stop bullshitting me, McGill. Natasha has already confessed. You have an app on your tapper that tracks Raash. Why would you have that if you weren't directing him? He is your asset, isn't he? Confess, McGill."

I was befuddled, rubbing at my eyes, and I wanted a beer real bad. I shook my head.

"I'm sorry, sir," I said, with amniotic fluid dripping off me on both sides. You would think something like that would cool a man down, like sweat, but it didn't. It was so hot out here, so muggy and humid, that it felt like hot soup had been dumped over my head. "Sir, you've got to believe me, I was tracking Raash because I was trying to figure out what the hell he's doing on our ship—just like you are. I'm not in control of him!"

"All right, then, level with me. Who's in charge of that big ugly lizard? Who's pulling his strings?"

I blinked a couple of times, and I finally decided to tell the truth—well, my own special brand of the truth.

"Tribune Winslade, sir. I cannot tell a lie," I told him.

"What kind of bullshit is this?" Graves began, but I cut him off.

"Just think about it, sir. Where's Tribune Winslade?"

"Back up on *Scorpio*, of course, overseeing this entire fiasco from a safe distance."

"Right, right, of course he is. He won't come down here until there's an air-conditioned Gold Bunker built to his specifications. But, he likes to have eyes and ears, and maybe he doesn't trust any Legion Varus man. Maybe he has a special Saurian friend to keep an eye on things for him."

Graves squinted at me. I could tell he was squinting, although the light was dim. My vision was coming back.

"You're telling me that lizard is working for Tribune Winslade?"

"It's obvious, sir," I said, throwing my arms wide. "Like you said, nobody else could have gotten him into a drop-pod. Who assigned him to our cohort without your knowledge or mine?"

"I don't know…" Graves said. "Maybe Natasha did it. She is a hacker, after all."

"Oh, come on, you already grilled her, right?" I said. "She's a softie. She'd cave the second you leaned on her."

"Yeah, yeah, she sort of did."

"What'd she say? That I wanted a tracking app? One to put on Raash, right?"

"Yes, that's what she said."

"Well then, you believe her, don't you? I wanted the tracking app to see what the hell he's up to. To help figure him out, the same as you're trying to do now."

Graves looked at me and then stared down at the dirt for a second. He frowned fiercely, then looked back up at me again.

"You're telling me that Winslade's behind this? That he's got some secret reason of his own?"

"That's exactly right, sir."

"Shit…"

It was a good lie, and I was proud of it. I was especially proud of how I'd come up with it on the spot.

Oftentimes, I came up with my most creative lies when my back was up against the wall. That's when my mind was a blank, and I was only half-alive—like right now. It was inspirational when those rare moments came.

"If I find out you're bullshitting me, McGill…" Graves said sourly.

"I get it, sir. My balls will be hanging from my chin strap, and there won't even be any skin on them."

"That's right, McGill. Now get your ass back to your unit, pull your people together, and take watch on the wall."

"Uh… the wall, sir?"

"Yeah, that shitty pile of sticks off to the north. You'll figure it out. I'm putting you on watch all night long."

"Well, sir, I want to thank you kindly for that consideration. That is a just reward for your hardest-working, most elite unit in this cohort. I don't even want to think about what it's going to be like on that wall at high noon. Giving me the night shift? Damn, that does me proud."

"Shut up, McGill. Get going."

Turning away, I marched off into the muddy night. I could tell that Graves didn't entirely buy my story. He never entirely bought my stories, whether they were true or false. That was because he'd been taken in too many times, just to discover later that my version of events was even more deeply false than he'd imagined at first.

"I'm going to check out that bullshit you said about Tribune Winslade," Graves shouted after me.

"You do that, sir," I hollered back over my shoulder. "Don't trust, verify!"

I turned my back on him and hustled away.

Naturally, I knew Graves would do no such thing. By putting the blame on Tribune Winslade, I had in fact performed an act of mental jujitsu on the mind of my superior officer.

You see, if Tribune Winslade had indeed installed Raash as a watchdog over our cohort—as I had falsely proclaimed—then Graves was in no position to countermand that or even to investigate it. It was his job just to deal with it, to follow orders without question from his rightful superior.

You see, right there, that's the trap I'd cornered him in.

What was likely to happen? Well, Graves could call up Winslade and ask him if it was true. Winslade would, of course, deny it.

And then what? What was Graves going to do after that? Either his tribune was lying—which was completely possible—or he was telling the truth. Either way, Graves would be in no position to verify anything. I'd thusly neutralized his nosy investigations.

Now, any sane, normal person, such as Adjunct Leeza, who was another relatively straight-laced person in my unit—possibly the last of her kind—would be wondering why the hell I didn't just tell Graves the truth.

Sure, I could have explained that Raash was working for Alexander Turov, the most infamous Public Servant on Earth. But I was already in a ton of trouble with the Turovs. I wouldn't be surprised to learn I was a single step from joining Drusus in his little brain tank—or to being permed for fun.

If people started making calls back to Public Servant Turov, they might mention my name as a source of information. If they asked about Raash or anything else, I might as well put my oversized skull into a guillotine.

In my universe, the truth had its place—but that was nowhere near the government of Earth. I'd learned after living under the semi-tyrannical government of Hegemony for many harsh years that a man rarely got into serious trouble for lying. No, sir. You got into real trouble when you told the truth. That was doubly so if the important people didn't want the truth in question to be spoken out loud.

Reaching my unit and gathering them all together, I did a little headcount. I found out that we were down by seventeen soldiers still—but that was good enough for me.

All the key personnel were walking and talking—by that, I meant the ones that did the fighting. The rest of them, the Natashas, the Kivis—all of the dumb women who put little blue flowers in their hair—they were still dead.

But I didn't need any of their type to man a wall in the middle of the night. So, I marched my heavies to the north and sent my lights beyond the barrier to operate as pickets in the jungle.

There were some big complaints about that, but I didn't care. I ordered them to walk out about 200 meters and patrol. In actuality, they went about a hundred and then squatted down in the grass. They went just into the tree line, far enough so that I couldn't see them, and hid themselves.

That was fine. They were just out there to give me some warning time. I was sure they'd sprint back to the wall for protection, firing over their shoulders as they ran, if anything big charged out of the jungle at them.

At the wall itself, I placed a line of heavies on top. They aimed out into the darkness, scanning the place with infrared and Lidar rigs. A few buzzers flitted over the area in cycles, looking for anything hungry that might come out of the trees.

"You want I should set up some 88s, sir?" Leeson asked me.

"Nah... I don't think we have any of them out from the lifters yet anyway. Do we?"

"No, no, it's going to be a while. I just wanted to put in the requisition right now, with a little signature saying my centurion was demanding it."

"Well, I'm not," I told him. "Arm your weaponeers with mini-missile packs and belchers. Spread them out, with one high-powered weapon every ten troops."

Leeson moved off, grumbling about short-sightedness, but I pretended not to hear him.

The wall itself wasn't much to look at. It was just like Graves had said, a stack of sticks, but in this case, the sticks ran vertically.

Built with big wooden growths that looked something like massive bamboo shoots, the wall was all strapped together and about ten meters high. The top of the wall was jagged, each of the tree trunks shorn off randomly. I guess the skunk people had cut these logs off wherever they felt like.

I turned to Leeza next. "I want you to cycle your lights. Put half in the field to patrol and skirmish if anything comes our way. Put the other half on the wall to play sniper and rotate them every few hours to keep them on their toes."

"You got it, sir," she said, and she trotted off into the dark. She began personally overseeing the positioning of her troops. I was impressed by that.

"You know what?" Harris told me. "Leeza kind of reminds me of a skinny-ass version of Barton."

I laughed at that. "Yep. They both came from a snooty legion, so I guess it makes sense."

We did have some issues with the fact humans were much taller than Nebra natives. The walkway didn't give a man enough room to stand and fire over the top. It was, in fact, built for someone who was skunk-high to peep over. That meant there was only about a meter of coverage, and unless you kneeled on the platforms, you were exposed.

I supposed it didn't matter much. I hadn't seen any armies of skunks with rifles marching around, shooting at us. But it did feel weird, like you had to sit on your ass to feel seriously sheltered by the structure.

"Boy, I'd give anything for a puffcrete machine right now," Leeson complained. He placed his weaponeers every ten meters along the top. "These bamboo shoots are bullshit."

"Yeah," Harris said, "I bet I could stick a force blade right through this so-called wall. We could slice it down like nothing. You want me to try?"

"No," I told him. "Remember, we're only here for show."

They grumbled, but I didn't much care. After reviewing my troops, making sure they were all placed well, I had some nice floodlights set up. These were immediately thronged by amazingly large and aggressive insects, so we turned them off.

I found my way down to a cool, reasonable spot at the base of the wall. I put my head up against it, and promptly took a quick nap.

Every hour or two, I woke up and reviewed the reports that were coming in from the troops in the field. There were sightings of stray animals, weird flapping things in the sky, and the occasional new troop who came in from the revival chambers to join us.

None of it mattered. It looked like a long, quiet night was actually going to be ours.

Overhead, Nebra's three small moons glowed in a clump. They were each smaller than Luna, but together they put out a pretty steady shine.

The silvery light was the most interesting thing we saw or heard until around 0200 hours. That's when a distant, loud, foghorn-like hooting began to echo across the jungle. For some reason, when that hooting came, a lot of other noises stopped.

The hooting died after awhile, but when it was gone, the other jungle sounds faded away with it. The buzzing insects disappeared. The flapping night-creatures, attracted to our lights, stopped dashing themselves against them like insane, oversized moths. They'd all vanished.

I was used to putting up with a lot of peeping and squawking out of the jungle all night long, and it was weird to hear it die away to nothing.

"Did you hear that, sir?" Harris said, whispering out of the dark. He was somewhere to my right.

"Hear what?" I said.

"That big, long, warbling hoot—then silence."

I listened for a second. "Don't hear anything now."

Harris stared into the dark. "That's just it. The whole place has gone quiet. It's fucking weird."

"New planet, new rules, Harris."

We sat listening in the dark. All the noises we did catch came from our unit's camp area. There were coughs and grunts. The distant clanking of men in armor, the crackle of fires, all from inside the large expanse protected by this half-assed wall the locals had built in the past. All of it seemed like typical sounds for an alien wilderness at night.

I frowned, having a sudden thought. These skunk-aliens had clearly built this fortification. They must have done so for a reason. What had it been built to keep out?

Even more disturbing, I came to wonder why the citizens of Nebra had given this fort to human troops. We'd come here to occupy their planet, and we were now squatting within their walls.

The locals weren't all that happy with the Mogwa, that much was clear. They were conquerors here. By extension, they probably weren't all that happy with the earthmen who'd come to serve those same Mogwa overlords.

Hmm... was it possible those little skunk-bastards had given us this place of refuge as a trick?

## -20-

The night was a long one. The jungle was dark and foreboding. The thickest tangle of forest was out past the wall to the north. There, the wildest region lay in permanent shadow. At our backs was the coastal city of the skunk people, a town I hadn't even had a chance to visit yet.

I awakened when someone shook me lightly. Being a man who's had a number of negative experiences over the years, I reacted uncharitably.

Lashing out, I flung an arm wide to smash away whoever was touching me. At the same time, I reached for the pistol on my belt with my other hand.

I heard someone shout in pain, and the rickety boards of the great bamboo wall rattled under my feet. I snapped my eyes open, looking around—but no one was there.

The troopers manning the wall on either side of me glanced over in surprise. Both of them looked at me as if I was crazy.

That's when I thought to look down. There, at the base of the wall were muddy footprints. In an instant, I knew the truth—because there was also a butt-print.

"Cooper?" I asked.

"No, you idiot, it's Della."

"Ah…" I said, relaxing somewhat. "Sorry about that. Need a hand up?"

I groped for her, but she didn't take my paw. Instead, she slapped it away.

If this had been Cooper, I would have ripped his stealth suit right off his ungrateful ass—but as it was Della... well, I'd always have a bit of a soft spot for her. She was Etta's mother and all.

"What's up, girl?" I said.

"Something's wrong," she said.

"Uh... like what? They haven't brought us breakfast yet, I can tell you that much. In my book, that's a crime on any given morning."

"No, James. I mean something's wrong in the forest. Just listen."

Listening again? I tried not to sigh and roll my eyes. I even did some listening for a time.

I had to admit that the place was quieter than it had been. Sure, there was still some peeping and squawking—and plenty of buzzing. There'd never been a jungle born that didn't have a couple thousand living things in it, making noise all the time.

"Sounds the same to me."

"It's too quiet," she said. "It's too quiet by half. I've been out here all night, walking amongst the trees. This is actually a beautiful planet, you know."

I grunted, unconvinced. I'd have to take her word for it. To me, I already had a sour taste for this place. It was going to be hard to convince me that Nebra was anything other than a disappointment.

"What's missing?" I asked her.

"There's a whole layer of sound," she said. "I'm hearing the winds. I'm hearing the insects. There are very few night birds here. But earlier, there were some loud howling noises. I thought they would go on all night."

I remembered that, thinking it over. "You mean all that hooting earlier? Bah, that's probably just some kind of big monkey out there in the trees."

"Maybe..." Della said.

"It's a new planet, girl. We've got to get used to the place, that's all."

"This is a new place... but my instincts tell me something's wrong. I used to be a scout back on Dust World—remember?"

"I surely do." I recalled pursuing her there and getting lucky in an underground hot spring. Those had been the days.

"By now, I've been a scout on a dozen other planets as well. I'm telling you, James, that something has changed out there."

"Okay," I said slapping my knee loudly, "you're the ghost. I'm putting you in charge of an investigation."

"An investigation?"

"That's right. I'll give Natasha the word. She'll send out a whole fleet of buzzers to search the forest. Uh... Natasha and Kivi are back from the revival machine by now, aren't they?"

"Yes," she said. "Both of them are back—but you should be forewarned, neither one of them seems too happy."

She left then, going about her duties. I thought to myself I ought to take her warning more seriously—but it just wasn't in me.

I got up off my lazy butt and went looking for my tech girls. I soon found they'd been revived—and they were in a sour mood.

Of all the ladies in my unit, I had to give Della her due. She hadn't made the mistake of decorating herself with a blue alien flower. Therefore, she hadn't marked herself as a target for the local megafauna. Hell, even I'd fallen for that trap.

Natasha and Kivi both came promptly to my summons.

"Good morning, ladies."

"It's anything but a good morning," Natasha groused.

"Yes," Kivi agreed. "I hate this planet and these people. You were right, McGill. They are skunks. We should torch their whole city for the tricks they played on us."

I laughed. "Hey, maybe in their culture, that's just how they have a bit of fun. Like a hazing ritual or something."

"James, a dinosaur ripped my arm off," Natasha said. "I bled out, howling on that road."

"That's nothing," Kivi said. "The beast that attacked me snapped my head off. I swear I can still feel, hear and smell that big mouth coming down over my skull and clamping down."

She gave a little shudder and closed her eyes.

"Aw, okay, then," I said. "Don't you think it's time for a little payback?"

This perked them up, but they regarded me with suspicion. "What do you have in mind, Centurion?" Kivi asked.

I lowered my voice as if I was imparting a great secret. "There's something going on out there in the forest. I want you two to fly every buzzer you have out there, double-time. Scan, sweep, and search until you figure out what's happening."

This lit them up, and the two set to work. Maybe, in the end, having died and whined about it at length had been for the best. Maybe the aliens had done me a good turn. They'd sharpened-up these two ladies. They now had their minds focused on the problem at hand. They weren't liable to be sucked into another trick anytime soon.

About a dozen minutes later, when I was relieving myself upon a fallen log, I heard another rustle. I almost lashed out again—but I stopped myself.

What if it was Della again?

I looked down, spotting the telltale footprints. Judging by the size of the feet in those invisible boots, I knew who it had to be.

With a sudden motion, I faked a yawn. Two fists flashed out at about head level. I felt my left fist graze something.

"Whoa!" he said.

It was Cooper, no doubt. But he'd managed to dodge the worst of my blow.

"Best not to be checking up on a man during his most private moments, Cooper."

"Just trying to be polite, Centurion. I was waiting until you'd finished."

I nodded—but I didn't believe him. Cooper had some of the worst instincts and an even worse reputation when it came to being a perv entrusted with a stealth suit. In any other legion, he would have been stripped of his rank and tossed out on his ear by now. The complaints women had lodged over the years alone were enough for that.

But the truth was, he was very good at what he did. He was highly experienced. And Legion Varus was always hurting for manpower. So, no one had ever kicked him out.

"What have you got for me, Cooper?"

"There's something odd going on out there—I mean in the jungle, sir."

"Something to do with blue flowers?"

"No, not this time. Something much stranger than that."

"Like what?"

"Well... I think a large number of our light troopers have fallen asleep."

"What?" I said, turning toward him in real concern.

"Yeah," he said. "It's weird. I've been walking around out there, you know, just checking up on things. That's my job."

I nodded doubtfully.

"I found a female recruit slumped over her rifle. And another one, passed out over a log."

"Both females, huh?" I said.

"That happened to be the case, yes, sir."

"Why didn't you report in by radio? Are they dead?" My face was twisting up into a scowl. I couldn't help it.

"No—I was able to awaken them."

"Not by... uh..." I said. "Not by touching anybody? Right, Cooper?"

"Don't worry, sir. There will be no complaints."

I thought over his carefully worded statements, and I didn't like the taste of them.

"Anyway, get to the point," I said. "What the hell's going on?"

"I'm telling you, there's a lot of our light troopers out there who aren't completely alert. And when they become alert, they seem to fall asleep again soon afterward."

"Huh... I don't like the sound of that."

I contacted Natasha using my tapper, and I asked her about Cooper's report. I demanded to know if she had seen any of this coming in from her buzzer feeds.

"I did notice some of our troops aren't moving..." she said. "But they're alive. Their vitals are all available online. If you looked at their autonomic systems on your HUD, you can see their pulse rates, breath rates... maybe they're a bit lower than normal."

I was flipping through the data as she spoke. "If you look at their motion-history… Damn," I said. "Most of those clowns out there haven't moved an inch in the last hour. What the hell's wrong with Leeza?"

Breaking the connection with Natasha, I immediately tried to contact Adjunct Leeza. I wasn't able to raise a response.

"Dammit, is everybody napping just because we'd spent a few late hours in the dark? This is downright unprofessional. Come on, Cooper."

I marched out to where I'd pinpointed Leeza on my trapper. It was only a few hundred meters away through the forest. Of course, it was on the far side of the wall, out in the jungle itself.

Near the tree line, I discovered her. She was just like Cooper had said—lying in the grass with a few bugs crawling over her.

"You sure she's not dead?"

"I don't think so."

I checked her numbers, and called for Carlos, our bio specialist. Her lifeline vitals were all good. Fortunately, she'd flipped her visor down. None of the creepy-crawlies had gotten into her suit with her.

Grabbing her shoulders, I gave her a shake. And after a vigorous effort, I managed to rouse her.

"Centurion? Oh, I'm so sorry," she said, struggling to her feet.

I helped her stand, guiding her up by the elbow. She seemed groggy.

"Are you tired, or have you been drugged?" I asked her.

She squinted at me, trying to think it over. "I'm not sure which, sir. I'm feeling intense fatigue. I don't understand it. Something… something's wrong out here."

"Right," I said. "Have your men sound off. If anybody doesn't answer, send a trooper out to bring them back to the wall."

This process began, and soon Leeza was shouting orders into her tapper. Surprisingly, not that many of her troops responded. I was beginning to realize just how widespread the problem Cooper had reported was.

I think it was in that moment, when we began the retreat toward safety, when the enemy took notice.

A warbling sound rang out. It sounded almost like a natural noise, the kind of thing some giant beast would make.

Another answered the call, then another. Less than a minute later, we heard a thunderous noise. It was the sound of hooves, or giant feet—something like that. Something living and large was crashing its way through the jungle in our direction.

"Centurion!" Natasha shouted in my ear. "There are several big contacts coming towards you—our whole skirmish line is under attack! You've got to get out of there, sir. Get the men back to the wall!"

She relayed imagery to my tapper. Heat signatures from her network of buzzers glowed an orangey-white.

They were indeed large contacts. Not quite the same as the brontosaurus-like dinosaurs that we'd dealt with the day before. No, these were different. They seemed to be something more akin to the size of draft horses rather than city buses.

But, instead of the rambling charge from beasts of burden like we faced the day before, this time the approaching creatures seemed more purposeful—and faster. They moved with the focus and speed of predators.

I glanced over my shoulder toward the walls where safety was. If I merely turned and raced in that direction, yes, I could reach the wall in time—but that wouldn't be good enough. I wasn't going to make onto the safe side of the wall. The nearest gate was several hundred meters away.

What was the point of being chased to the wall and then standing there? Possibly, my men up on the battlements could stop these attackers with focused fire...

But then again, maybe they couldn't.

"I'm making my stand here," I said. "Leeza, if you can't get your people back inside the walls, tell them to stand and fight. We're being rushed."

"By what, sir?"

"I don't know, and I don't care. By the looks of it, these things are alive and that means they can be killed. So, kill them all."

That's when the first one broke into the open.

It was massive, alien and furry. To me, it looked something like a cross between a saber-toothed cat and a woolly rhinoceros.

The skin was leathery. The head was fanged. The feet didn't have retractable claws like a cat, they were much more lumpy and thick and black—like a dog's claws.

Those dark eyes caught me, and they narrowed. In its primitive mind, I'd become the target.

The monster charged toward me, roaring. The mouth opened, and I saw that it indeed had some serious predatory teeth. Fangs, top and bottom, that protruded from the face. These fangs were each longer than my fingers and curved. I had no doubts they were serrated as well, built to rip meat from the bone.

I started off by firing a grenade from my morph-rifle. I popped it right at the beast—which dodged with surprising agility.

Still, the blast rolled it over on its side. It got up, shook its head, and came at me again.

I began firing explosive rounds, shredding it. The thing was just too massive, however. Too full of vitality and life to die before it reached me.

It hit me more with its bulk than with its teeth. I think it was already dead on its feet, but its brain hadn't yet received this important information from its wrecked body.

I was smashed aside, and I rolled into the jungle ferns. One of the massive clawed paws slammed down onto my leg painfully. There was a cracking sound, but I wasn't sure if it was my bone or the monster's.

The beast was dead. I sat up, groaning, and managed to roll it off me. Cooper was there, helping. I could see the extra set of hands on the fur.

Naturally, he'd been of zero help during the actual combat. He'd dodged aside and probably hadn't fired a shot. That wasn't really a huge mark of cowardice on his part. Our ghosts weren't trained to fight straight-out battles like this. They were snipers, assassins, and spies. They only attacked when the enemy was unaware. Lightly armed and completely unarmored, they didn't stand much of a chance in a fair fight.

So, in this case, with the charging monster bearing down on me so swiftly, Cooper had wisely chosen not to engage until the matter had been decided.

Limping rapidly, I headed for the walls. The monstrous predators in the jungle were running around all along the tree line, slaughtering Leeza's light troopers. Apparently, a large number of them were still asleep.

When I reached safety, I wasn't sure how the battle was going to play out, but I was sure of one thing.

We were under attack, and those fucking skunks were behind it all.

## -21-

The jungle predators retreated after eating half of my light troopers. Carlos died too—he'd somehow managed to get killed while he was checking into why Leeza's soldiers were falling asleep on duty. Disgusted, I headed back to camp and leaned my shoulders up against the inside wall.

I was confronted immediately by Harris. "Leeza's dead," he said, "isn't she?"

"Yep, that's what it looks like." Both of us were checking the red names on the inside of our officers' helmet. Each one of them indicated a dead man.

"How is that possible, Centurion?" Harris complained angrily. He'd never liked anything deadly—unless he was wielding it. "This just *sucks*. It totally sucks!"

"Bad things happen, Adjunct."

Harris went on as if he hadn't heard me. He was mostly talking to himself. "You put some scouts out in the woods, sure. That might have been a bit of a risk—but it was reasonable. Then, some-frigging-how, those tricky skunks drugged our men and then herded a whole army of predators right out of the jungle into our ranks."

My breathing was slowing down now, after the big puffing run from the jungle back to the safety of the compound. I thought about it, and I nodded. I figured Harris had to be right.

"And those big animals weren't total retards," he continued. "No, sir. They came out to the tree line and stopped right there. They snapped off a few heads for fun—and they lost a few. But then, they wisely raced back into the trees again."

"What's your point, Harris?"

"That this was no natural animal attack. None of this was an accident, mark my words."

"What's more impressive is they're gone now—no trace left behind."

He waggled a finger at me. "They're smart! Smarter than Natasha and Kivi and all their worthless drones. I bet they know what kind of range we've got with our detection gear. They pulled back to where we can't see them. Maybe they'll come at some other spot on our lines—hell, I don't know."

Drones had never operated very well in jungle terrain. Even when they did, they had a fairly limited range. Those big predators were probably two kilometers away by now.

"Hit and run," Harris said, shaking his head. "You've got to go and shake him down."

"Shake who down?"

"Tribune Winslade, who do you think?"

I'd actually been thinking about Sateekas himself. After all, the grand admiral had clearly screwed us. He'd puffed us up with praise. Talking big about how we were special and trusted and somehow competitive with better outfits like Victrix and Germanica. Then, he'd played upon Winslade's greed for an easy assignment.

"Maybe I should talk to Sateekas instead," I said.

Harris flashed me some eyebrows. He was impressed. "What are you going to say to that snooty alien?"

"I now suspect he was perfectly aware of how shitty this deal was the whole time he was hard-selling it to us at a bargain-basement price."

"So what? Isn't that his job? To get a good outfit to fight for him as cheaply as possible?"

"Yeah... I guess it is..." I grumbled. "I still don't like getting screwed even when it is someone's job to do it."

"So what if that old spidery-bastard buttered us up, oversold the deal until we cut our prices, then led us into a slaughterhouse? That's not his failure—that's Winslade's fuck-up."

My jaw was a firm line, sticking out a bit from the rest of my face. I was pretty damn sure we'd been hoodwinked. The grand admiral always had been better at negotiations than he'd been at tactics. He was more of a political animal than he was a military one.

I stood up suddenly, and I straightened my back. I shook off the sore leg, the sore everything.

"Uh-oh," Leeson said, seeing my posture and sidling near. "McGill's got an idea! Everybody better look out!"

"Leeson," I said, "you're in charge until I get back."

"Crap…"

Leeson turned and stumped away, shaking his head. He didn't even bother to ask what I had planned. He probably didn't want to hear it. The fewer details he knew, the less someone could beat out of him later on when there was an investigation into the matter.

Harris stared at me. "What're you going to do?"

"I'm not sure yet," I said. "I'm going to try to get to the bottom of this."

Harris shouted encouragement, but he was already talking to my back. I left the wall and our encampment behind.

As I left, I saw Leeson walking among the wounded. He checked each injury personally, shooting those who were too weak to keep fighting and needed a recycle. He did this methodically, not listening to pleas, excuses, or reassurance. He simply trusted his own eye, and with a single shot, dispatched more of Leeza's troops. Soon, six fresh bodies were bound for the recyclers.

By this time, the Legion Varus engineering crews had finished their first bunker. Unsurprisingly, they named it Gold Bunker.

They were working on a second one, and by the time dawn broke, they'd have it done. That was destined to be Blue Bunker. I was happy about that. If I died again, at least I wouldn't have to be revived in some hot plastic tent like an animal.

At the entrance of the new Gold Bunker, I was challenged by a couple of veterans. I quickly shunted them aside with my rank.

It was right then, when I entered the relative cool gloom of the interior, that I got the sense I was being followed—but I gave no hint that I was aware of it.

The bunker was pretty barebones. They'd yet to properly floor the deck, paint anything, or even hang doors in the big puffcrete cutouts they'd left for that purpose. The doorways were yawning rectangles on both sides of the passageway.

In a quiet spot, I stood stock-still for a moment. No one else was near. I listened, and I thought that… Yes, there it was. Soft footsteps—very soft.

I turned slowly. There was no one there.

"Della?" I whispered.

"How'd you know it was me?"

I smiled, and my hand eased away from my pistol. My other hand, which was resting on my combat knife, relaxed as well.

"I figured it was either you, or Cooper," I said, "but your step is much lighter."

"That's a high compliment, sir," she responded, and I could tell she was truly happy. There was nothing you could tell a ghost that made them prouder than to compliment their stealth.

"Why'd you follow me?" I asked her.

"I thought I might be able to help."

"How so?"

"Cooper told me what happened out there in the jungle. He ran off in the middle of the fight, you know. After the predators left."

"Right, right," I said, having been aware that he was no longer with me by the time I reached the wall.

"We both wasted some time running around in the jungle, looking for a skunk—maybe one with a whip."

"Find anything?"

"Nothing at all. They sent that raging horde of predators at us, and they got away cleanly. I would like to report that we started feeling sleepy out there after a time. That was odd, so we retreated to the wall immediately. Anyway, I decided to follow you, in case I could help."

"What possible help might you be, ghost?" I asked her.

"I already got past the guards and into Gold Bunker, didn't I?"

I shrugged. "Any ghost could have done that."

"Right," she said, "but if something goes wrong down here, when you confront certain parties, what other ghost will have your back?"

I folded up my lips and nodded appreciatively. "Okay," I said, "follow along. If you get caught, I'm going to say I had no idea you were down here, and you should be put into the stockade."

"Challenge accepted, Centurion."

It felt good to know I had a friendly blade watching my back. When I reached the end of the corridor, I raised a big fist and hammered on the only door they'd installed so far.

Normally, there'd be a heavy trooper from Blood World on guard—but not today. There wasn't room aboard the *Scorpio* for their kind. In fact, there was barely room for full-sized humans as it was.

No one answered the door.

Undeterred, I raised my fist to hammer again. After another dozen thuds, the door was finally snatched open.

A sour-looking man stared up at me. To my disappointment, it wasn't Winslade, but Primus Gilbert instead.

"Oh... hello there, sir," I said, faking good cheer.

"It's very early, McGill. The tribune is not yet ready to receive visitors—especially random centurions without appointments."

"But I've got something unique and important to report, sir!"

"Very well..." He stood there, waiting patiently.

I said nothing. I simply continued to grin like an idiot and sway slightly on my big boots.

Gilbert crossed his arms, and his face soured. "Well? Out with it, man!"

"Uh..." I said. "Isn't Winslade back there somewhere?"

"You can make your report to me, Centurion. I will see that it's handled and relayed as necessary."

I leaned forward intrusively, taking a little peek over his shoulder.

Going from incredulous to irritated—and then to outright anger, Primus Gilbert lowered his hands and put them on his hips. He rested one hand on the butt of his pistol. The other fondled a shock-rod he'd tucked into his belt.

It has to be said that the choice of a shock-rod was a bit odd for a Varus man. We normally preferred something deadly as a secondary weapon—like a combat knife—but not Gilbert. He'd always liked the rod, and he rarely spared it when he sensed discipline needed to be meted out upon the skull of a lower-ranked soldier.

He began to draw this item out, in a manner which he might have imagined to be threatening.

I kept up the grin and the dumbass expression. Already, I was preparing a list of lies and platitudes—but these never left my throat.

To my surprise—and Primus Gilbert's utter horror—his shock-rod turned itself on. Worse still, the thumb button was depressed.

There was a crackling sound followed by a sizzle. A moment later, Gilbert was on the floor, curled up in a fetal ball. He made a few mewling noises like a barnyard kitten.

"What the devil is going on out here?" Winslade shouted. He'd finally decided to come out and see what all the hullabaloo was about.

There I was, in a compromised position. I stood over Primus Gilbert with my hands on my knees, offering helpful advice.

Gilbert was down, his teeth clenched together, unable to speak.

Winslade marched closer and raged. "What in the nine hells—McGill? What did you do to my staffer? Did you assault a superior officer *again*? I'll have you flogged for this!"

"I did nothing of the kind, sir," I said. I noticed that on my tapper, a short clip of video footage had just arrived. I surreptitiously tapped on it and viewed it in silent mode. Winslade, during this interlude, proceeded to verbally ream me a new one. He declared me a menace to the entire legion and society at large.

Fortunately, when he paused to take a breath, I was able to show him the video playing on my arm.

"You see this here, sir? Just take a look at this camera file."

When Winslade paused to catch his breath, he eyed the feed with suspicion. "Do you have a drone in here or something? That's against regulations, McGill."

"Ah!" I boomed. "I see the problem! Looky here—see when Primus Gilbert pulled out his favorite weapon?"

There was a loud snap and a flash. Winslade winced as the video played.

I clucked my tongue and shook my oversized head. "You know, a man really shouldn't keep a shock-rod with a hair trigger that close to his balls. It doesn't bear thinking about."

"Ugh…" Winslade said.

I helpfully replayed the vid. Again, he winced and recoiled when a bright spark jumped from Gilbert's non-lethal weapon to his groin region.

I tsked loudly and made sympathetic noises. "I bet old Gilbert will have a bald patch on the left side of his nut sack after that."

While we discussed his stone-cold idiocy, Gilbert began to moan and recover. He was conscious and able to move again but obviously still in a great deal of pain.

"It looks like the fault is yours, Primus," Winslade said to him. "What kind of a fool keeps a weapon like that on his hip, fully charged—and apparently switched to the highest possible power setting?"

Gilbert muttered and groaned, but none of it was actually intelligible.

Winslade sneered down at him, then returned his gaze to me. "All right, McGill," he said, "follow me into my office. You've already ruined half my morning, so you might as well finish the job."

He turned and walked smartly away. I took this opportunity to reach out a hand and point toward the exit behind his back.

"Are you sure?" Della whispered.

"Yeah—get out of here."

There was a light thumping sound as Della leapt over the sprawled-out Primus Gilbert. Her invisible butt made haste as she trotted away toward the exit.

She had pushed her luck with that stunt, but I had to admit, it had been as funny as hell. Poor old Gilbert was never going to figure out how he'd fried his balls with his own shock stick before he'd even gotten it off his belt.

Tribune Winslade wasn't in a good mood. I stood in front of his desk at attention and made my report about the evening's watch on the north wall.

"Yes, yes, yes," he said, "more tricks from the locals. I've heard all this already, McGill. You're boring me with details you probably find scintillating. Well, I can tell you, they're not. Similar attacks were made throughout the night on several fronts."

"The skunks have got to be behind all this, sir," I said.

"Yes, of course, they are. Do you have anything else for me? Anything worthy of my time?"

"I surely do, sir!"

He sighed and shook his head. "I know I'm going to regret it, but I will ask. What is it?"

"Where are the Mogwa, sir? Where's Grand Admiral Sateekas and his family? Aren't they supposed to be on this planet?"

"That information is beyond privileged—it's classified."

"Very good, sir," I said. "I'd like to formally volunteer to lead the Grand Admiral's personal guard."

Winslade scoffed loudly. "Are you a madman? You're the last human being in this entire legion I would assign to our principal benefactor. He's the one responsible for paying our contract. Without him, we wouldn't have any of this to be thankful for." He made a vague gesture toward the entire encampment.

Primus Gilbert had managed to get to his feet and was now limping around in the outer office. He had a terrible scowl on his face when he caught me looking his way.

A part of me wondered if he'd have the guts to draw his pistol and shoot me in the back. I would have had more respect for him if he did—but I very much doubted he'd do it. He just wasn't that kind of man.

I turned back to Winslade and grinned. "Are you calling Grand Admiral Sateekas our benefactor, sir? Did I hear that right?"

"Yes, apparently your ears are operable. They're as large as an elephant's flaps. I'm surprised you can't hear the fish farting out in that equatorial ocean with those things."

"Yes, sir," I said. "But what I meant was, it occurs to me that the grand admiral pretty much screwed us with this entire deal."

Winslade stared at me for a moment. He narrowed his eyes, as if he suspected I was somehow involved in this screwing I was talking about. "Go on, McGill…"

"I was there, sir, during the negotiations. I think we were played for suckers. I'm talking about you and me—all of Legion Varus."

"By whom?" Winslade said, leaning back and crossing his skinny arms over his even skinnier ribs.

I shrugged. "Pretty much everybody. Think about it. This deal was sold to us as a safe, smooth-as-glass escort mission. We cut our prices hoping to steal the deal from Victrix and Germanica. Lo and behold, we succeeded."

"Yes, yes, go on."

"Well, sir, that's the whole story. Sateekas knew this was no walk in the park. Possibly, just maybe, those two pukes from Germanica and Victrix were in on it, too. Hell, maybe even Wurtenberger knew the real score."

Winslade eyed me as if he'd never had this thought before—and I could tell he didn't like the flavor of it.

Suddenly, he spat and hissed. He stood up and began walking around in a circle, gesticulating in the air with his fingers. He was so mad he couldn't even speak properly.

After several seconds of this odd behavior, he whipped around and pointed an accusatory finger in my direction.

"You're right," he said. "They *did* play us. I was a fool! Twenty-five percent off? The sheer madness!"

He then continued to curse and strut, but I figured he was cursing at himself, so I relaxed.

When he was done and calming down, I spoke up again. "So, uh... sir? What about my request?"

"What?" he said. "What request?"

"How about you putting me in charge of the grand admiral's private security detail?"

He stared at me again, thinking that over in a new light. Finally, he began to smile.

"Yes..." he said. "In this singular instance, I'm beginning to appreciate your devious nature, McGill. It's true, you're a five-thumbed ape who has less luck than a broken mirror to draw upon. You're an ignoramus and a menace to everyone who dares come near you. But... possibly, just possibly, you're precisely the individual who *should* be responsible for the grand admiral's personal protection."

## -22-

I might have arrived at Gold Bunker on Nebra as a pariah—at least in Primus Gilbert's wet eyes—but I left with the status of a hero.

Winslade made a special effort, contacting the Mogwa garrison commander to sell him on a reassignment. I was thusly elevated from the status of a pathetic wall-duty guardsman to the head personal bodyguard for a planned planetary tour.

Apparently, Sateekas hadn't bothered to land with the rest of us grunts. I could hardly blame him, what with how dirty these skunk-people were. Today, however, was the big day—the official arrival of the new Mogwa overlords who'd so recently annexed this miserable planet.

There were a few details involved that I didn't like. For one thing, I wasn't going to be allowed to bring my entire unit along. A single platoon was all that was required, I was told by a stern-faced Mogwa soldier. He was obviously jealous of my status and probably didn't want me along for the ride at all.

But Winslade had some pull. He convinced the garrison commander that I should be included to ensure the safety and well-being of Sateekas and his consort, Governess Nox.

Whatever the case, I got the assignment, and I handpicked a platoon of men to go with me. I chose mostly heavies with a few specialists to round out the team.

Both Harris and Leeson were incredibly relieved they weren't expected to go on this tour of Nebra. They'd already wisely concluded that the locals were not apt to give the warmest welcome to Sateekas or anyone who dared to escort him.

We polished the last scuffs out of our armor. Eventually air transport showed up. We boarded at a trot and were whisked away to the city center to meet the Mogwa VIPs.

The transport ship settled down into the grass near our encampment on three heavy skids. The rearmost of these crushed a tent.

Fortunately, only two light troopers were crushed—no big loss. The others had been able to scramble out in time, cutting and crawling their way out of the plastic before they were killed.

There was a lot of whining about this on my unit's tactical chat channel. To me, it was a shrug of the shoulders situation. Of course, the Mogwa air transport pilot gave less than zero shits about endangering humans. Indeed, the only remark he made was to complain that we'd placed our tents too close to the northern wall.

I wasn't exactly sure where else we were supposed to set up camp, but I didn't argue. For one thing, I knew there was no point.

I also knew the proper response to this grave insult. Few men of Earth did. Accordingly, I went out to greet the smug alien bastards.

Two Mogwa were on the ramp leading into their ship, blocking our way. They were carefully stalking around in their little walking tanks. The metal spider-feet clicked on the ramp furtively.

"I'm so sorry, sirs," I said, bowing at the waist and making a big sweep of my hand. If I'd had a cap to pull off and wave around, I would have done that, too. "May I bring my company of men aboard your transport now, master pilot?"

They eyed my troops with a mixture of disdain and distrust. This was always the case. Mogwa viewed humans the way housewives viewed untrained dogs.

The main gun of each Mogwa tank swiveled, perfectly tracking the movement of their eyes. These turrets aimed at us in a disconcerting fashion. Each black, flat muzzle zeroed in on any human who happened to be under their scrutiny.

As I spoke, they both focused on me, but I didn't shy away and wet my pants. I stood tall and proud.

"Yes, yes," the Mogwa pilot said at last. "Herd your savages aboard. This whole thing is a waste of time, anyway. I don't even know why Sateekas hired you apes."

"We're bullet-catchers, sir," I said.

"What?"

"We're blade-stoppers—shields made of meat."

"What are you talking about, idiot human?"

"That's our purpose," I explained. "We are here to block the skunk-alien rebels. We will die so you don't have to."

"Skunk-aliens? Are you talking about the Nebrans?"

"Uh… yes, sir," I said, realizing that the term 'skunk-alien' probably didn't make sense for the Mogwa after it was translated through his tapper into Imperial Standard.

"Ah…" he said at last. He'd finally caught my meaning. "Meat-shields? Yes, I understand that concept. Perhaps the grand admiral is wise…"

"Of course, he's wise," the other Mogwa said sharply.

"Right, right," the pilot said. The two of them gave each other odd glances.

I knew how it went. In general, all the military personnel who worked for Grand Animal Sateekas eventually became contemptuous of his leadership capabilities. But although they probably scorned him in private, they all knew it wasn't their place to complain openly—especially not in front of losers like us. We humans were so low on the totem pole, we were nothing more than slave troopers to the Mogwa.

After that, they finally stepped aside. I marched my men smartly up the ramp into the belly of the Mogwa ship.

I had chosen a single scout to join my team. It was Cooper's turn this time, as Della had already done me a special service on this mission. She didn't deserve to be associated with a mission that was as apt to go horribly wrong as this one so obviously was.

For my bio specialist, I'd dragooned only one man: Carlos Ortiz. He was an asshole and always deserved the worst of the worst. I had no compunction about making that choice.

To play the role of my chief noncom, I'd considered both Sargon and Moller. I'd decided to discard both of their names from the list and chosen instead a new individual. A man named Washburn had risen in the ranks recently. He'd once been a weaponeer but had now been elevated to veteran.

Washburn needed field experience. He needed to learn the harsh realities of small-unit command in Varus. I wanted to show him how to do it, McGill-style.

When it came down to the technicians, the choice was obvious. I took Natasha. If I'd chosen Kivi, Sargon might've been upset because I would've split them up. Besides which, Natasha was more adept at working with alien hardware. She was quite possibly the only member of my entire handpicked team who was absolutely ecstatic about me having chosen her. The rest seemed fairly glum.

We lifted off the planet surface, watching through tiny portholes as exhaust and gravity waves dumped down from the ship's belly. This gush of heat and pressure flattened more tents and tall grasses below us.

The majority of my team appeared resigned to this new fate. A few, however, looked hopeful—even adventurous.

Sure, they'd had a long, hard night hugging the north wall, and many of them had already died at the hands of Nebrans. A couple of them had even managed to do it twice already.

But still, we were now huddling in the belly of a new beast. Maybe things would turn out to be better than we dared hope.

To my surprise, the air transport rose up and up, higher into the sky. It had been my impression we were supposed to go directly to the capital—but this was not the case.

Instead, we flew up into the stratosphere and beyond. Once the air grew so thin that it was down to a few molecules every cubic meter or so, we were actually at the edge of space.

There, hanging in orbit above Nebra, we docked with one of the large battlecruisers that Sateekas had so carefully built over the preceding decade.

Moving my team to the docking zone, we were ordered to stand at attention. Our backs were to the walls, and our eyes aimed straight ahead.

The Mogwa soldiers stood in the middle, and they opened the hatch that allowed pressure to equalize between the two ships. After a lot of hissing of pipes and groaning of metal, the passageway was finally open and secure.

Finally, at long last, Grand Admiral Sateekas made his appearance. I recognized him, daring to take a couple of sidelong glances in his direction.

He looked pretty good—for a middle-aged spider-alien. He probably hadn't died much lately, possibly not since the Crystal World campaign or even before that.

Seeing Sateekas himself wasn't that big of a surprise, what made me take notice was the identities of the other civilians in his wake.

The second in the group was also recognizable to me. It was none other than Nox, the sleek, black-widow-lady.

Nox was Sateekas' consort, his mate. I wasn't really sure that Mogwa families went in for the whole husband-wife thing, but they definitely mated for life, and these two had a professional relationship in addition to a family that produced offspring.

I could tell by the bulge around her middle that Nox was probably pregnant yet again—or she was carrying another kid in her forward pouch.

Behind her, I caught sight of two smaller Mogwa. These were different than any I'd seen since the City World campaign. They were children. One was a young male, the second an even younger female. Could these be their kids? It was my impression that they were.

Sateekas paused when he reached our air transport, and he slid his numerous eyes over the humans who stood in a line like chrome-covered robots. We stood, all polished and shiny, in two rows on either side of the chamber.

"These are the humans?" he said.

"Yes, Grand Admiral," the garrison commander responded. "Just as you requested. They've been hand-picked by the tribune of the slave legion."

Sateekas looked somewhat annoyed. He walked among us, eyeing us as individuals. When he got to me, he paused and turned toward the garrison commander.

"They appear to be suitable," he said, "but I've failed to understand why this one—" here he pointed a lanky, multi-jointed limb in my direction "—is so much larger than the rest. The row on the right here seems uneven. It's not smooth to the eye. Didn't I specify regularly shaped and sized humans? Can't you get the most basic details done correctly?"

"My apologies, Admiral," the garrison commander said. "I wasn't responsible for the individuals that were picked out."

Sateekas made a blatting noise. The Mogwa often did that. Whether they were laughing, angry, dying in agony, or sighing in defeat, it all seemed to sound about the same to me.

Walking closer and displaying a bad attitude, he regarded me more closely. Suddenly, he peered and even cocked his head a fraction.

"McGill...?" he said, incredulous.

"Hello there, Grand Admiral!" I dared to raise a hand and wave it in his direction.

"Shut your filthy hole!" the garrison commander boomed. His mini-tank marched toward me with squeaking, whirring joints. The spider-like vehicle instantly aimed every gun it had in my direction, ready to fire.

I lowered my hand slowly. My movement had apparently been seen as an insult, or possibly a threat toward the grand admiral.

"McGill..." Sateekas said again. "How is it that I am unable to evade your presence?"

"I don't rightly know, sir," I said. "Maybe it's all a happy coincidence."

"No... It's neither a coincidence, nor happy." He turned around and addressed the garrison commander. "This beast haunts me. Who chose these individuals for this mission? Who has been charged with the protection and maintenance of my person?"

"The humans made their recommendations to me, sir."

Sateekas turned back to face me again. "And you saw fit to take the advice of grunting primitives? Incredible."

"Uh..." I said, not quite sure what all the fuss was about. "I volunteered, sir, and Tribune Winslade approved it."

"Why?" Sateekas demanded.

"Well, sir, because I know you rather well. I know your likes and dislikes—that kind of thing."

"Is that so?" the Mogwa said. "What emotion do you think I'm feeling right now?"

"Uh..." I said, thinking it over. "Loathing, maybe? Disgust?"

"Precisely so!" Nox said. The female Mogwa advanced suddenly. She'd been listening but hadn't said a word up until now. "Disgust! That's the right term, McGill. The last time we were on a mission together, we were lured out into the frontier and beyond by that skulking deceiver, Winslade. You and Primus Graves connived by your own designs and destroyed the space cannon. That destroyed the coalition we'd worked so hard to support."

"I've been hearing nothing but complaints about it since we left," Sateekas added.

"Exactly," Nox said. "According to every report I've read, this creature was instrumental in the destruction of the most valuable artifact found during that entire campaign."

My mouth was gaping by this time. At the meeting where we'd hammered out the contract, Sateekas hadn't bitched about me being there. So where was all this hate coming from now?

My eyes slid to Lady Nox, and they stopped there. She had to be the source of this hissy-fit.

"Hold on, overlords," I said, daring to lift my hands again. My fingers spread wide.

The Mogwa troops again focused their cannons on me and my possibly dangerous hands. Remembering my manners, I let my arms slowly drop back down to my sides once more.

Then, I went into my usual denial speech. I regaled them with my "I-didn't-do-nothing" excuse list.

For me, this recitation was well-rehearsed. I was like a musician playing his top hits long after he's retired. Every word, every syllable, every utterance of dismay had been practiced hundreds—or maybe even thousands—of times.

Finally, Lady Nox accepted my apologies and the Mogwa VIPs passed us by. As they left, she said something about me not being allowed to get in her way again.

I assured the bitchy Mogwa princess I'd be as faithful as a church mouse and as quiet as a bear in the woods… or something to that effect.

## -23-

When we were all outside in the courtyard, Sateekas took it upon himself to approach me.

"Of all the creatures to be assigned to my personal guard," he began, "the last I expected was you, McGill."

"Thank you, sir," I responded, "I guess today is your lucky day!"

He glowered at me and shuffled his limbs in a restive manner. "I think you have possibly misconstrued my commentary."

"And for that, I apologize deeply, Grand Admiral."

"Whatever. I suppose one pack of armored human shields will serve as well as another." After this rude statement, he turned to his Mogwa troops and gave stern orders. "Garrison commander, escort me and my family to the floater. You and your men will form an immediate ring around my vehicle. You will personally hold the tether."

I frowned a bit at this conversation, wondering exactly what kind of vehicle this floater was going to be and why it had a tether. I was curious about it, I don't mind telling you.

"The humans," Sateekas continued instructing the commander, "will be arranged in a pattern around this central concentration of importance. It will be up to you how to deploy them, and you will bear full responsibility for any mishaps that arise from this tour."

Lady Nox, was listening to all this, and she seemed disquieted.

"Sateekas," she said sternly, "are you certain that this is a sane plan?"

"Of course, it is," Sateekas said, "otherwise I would not have dared propose it."

"But here we are, walking among the Nebrans. These people are the most dedicated of saboteurs."

"That is precisely the point. They will not be expecting this tour de force. We have hired extra guardsmen. There should be no serious danger presented."

"But you don't know that. Here I am with my young…"

"Bah—all of them have been body-scanned."

Lady Nox snarled at this. "Body-scanned, yes, and mentally stored. But I don't want my children to experience their first death in the squalid streets of this rebellious shithole of a planet!"

I, for one, had to admit that Lady Nox had a point. Parading around a bit on a conquered planet, well, I could understand that. Sateekas could take that risk. Maybe his wife as well. But… the kids? That seemed like a step too far to me. Even if they were revived an hour later, it would have to be traumatic for a young child to experience violent death at the hands of rebels. I wouldn't have chanced it if it were my family.

But old Sateekas was nothing if not an alien who consistently overestimated his odds of success in any endeavor. He seemed to take insult from his female's lack of faith.

He straightened up to his full height—which wasn't all that high. If the truth were to be told, as he was only a tad over a meter tall.

He spoke stiffly. "If your feminine fear overwhelms you, I will allow you and the younger children to retreat to our ship and huddle there, awaiting our return."

Nox was offended, but she seemed to see the offer as an opportunity that was too good to be passed up.

"I will do just that," she said, reaching down and grabbing the limbs of her two kids.

Sateekas, however, raised a foot-hand and bade her to stop.

"Hold," he said. "You may take the pouchling and our daughter—but my son is destined for greater things. He can never be seen quailing from a confrontation. We have discussed this previously."

"I don't see how this minor grandstanding event will be meaningful. How can such a risky display make the slightest difference to our son's career and eventual status? No Core World citizen has ever pondered this planet for an instant."

"That's where you're wrong," Sateekas said. "For I have pondered this dirty orb at length. Experiences like this one are crucial to the development of a future tyrant. Our son needs to experience vicious peasantry, and he needs to greet such encounters with enthusiasm."

Nox made a funny, windy sound. I figured it was a noise indicating disgust. She turned around, taking her daughter and her pouchling back inside.

Sateekas stood stiffly in her wake, looking annoyed. "If that female were not so comely and well-positioned in the social networks... Ah, but never mind. Come, son. It is time for us to tour this squalid city."

Sateekas' son, who all this while had been carefully watching the interaction between his parents, finally decided to speak up. "Will I get to see any of them die, Father?"

"Any of what?"

"The humans, Father—or possibly the Nebrans."

Sateekas laughed. "It's possible, son, it's possible. I'm making no promises, but some sort of violent altercation is more than likely in this city. Come now, let's head for the floater."

Sateekas marched ahead then, followed by the Mogwa troops, who were in turn followed by my platoon of men.

The garrison commander gestured angrily for us to march in his wake. We did so, doing our best to line up and move our bodies in matching precision. We'd had plenty of practice marching around parade grounds, but it wasn't really our strong point. Legion Varus was a combat outfit, much more than it was a color guard.

Once we were in position, a large floater descended into our midst. It was precisely as one might imagine: a bubble-domed platform, oval in shape.

The contrivance reminded me of nothing more than a turkey platter with a cover on top. The cover in this case, however, was transparent. You could only see a faint shimmer in the air where the forcefield enclosed the interior.

Suddenly, I understood the plan behind this coming fiasco. It seemed to me to be even more insane than I'd thought it would be the first time I heard about it.

The platform, which was about four meters long and three wide, was to be stood upon by Sateekas and his son. The two of them were enclosed underneath a protective barrier, which would at least deflect basic ballistic dangers—things like bullets.

Beneath the vehicle was a repelling glow that lifted the floater half a meter in height. That blue, shimmering region had anti-gravity forces at work. Intelligent repellers were operating in coordination to keep both the floater and its occupants from touching the dirt roads that we would be marching over.

I had a device like this of my own back home at Waycross. I used it as a coffee table. That unit, of course, was only about the size of a surfboard, but it had provided me a lot of entertainment over the years.

There was a tether attached to the front of the floater. Normally, these things used control wires and buttons to guide the craft. That's how I would have done it if I were piloting it personally.

But no Mogwa overlord, especially not one so highly self-regarding as Sateekas, would be caught dead piloting his own vehicle. The grand admiral was content to allow the garrison commander to do the honors of dragging his floater through the city.

The tether wasn't a simple rope, nor even a wire—it was an intelligent guidance device. I could tell this because the tether did not hang loosely. It didn't dip down and touch the flagstones of the courtyard, even when the slack should have caused it to do so.

Instead, it wriggled around and lifted itself so as to avoid touching the earth. It was almost like a living snake of some kind instead of a simple rope or wire.

In addition to this, I got the distinct impression that it was terminated by some kind of control mechanism, which the garrison commander was able to manipulate as soon as he touched it. He caused the protective dome to completely enclose his two charges of importance, and then to slowly rotate them toward the gates. These movements were definitely not occurring because the garrison commander was dragging the vehicle around with a rope. He was directing it remotely.

"Primitives," the garrison commander called out, "close ranks around your lord. Do not allow a single grunting peasant to approach. Cast aside any who do—and if they persist, cast aside their dead bodies instead."

Impressed by this fierce order, my men gripped and re-gripped their rifles, wondering what they were in for. Sure, these skunks were small, but they were also tricky. I got the impression from the Mogwa commander's attitude that he had no illusions as to the nature of these conquered people, either.

As the commander spoke, the forward gates swung slowly open. This was done through some means of automation, as I didn't see anyone pushing on it.

At last, beyond the floater and squad of Mogwa soldiers that surrounded it, I could see the open city streets of Nebra City. It was my first glimpse at an actual habitation of any size and consequence built by these skunk-aliens.

Right off, I have to say I wasn't impressed. It looked to me like something from an archaeological textbook. The buildings on either side of the street were built in a haphazard style. It seemed that a substance—I had to assume it was probably bricks made of mud—perhaps adobe baked in the sun, had been used in the construction process.

While the street itself was wide enough, much narrower, spoke-like streets went between the buildings on either side of us. That only made sense. These skunks probably wouldn't need any street wider than two meters, given their own relatively small stature.

The main thoroughfare, however, was quite a bit larger, at least twenty meters wide. A throng of the locals was already there to greet us.

"Looks like they got out the welcoming committee, Centurion," Veteran Washburn said. I could tell he was impressed.

I, however, was not.

I didn't look at their waving paws, their seemingly happy smiles. They threw their arms high in the air as if cheering. They made odd warbling sounds in their inhuman throats as well.

It all sounded rather festive and inviting. There had to be a throng of close to a hundred of them directly in our path. They all seemed very excited to see us—and their conqueror on his floating platform.

"I don't trust these fuzzy little bastards, McGill," Carlos said to me.

"I hear you, Ortiz," I said. "Washburn, you take the left flank. Walk up front, directly in front of the floater. I'll take the right."

I then called out a series of names, placing five more heavy troops between the two of us. I wanted a thick wall of marching metal-clad troops between Sateekas and the cheering crowd of diminutive natives. As we moved into this formation, the garrison commander made appreciative noises.

"Yes, yes!" he said. "That's it! Sateekas has assured me that you primitives have the minds of killer-apes, as simple as beasts of the jungle. But you're filled with a natural cunning for the tactics of the battlefield. Perhaps that high praise will be proven correct today!"

"I can assure you, sir," I said, "Legion Varus will not disappoint."

"See that you don't."

We took up our positions, making a firm wall between our charges and the adoring crowd. We began to march at last. We proceeded slowly but inexorably toward them.

Under most normal circumstances, a crowd of tiny creatures like this would have melted away upon our approach, but these skunk-aliens were persistent. They thronged us, running their tiny paws over our thighs and kneecaps. Some of them thrust things up to us, gifts, effigies of tiny skunk-shaped maidens, shiny cut-glass jewels—even food offerings in colorfully laid out dishes.

But then I saw something I liked even less than these others, none of which I trusted. I saw one of those blue flowers in the hands of one of the female aliens. She was offering it up to me, from both of her hands, toward my gauntlet. I reached out, grabbed the flower from her, and crushed it into a pulpy mass. The flower dribbled purple gooey juices onto the roadway.

She looked aghast. I then tossed it down and stomped on it with my right boot heel, crushing out the last of its juices. It left a dark stain on the dusty road.

The native looked shocked, horrified, and then angry. She showed me a flash of her sharp white teeth, and then she vanished into the throng again, from whence she'd come.

The aliens in general fell back before us. We moved slowly, attempting not to trample them. There was no need for bodily injury if it wasn't absolutely necessary. But then again, we weren't taking any guff from these frisky fellows. We'd already seen what their gifts and their hospitality were worth.

So we nudged them away, knocking them in the chest with our metal-capped knee pads, slapping them lightly with the butts of our rifles until they staggered back, grabbing at their skulls.

But we didn't crack any heads. We didn't stomp upon their probing, clawed feet. We just kept marching and shoving until they fell back away from us.

After a couple of minutes of this, during which the alien throng was unable to penetrate past our retinue of guards to the Mogwa floater itself, the crowd suddenly relented. They fell back as if upon a silent signal. What had once been a street teeming with aliens was now rapidly emptying out.

"Looks like the sugary part of this welcome has ended," I told my men.

"That's right," Carlos answered. "Now, they're going to pull out something more spicy."

I didn't tell him to shut up because I figured he was probably right.

## -24-

Once all the friendliness had drained out of the skunks, their true nature began to show. Instead of thronging us, casting flowers and other gifts, they began to slink away. The streets emptied, but I got the sense that they weren't done with us yet.

I noticed a channel blinking on my HUD, and I engaged it. It was the Mogwa local channel, and I was able to overhear the voice of Sateekas as he was talking to his son. Despite the fact this was an official audio channel shared by a military team, it pretty much consisted of Sateekas giving a sermon.

We marched down the main thoroughfare without incident. But to me, things looked suspicious. These skunks were clearly planning an interruption of our little tour-de-force. Sateekas seemed oblivious to all this.

"You see, son," he said, "first they thronged us with gifts of adulation. Now, that small crowd of peasants has given way to the larger populace, which is clearly cowardly in nature. They hide from us. They *fear* us—which is a very good thing. They—"

"Why is that a good thing, Father?" The impertinent son said, speaking up out of turn.

Sateekas paused, probably in annoyance. I could almost hear him shuffling his limbs around. When he was in the middle of a speech—which he pretty much always was—he didn't like to be interrupted. But he seemed to make a special case for his son.

"A good question, which I shall indulge," Sateekas said. "When creatures fear you, they tend to obey you more readily. They may also obey you when they feel slave-love. But which of these two emotions do you think is more likely to be forgotten when times are difficult?"

The kid thought that one over. "You mean like when we're in the midst of a rebellion?"

"Yes, exactly."

"Well, of course, they would forget their love, not their fear."

"Excellent!" Sateekas said. "Let that lesson sink in. It will guide you to a better future. A tyrant has to know these things."

"Still…" the kid said, "it can be nice to be loved by your people."

Again, Sateekas made that kind of growling, thumping, annoyed sound. "Disappointment. You've already made the logical leap to which of these two emotive responses is superior. Do not sully your mental advance with frivolous niceties. In the end, rulership is easy until it's not. Everything we do as a ruler is in preparation for that moment of difficulty, which will always come in the end."

"Whatever," the kid said.

One more time, I heard Sateekas utter a near growl of frustration. I sensed that Nox was probably spoiling this boy. He had a bit of an attitude in him.

Every Mogwa had an attitude, mind you, and every human teenage kid did as well. I imagined this sort of thing pained Sateekas just as much as it had pained every father throughout time.

"What the hell's that?" Carlos said suddenly.

My eyes began to scan the scene. Carlos was marching along at the rear of the column, so I swung my attention that way.

Among all the troops here, Carlos was probably the most experienced. He wasn't a weaponeer or even a heavy, but he had served in the capacity of a combat soldier in the distant past. Sure, he was just a bio now, but that didn't mean he didn't know how to fight and recognize when something bad was coming.

"What's wrong, Ortiz?" I boomed over our tactical channel.

"Don't you see it? Don't you see *them*?" he asked.

I looked in the direction he indicated with a pointing arm. I squinted and adjusted the visual gain on my helmet.

The sun was beating down on us, and you could feel it even through the air conditioning systems inside our suits. It was hot out here. That bright sun had, despite our lenses and the polarization of our visors, made dark pits out of the alleyways that led off to either side of the main road.

But there, in between a series of earthenware urns... Yes, I saw some bumping shapes, some flashing eyes. What were those? Fuzzy heads? A few snouts sniffing at the air?

There were creatures hiding in between those urns. Under normal circumstances that'd be no big deal. After all, we were walking through a whole city full of these skunk-aliens. Maybe a few of their kids were out watching the parade. Maybe they didn't want to be seen out in the open. These guys would naturally like to skulk in the shadows of an alleyway and peep out at us as we marched by from a safe vantage point. They were like wary animals, uncertain if they should completely reveal themselves.

But then I saw it. I saw what Carlos must be talking about. A flash of bright metal. A glint of steel, perhaps? Or something else?

I wasn't sure. But this group of aliens, the guys hiding behind the urns in an alleyway, they were carrying something. Was it a long pole, perhaps? I was confused.

"Company, halt!" I shouted over tactical chat. I switched immediately to the Mogwa channel, where Sateekas was now lecturing his son upon the finer points of selecting a servant for one's household. I broke in on the conversation rudely.

"Sirs, we have a sighting," I said. "Possible hostile on our left flank."

"Is that why you've halted, you moron?" the garrison commander demanded. "If these aliens are planning something, our best move is to get past them as fast as possible. Start moving your lazy feet, animal!"

Naturally, I disagreed. If there was one group of skunks carrying around a mysterious length of metal, there were probably more of them ahead of us.

But I wasn't in charge of this show, so I gave orders for my men to advance again.

"Pick it up, double time!" I boomed.

Moving at a trot in our ridiculous, chrome-dipped armor, we surged ahead. Right behind us, the Mogwa commander was hauling on the tether, urging the floater containing his charges to greater speed. This resulted in a barely perceptible increase in our pace. I frowned and shook my head at that. It would have been much better for the family members to be inside of a regular aircar. Sure, they couldn't see everything as easily, and the populace couldn't see them either if they were sitting inside of an enclosed vehicle. But if they had been, they could have fired up into the sky and immediately been safe from whatever was about to befall our procession.

The skunks, for their part, saw us advance at a jog. They decided to accelerate their plans as well. From both sides of the wide street a large number of skunks emerged.

They came in teams of six. Each team carried a long metal pole.

"Spread out!" I shouted. "Push them back!"

"Shall we use deadly force, sir?" Washburn demanded.

I hesitated for a moment, but then made my decision. "No, not until they do something that deserves it."

In my heart I wondered if this choice was a mistake, but I couldn't order my men to fire now. After all, I didn't want to slaughter a bunch of unarmed civilians who were possibly setting up a celebration—even if they were about the most untrustworthy bunch I'd ever run into.

The skunks suddenly stopped their advance on all sides of us. They didn't come all the way up to our lines, but rather halted, busying themselves with their odd metal poles. Each group of six raised their pole to a vertical state, standing it up in the roadway.

We were gritting our teeth, expecting something weird. Perhaps we'd be treated to a shower of bomblets—or maybe jolts of released power from a Tesla coil.

But nothing of the kind happened. Instead, the poles grew taller. With a whirring sound, each of them stretched up from two meters in height to about four. At the top of each of these tall poles, a flag suddenly unfurled.

Flagpoles? Were these just flagpoles?

We gawked in confusion. Each of the flags depicted the Mogwa standard I'd seen previously. It looked sort of like a spider with a weapon in its hand, crouching upon a large planet.

"Ah!" Sateekas said in relief and recognition. "They honor us! All halt! I will not miss this obsequious ceremony!"

We stopped marching, and so did the Mogwa soldiers. Their small tanks prowled warily, attempting to aim their turrets in every direction at once. They were nothing if not paranoid.

"My bodyguards are overzealous fools," Sateekas said to his son. "You see that flag? That is the banner of House Trantor. This is a grand sign of adoration and allegiance. Do you recall when I spoke upon fear versus love?"

"I've forgotten nothing, Father. I endured your lecture only minutes ago."

"Yes, yes. Well, here is an example of unbidden affection. This is the best kind of slave-love. Sometimes, incredible though it might seem, such displays are presented spontaneously. Mogwa xenologists have long puzzled over the phenomenon. They theorize that conquered peoples begin to take comfort in their pathetic state, coming to imagine themselves protected by a superior intellect. These delusions—"

Here, Sateekas cut off his speech. The situation on the ground had altered further.

While we were standing around in befuddlement, gawking upward at these six flagpoles which now completely encircled the procession—the skunks had been busy.

"They're taking off!" Carlos said. "Look at those little fuzzy feet run."

I turned my gaze downward from the high flags, which everyone was marveling over, and noticed it was true. The skunks were retreating, vanishing back into the dark shadows among the urn-lined alleyways between the buildings.

I frowned. This development seemed odd to me.

My mouth opened wide, ready to give a further warning to the Mogwa garrison commander—when a mysterious buzzing sound began. It was coming from all six of the flagpoles surrounding us.

At the base of each, my troops were staring and walking around in wonderment. A few of them had even put a gauntlet upon the metal poles. Those few men were the most unlucky of individuals.

A massive electrical charge was released. The soldiers who'd witlessly grasped a pole were electrocuted instantly. Worse than that, all the poles were now tipping over in concert, falling. I quickly realized that they weren't just toppling over, they were indeed all converging upon the domed floater in our midst.

"Our metal armor," Natasha said urgently. "Your men could form a circuit and short out these flagpole things. James, you can't let them touch Sateekas' vehicle!"

It was an impossible situation. Within a second or two, all the poles toppled. I ordered my men to smash them away with their rifles, and to shoot after any running skunks. We kicked at the dirt roadway, attempting to find the hidden cables that had to be buried under our boots.

But there simply wasn't time to do any of these things. In the end, three of my men were electrocuted. The Mogwa garrison commander, to his credit, drove his tank directly into the path of one of the falling flagpoles, the one that was coming from the front. He blocked its descent with his mini-tank's chassis. Inside the cockpit, I saw him do a deadly dance as he was electrocuted and transformed into a steaming corpse.

We managed to knock away four of the falling poles, but two of them got through. That was enough. They sizzled on the forcefield. Sparks flew.

None of us dared to touch the poles directly. To do so was to be immediately electrocuted. I ran forward and grabbed the tether from the garrison commander, who was quite dead and unable to maneuver it.

I yanked on the heavy cord, unable to understand the controls as I'd never been instructed on how to use them. Pulling on the cord as if it were a rope attached to a boat, I hauled upon it, attempting to drag the floater free of the trap.

To some extent, I was successful. The dome was going orange. That's what these forcefields did. They went through a series of colors until they flickered out. It was still protecting the two Mogwa inside, who were in a snarling huddle at the center of the floater, clearly expecting death.

I managed to pull the floater a few meters away from the trap by sheer force. One of the two poles that had made contact with the dome slid away and fell into the dirt. This pole brought great misfortune to another of the Mogwa soldiers, who was shocked to death when it fell on his vehicle.

There was just one pole left, just one that seemed to cling upon the floater's dome, unwilling to let go.

The forcefield flickered, it was buckling. It was beyond orange now, going into a fuzzing brown-red glow.

It flickered out at last, but due to my efforts, the pole struck the end of the floater rather than crashing down onto the heads of the two Mogwa. It gave a nasty jolt to the feet of Sateekas and his son.

They yelped in pain, but they didn't die. Their bodies didn't steam and cook.

The pole then slid off the floater, which many of my men were now pushing and hauling upon with me, trying to drag it to safety. We left the last of the poles in the dirt, where it buzzed and flashed. The surviving troops stepped over it gingerly, careful to be sure they didn't make contact with the deadly device.

I managed to drag the floater another dozen meters along the road before we all stopped and reformed our circle of arms and armor around the two Mogwa in our midst.

"That was a close one," I said.

"It was beyond close," Sateekas shouted, daring to stand tall again. "Where is my garrison commander?"

"I'm afraid he died, sir," I told him. "He stopped one of those falling poles with his own hand."

"Did he die in agony?" Sateekas demanded.

"I believe he did, your overlordship."

"Good! He has failed me. Here I am, exposed to this foul planet's glaring sun, while these vicious mammalian rebels are no doubt plotting their next attack upon my person. Who is in charge of my safety now?"

"Uh…" I said, looking around. There were a couple of Mogwa soldiers left alive, but they were just grunts in their tanks. There wasn't even a noncom among them. "I guess I am, sir. Since I'm the only officer that's still breathing."

"Very well, McGill. Let's finish this tour of this despicable town. This place is a cankerous boil mounted upon an unsightly creature's rump!"

"Uh…" I said, "finish the tour, sir? I don't think I can get that force dome up again. It's fried."

"The floater still works. Proceed!"

"You might have to walk," I said. "I don't know how to pilot this floater of yours. Hell, I don't even know which direction we're going."

"What are you grunting about? I will not be defeated in this fashion, you disgusting ape! This is *my* planet. It is my son's birthright, and these people will accept their annexation. I will not give them an easy victory. They will not cheer in their burrows tonight about how they chased off their rightful overlord."

"But sir…"

"I can handle it, Centurion," Natasha said, stepping up and gently taking the tether from my hands.

It had a strange control system, but she seemed to have no trouble with it. Go figure. Natasha had flown more than a few alien spaceships. I guess it was no brain teaser for her to drive what amounted to a floating hay-hauler through this alien town.

"Okay, then," I said, with a shrug and a shaking head. "Saddle up, boys. The day isn't getting any younger."

## -25-

Sateekas demanded that we continue our tour of the city, despite my paranoia and the fact that the skunks had already managed to take down his protective dome.

"Two bullets, that's all it's going to take," Washburn said.

Carlos laughed. "They don't even need bullets. A thrown rock will do the job."

"Shut up, you two," I told them.

A number of my men laughed roughly. It was general knowledge that the carapace of any Mogwa citizen was remarkably thin. Their bodies would pop like melons if they encountered significant force of any kind. That's why they rode around in walking tanks all the time.

I thought wistfully about the three tanks that we'd left behind, with dead Mogwa soldiers inside. Hell, if we just dragged them along, maybe I could have talked Sateekas and his kid into getting into a couple of them.

Forget about it, I told myself. The customer is always right, and today, Sateekas was paying the bills. If he wanted to risk death, that was his business.

We continued on, with frequent radio traffic flying every time anybody saw a skunk who looked like he was ready to take a leak. We marched along in relative peace, however, and we even began to believe the scary part of this adventure was done with. We were more than halfway through the loop now, which would eventually lead us around to the central palace again, where we had started this escapade.

Our spirits rose when we rounded the third turn along the great square road. We were now three-quarters of the way through this insane city tour.

But then, we saw a body lying in the road. It was a skunk-alien female. She was motionless, her fur puffing in the wind. There was not another skunk to be seen.

"I don't like the look of this, sir," Washburn said.

"Why not?" Carlos said. "The only good skunk is a dead skunk. That's what I say."

Again, there were a few chuckles, but everyone was nervous. My troops were aiming their weapons this way and that. We all had the feeling this could be another trick.

"What's the delay?" Sateekas demanded when he noticed we'd slowed down.

"There appears to be a local citizen lying in the roadway," I informed him.

"What of it?" Sateekas demanded. "Kick the corpse aside. Don't show fear before the enemy. They will never bend the knee if you do."

"Is that another axiom, Father?" Nero asked at his father's side.

"Yes, consider it so, my son."

I signaled for Carlos, who jogged forward, grumbling along the way. "What if this thing is laced with bombs or something?"

"In that case," I said, "you should have been born a tech."

It got a laugh from a lot of my men, but we all watched warily as he knelt and examined the body. "Still breathing. I don't see an injury. I'm not quite sure why she's—"

"What is this unholy delay?" Sateekas roared all of a sudden. "Soldiers, forward! Take the tether, pull me through this."

Carlos and my front line of men stumbled aside as the floater surged and began to glide forward. The three Mogwa soldiers who were still breathing dragged the floater closer to the body in the street.

The rest of us parted before them, our chromed legs clanking as we stepped aside. I was relieved to see that at least the Mogwa soldiers did not drive one of those spiky, spider-like legs of their mini-tanks down and crush the poor alien skunk-lady. Instead, they walked around her and kept on going. We fell in on either side of the floater, forming two columns.

We marched along at a reasonable pace. But then, as the floater glided over the body in the road, I heard an awful noise. It was kind of a squelching sound. I thought I heard a small squalling sound as well.

"Whoa," Carlos said, "some of that got on my boot."

I looked under the floater, and I was immediately horrified. The skunk lady's body had kind of... imploded.

That was the thing about these floating vehicles and their gravity repellers. They didn't really make the floater itself weigh less. Instead, they transferred that weight, in this case in a downward direction, so that essentially the weight of it was immediately applied to the ground below. The body of the tiny alien that the vehicle was passing over had taken the brunt of it.

The floater had crushed her. If she hadn't been dead before, she was quite dead now. I had to wonder if the whole "dead skunk in the road" thing had been a trick. Perhaps a ruse designed to slow us down. If it had been, she'd paid for the trick with her life.

After that fateful moment, everything changed. The streets had been empty. They'd been windblown and quiet. Now, they transformed before our eyes.

Dozens of skunks, then hundreds—no there probably had to be more like a thousand now. They surged into the street within a minute's time. They came rushing out of the houses, out of the side alleys, from the road ahead and behind. They thronged us in a growing crowd, and not a damned one of these guys looked happy.

They showed us their sharp white teeth and their angry, slitted eyes. There were snarls and hisses.

The mob had things in their hands: weapons, tools—some even held rocks, but they all looked furious and determined.

"Uh-oh," Carlos said. "Who could have figured that if you just made one skunk pie in the middle of the road, these guys would all go crazy on us?"

"What is the meaning of this?" Sateekas shouted. "Why are you slowing down? Push through them! Don't stop!"

Following his orders, we surged forward, shoving aside any skunks that dared stand too close in their growling, growing circle.

We began making some headway, but I heard something behind us. I craned my neck, as did others.

It was a familiar noise, a clanking, squeaking sound. Then I saw the first of them. A Mogwa mini-tank was driving up on our six. It was being driven by one of the skunks. Behind him came the other two machines.

They had dragged the bodies of the Mogwa out of them and figured out how to use them. They were rather easy to pilot, and now they were charging in on our rear. The skunks piloting these contraptions looked just as angry as the ones who were surrounding us in the street. Behind these three mini-tanks were a number of other armed skunks. In two to three-man teams, they were carrying the weapon systems of the Legion Varus regular heavy trooper. They had morph-rifles.

"Damn it," Washburn shouted. "Permission to fire, sir?"

I hesitated, gritting my teeth. "Lord Sateekas," I said, "what are your orders?"

"Kill them!" Sateekas shouted. "Kill them all!"

Maybe those words were the ones the skunks were waiting for, and they certainly did electrify my men, too. Whatever the case, the two sides fell upon one another.

We were in close quarters. We were stronger, more organized, and better armored compared to the skunks. Still, they got a few licks in. Some of my men had their ankles hooked, and they were pulled down. A horde of angry, squalling skunks surged in with vicious growls. Washburn was one of the first to go down. He scrabbled on the roadway. His force blade sung and slashed through smoking hair.

Body parts flew. Growling skunks shot, stabbed and beat upon my men, at least a dozen working on a single man.

Setting our morph-rifles to full auto, we fired thousands of explosive rounds at point-blank range. The skunks were torn up and thrown back. If they hadn't been in so close, they wouldn't have had a chance.

But then the squeaking and the stomping of the walking mini-tanks coming up behind us joined the fray. They unleashed gouts of energy and a hailstorm of explosive pellets that popped and shattered the armor of my men. Those troops at the rear were people like Natasha, the least armored and the lightest armed of the entire guard. They were torn apart.

Our own Mogwa soldiers, however, surged forward to meet this threat, and it became a battle between two sets of mini-tanks. Even with the help of the countless skunks and the stolen weapons they'd taken from Legion Varus men, the skunk rebels were overwhelmed. They simply hadn't had the training. Their ferocity and rage were not enough to carry them through. We killed them until they broke, and they melted away into the streets around us.

"Sound off!" I shouted. A dozen voices answered. Six more groaned in pain. About half my command had been lost.

Cursing up a blue streak, I turned and walked to the floater we'd been protecting this entire time. There, I found Sateekas with folded-up legs. Those legs enclosed a smaller body beneath him. The old Mogwa was dead, but he had protected his son, who was relatively uninjured beneath him.

Nero shoved his father's body aside, looking at it briefly. "This is strange," he said. "I've never seen my father in the repose of death."

"I'm sorry about that, kid," I said.

The Mogwa youth left his father behind, clattered across the platform on six churning foot-hands. He experimentally fooled with the piloting tether. "This vehicle is disabled. We must abandon it."

"Yep... looks that way."

Nero peered up at me. "How am I to be transported, McGill-creature?"

"Well... I guess you could walk. It's not that far, probably just about a kilometer or so."

The Mogwa brat blasted out a spray of nasty, sticky stuff. I think it was from his nostril—at least, I hoped it was.

"An absurd suggestion," he said. "Now that my father is gone, I am in charge. You will obey me, human."

I sighed and strongly considered giving the kid what he so richly deserved at that moment. But I contained myself.

"What do you suggest, mighty and worthy son of Sateekas?"

"I will climb upon your back. You will bear me as might any beast of burden. I recommend you do this quickly, as the rebels seem to be gathering a new force ahead."

He pointed with one skinny foot-arm, and I followed that gesture. It was true—up ahead of us was another swarm of skunks. The crowd was nowhere near as large as the one we'd just broken through, but...

"All right," I said. "Troops, I want two ranks in front of me, two ranks behind. If you can't walk, let me know. I'll shoot you now."

This got several injured men to their feet. They staggered in our wake.

The Mogwa kid, Nero, was agile enough despite his age and breeding. He leapt onto my back and rode there. It was kind of like having a monkey cling to your pack.

I set off at a jog. Seeing us coming at them aggressively, the skunk crowd melted away again before we even reached them. I got the feeling they'd had enough. One slaughter was more than sufficient to convince them today. I was happy about that.

We broke through and kept on jogging all the way back to the courtyard at the end of the street. There, when the great gates opened, we were not met with cries of happiness and joy from the Mogwa garrison. Far from it.

A surprised Mogwa captain backed up a step. "Master?" he said to Nero. "Where is our Lord?"

"Sateekas has fallen," Nero told him. "Until he has been revived, I'm in charge. You will obey my every whim."

The Mogwa captain looked very unhappy to hear this. He squirmed around a little bit, but he didn't speak. I could tell he was processing this statement from Nero.

"Did you not hear me, Captain?" the punk asked. "Must I have you dragged from that tank and flogged to death for impudence?"

"This is a most unusual situation," the captain complained. "Your father will be revived shortly, but I will acquiesce to your authority with a single exception: I'm in charge of all military matters."

"I accept your conditions," Nero said. "These animals will now escort me into my chambers. I will be reunited with my mother and siblings. In this matter, I will not be denied."

I could tell the captain wanted to execute all of the humans on the spot for having failed to guard Sateekas. He snarled and groused. His mini-tank squealed as he marched around in a circle, causing the spiny legs to scratch the flagstones. Sparks showered up underneath the chassis.

"Very well," he said at last.

I was impressed. Nero had successfully intervened on our behalf. Had he done this out of a sense of loyalty and justice? No, I doubted that. He'd probably made this choice for his own personal benefit. He liked having a squad of humans under his command, a personal guard of his own. Whatever the case, we were allowed to accompany Nero back to the private quarters of the ruling family.

There, we met up with a very angry Lady Nox. She scolded us and her son. She demanded to know who had made the grievous error that had caused this disaster to occur.

Nero was a punk, a teenager with big ideas. He was the kind of guy who liked to write checks his little body couldn't cash, as we like to say down in Georgia. But in this instance, he did a good job of concisely describing the sequence of events that had led to this disaster.

Lady Nox sighed, her shoulders slumping. "Such a fool..." she said, and I knew she meant Sateekas himself. "You have done well, son."

She gave him a pat, which he half-dodged. He was like any kid his age. He didn't want the touch of a clinging mother when adulthood was right around the corner.

Lady Nox turned around and glared at me. "By all rights, I should have you tortured to death, McGill—then tortured and executed again after you are revived. This process would normally repeat to deliver the full three rounds of punishment you so richly deserve!"

"Uh..."

"But I will do none of these things. Not today. You should all pray that when Sateekas returns, he is as considerate and generous as I am." With that, she slammed her double doors in our faces.

My men all cast sour glances at one another. There were a few whispered threats, which I quelled quickly, waving for silence. "Sure, Lady Nox is an ungrateful witch, but she's in an emotional state, boys. No mother is reasonable when her kids are threatened."

"We deserved better than that shit," Carlos complained.

"Babies! I'm surrounded by overgrown babies who got their feelings hurt. It's not our place to demand praise or even the slightest hint of justice!"

"And we sure didn't get any," grumbled another man.

I thought about cuffing him one, but I passed.

"Quit whining and suck it up," I told them. "Now, let's go see if these hoity-toity Mogwa have any food worth eating downstairs."

## -26-

We didn't find much to eat at the Mogwa stronghold. They had food, sure, but it was pretty much garbage from the human point of view.

These guys like to eat mollusks—flying mollusks. If you want to know what a mollusk is, think of a snail. That's a mollusk.

Now, think of one that flaps around with some wet, mucus-layered wings. Not too enticing, huh?

Me and my men were pretty disappointed until we ran into a Nairb. What was strange was the fact I knew this Nairb. I knew him well.

"Seven?" I said, incredulous. "What the hell are you doing all the way out here at Nebra?"

The green seal-like being shrugged at me. He had developed quite a few human habits during his long years of service on Earth.

"I thought you worked for us?" I said.

"I do, human," he said, "but I'm a freelancer. What's more, the Nairb people live in the mid-zone. This is my home territory."

"Huh…" I said, thinking that over. "You got a planet near here then?"

"No," he said, "I would not call it nearby. My homeworld is many thousands of light-years away—but I suppose it is close in relative terms."

"Okay, good enough then. So, you're visiting your home stars. That's what this is all about?" I was suspicious. Why would a Nairb be here on Nebra unless he was either representing Earth or the local Mogwa? As he'd admitted, he was several thousand light-years from his own home, so it didn't make too much sense to me that he was here just visiting a sick friend.

The Nairb squirmed a bit. "First, I must ask you what you're doing here?"

I answered at length, explaining how we'd been the personal guard of Sateekas, and we had somewhat failed him as he had died during the procession. A number of our own troops had died as well, and while we were waiting for everybody to come out of the local revival machines, I decided to see if I could find something to eat and drink.

This, for the very first time, perked up the Nairb. "A drink?" he said. "You are searching for a drink?"

"I always am," I admitted, laughing. I remember then that this particular Nairb, of all the ones that I've met, had a real taste for alcohol.

"But I'm afraid," I said, "I haven't found much here in the kitchens. I don't think the Mogwa drink alcohol at all."

"No," the Nairb said, "they certainly do not. It's a shame. But… possibly, I could be of assistance in your quest."

"Uh…" I said, "what are we talking about, again?"

"Alcohol, of course."

I stared at him, and he stared back at me. "Are you saying you've got some alcohol, you old devil?"

"I might have a bottle or two," he admitted.

"Whoa! All right, then. Come on, share it up with an old friend!"

He humped away and came back a minute or two later with a big floppy container. I was disappointed immediately, as it appeared to be one of the flaccid plastic containers that they normally use for water among the Imperium.

"It doesn't look like much," I said.

"Taste it before you make any rash judgments," Seven said.

"Alrighty."

I produced a cup, which was really part of my basic mess-kit, and he poured me a dollop. I touched it with my tongue, winced, and then threw it down.

"It put some fire in my belly, I'll tell you that," I said. "Not a lot of flavor… but pretty powerful. How about you pour a glass or two for all my boys, here?"

The Nairb looked around at my surviving troops. They were large and numerous.

"That would be costly," he said.

"Ah," I said, "you don't have that big a supply, huh? I understand. When a man's low on hooch, his generosity fails him every time. But hey, how about I pay you a bit for it?"

The Nairb perked up. "An excellent suggestion."

He came up with a charge, and what's more, it was in Imperial credits. That only made sense as Earth money certainly wasn't much good out here in the Mid-Zone. It was expensive, but I paid up.

The Nairb humped away again and came back with more of the sloshy bags of alcohol. We poured them out to my troops. Each man grimaced and winced and squinted as he slurped it down. Pretty soon, everybody was in an elevated mood.

"Is my product acceptable?" Seven asked.

"It sure as hell is. Where'd you come by all this stuff?"

"I made it."

"Ohhh…"

All of a sudden, my brain was clicking. We'd given this Nairb the formula for alcohol distillation. When I say we, well, Primus Collins and I had both been there, mind you. But I'd really been the one who'd transferred the files to him with my tapper.

"I'm kind of surprised you're not sloshed yourself right now," I said to Seven.

"I make an effort not to consume when I'm working."

"So… you're working right now?"

He made a gesture with his flipper, rolling it over so I could see the underside of it—which was grayish-green and kind of nasty-looking. "I've just made three sales, haven't I?"

I laughed. "You sure did, didn't you, you old sly-boots? Okay, so you've got a little side-hustle going. You're making booze and selling it. Who are your main customers? The Mogwa?"

"No," he said. "They have no taste for this fine spirit. Other Nairbs, however, are quite easily seduced by this substance from Earth."

I laughed. I offered him a free drink out of one of my own bottles, which he accepted. Pretty soon, everybody in the room was laughing and happy.

Seven and I were reminiscing about old times when another individual showed up. Before he appeared, however, I heard a warning beep on my tapper. I checked it and noticed with a frown that it was the one I'd had Natasha create for me.

My mind was fuzzy, but I recalled that I'd had her set up a tracker on Raash. Apparently, she'd had the forethought to set the tracker up to give me a warning beep if Raash was quite close.

Well, all of a sudden, he was.

Raash was someone I'd been hoping not to see again today—or maybe not ever. He came rasping in, dragging a long, scaly tail. He spotted me and immediately made a beeline toward my position among the partying men and the single Nairb.

"Raash?" I said. "Hey, look! It's the original party-crasher!"

"I am driving no vehicle," he said. "Therefore, crashing is impossible. Besides which, this is not a party."

"I disagree. Have you ever tried alcohol, Raash?"

"I have. It is disgusting, and it injures my intestines."

I thought that over, and I squinted. Raash was already a pretty stinky guy. When he dropped a deuce, it chased all the secretaries right out of the henhouse, if you know what I mean. Therefore, if he said it upset his intestines, I wanted nothing to do with it.

"Okay, then," I said. "No booze for Raash, everybody!"

"Why do you celebrate?" he asked me.

I told him briefly about the tour-de-force we'd performed today in the Nebran town. He seemed unimpressed.

"You have described abject failure—even humiliation. A criminally negligent series of blunders that are worthy of military punishment for the commander."

"I bet that's happening right now," I said. I described the garrison commander, who had been revived by this time. "That's the poor bastard who was in charge of this disastrous operation."

Raash hissed. He stepped from side-to-side on his clawed, scratchy feet. He made bad smells and sounds. He seemed frustrated.

"The garrison commander was not the only one at fault," he said at last. "You took over at his termination. At that point, you became responsible for—"

"Come on, Raash," I said, trying to get him to loosen up. This lizard was a one-track reptile most of the time.

I thought about making a joke about his tail but passed on the idea. He wouldn't know a joke if it came up and slapped him in the snout. Jokes usually made him angry, and he was already in a foul mood.

"You tell me your story now," I said. "Why have you been following me around from planet to planet?"

"I have a very specific purpose," he said. "And this one here," he flicked a long finger with a hooked claw on the end of it toward Seven, "this one is not worthy of hearing my words."

"Good enough," Seven said, taking his flaccid alcohol bags and humping away with them. I had the feeling he was going to get a few more and try to sell them to my men now that they were drunk. He was like a drug dealer who knew he was in a target-rich environment.

My attention returned to Raash, who was studying me intently.

"You have done nothing but attempt to evade me since Earth," he said.

"That's right, buddy," I told him. "You've been following me around like a chimp trying to hug onto his mama."

"I am no primate! Your statements are inaccurate as well as insulting."

"Yeah, yeah. Come on, Raash, you haven't told me the truth yet. Why the hell are you after me?"

He stomped around and made some hissy, stinky sounds for a bit. It was like he was thinking hard. I wondered if I was going to see a little bit of lizard brain dribble out of his near-invisible ear holes.

Finally, he turned back to me. "I will tell you. I know that your legion has sided with the Mogwa in this conflict."

"Yep. We got hired by them, if that's what you mean."

"That was a mistake," he said. "This contract should never have been signed. It should never have been allowed!"

I laughed. "Who the hell's going to get in the way of something like our contract?"

"I think you know who."

I stared at him. He stared back at me for a minute.

The alcohol was kind of slowing my brain down, and that was a big deal when you started with a pretty slow brain to begin with. But then, I caught on. "You mean Alexander Turov?"

"The same," he said.

"Ah… so you're still working for old Alex. Okay. What's he want out of all this?"

"He does not want this planet to be conquered and acquiescent to the Segin Mogwa."

"Why the hell not?"

"Because that will elevate the status of their planet to that of a minor kingdom."

I squinted, thinking over his words. I remembered learning about the many levels of civilizations back in grade school. I recalled that a Tier One civilization was a species that was at least capable of space flight—but only possessed a single planet.

Normally, for any frontier worlds, that was as high as you could go. Earth had been grandfathered in because we'd already had a second colony before the Mogwa had annexed Earth. That meant that we'd achieved a level two civilization status prior to their arrival.

Since then, we'd progressed to Tier Three, having taken as possessions quite a number of planets. This was only possible, of course, due to a temporary permission granted us by the Core Worlds.

The Empire was in decline. There was a lot of civil war and strife in the core of the galaxy, and they needed strong, supportive vassal states like Earth out on the frontier for the purpose of keeping order.

Old Battle Fleet 921 never came out to our province anymore. As far as I knew, it had been completely destroyed long ago. Earth had taken over the fleet's role as local enforcers for the Galactics.

I thought about all this, even though it made the nice, happy fog in my mind begin to be a problem instead of a bonus. I was having to fight against the alcohol in order to think clearly.

Dammit, what the hell had Seven put in this stuff? It had quite a kick. I suspected he'd distilled a damn near pure level of alcohol. Next time I had a drink, I was going to have to make sure I had a big fruity mixer of some kind.

I looked around the room, noting that many of my men were already sawing wood. They were flopped out on chairs—even tables. At least they were enjoying themselves.

"Okay," I said, "so old Alexander doesn't want the Mogwa from the Mid-Zone to expand to an even larger civilizational state. I guess I can sort of understand that. I don't know why he cares, but at least it makes some kind of sense. What do you want me to do about it?"

"Aaah," Raash said, making a sound that was somewhere between a satisfied sigh and a hiss of pleasure. He stepped forward, and his claws flickered up in front of my eyes. Due to my inebriated state, I didn't flinch away but simply stared back at him.

"And now we come to the true reason for my visit with you today. McGill, I wish you to accompany me. I wish you to meet an individual of great importance here on this planet."

"Uh…" I said.

I looked around the place again. There were no girls worth hitting on, and my men had only just begun to come back from the revival machines. Seven had disappeared after dispensing his three bottles of heavenly liquid. There'd been no sign of Sateekas yet, either.

I smiled at Raash and his claws. I reached up a hand, and I grasped his thorny paw in mine.

"All right, buddy," I said, "you've got yourself a deal. Let's go meet this dude. I'm in the perfect mood to meet someone new."

## -27-

Raash led me out of the Mogwa compound. He didn't do this through the front gates, mind you, but rather some little side exit that was obviously meant for servants and tradesmen.

The doorway in the wall was pretty small. We both had to hunch over, almost going down on all fours to get through it.

Once we were through the wall and out in the streets again, I got to admire the Nebran town in a state that I'd never seen it in before. Instead of looking war-torn, or full of angry crowds, it was a straightforward place of commerce.

Skunks walked in singles and pairs along both sides of the road, which was kind of narrow but wide enough for a human to move along without causing undue disruption.

Raash had me leave my armor and weapons behind. Naturally, I'd kept my combat knife and a pistol, but gone were all the chrome plates and the heavy morph-rifle full of explosive pellets.

Still, the Nebrans didn't look happy to see us. I got the feeling they recognized me as I passed. They curled their lips, flashed white sharp teeth, and skirted away. Usually, they ducked into side passages or doorways—anywhere they could take refuge from the big bad man from Earth.

I felt a little bad about that, but I supposed I was going to have to get used to it. After all, I could hardly expect to be greeted with joyful cries and open arms after I'd slaughtered hundreds of them just today.

The skunks didn't seem to like the looks of Raash, either. He had to be even stranger in appearance and mannerisms than I was. Hell, he wasn't even a mammal.

"Right this way, McGill," Raash said. "I'm surprised you were so easily convinced to accompany me. I would have thought you lacked the tail for such an outing."

"Yeah, well," I said, "after you've seen one occupied planet, you've pretty much seen them all."

"Your comments are nonsensical," Raash said. "I'm beginning to doubt my wisdom in bringing an inebriated ape with me to meet an important personage."

"Don't worry, Raash, old buddy," I said. "I can hold my liquor."

I was, in fact, swaying a bit as I walked. Not exactly stumbling and staggering, mind you, but I was definitely feeling it. Seven's white lightning concoction had hit me squarely between the eyes.

Reaching for my canteen, I upended it and guzzled some water every now and then. I was hoping to clear out my guts with some good, sweet, non-toxic liquids.

"Are you feeling weakness in this heat, human?" Raash asked. "It is not the same for me. I am relishing this warmth. Most planets I serve upon are icy-cold, numbing to my body—including Earth."

"Is that so?" I said. "Oh yeah… you're from Steel World. That's a fricking inferno."

"It is warmth personified. Our young quicken in their eggs without being squatted upon or buried."

He sounded like he was proud of this tidbit about his home planet, so I decided to let him have it. "That's great, Raash. But… uh… where the hell are you taking me?"

"Our destination is unique, and it is near. The Nebran leadership wishes to stay near the Mogwa fortress. They wish to track every action taken by their oppressors."

I squinted, thinking that over. "Who the hell would want to track the Mogwa?" My mind was fuzzy, but it was clearing a bit. Maybe it was the water that had flushed my innards clean. I felt the urge to piss, so I wet down a squatty doorstep. A skunk hissed at me. I waved my apologies over my shoulder.

"You pass waste to insult the natives?" Raash asked. "An interesting stratagem."

"Well, no, I just had to go, see. But… wait a second." My mind was clearing. Something Raash had said stuck out in my dim bulb of a brain… "Are we going to go talk to some skunks?"

"Skunks?" he said. "Stripe-furred animals from Earth? No, there are no such beasts here. In fact, I would hazard to say that you're the only uncivilized animal capable of producing a great stench in this city."

"You got the right of that," I said. "But I'm talking about the Nebrans."

"Of course, we're going to see the Nebrans," he said. "Who else did you imagine might want to meet with you and I? Who else might you imagine is even here on this planet?"

I thought about that, and I realized that I'd been a fool. Of course, Raash was taking me to talk to some skunks. We were in the middle of Skunk City.

Then I took a deep breath. The entire situation seemed clearer to me, and I stopped walking. Raash took one more step, his reflexes being a bit slower than mine, then he halted and swung around. His tail lifted high, pointing up in the air. This was a questioning pose for any Saurian.

"Do you fear?" he asked. "I'm surprised by this and ashamed to be in your company."

"I'm not afraid, you damned lizard. I just don't know if I should be talking to someone who's a clear enemy of the Mogwa and Earth."

"Fear," he said. "Yes, fear. You shame me. I will turn now. I will walk down this street to disassociate myself with your tainted presence. Our destination is not far, should you dare to follow me. If you do not, it is because you are an abject coward."

"Hold on a minute!"

"No!" he said, jabbing one of his claws in my direction. Raash was always the kind of guy who got angry fast over the strangest things. "If your guts are too filled with terror to speak with a few of the local natives, then I have misjudged you. In fact, I do not want your company. Shame is like a disease that infects the proud. I'm done with you."

He spun back around and began trudging away. I looked after him, frowning.

This was an unusual situation. As I watched Raash stomp away, I grew just a bit ornery in my heart. After all, I'd had a damnably long day. I'd suffered countless skunks, both during the patrol and walking by right now. Every one of them sneered at me. At least they were giving me a wide berth now.

Raash was the one who was really pissing me off. He'd gone and taken a squat on my pride.

Was I about to talk to the enemy? Well, I'd done worse. My mind argued that just meeting with some skunks wasn't exactly an act of treachery.

Picking up my heels, I marched after Raash. I caught up after another dozen steps, and he grunted. He didn't even seem surprised I'd followed him.

He led me into a side road, one of those dark tunnel-like alleys in between the buildings. Suddenly, he stopped, bent over, and grabbed hold of a large urn. His muscles bulged. I could tell it was heavy, probably full of sloshing oil or some other liquid. He shunted the large urn aside.

Behind it, I saw a hole.

"Oh, jeez," I said. "Don't tell me I've gotta crawl into that thing?"

"This is the only entrance," Raash said. "Do not despair. It is much larger on the inside."

"Yeah, well, you first."

Raash hissed and complained a bit, but he finally squatted down and crawled inside the hole. Saurians were tunnelers back on Steel World, so I guess for him it wasn't that bad of a deal.

I followed him, feeling far less comfortable in the enclosed space. But as he'd promised, once we'd gone through a short distance of broken adobe bricks and powdery dirt, we were able to stand up again.

I turned on my suit lights, and there was a hell of a lot of hissing to be had when I did so.

"Douse that light!" came a high-pitched voice from out of the dark.

I reached up and twiddled down the gain on my chest light. It dimmed down to a wan glow instead of a searchlight's beam.

That's when I spotted the speaker. He was one of the skunks, of course, and he sat upon a throne of sorts. The throne was built of bones, as far as I could tell—big bones.

I pointed a finger, smiled, and took a step forward. Numerous skunks all around the chamber scrambled. My movement was taken as a sign of aggression. I didn't care. I was too swept away with the recognition of what that skunk was squatting upon to worry about all these little guys pissing themselves.

"That's a bone throne!" I said. "Those are dinosaur bones, aren't they?"

The skunk squatting on the throne blinked at me, squinting his eyes. He looked like he wanted to chew my finger off.

"Dinosaurs...?" he said. His translator box was obviously doing a bit of searching, "large reptilian creatures... Yes, you are accurate. This throne was built with the bones of reptiles from the jungle. It is an heirloom passed down to me through generations. The founders of this great city had to conquer it to take it from the forest dwellers who owned this place before us."

The voice this skunk dude had was kind of different. It was a bit higher-pitched, as you would expect from a smaller creature, but still definitely masculine. It was also a bit raspy.

"This throne is a relic," the skunk explained, but I was barely listening already. "It is an heirloom for us and my birthright."

"Birthright, huh?" I said. "So, what? Are you, like, the prince of skunks or something?"

"I am no prince. I'm no spoiled offspring of a royal family. No, I am an elder. I am the sovereign. I am the Nebran king."

"Oh..." I said, slightly impressed. Deciding to kiss his fuzzy little ass, I swept off my beret with a dramatic flourish. I held it at my waist, and I bowed deeply.

"It's a real honor to meet you, King," I told him. "What's your name, Sire?"

"Vorhoos," he said.

"Of course... King Vorhoos. You made my day just agreeing to see me."

The skunks all glanced at each other. They appeared somewhat surprised and wary.

Surreptitiously, as I did my little bow maneuver, I lifted my arm and checked my tapper. Yep, I had a signal, despite being buried inside of a brick building and in somebody's basement. That made me smile.

I wasn't all that far from the Mogwa stronghold. I'd catch a revive for sure. That meant that if I wanted to go out in a blaze of glory, well, this was a good place to do it.

I considered knifing skunks until I died in a puddle of my own blood with my throat torn out. I'd kind of already figured out I was a dead man. I was even wishing I'd brought along a plasma grenade to take the whole pack of these bastards with me.

But the skunks didn't attack. They didn't swarm me. They clearly didn't like me, but they kept their distance and stayed polite.

"Raash has arranged this meeting," King Vorhoos said, "because he believes you are a uniquely reasonable human, and he tells us you lead the human forces here in the city."

I glanced over at Raash in surprise. He gave me that stony-eyed reptilian stare in return. There was no expression on his face that I could read.

Trying to figure out what a lizard's thinking by looking at him is damn-near impossible. Unless he's angry, hissing and ready to strike, I doubt any human could figure out if one of his kind were ready to kiss you or dance the hokey-pokey.

Getting no help there, I turned back to Vorhoos. "Uh..." I said, "what exactly have you got in mind, King?"

"Human, we offer you a cessation of hostilities. No more tricks. No more humans will die in the night. Your people have suffered great losses, and ours have suffered today as well. This is an unnecessary state of affairs."

"We have our mission to perform," I said. "It's nothing personal."

"It's very personal. Hundreds have died on both sides already. You should not serve the Mogwa. We are subjugated by them, just as you are. We should be brothers, not enemies."

"Well, now, that's sort of true," I admitted.

"No, it is precisely true," Vorhoos continued. "The Mogwa are playing us both for fools. You are a slave race, and they wish to make us the same. We see you humans as victims of these most vile Galactics. We offer you an alliance."

I laughed, which wasn't met well by the skunk-boys. They did a lot of hissing and slinking around. Many of them ruffled their hair, fluffing up like birds on a wire. I could tell they weren't happy with my laughter.

"What amuses you so, human?" demanded the king.

"Well, I'm just finding it kind of funny that you aliens figure we're all in the same boat. Because we're not—not really. You see, for one thing, we earthlings haven't lost a single man since we landed on this planet—at least not permanently."

"What? What's this? What are you talking about? We have seen your blood. We have seen you die. In fact, you were the commander of the marching group that went through our city streets, humiliating us just today. We counted no less than twenty-nine of your kind dead in our streets. Those are bucks that will not go home to their families!"

"Well now, hold on just a minute," I said, raising a finger.

"McGill," Raash said suddenly. "You should speak no further."

"Huh? Why not?"

"Do not be foolish," Raash said. "Simply listen to the king and make your decision about how you might proceed."

"Well… all right, I'll hear him out," I said. "What exactly do you want to do? How do you want to make this work for us?"

"It's simple. Your legion and our masses together greatly outnumber the Mogwa on this planet. We wish for you to exterminate them. You're in a much better place to do this than we are, as you are trusted soldiers in their midst. Throw off your slave collars and slaughter this enemy that we both share!

In turn, we will kill no more humans. We'll do whatever we can to aid you to return to your home planet."

I shook my head sadly. "That's not really gonna work, see?"

I tried then to explain a bit about how the whole galactic system operated, and how Earth was a vassal of the Mogwa. We served them in more ways than one.

The skunk-king was hissing inconsolably. He argued with me for a time, but then finally came back to one important point. "Earlier, you stated that none of you had died. Please explain that, human."

"That is enough," Raash said suddenly. "I call this meeting at an end." He stood up, his tail lifted high. A couple of nearby skunks skittered away. "We will be taking our leave now, great king."

King Vorhoos made a guttural noise. All of a sudden, there were a heck of a lot of skunks around us with weaponry in their hands.

They had blades and several of them had morph-rifles. This kind of surprised me, but I guess it shouldn't have. It took a team—kind of like several men running a machine gun nest—to handle one of our morph-rifles, but they managed it.

Since I was unarmed and unarmored, I was concerned. I put my hands up high. "Hey, hey! Settle down, little guys. This is supposed to be a parlay."

"It is, and you are free to return to your homes, but first you must answer me one question, human."

"Okay, go ahead. Shoot."

"Shoot? You yearn for an immediate death?"

"No, no, that's just an expression. I mean, go ahead and tell me what the heck you're talking about."

"You said that none of your people had died. Answer me, why?"

Before Raash could start squawking about it again, telling me to shut up, I went ahead and blurted it out. "Because we have revival machines. Don't you guys know about that? A lot of our men died today, but they'll all be printed out again. They'll be fresh and new and marching around tomorrow. That puts us on a different footing than you skunks. When one of you dies, you stay dead."

The king did not take this well. Neither did his numerous subjects.

They rattled at each other in their own language for a time, but my translator didn't have an application to convert their words to mine.

Raash, in the meantime, had laid a hand on my elbow and was beginning to tug me back toward the entrance. He seemed to want us to crawl out through the adobe wall again.

"You are a huge fool, human," he said. "A monstrous fool of unlikely proportions."

Vorhoos called to us as we attempted to retreat. We turned back to look at him.

"You have forfeited your lives," the skunk said. "Possibly, you two will be printed again. But you will not freely kill our people without suffering at least the pain and anguish of one death!"

"Wait!" Raash said. "You are breaking our agreement. We were to be given safe passage. We came to parley a deal. You cannot simply execute us!"

"We're not," Vorhoos said. "Just as your pet human has said, your deaths aren't permanent. They are mere inconveniences to you. On the other hand, it will provide us with great pleasure to watch you die."

And then the morph-rifles began to flash and rip the air with fire.

Fortunately, being gunned down at point-blank range by automatic weapons was a quick process. I'd experienced the sensation before.

I went down first, then Raash toppled on top of me. With my last gasping effort, I reached an arm across his body to touch my wrist to his.

There was a single tingling shake. It was done. I'd scanned the dead lizard's tapper.

With any luck, both of our deaths would be recorded at the Mogwa stronghold, and we would live again.

## -28-

When I eventually reawakened, my first sensation was of… *heat*. I was in a hot place—a hot, sticky place. That was a bad sign.

"Urgh," I groaned.

Was I back at my legion camp? That was my first impression. Perhaps they hadn't moved the revival machines to Blue Bunker yet. Could they still be reviving people in tents?

The next thing I expected to experience was a bug bite—but that didn't happen. Instead, I heard odd clicking and warbling noises. My hazy mind tried to recollect what language and what species generated those strange sounds…

After a bit, I had it. The Mogwa sounded like that.

My eyes snapped open, but they squinched back closed again due to the glaring brightness of the room.

"Ah, he is awake," a translated voice said.

I tried to peek toward the sound, but when your eyes are freshly regrown and blurry, one Mogwa looks very much like another. And that's who was reviving me—two Mogwa.

"McGill?" the first individual said. "I am the garrison commander. We have questions."

I mumbled something incoherent in response.

After that, I was fussed over, prodded and poked. The Mogwa took tests, they quoted numbers—but I was essentially unresponsive.

This was always my first line of defense when I was revived in a potentially hostile situation. I liked to play possum in these situations, and I was pretty good at it by now.

In the meantime, my mind was knitting back together. It made sense to me—now that I thought about it—that I was being revived by the Mogwa. There were no soft, human touches. Nothing like the sweet caress of Dawn's hands.

No, I was getting the raspy, foot-hand prodding of an unforgiving race. I'd died quite close to the Mogwa headquarters, and I was now officially assigned to Sateekas' personal guard. It only made sense they'd revive me in their own fortress, rather than bringing me back at the human encampment.

What had the garrison commander said? Something about having questions? That wasn't good.

Eventually, as I continued to play for time, they decided to bring in an expert. This so-called master-class individual was none other than the bio-specialist known as Carlos.

"That's him, all right," he said. "I'd recognize that big, tall lump of stupid anywhere."

"He is remarkably unresponsive," the garrison commander said. "We're at a loss to understand his status. Have we made an error of some kind in his duplication?"

Carlos prodded at me now as well. He took various measurements and tests. He knew me well, and there was no way he didn't know I was faking—but he went with it anyway.

"Nah," he said. "He's a good grow. He just needs a little extra time to recover. I'll tell you what, I'll take him off your hands. Let me give him some of our special human revivification brew, and I'll have him up and hopping within thirty minutes."

"Thirty minutes?" the garrison commander echoed disappointedly. "That seems like an absurdly long recovery time."

"Okay, then. He's all yours. You can figure out how to fix him."

The two Mogwas made some blatting noises, talking it over. At last, the bio Mogwa spoke.

"No," she said. "He's already been stinking up the place for long enough. He smells of digestive fluids and flatulence."

"Yep, that's McGill for you."

"Take him with you," the female ordered Carlos.

The garrison commander wasn't happy. I'd hoped to slip away and be forgotten—but it wasn't to be. "He is to report to my office within thirty minutes," he said. "Or I will send troops to fetch him no matter what state he's in."

"Okay, you've got it," Carlos assured the irritable aliens. "Thirty minutes, or I'll eat my air hose."

"That would be both unnecessary and destructive. You two are miserable servants."

"Oh no! Anything but that! Say it's not so, Commander!"

"It is so," the Mogwa said stiffly. "You're dismissed."

Carlos sniveled, pretending like he cared what the Mogwa thought about anything, and he helped me up off the gurney. I made a big show of needing lots of extra support, throwing an arm around his shoulder. I leaned on him so heavily that he grunted.

Fortunately, Carlos was a sturdy man, even if he wasn't all that tall. He threw his shoulder into my armpit and helped me stagger out of the place. As soon as we were out of the passageway, I whispered to him. "Are we clear?"

Carlos swiveled his head this way and that. "Yeah, get off me, you big lump."

I straightened up and walked upright.

He threw a uniform at me, which I pulled on over my sticky skin.

"Why are you faking so hard?" he asked me.

"Well, they said they had *questions*…"

"Whoa," Carlos said, "questions? A Mogwa with questions? That's a bad thing for old McGill. You're always guilty of something."

"That's right."

"So, what do we do now?" Carlos asked.

"First off, we're going to scare up some of that special revival brew you were talking about."

We headed for our small commissary, which was dedicated to the palates of humans. Now that we were permanent residents here at the Mogwa fortress, we'd been provided the basics of human comforts.

Carlos' special brew turned out to be exactly what I'd expected: a half-cold squeeze bottle of beer. He pressed one into my paw, and I nursed on it.

My favorite food after a hangover or a hard death was eggs benedict, but we had nothing like that here. Instead, I got a mess of creamed meats on flatbread.

"Shit on a shingle," Carlos said. "That's what the boys are calling this stuff."

I ate the meal unhappily.

"Hey, listen," Carlos said, leaning forward. "You've only got about fifteen minutes left. What are you going to tell that Mogwa prick when you report—or are you going to report at all?"

Carlos gave me a meaningful look. He knew me very well, possibly better than anyone else in my unit. We had, in fact, joined up with Legion Varus on the very same day, having more or less tricked one another into signing with the most infamous outfit on Earth.

I thought about what he was saying. What were my options? I'd been assigned to the Mogwa leadership as a personal guardsman, and I'd fought to get this assignment. That meant I couldn't very well call up Winslade and ask for a new post. He would scoff at me and tell me to suck it up.

Heaving a deep breath, I drank the rest of my lukewarm beer and stood up. "I'm going to march back up there and bluff this through."

"That's my boy," Carlos said. "Don't you let a single word of truthfulness exit that face of yours. It'd burn your lips."

I exited the tiny mess hall, feeling ready for anything. Adjusting my uniform and marching straight, I arrived at the office of the garrison commander.

To my surprise, the prick of an alien didn't even interview me personally. Instead, he walked me down the hallway to a set of double doors where I'd recently escorted Lady Nox and her family.

I frowned at the closed doors. Then I frowned at the garrison commander as he politely chimed on the doorbell.

"Uh…" I said, "hey, Mr. Commander, sir? I was kind of thinking you were going to talk to me—or maybe Sateekas himself would."

The Mogwa looked at me for a moment. Then he looked down, and back up again. It was a rare moment of indecision for his kind. "Sateekas has not yet been revived."

"What?" I squawked in surprise.

Then, the door opened. It was yanked wide, and inside I saw Lady Nox.

The kids weren't there. Not even the little pouchling, the youngest, was present. Apparently, she'd stashed all her offspring somewhere else.

Lady Nox's pouch hung flaccid in front of her belly. It was an unsightly thing to look at, so I tried not to stare.

"Come in, McGill," she said.

I walked inside, and she caused the doors to close silently behind me. She moved to a pair of thrones in the back of the large chamber. She squatted on the smaller, but more ornate, of the two.

"Is that other chair over there for Sateekas?" I asked.

"It is indeed. You are most discerning."

"Not really," I said, "but one thing I did notice is that Sateekas isn't sitting on it."

Nox stared at me for a moment. "No, he's not."

I squinched up my eyes, and I thought about this for a moment. I shook my head. "You know, the only person I can think of who could delay the revival process for Sateekas would be you, Lady Nox. Tell me that's not so."

She didn't say anything. She just stared at me for a moment. Finally, she let loose one of those long, low, blatting noises. I held my breath in case there was a foul gust to follow.

"I don't know what to do with you," she said. "I've reviewed all the videos of today's action. You fought hard. You did your best to save my foolish husband and my young son. In fact, you returned with my Nero still alive."

"That's right. He was riding on my back like a happy monkey."

"An offensive statement, but forgivable in this instance. Anyway, Nero is now displaying an odd attachment to you, McGill."

"He is, huh? That's cool!"

"No, it isn't."

I laughed. "He's probably just feeling affection for his protector. It's a natural thing."

Nox mulled that over. "I suppose I might be willing to classify you as a large, loyal house pet. An animal guardian of sorts."

"Do you have guard dogs on Trantor? Or anything like that?"

"No, but we are familiar with the concept. In my son's mind, I think you've taken on that role. It's upsetting."

"So, why is Sateekas still dead?" I dared to ask again.

She glared at me. "Let's set that aside for the moment, McGill."

"Okay." To my mind, if Nox wanted to keep her husband dead for a while, that was her business. Maybe she wanted to punish him for doing something so shit-off stupid it nearly got her son killed. A long-standing rule of mine was not to get involved in domestic situations.

"I've been reviewing more videos," she said, "not just of today's tour-de-force."

"How's that, ma'am?"

She made a flicking motion over her tapper. One of the screens between the two of us lit up. A holographic, three-dimensional representation took shape between us. I recognized the scene. It was the dark, dingy pit where I'd met the skunk king squatting on his throne.

"Whoa, look at that!" I said. "It's almost like it's real. How'd you know I dreamed about that same place just two nights ago?"

"You're spouting nonsense," Lady Nox said. "Tappers do not record dreams."

I laughed. "Well, ma'am, maybe not Galactic-made tappers... You see, human-made tappers, well, they've got a few nits and lice, if you know what I mean. They're buggy."

She squinted at me, looked through the files, and then squinted at me again.

"I don't believe you," she said. "This is a depiction of recent reality. Who is that Nebran you're talking to? What rebel dares squat upon a throne?"

"Uh…" I said, realizing that my entire scam about it having been a dream wasn't working, "I don't rightly know, I said, "he never gave me a name or nothing—not even when I was dreaming about him."

Lady Nox made a very unladylike noise, but I kept on bullshitting like I didn't notice.

"Sometimes, you know, when you meet up with a skunk in your mind, your subconscious makes up a name for him. But not this time. I guess my old dream-factory wasn't up to the task."

"McGill, stop with your ham-handed obfuscation. This is serious business. This entire military operation is at risk."

"How so?"

"Are you aware of our political status back at Segin?"

"Uh…" I said, thinking about it, "aren't you the king and queen of that planet?"

"No," she said, "we're not monarchs. It's disgusting, but we are democratically elected representatives."

"But… you sort of act like monarchs…"

"Of course, anything else would be absurd. We, like all beings who've ever been elected to high office before us, desire total despotic control."

I nodded, because it did seem to me that that was the natural state of man and alien alike. When you gave a politician a little bit of power, they always wanted more—and they never wanted it to end.

"Well," I said, reaching up and giving myself a scratch, "what's the problem exactly, and what can I do about it?"

"Two very pertinent questions at last," she said. "My problem is twofold. I need to quickly achieve an annexation of this planet, number one. And number two, my husband is a fool."

"Huh…" I said, thinking that one over. She was definitely right about the second point, but I wasn't going to tell her that. "I still don't see how I fit into all this."

"The garrison commander here on Nebra is losing faith in us—in this mission. We're on the very brink of losing the required political will to continue this campaign back on Segin as well."

"Are we talking about an election or something?" I said, scratching myself again.

"Yes, you idiot. Of course, we are. These soldiers are conscripts—all of them. After the City World campaign, we managed to get the Mogwa on Segin to agree to a conscription system—but Mogwa do not like to fight their own battles."

"Oh yeah, I know all about that."

"Fear caused them to back us at first, after the invasion of their planet. We managed to build an army and a fleet. We used these forces to invade several weak, local planets. This world is the last and the most critical of them all."

"Uh… how so?"

"Our plan is to build a Tier Three civilization. But those plans are beginning to fall apart due to stiff resistance on Nebra and the spineless nature of our citizens. In short, the Segin conscripts want to go home."

"Tier Three…" I said, squinting and letting my jaw sag low. It always did that when I thought real hard… "Oh yeah, the Galactic rules on civilizational status. Having one planet is Tier One, two planets is Tier Two and what… seven gets you to Tier Three?"

"Exactly," she said. "Earth has already superseded this result. In fact, you're burgeoning on to Tier Four."

"Huh… What's the definition of a Tier Four?"

"A civilization that spills out of a single province."

"Oh! We're kind of doing that, aren't we?"

"Yes. It's highly threatening and wouldn't be allowed under normal circumstances, but the Galactics at the Core are weak. We are not unified, and our rules are going unenforced."

"Yeah… All those civil wars and everything else…" I said. I'd been hearing about the chaos in the heart of the Empire for decades. "But I still don't get it. Why does Segin need to become a Tier Three civilization?"

"Because," she said, leaning forward and lowering her voice. She sounded conspiratorial. "Trantor could then pass one of our most severe hurdles. The Mogwa people have been barred from achieving their logical apogee."

"Huh?"

She sucked in a deep breath and sighed. "I'm not sure if you are an idiot, or merely ignorant."

"I would say 'yes' to both of those, Lady," I assured her. "Maybe you could explain it kind of… slow-like."

"Very well. You know that there is no emperor on the Galactic Throne, yes? That there has not been one for a century now?"

"Yep. Yep. I've heard that."

"What you probably didn't know is that the Mogwa people have never put forward a name to rule the entire galaxy."

"Wow. Why is that exactly? You people seem plenty ambitious to me."

"We are," she said, "but one of our natural predilections has been holding us back."

"Which one is that, ma'am?"

"Every Mogwa's natural desire to live on Trantor itself."

"Oh yeah! That's right, you guys are like salmon or homing pigeons."

Lady Nox seemed disgusted again. "Such repulsive comparators. We simply adore our home world, and we've layered our great city into a single mass to support our populace."

I suppressed a shudder. Such an incredible level of overcrowding seemed abhorrent to a country boy like me. I'd been on Trantor, and it seemed like an overloaded beehive to me.

"Due to the concentration of our population," she continued, "we have few outlying territories that are inhabited by our citizens. Therefore, our technical qualifications to ascend to the Imperial Throne have always been in doubt. But, with the addition of another Tier Three civilization that's ruled over by colonist Mogwa…"

I suddenly got what she was trying to explain. Some bureaucratic bylaw had been cock-blocking the Mogwa for years. But, if Trantor could reunite with Segin and claim to be a higher-status civilization by Galactic standards… that impediment would be removed.

"But… wait a second. Are you talking about putting some Mogwa on the Throne? To rule the whole Empire? The whole frigging *galaxy*?"

"And why not? Who is more worthy than us?"

"Uh… what name would you put forward, then? I mean, yours… or Sateekas?" I was wincing already, hoping it wouldn't be Sateekas. Damn, that boy could hardly run his own household, even if his heart was in the right place some of the time.

"No. Sateekas would not be acceptable to anyone. Honestly, I wouldn't be well-received either. But there is an individual who is at the center of all of this. One who, if he was declared the rightful monarch of Segin and all of Segin's seven possessions, therefore controlling a Tier Three civilization, would be a prime candidate. Who do you think that might be?"

I squinted at her. The only person I could think of would be that skunk-king guy, Vorhoos. I didn't think the Mogwa would go for that. I shook my head. "No clue, ma'am."

"Fool," she snarled at me. "I'm talking about my son, Nero, of course!"

"Huh? You mean your kid?"

I must have said this with a scoffing tone because Lady Nox seemed to take offense. She drew herself up, becoming angry with me. She shook a raging foot-hand in my direction.

"And why not?" she demanded. "He's the very best of us. He's unsullied by the failures that plague his parents. He has the best of our genes—and none of our questionable history."

"Huh… okay," I said, realizing that I had just gotten a tiger mama to start bragging about her offspring. That was never a position anyone wanted to be in.

"Nero is the best," she insisted. "There's never been better."

"You're right about that!" I said with false enthusiasm. "But… I'm a bit confused."

"About what?"

"About why Sateekas is still dead—and how I fit into all this."

Nox shuffled her limbs around furtively for a bit, and then she began to explain.

## -29-

Lady Nox looked kind of like a big spider, and she was something of a web-spinner in real life. She'd come up with a complicated plot. It was more than a plot, actually. It was a full-blown scheme.

Sure, her plan was insane on the face of it. I didn't think for one second that Sateekas and Nox were going to get away with foisting their own kid on everyone as the next emperor.

Nero? The Emperor? Not just of the Mogwa people, mind you, but of the entire galaxy? It didn't even bear thinking about.

But she was hot on the topic. I could tell she spent most of her days plotting to get her son's nasty self onto that Throne. For my own part, I was in a state of serious admiration. Her unique mix of crazy and overreaching was astounding.

While she wove a complex tapestry of unlikely bullshit in the air, I continuously grunted "uh-huh" and appeared to listen to her, enraptured. While I consider myself to be a master of the fine art of deception, I'm not all that good at pipe-dreaming. Lady Nox put me to shame in the art of self-delusion.

She was pacing around in front of me now, ignoring the two thrones and me. I could have killed her, of course, if I'd wanted to—and she knew it, too.

But both of us knew I wasn't likely to do it. First of all, I was a pretty loyal guardsman, and secondly, she'd just catch a revive and come out hopping mad a few hours later.

The sole reason why I *did* consider murdering her, of course, was to help out Sateekas. Lady Nox was keeping him artificially dead. She had an excuse or two all lined up for that, but the real reason was she felt he'd screwed up with his public marching around and grandstanding. Just as importantly, he'd nearly gotten her son killed for his first time.

She was very protective of that boy, quite the opposite of Sateekas who was trying to give him helpful life-experience. She seemed to feel that if the kid died, he'd undergo some kind of a mental break that he wasn't prepared for.

To me, that was flat-out overprotectiveness. She was coddling her kid. Hell, if any kid learned how to die and come back early on, it could only turn out to be a strength later. At least, that's how the Legion Varus philosophy went.

"Are you even listening to me, McGill?" Lady Nox suddenly snapped. She'd stopped pacing at some point, and she was now standing in front of me, glaring up angrily.

I realized that I'd stopped listening some time ago. In fact, I no longer had any idea what the hell she was talking about.

"Absolutely, ma'am!" I said with conviction. "You just go right on ahead. I'm hanging on every detail. I'm taking notes on my tapper, in fact… uh… back behind my back."

I was, in fact, leaning back in my chair with my fingers knitted behind my head. I was bored, hopelessly bored.

"Very well, then," she said. "What's your answer?"

"Uh… to which part exactly, Lady?"

She glared some more at me. "Will you or will you not support me if the garrison commander attempts to take action against me?"

"You mean, like, if he tries to shoot you?"

She nodded seriously.

"Hell yeah, I'll stop him! I'll be right in there, blocking bullets like nobody's business. You'll think you had a dozen sandbags plus me standing in the way."

"No, no, not just that," she said, slapping a foot around in the air. "I want you to have my back *politically*."

"Meaning what exactly, ma'am?"

"If he marches in here through that door right now—"

"Uh-huh?"

"—or he demands that we withdraw our troops from Nebra—or worse yet, he demands that I hand over command of this expedition to him, I want you to execute him for treachery instantly."

"Oh…" I said. "That's not the kind of thing I was hoping to get into."

"But will you support me? You are the McGill-creature. I need your help."

I had to give the situation a hard think. If Sateekas had asked me this exact same question, I would have automatically responded in the affirmative. The problem here was, Lady Nox wasn't really in charge. Not officially. Sateekas was the military commander of this entire operation. He'd hired Legion Varus personally—hell, I'd been a witness.

Nox had usurped him, and she was obviously keeping him dead. Therefore, logically, the garrison commander had the right to be concerned. He was the next officer down in the official chain of command. That gave him every right to shunt her aside.

"Damn…" I said, shaking my head. "I don't know, ma'am. I think you should be having this conversation with Tribune Winslade. If he ordered me to back you in the manner you're describing, then of course I'd do it."

She glared at me, thinking hard. "I've got no leverage over Winslade," she said. "He's a conniving beast. He's going to want something large and expensive for such a breach of protocol. I was hoping to draw upon your sense of loyalty, combined with your near-idiocy, to secure your aid."

"Well, ma'am…" I said, "maybe what you ought to be doing is reviving Sateekas. I suggest you should have this talk with him. Explain your reasoning, and you can probably get him to do what you want."

"How? He's a most obstinate male. Even more so than you are."

"I suspect that's true. But why not use the classic tools of feminine wiles to get your way? Any human woman could persuade her mate to do practically anything."

Nox considered this thoughtfully. "What would a human woman do in this situation?"

"Well… uh…" I began ticking off things on my fingers. I described to her at length how countless women sitting behind countless thrones had badgered, hectored, seduced, cajoled, and thrown hissy-fits until they got their way.

"You see? The way I see it, you've got the upper hand in this situation because of your son's near death. He was greatly threatened, and your husband put him in that state. That's what's at the core of all this, right?"

"Yes…" she admitted.

I felt I was beginning to understand old Lady Nox. She may not look anything like a human woman, but she still had that mother-bear instinct they all did.

"Okay, then," I said, "you just got to play up that angle the way any woman would back on Earth."

"Elaborate."

"Uh… he screwed up. So, you've got to push on his buttons until he relents and gives you what you want."

She blinked at me a couple of times with her many eye-groups. "I'm not following what you're saying, here."

"Oh…" I said, "well, it's, uh, become apparent to me over many years that old Sateekas is a randy old goat."

"Randy old goat?" she said, puzzling through the idiomatic expression on her tapper. "Oh… an overzealous participant in sexual acts?"

"Yeah, that's right."

"I would have to agree with that description," she admitted.

"Well then, all you've got to do is withhold certain… favors, let's say… which you might bestow upon him in a nightly fashion. Tell him he gets no more sugar until he gives you what you want."

Nox frowned, making an odd expression. "Are you suggesting I refuse to mate with him until he does what I wish in a geopolitical sense?"

"Yeah," I said, "you've got it."

"That is highly unethical," she said, "a Mogwa female who's married to a respectable Mogwa male doesn't resort to such tactics."

"You mean you never say no to your husband?" I asked, surprised.

"Never."

"Wow! Maybe I should marry a Mogwa," I joked. "But in any case, that's what an Earth woman would do."

"How can I justify such a thing?" she pondered.

"Because of Nero," I reminded her. "You can pretend to be even more upset than you already are."

"Right... I could claim a great state of agitation. That fear and anger have overcome me. I'll pretend I'm no longer able to..." she trailed off, contemplating. "You know, McGill, this is a repugnant idea—but it might well work. No wonder you humans are so driven."

"I take it then that you're going to revive Sateekas?"

Nox heaved a sigh. "We're at such a critical juncture. If I could keep him dead just for a few more months, we could finish out this campaign. But it's such a balancing act. The garrison commander wants to pull out. He demands it every day. And what did Sateekas do today? He gave the commander yet another excuse to request that we return to Segin. It seems like there's a new setback every hour. This is why we went and hired Legion Varus, you know. Your Earth legions were to help us put these people down once and for all."

"Yeah, okay," I said, without caring one whit. "Are you going to revive Sateekas or not?"

"I might. I haven't decided yet."

I rolled my eyes. Fortunately, Lady Nox didn't seem to understand the meaning of that gesture.

"Let's talk of another matter," she said. "The creature you met with in the city is a rebel."

I gasped and almost swooned. "What!? How's such a thing possible! No wonder he was so vicious. He shot me down like a dog—you saw that part, didn't you?"

She stared at me for a moment. "You said the whole thing was a transcription of a dream you had."

"That's right. A frigging nightmare!"

"McGill... how are you connected with this rebel king?" she asked.

That stopped me right there. She *knew* he was the Nebran king. I'd never mentioned that before. Old King Vorhoos was still screwing me from the comfort of his dinosaur bone throne…

"Well…" I said, "I basically got convinced to go down there to have a little parlay with him and got myself killed. So, I can't say I'm a super big fan of this guy."

"I can believe that," she said. "Why were you meeting with him in the first place?"

"I was led there by Raash."

"I know that agent of Earth. He's a spy, and he's unwelcome here."

"Well, you'll have to take a number to start hating on him," I remarked. "There's a long line of folks in front of you."

Right then, a wild thumping began at the door. Lady Nox did not move to open it.

"Who demands entry?" she said into an intercom.

"It is I, the garrison commander."

Lady Nox made a few gestures over her computer. Cameras in the hall outside activated, and the scene beyond the door was depicted on the door itself. The effect looked kind of cool, like the door had transformed into a window.

We saw it wasn't just the garrison commander at the door. He had a full squad of twelve Mogwa soldiers behind him, all in their mini tanks.

"Damn…" Nox said quietly.

I looked around for a weapon, but I didn't find anything suitable. Certainly nothing that could stop a squad of alien troops.

"I'm going to have to acquiesce," Lady Nox said. "But this game is not yet over."

"Uh…" I said, thinking I wasn't sure if I was going to live or die over the next few minutes.

The rapping came again, and Lady Nox suddenly triggered the doors to open.

The garrison commander looked somewhat surprised. He stepped inside while his troops remained in the passageway beyond.

"Lady Nox?" he said, "I am here to assert command over this occupying force. As Sateekas is no longer in the revival queue, and I am next in the chain of command, I—"

"Hold it," Nox said calmly, putting her foot-hand in the air. "Sateekas is in the revival queue. In fact, he's currently undergoing the process."

The Mogwa commander seemed quite surprised, even befuddled.

"He is?"

"Yes. Head on down there this instant and oversee his revivification. When he is capable of locomotion again, I will have McGill bring him to me so that I may nurse him back to health."

"I must talk to the appropriate authorities about this."

"You will," Nox reassured him. "The proper authority in this case is Grand Admiral Sateekas himself. I recommend you take your guards down there and await his reinstatement as your proper commander."

The Mogwa garrison commander didn't seem to know quite what to do. I could tell he'd screwed up all his courage, gathered together his men, and marched on Lady Nox. He'd planned a coup of sorts.

But now here he was, outmaneuvered. He kept glancing back at his own noncoms and troops. They were not the most forgiving sort. I'd dealt with them many times in the past. They were, in fact, rule-sticklers of the worst kind, downright close to being male Karens, each and every one of them. He'd have an easier time convincing a pack of Nairbs to rebel against their rightful masters.

I had to smile a bit. Lady Nox had called his bluff. He'd probably gotten this squad of soldiers to follow him in this coup attempt, based entirely on the idea that Lady Nox was irrationally and illegally holding her husband's revival in check.

But now, that problem had been solved. He therefore had no leg to stand on. Seeing as he was a six-legged, crab-like dude, not having a leg to stand on was a big deal.

"Very well. I shall await my rightful commander's return," he spun around and marched out.

Lady Nox slammed the door behind him. Then, she turned to me.

"I want you to go down there and oversee my husband's revival. I'm rearranging the revival queue now—"

"You mean Sateekas isn't really being revived yet?"

"Of course not, you imbecile. Listen: I doubt the garrison commander will try anything drastic, but you need to get my husband back up here and into these apartments so I can have a private discussion with him before he makes any further rash decisions."

"Gotcha," I said, figuring that she was about to employ the tactics which human women had employed since time immemorial to hamstring their husbands.

I marched out the door and downstairs on the double. I had to push my way through a crowd of snarling troops to get into the chamber first.

Lady Nox had pulled off a nice move. She'd come up with a bluff and played it to the hilt. Instead of agreeing to the garrison commander's demands, she pretended she'd already given the order herself. That meant she was still in charge, and the garrison commander hadn't badgered her into doing anything.

All of that was a lie, of course.

*Sheer genius...* I thought to myself.

If Nox had been human girl, hell, she was tricky and evil enough to be one of my girlfriends. Too bad she was sinfully ugly, a married mom, and an alien to boot.

## -30-

When I got down to the revival chamber, I found Sateekas was fresh out of the oven.

"What's that foul smell assaulting my nostrils?" he demanded. "My olfactory organ is overwhelmed by a distinctly alien stench."

"My apologies, Grand Admiral," said the Mogwa bio-operator. "There's a large ape-descendant in the chamber with us. That must be the source of the odor."

The Mogwas all twitched their faces a bit. I figured they were snuffling. I was beginning to feel a mite offended by this display.

"Hiya, Grand Admiral," I said, shrugging off any sensation of being unwelcome.

The grand admiral peered in my direction. "I see a heinously tall blob of meat. It must be the McGill-creature, am I correct?"

"You certainly are. Got it in one."

"What are you doing here, McGill? This is not my finest moment."

Sateekas was moving weakly, trying to organize his thoughts and his nervous system. I had sympathy for all that, but I also had orders from Lady Nox.

I thought about how I could break all the bad news that was coming his way. I had to do it in a manner that would cause him the least amount of anxiety—and invoke the least amount of rage.

"I'm here to guard your person just like always, sir," I told him.

"How absurd. I'm in the Mogwa fortress. Nowhere could be more secure."

I fell quiet while the rest of the revival team went through all the motions. They quoted numbers, gave him various tests, and endured some foot-hand slaps from the admiral as he irritably questioned their intellects.

When Sateekas was finally released, I trailed after him.

The garrison commander was right there at the door, and he tried to take over. "That's enough, McGill," he told me. "You are relieved of your duties. Return to your barracks and shut down."

"Uh…" I said, "I'm actually under orders from Lady Nox, Mr. Commander, sir."

"Lady Nox?" Sateekas demanded, cranking his orbs halfway around and looking at me. He peered suspiciously through his squinty, fresh-grown eyes.

"That's right, Grand Admiral," I said. "The good lady wanted to make sure that you got up to your apartments safely."

"What nonsense…" He turned back around and grumbled as he thumped and staggered his way toward the upper floors.

Mogwa weren't much for stairways. They tended to use ramps for climbing up levels. I trotted along on the ramps behind him, following in his wake.

The garrison commander seemed annoyed, but not enough to attempt to intervene again. He threw me a hateful glance at the second ramp, and bade Sateekas farewell. Then, he disappeared, heading for his military headquarters chamber.

Once he was gone, Sateekas stopped walking and peered after him. He waited until he was a goodly distance away before he spoke in a hushed tone.

"He's an assassin, isn't he?" he said. "I've always suspected…"

"Uh…" I said. "I'm not sure about that, sir."

"Then why, by the blackest of the blackest of holes, did Lady Nox order you to escort me all the way up to her apartments?"

"I don't rightly know, sir, but I'm certain she's concerned for your personal safety and well-being."

He made a nasty snorting noise. Something wet and sticky splatted on the ramp between my boots. I tried not to look too disgusted.

"What utter nonsense," he said. He turned around and made it up a couple more floors up the ramps. As he moved, I could see he was now operating his body with greater agility and purposefulness.

When we got to the last passageway, the one that terminated in the large double doors that held Lady Nox's apartment, I was very surprised to see a total lack of guardsmen. Instead, I counted no less than seven of the skunk-aliens.

They all stood there, staring at us. I halted, as did Sateekas.

"What are these creatures doing here?" Sateekas demanded.

I took a dim view of the whole thing, having dealt with these aliens on multiple occasions. I stepped ahead of Sateekas defensively. My hand fell upon my pistol, but I didn't yet draw it.

"Hey there," I said. "You skunks! What are you doing in this hallway? There's no cause for you to be here."

One of them produced a broom. He began sweeping in an unconvincing manner at the floor. The other six just continued to stare.

"Ah..." Sateekas said. "They are mere servants, sent here to clean up. It's about time some of the locals volunteered to service my whims... No Mogwa should be required to perform such a task—and you humans are far too overpriced to be wasted on this kind of menial labor."

He began to trundle forward again, but I stopped him by putting a hand down in front of his face. He made some rough snorting noises of surprise and anger.

But I glared at the skunks with suspicion. I drew my pistol and aimed it in their direction.

"Get out of here," I ordered them. "This passageway is off limits to your kind."

The skunks froze. Even the one who was fake-sweeping paused. They all stared at me for a moment.

I took a menacing step forward, thumping my boots loudly and leveling the pistol at the nearest.

That was all it took. They bolted. They ran off in a half-dozen different directions and disappeared down side passages.

I walked around a bit, making sure the coast was clear. During this time, Sateekas grumbled and complained about paranoia and delays.

At last, I knocked for Lady Nox to open the door. She did so, and Sateekas scuttled inside. I moved to follow them, but I was not allowed to enter.

"Your services are no longer required, McGill," Sateekas said as he snaked one of his arms around Lady Nox.

I have a hard time reading regular human woman's expressions, much less a Mogwa's, but to me, she looked resigned and annoyed.

"Good night, McGill," Lady Nox said.

Then the door closed in my face.

As I turned around and began to walk down the passageway again, I saw one lone skunk alien, still wearing his servant's uniform. It was the one with the broom. He stared at me as I approached. I considered giving him a kick, but decided not to, stepping aside instead.

He reached out with his broom and poked at my boot experimentally.

I stopped and put my hands on my knees, looking at this single, fluffy and deceptive creature.

"What do you want, skunk?"

"You have failed us," he said.

"How so?"

"We discussed our arrangements with you in the city," he pointed vaguely off over his shoulder.

I immediately got the feeling he was talking about the time I'd been taken to King Vorhoos and given an ultimatum, followed by a very distasteful dismissal.

I laughed at the skunk. "What did you think? ...that I was supposed to listen to you after you went and shot me to death? Where I'm from, we don't take kindly to murdering skunks."

He looked at me quizzically for a moment, cocking his head. "You claim not to be in our employ?"

"That's right, I'm not in your employ at all. I don't even like you guys much."

"I thought all was made clear," the skunk said. "We made our argument of injustice. I thought that you, as a fellow slave-creature—"

"Well," I said, "you thought wrong. You can go back home and tell Vorhoos that."

The skunk dropped his small broom and scuttled away. I watched him leave and looked around to both my flanks and my six—just in case there were more of these aliens sneaking up on me—but I saw nothing threatening.

These Nebrans reminded me of the gremlins of Blood World. In all honesty, those guys were probably worse, but these skunks came in a close second when it came to skullduggery and vicious shenanigans.

Shaking my head, I returned to my guard barracks and bunked down for the night.

\* \* \*

In the middle of the night, I was treated to a rude awakening. All my troops in the barracks shared the experience.

Without warning or preamble, several Mogwa guardians marched into the place in their little tanks and threatened us. My men rolled up out of their bunks, scowling. They reached for weapons, but they didn't immediately aim them in the direction of any Mogwa.

Carlos and Sargon, being men that had frequently dealt with the Mogwa in a personal sense in the past, both appeared behind them. They weren't carrying guns, but rather clubs.

I knew what they were thinking. One of the best ways to take out a Mogwa in his tank was to get in close and simply beat him to death with a large, heavy object.

I put up a single hand, palm high and flat, signaling them to hold off.

"What's this?" the garrison commander demanded. "A sign of surrender and obsequiousness?"

He didn't even seem to get the fact that I was signaling the men behind him—which he had not even noticed yet.

The Mogwa were masters of deception and sheer pig-headed arrogance, but they weren't terribly good at tactics. They had a rather poor sense of fighting and predatory behavior.

"What can I do for you this morning, Mr. Commander, sir?" I asked.

"You have brought an alien spy into our midst," he said.

"What? You mean that skunk with the broom?"

"Stop your worthless chatter. There's a creature, a creature of unrelenting filth, and of a highly predatory nature," he said. "He apparently died at one point, and we were directed to revive him. He keeps saying he's a member of your company. When he was brought back to life, he severed two of my bio-officers' limbs."

That's when I noticed something about the second Mogwa in the group. He wasn't wearing a combat suit, and he did seem indeed to be missing two limbs. He looked as if he was in great pain, and his stumps were wrapped with an artificial-skin container.

"Oh..." I said, looking at that and frowning. "Did you happen to catch the name of this individual?"

"The name is Raash," another loud voice boomed from the back of the group.

I peered, and indeed, I saw Raash.

Blue scales and teeth presented themselves to me. His yellow squinting eyes regarded me with hate. His tail was rigid and upright, a sure sign that he was angry. He was nude as well, but for a Saurian, that didn't mean much. They weighed over two hundred kilos on average and stood about two meters tall. A Saurian male didn't need a weapon or a uniform to be dangerous.

"This is the creature in question," the Mogwa commander said. "He broke free of the revival chamber after having injured my medical officer. I now declare him to be your responsibility. Any further misbehavior on his part will be directly attributed to you and your platoon."

I sputtered a bit at this, as did Sargon, but the Mogwa commander wasn't interested. He marched out of the place, shuffling aside any human who got in his way.

The bio-officer glanced over his humping shoulders, nursing his injured limbs. He hissed and spat as he exited the room last, directing a volume of ejectus toward Raash, who was standing tall.

I turned toward the lizard alien who pridefully regarded me in return.

"Raash…" I said, "so let me get this straight. Somebody ordered you to be revived here with the Mogwa garrison by mistake. Then… you took that opportunity to chew off your own reviving physician's arm?"

"Your statement has multiple inaccuracies."

"Okay, let's just forget about all that," I said. "What do you want here?"

Raash pointed a very long claw in my direction. He made a stabbing motion with it, but I didn't quite let him reach me.

"My demands are simple and inescapable," the lizard said. "You will add me to your guardian group. You will treat me as you would any other member of your combat team of soft humans."

"Oh yeah?" I said. "And what are you going to do if I don't do that?"

"Then I'll expose you, James McGill. I'll inform Sateekas of your interactions with the rebels of this planet. You will be ejected from this fortress and prevented from returning."

I thought that over, frowning. Lady Nox already knew I'd talked to the skunk-king… but… "Okay, whatever. Morales?"

"Yes, Centurion?"

"Get out of that bunk. You've been replaced by this here lizard."

Looking shocked, Morales was ejected from his sleeping place. Raash stretched out upon the bunk instead. Immediately, the fabric of the sheets and blankets ripped underneath his thorny, scaly skin.

Sargon stepped up to me, looking doubtfully at the lizard who was stretching out and making himself comfortable.

"You want I should get him a blanket or something, sir?"

"Unnecessary," Raash said. "Human beings are such delicate creatures. The interior of my mother's egg wasn't this comfortable on Cancri-9. I would be embarrassed to require this much padding, even in my own grave."

"Seems like he's fine, Sargon," I said, heading back to my own bunk. It was not yet dawn, and I wanted to get a few more hours' sleep.

"I do have one requirement, however," Raash announced.

I swear, with every word he spoke, some of the fetid stink from his unbrushed, curved fangs managed to reach my nostrils after it wafted across the barracks.

"What is it now, Raash?"

"I require that you turn off the air conditioning," he said.

"What?" Carlos squawked, finally speaking up. "You don't want a blanket, but you want us all to fry in our beds?"

"The natural temperature of this planet is perfect," Raash complained. "You humans are the ones altering it to your own convenience. You have no right to discomfort me in this manner."

A number of surprised-looking expressions shifted to gaze at me. I frowned, thinking over Raash's request. Finally, I nodded.

"All right. Turn off the A.C., Carlos."

"Aw, hell," he complained. But he walked over, and he did it.

The rest of the night was hot, sticky, and full of the raspy sounds of Raash's breathing.

## -31-

Any sane human—or Mogwa—would've figured that the last thing Sateekas should want to do the day after he'd been revived was go on another showboating patrol.

But they all would have thought wrong.

"McGill, attend me," Sateekas said. I hustled forward, jangling and clanking in my armor. Behind me, dozens of other troops did the same. It was a goodly two days after the disaster in the streets of the Nebran capital, and all of my men had been revived by now.

The Mogwa garrison commander looked chagrined. "I find it unnecessary for this color guard to—"

"Stop right there," Sateekas said, putting up a foot-hand in his face.

The commander bristled, his mini-tank betraying his own personal reactions as would an exoskeleton. These tanks responded immediately to the movements of the Mogwa occupant, and they tended to reveal the inner thought patterns and emotions of the pilot inside.

"It is you who shall not be attending me today," Sateekas told the garrison commander. "You will stay here where you belong, inside the fortification. McGill and his troops will provide all the protection I need."

The garrison commander seemed aghast. "But Grand Admiral—"

"I will hear no more of it," Sateekas said.

"Well, sir, then perhaps you can at least tell us where you're headed so that we may make arrangements and can possibly scramble a rescue party to your location."

"Unnecessary and counterproductive," Sateekas boomed back. "You will stay here—all of you. You will follow my orders in this matter, or you will be removed from your duties."

The garrison commander and his tank shuffled a bit. His gun was aimed up directly into the sky, as was traditional and respectful when in the middle of a non-combatant situation, but it was twitchy. I suspected that possibly, just possibly, he wanted to aim it at myself or maybe the grand admiral himself.

"Very well, sir," he said, at last. "It will be as you command."

"Of course, it will be! Out of my way!"

Sateekas headed for the exits with his typical, wobbly gait. As before, there were two of them, Sateekas and his son Nero. My platoon hustled behind them. I made it a point to tuck my troops in close, surrounding and enclosing our charges.

So far, Nero hadn't said a word. He was merely staring and listening. I got the feeling he was absorbing all that was said—he wasn't a dumb kid.

Maybe there was hope for the boy yet. Maybe, he had inherited the brains of his mother and the bravado of his father. It would be a nice combination if it was possible. He certainly had the arrogance of both.

We headed out into the courtyard where a transport waited. Vapor rolled off its flanks. A ramp uncoiled from the side of the craft, and we marched aboard.

Inside the small suborbital craft, it was a tight squeeze for forty men—plus one lizard. It was only when we were aboard and Sateekas was berating the pilot that he took note of the single extra member of my guard detail.

"What's this?" he demanded. "That's no human—and it's no Nebran, either. Who brought this unknown beast onto my transport?"

His legs churned, and he moved at a crawling pace towards Raash, who was sitting in the back. I followed Sateekas, and I offered my apologies. I'd kind of hoped to sneak the lizard aboard without him having noticed.

"This is Raash, sir," I said.

Sateekas stopped in front of the blue lizard, who was already hissing and showing a few extra rows of curved fangs. "What purpose might a Saurian serve aboard my transport? Besides sabotage?" Sateekas directed a foot-hand in the direction of the interloper. "Remove this animal, McGill," he said. "We won't be taking off until you do."

"Hold on there, Grand Admiral," I said. "This is Raash."

"I don't care what kind of medical problems he might have," Sateekas said.

"I am no pet!" Raash declared unhelpfully.

"Settle down, Raash," I said immediately, knowing that he was apt to run his fanged mouth at the worst moments.

He did some more hissing, but he spoke no further translatable words. I got the feeling he was cursing in his own language.

"Impudence as well as a beastly manner," Sateekas complained. "What odd sub-servants you employ, human."

"You have to understand, sir, this guy's got special powers when it comes to combat and personal protection."

Sateekas looked at me in a disbelieving way. "Explain yourself, McGill-creature."

"Well, you just need to see him in action. This lizard—he's big, he's strong, and he's powerful. He doesn't even need armor or a weapon."

There was another long, low hiss from Raash. Possibly it was a warning sound, but I paid no heed. "I just keep him on a chain most of the time, see, because he's kind of dangerous. But when I let him off—bam! He'll run off like a hunting hound to ferret-out any skunk who dares to lift a hand against his rightful ruler."

"The circumstances you describe are beyond unlikely," Raash complained.

"Silence, lizard," I told him. "You'll get a treat later if you're good."

There was more hissing unpleasantness.

Sateekas looked intrigued. "So... this is some kind of scouting creature? A hunting hound, as it were?"

"Exactly," I said.

"Hmm... that is most innovative. I didn't realize the human legions maintained primitive subspecies like this for such purposes. I approve—but keep it away from me. It's exuding an even fouler set of odors than you are."

"You got it, sir," I told him, and I led him back toward the front of the suborbital craft. "He won't bother us for a second."

Behind Sateekas' back, I made many calming gestures toward Raash, attempting to indicate with my hands that he should shut up and bide his time.

Once I had Sateekas up at the front of the craft and Raash at the far back, both of them seemed happier, and we were able to take off.

"Uh..." I said to Sateekas as we took to the air, swung south, and began zooming across the landscape. "Where the hell are we headed, sir?"

Quickly, we broke out over the ocean and skimmed low over the waves.

"It's best that you do not know," Sateekas said. "Even the pilot has only coordinates to guide him—and these were received in the last few seconds."

"Wow," I said, "that's a whole lot of secrecy. Do you expect any trouble?"

"I always expect trouble on Nebra. This planet is a hive of villainy. Even my own officer corps seems at times too—well, never mind."

Sateekas didn't finish the thought, but then he didn't really have to. I had long thought that he had dissenters in his own ranks. In fact, if I had to put my finger on it, I would say that the garrison commander wasn't too keen on this mission.

We flew onwards for a few hours until we found ourselves hovering over a jungle plateau. I waited until our skids were setting down in a swirling dust-devil of grit before I questioned his wisdom further.

"Uh... Grand Admiral, sir? It would kind of help us to deploy more effectively if we knew what we were up against."

"I expect little resistance—but you are here, just in case."

I sent a dozen of my troops clambering down the ramp in the lead. They spread out in a fan formation, and I had them move to both sides of the aircraft just to check that there were no dangers present on the landing zone we'd come to rest upon.

When they reported "all clear" I appeared at the top of the ramp. My rifle was out, and I scanned the horizon.

We were on top of a flat table-like land. It was grassy and only sparsely carpeted by trees. The trees looked to me like they were similar to a type found on Earth known as the palmetto, and indeed, the vegetation in the area was made up almost entirely of palms.

Sateekas immediately appeared behind me, even though I'd not asked him to move forward yet. He always had a mind of his own.

Nero, of course, was immediately in his wake. He peeked out past his father's tangle of limbs. Sateekas peered at the environment suspiciously and critically.

"Where is that lizard of yours?" he asked. "I don't see it running about."

"Uh… oh yeah. Let me get my tracker onto the field and get him hopping."

I snapped my fingers for Rasha's attention. He hissed at me in return, and I waved furiously for him to approach.

These motions were done behind Sateekas and Nero's back, of course. It wouldn't do for them to see just how uncooperative my "scouting lizard" truly was.

Finally, after ambling forward in a rather lackadaisical fashion, Raash dragged his raspy tail over the deck of the craft past the boots of my chrome-armored troops. From the bottom of the ramp, he surveyed the scene outside.

"This is no city," he complained.

"Where we are and what we're doing here is none of your affair, Saurian," Sateekas said. "Go now. Perform your function. Scout the landscape before us and give me your report. So far, I must say, I am less than impressed by your alacrity."

Still making syllabic noises, which I suspected were Saurian curses, Raash marched into the palmettoes. He walked unhurriedly about, inspecting the greenery. He showed no signs of attentiveness.

Sateekas watched in disgust and gave his son Nero a lecture about treating poor performers harshly. I assured him repeatedly there was a beating in Raash's near future after this insolent performance.

Sateekas seemed to accept this. "But I urge you, do not spare the battery when you apply a shock rod to this recalcitrant reptile!

At last, I grew tired of the "scouting game" and ordered my men to advance. They did so, moving in all directions. They walked among the palmettos, searching for any sign of danger. They found none.

"So…" I said, "you're sure this is the right place, huh, sir?"

Sateekas seemed mysterious. "Let us proceed to the east, in the direction of the local equinox."

Shrugging, I followed him, as did my men. We formed two columns on either side, and when I took a glance around, I realized that Raash had actually disappeared.

Had he slipped back up inside the transport while no one was looking? Or was he off in the palmettoes somewhere, taking a dump-squat?

I shrugged, because I really didn't care. I'd only agreed to bring him along because he was blackmailing me. Hell, if we accidentally left the lizard on this lonely plateau, that would be just fine with me.

We marched in the direction Sateekas had indicated and reached a rocky outcropping at the far eastern point of the tableau. From up here, we were afforded an amazing view.

Rocky cliffs, at least a kilometer high, swept down upon a verdant valley of monstrous green trees. Dinosaurs—or something very much like them—crawled around down there in herds, eating one another.

I began to frown as we approached the rocky outcropping. It began to look less and less like a random pile of rocks, and more like a temple of sorts. In fact, as I examined the place, I realized that there were a large series of hexagonal, black basalt stones. Each of these was several meters in length, and they've been stacked up in rows and in stair-like piles.

Altogether, the stones formed a ziggurat which rose up out of the palmettos. We climbed the central stair. At the summit of this pyramid-like structure, we found what had to be offerings: food in baskets, sacrificed meats from disemboweled animals—all of it was laid out upon stone bowls.

As my men poked curiously among the artifacts, remarking upon them, a figure rushed out from the center of the shrine. He waved his two furry arms at us, squeaking. He was one of the skunk-aliens, and he seemed highly agitated.

This skunk wore a series of wrapped headscarves around his skull, and as we watched, more skunks appeared behind him. They were all similarly dressed and agitated.

My men became wary. They halted and stopped chattering. They lifted their rifles and leveled them at the skunks.

"You want we should blast them, Centurion?" Sargon asked.

"Hold on just a second," I said, approaching the leader. I urged calmness with hand gestures aimed toward both sides.

"Hey, Reverend," I said. "Listen, we don't mean any harm. We just came down from the sky—in that big bird, see?"

I pantomimed some gestures for him and turned my translator on my tapper up to maximum volume.

These guys clearly didn't have tappers of their own. My arm did it's damnedest, translating my words into a series of squawks, squeaks, and grunts. As I spoke, the lead skunk took another step forward despite the bristling number of guns pointed at him. He gestured wildly past me.

I thought perhaps he was pointing back toward the distant vehicle that had transported us to this sacred place. I looked over my shoulder then, turning around to see what was making this miniature preacher so upset.

That's when I saw Raash had followed us. He was at the rear of our platoon—but that wasn't the surprising part.

What I found shocking was the fact he was helping himself to the offerings that were laid out upon this obviously holy ground. He was, in fact, busily desecrating a large black stone bowl of questionable meats.

He chewed on these raw delicacies, spitting out the bones. Blood ran down from both sides of his ghastly mouth, and although I've never been an expert upon reptilian expressions, it seemed to me that he was grinning.

## -32-

"God damn it, Raash," I said, "I should have left you behind!"

Sateekas turned around, and Nero squalled. "What is that cold-blooded monster doing, Father? It's disgusting!"

Sateekas considered, and he watched as I marched down the hill to the Saurian and began to admonish him.

Finally, Sateekas spoke: "Stand down, McGill!"

I looked back at him, my mouth gaping in utter surprise.

"You misunderstand the situation," he told me. "Perhaps that lizard of yours is not as useless as I'd once thought. I like the cut of his jib, as you apes say, and we will proceed in his shadow. All of your men should mimic this toothy monster."

"Uh... what?"

"You heard me. Desecrate this temple! Lay waste to the offerings! Crush down every flower under your boots! You there, tip over that raw milk. And you, massive lummox," he said, waving at Sargon, "spill that bowl of nectar. Leave not one drop of scrumptious juices behind! I demand it!"

We all gaped at one another, not quite sure what the hell was happening.

Even Raash halted his depredations. He seemed as surprised by Sateekas' reaction as anyone else. In fact, I got the impression that he'd figured he had pulled a fast one by damaging Sateekas' reputation with his rude behavior.

But Sateekas had different ideas swirling around in that weird, soft skull of his. He clearly planned to expand upon Raash's efforts—and in fact, to double-down.

My men stood around, milling and confused.

Frustrated, Sateekas took action himself. He picked up dish of fine blackberries, and he shattered it, spraying berries in every direction. He then picked these berries up and began pelting the squalling skunk priests with them.

Nero did the same, laughing. Purple juices flowed from the priests white and black fur, and even came to drip down from the tied and layered scarves of their headdresses.

The two Mogwa continued their vandalism until the skunks became wide-eyed and driven mad with fury. The lead skunk-priest finally charged toward Sateekas. Something the Mogwa had done—possibly when he sprayed waste into a sacred bowl—had been too much for the priest's mind to bear. He lost his cool and attempted to stop Sateekas' desecrations physically.

Without orders, Sargon interceded. He didn't shoot the skunk, but rather thumped the butt of his rifle into the small, angular skull. The priest toppled to the ground, senseless.

That was it. The rest of them went berserk. They produced curved knives and charged. My men surged forward. They had no orders from me, but definitely had the approval of Sateekas.

"Protect me!" the Mogwa shouted. "Perform your duties, human beasts! Gun them down!"

My troops opened up with a withering volley of fire. The charging skunks, who were clearly apprentices of the first one Sargon had brained, were blasted apart. Within a few seconds, they were all shredded by explosive pellets.

When it was all over with, the hilltop grew quiet again. I heard the wet slapping of two foot-hands coming together.

"Well done, Father," Nero said.

"Do you think the desecration was performed adequately?" Sateekas asked.

"Yes, I'm quite impressed. This has to work."

"What the hell was that shit... sir?" I asked. "These Nebrans didn't do anything to us. How is this supposed to calm them down?"

Sateekas made as if to answer, but Nero stood tall and raised an appendage. "May I explain it to the primitive, Father?"

"Yes, be my guest."

"You see, human beast," the young Mogwa lectured me, "there is a long but predictable sequence of steps that must be followed to pacify a reluctant subspecies. At the end of that series of steps, the result is always preordained."

"What?" I asked. "That they rage and charge at you in a suicidal red-hot fury?"

"That's not the endpoint of the sequence," he said, "but it is always a step in the process on the way to the final stage. These beasts must learn to fear us, to know they're helpless beneath our rule. Only when they've been broken and know they cannot stand against us will they accept their fates."

I gaped at the little shit as he and his father marched away, laughing to one another about the destruction they'd created.

Sargon was prodding at the single elder priest that he'd bashed with the butt of his rifle.

"Is he still alive?" I asked.

"I'm not sure, Centurion," Sargon said. He sounded a bit regretful.

My bio-specialist, Carlos Ortiz, kneeled beside the fallen skunk and ran a few tests.

"He'll live," he said. "He'll have a big headache tomorrow, but he'll live."

"All right, then. I guess we should get out of here."

Together, my men retreated into the palmetto forests and made our way back to the transport.

During this march, Raash slithered up beside me and struck up a conversation. "I am at a loss to understand the Mogwa's behavior."

"So am I," I admitted.

"What do you think might have been his purpose?"

"I think he wants to piss off these aliens. I think he wants to get the skunks so angry they attack us, and we're forced to destroy a lot of them."

Raash mulled that over. "Diabolical," he said at last. "I wonder if that will work."

I shook my head because I didn't know any more than Raash did.

We returned to our transport vehicle. Again, Raash sat in the back while Sateekas and his son sat in the front. I sat near Raash, and I settled in for a nap.

The trip back to the capital city was a fairly long one. I hadn't made it an hour into the flight, however, before I got a rude call on my tapper. It answered itself, opening the screen and flashing up an ugly view of Winslade's face.

"McGill?" he said, "McGill, are you sleeping on duty again?"

"Not at all, sir," I mumbled, coming awake and lifting my arms so I could look at my commanding officer.

Winslade had a permanently pinched face. He always seemed to be angry about something or other.

"What seems to be the trouble, Tribune?"

"Troubling reports are coming in—no, they're more than that—they're formal complaints."

"About what, sir?"

"About you, of course. You and your band of marauding savages who apparently found it necessary to desecrate the holiest site in the entirety of the Nebran religion."

I scratched my head, thinking about that for a minute. "Are we talking about that temple-thing on top of, uh, a tabletop mountain?"

"Yes, McGill, exactly that. Whatever possessed you to fly there and—according to these reports—produce waste that overfilled their sacred bowls? Then, as a follow-up, murdered a dozen members of their priesthood?"

"Uh..." I said, "I think there's some kind of misunderstanding here, sir. I didn't do any of that—except maybe for some of the killing. We did do some killing."

"What possible reason—?"

"Sateekas took us out there, I didn't even know where we were headed until—"

Winslade growled. "Do you honestly expect me to believe that? Do you remember Jungle World, McGill?"

"Uh..."

"Well, I do," he continued. "On that benighted planet, you purposefully irritated the ape-like locals. You poked at them with drones and murdered all who objected."

"Now, hold on. They charged my men with deadly spears, Tribune."

"Whatever. This has your kind of violence scrawled all over it. I refuse to believe you weren't materially involved."

"Well, I *was* involved... sort of. But again, it was all Sateekas' idea."

"Now you're attempting to pass the buck. Have you no shame, McGill? Can't you be a man and simply own up to your natural, bestial impulses?"

I thought that over and I nodded. "I do have some of those impulses you're talking about, sir, especially when it comes to the ladies. But in this case—"

Winslade interrupted me again. "Yes, yes, yes, I can see I'm not getting through to your depraved brain. You're going to persist—that's the bottom line, isn't it? You're completely innocent. You're as fresh as windblown snow."

"Now you've got it, sir."

He glared up at me. A single arm hair had sprouted more or less where his nose was. I plucked at it, and it warped his image grotesquely.

"Well," Winslade continued, "I'm not buying it. As a direct result of your depredations, Legion Varus is being required to move a large portion of our troops from the encampment outside of the capital city to support the central Mogwa compound."

"We are, sir? How many men are they requesting?"

"A full cohort."

"A whole cohort, huh?" I thought that over and gave my head a shake. A cohort seemed like too many troops to me. "Who drew the lucky straw this time?"

"3rd Cohort, of course," he said.

"Aw... why's that?"

"First off, because you are one of the units involved, and you're already there playing instigator-in-chief for the grand admiral. Secondly," Winslade ticked off another of his long, skinny fingers, "because you caused this entire fiasco."

I attempted to object further, but Winslade had already shut the channel down. Heaving a sigh, I crossed my arms and tried to go back to sleep, but it simply wasn't going to happen. Soon, my tapper began to buzz again, and this time it was Primus Graves.

"What in the nine hells have you gotten us into this time, McGill?" he demanded.

I played dumb. "I don't get it either, sir," I said.

"He transferred my cohort, ordering us to deploy under the garrison commander at the Nebran city capital."

"What? You're telling me Winslade just up and went crazy?"

"This is a vast disruption. Is it really necessary to have a full cohort to guard a few Mogwa civilians?"

"Well," I said, grinning, "you can leave that special duty to my boys. We'll stay inside and play watchdog for Sateekas. We'll make sure his feet are dry and his shoes are shiny—while you guys man the wall in the rain."

Graves slowly shook his head. "That's not how it's going to work, McGill. Not this time. You're going to be on those walls with us—at least until the Mogwa family is threatened directly."

He closed the channel just as abruptly and rudely as Winslade had done. After that, I found myself unable to go back to sleep until we reached the Nebran capital.

Throughout this process, Raash had been sitting next to me. He'd observed the conversations with interest. His stinking breath came in a raspy series of gasps, and when Graves hung-up, he finally spoke. "I am pleased."

"How's that, Raash?"

"I was uncertain as to how I was going to stop this campaign of subjugation, but now it appears I'm not going to have to."

"Huh?"

"That fool Sateekas has arranged everything for us. These aliens are far from pacified. In fact, the Mogwa garrison commander is already calling for reinforcements. A bloodbath is coming. That's what I predict. Their filthy dirt roads will run red with their lifeblood. With any luck, this planet will never be annexed."

I peered at him and squinted a bit. I decided it was time to have a bit of fun with him. "So, that's your real mission, huh?"

"What? I've said nothing of the kind."

"Yeah, you just did," I said, poking at him. "Admit it. You're here to make sure the Mogwa fail. That's why you started eating out of the sacrificial bowls."

"You speak with falsehoods. I refuse to listen. I will recommend that all others do the same."

I grinned at him. Raash was a spy of sorts. He excelled at sneaking into places and getting himself a job working for whoever it was he wanted to spy on at a given moment. Despite that, he was extremely poor at covering his tracks. It was always easy to bamboozle him into giving up the truth about his missions.

The Nairb Seven had already told me Raash was working for Alexander Turov. His mission was to stop the plans of the Mogwa. But now, both Sateekas and Raash had decided to make the same move by pissing off the skunks.

I didn't know how this was all going to end, but I was sure it wouldn't be dull.

## -33-

As we made our final spiraling approach over the Nebran capital, I frowned in thought. I was still trying to puzzle out the bizarre series of events that had occurred earlier today.

Sateekas wanted the aliens angry and warlike so that he could crush them. Raash wanted them in a fighting mood, hoping the Mogwa would eventually accept defeat and go home. I had to wonder which one of these two was going to get their way in the end.

By the time we landed at the Nebran capital, I was unsurprised to see an entire lifter from Legion Varus settling down in the courtyard. It could barely fit in the space, and our transport was indeed forced to land in the city streets outside the fortress.

Hundreds of men had already deployed, trotting down the large ramps. They brought with them all sorts of supplies, weapons, and gear.

Once my own guard unit had disembarked, we marched through the front gates and into the castle-like structure. Soon thereafter, we got Sateekas and his son safely inside the center of the compound. The transport then lifted off and flew away.

My men were immediately ordered to join the general deployment of 3rd Cohort, and I was happy to see members of my own unit come down the ramp to greet us.

Graves came and sought me out while I was glad-handing my men.

"You're going to be deployed on the walls, McGill," he said, pointing to the main gates.

I squinted in that direction. "There's barely room up there for a full unit, sir, much less this entire cohort."

"I'm not putting everyone up there. Most are going to be posted on the new fortifications we're building."

"Huh?"

Graves looked annoyed. He could tell I wasn't keeping up with all the memos and briefings headquarters threw at their officers every day. "To save time, I'm going to tell you what everyone else in this cohort already knows. We're going to start off by evacuating the entire city for a full block in every direction. Then we're going to level their dirty little huts, knocking them down to the bedrock."

I was already gaping at him in a state of shock and horror.

"After that," he continued, ignoring my stare, "we'll put a secondary wall farther out, made of puff-crete. We've already got the machines churning out sheets and bricks down over there."

It was true. I could see a few buzzing pigs had dragged a puff-crete machine out and set it up. Techs were operating the console.

"We'll use the same technique we've been using for years," Graves explained. "We'll set up a couple of force fields and pour puff-crete between them, filling up the space and making an instant wall. That should stop a skunk, huh?"

"But sir… we're actually going to destroy a part of their city to make room for this new construction?"

"That's what I just said. Don't tell me you were listening to the wind blow through your ears instead of your superior officer again, McGill."

"No sir… I just think this whole idea is plumb crazy. How the hell do you expect to pacify aliens if you're wrecking their hometown?"

Graves shook his head. "You haven't heard yet, have you?"

"Heard what, sir?"

"About the general rebellion. The skunks have called all their little skunk friends. They're mustering an army—and their target is this compound. Sateekas has decided to make a stand right here. He doesn't care if a million skunks come up against these walls. In the next few days, he wants them all put down—and I applaud the notion."

"That seems extreme, Primus."

"Look, you bleeding heart, we've been playing softball with these clowns long enough. Do you realize that every night since you left for this cushy job here at the capital, they've never stopped harassing us? They've sent waves of their worthless dinosaur cattle raging at us, poisoned our water, and given us free food that crawls with deadly maggots. I'm talking about things that will burrow right through your guts in the middle of the night."

I bared my teeth, thinking about that. It did sound like the kind of thing these aliens would do. They weren't much for a standup fight, but by damn, they were good at the more indirect methods of warfare.

"That's... uh... not good..." I admitted. "How long do we have before their army gets here?"

"It's already gathering in the jungles outside the city. We don't have time to kick all the aliens out and put a wall around the entire town, so we're going to have to make do."

"What about our main encampment?"

"They'll take care of themselves," he said. "We built up the fortifications there already. I'm hoping the regular legion will break their army before they even get here—but we'll have to see."

"I don't know, Primus. This whole—"

"Look," he said, backhanding me in the breastplate. "We're not running this show. Sateekas hired us. We're just doing what he wants us to do."

I thought that over and felt further misgivings. If there was one area where Grand Admiral Sateekas consistently failed, it was in the general zone of strategy. Whenever he chose an option on the battlefield, it was almost certain to be the wrong one.

So I sighed, gathered all of the troops of my unit together, and headed toward the front gates. We deployed exactly where Primus Graves had assigned us.

"Here's where we're going to make our stand, boys. Leeson!"

"Ready to serve, Centurion!"

"Set up the 88s!"

He rushed off with a grin on his face. He liked artillery best of all. It kept the enemy at a distance, and it frequently made them dead before you had to think much about them.

Roughly a thousand other men were faced with the grim task of clearing the local region of the city. After chasing the local populace away, they began methodically demolishing dozens of buildings.

I watched as Adjunct Leeson set up two light artillery 88s, each on the shoulders of the big front gate. The walls were no more than ten meters high, but that would have to do. I guess for these skunk aliens, ten meters was an amazingly tall wall.

Out in the streets there were explosions, dust, and fire. The locals were being driven away, and their buildings were being brought down in rapid succession. Seeing as they were made of simple local bricks, a single missile strike at the base of each structure brought it down, instantly converted into a stack of loose rubble and dust. Refugees streamed away in every direction down the streets, farther into the city.

I winced and squinted with each strike. I didn't like to see it. Sure, we were allowing the locals to escape, but I was pretty damned certain there were a few who hadn't made it out alive.

"What's the matter, McGill?" Adjunct Harris asked, coming up and standing next to me on the wall. "Don't tell me you're crying over these skunks? They've been giving us hell out there at the legion camp, you know."

"Yeah…" I said, "I'm sure they have. But what if it was us, Harris? What if this was our planet, and these guys were invading? Or maybe they were Rigellians, or somebody else. Wouldn't we do everything we could to try to kick them off Earth?"

"Yeah," he said, "sure, we would. But, these guys aren't very smart and they're just not doing it right."

"Aren't doing *what* right?"

"They aren't resisting their oppressors properly, that's what. You know, like when you're outclassed, you run away.

You hide out in the woods, maybe. Then, you wait a generation before you come back at them. You wait until they're tired of the expense and the little nicks and pricks you've given them all along the way. That's how you run a guerilla war. That's how you win if you're the little guy"

I thought about that as Harris turned and walked away. Yes, he was right—but he was also partly wrong. It was the nature of all species to fight for their territory up front. Only when they were fully defeated would they revert to the kind of tactics he was talking about.

Unhappy with my lot in this war, I placed my men as wisely as I could. I knew the skunks were coming in the morning, and I wasn't entirely dismissive of their capabilities to wage war. They'd already tricked us many times, and I was pretty damned sure they had a few more surprises tucked up into their fuzzy sleeves.

## -34-

The new outer wall of "Skunk Castle"—which was what we were all calling the Mogwa fortress by now—was thin. In actuality, it was only about ten centimeters thick. The only reason it stood up straight at all was because it was made with puff-crete, a weird, almost alchemical substance that was tougher than steel. We all figured it could withstand the best efforts of these wimpy aliens and their dinosaur pets.

What I didn't expect was the delay. The sun came up and kept rising into midmorning without any attack incoming. Everyone was somewhat befuddled.

"Well…" Harris said to me, "maybe these skunks just figured out what I was saying yesterday. They should lie low and cool their heels until things get better."

"Maybe this is all a trick," Leeza said, coming up on the other side of me.

"How do you mean, Adjunct?" I asked.

"I mean… what if they behaved aggressively to send us into a panic? We've deployed a cohort right in the middle of the capital city. We knocked down a hundred of their buildings and we put up an artificial wall. Perhaps that was their goal."

"What do you mean it was their goal?"

She inhaled and tried to explain to my slow brain. I felt for her. I really did. "I'm saying they might have goaded us into actions that help their cause," she said.

"Diabolical!" Harris said. His big eyes were even bigger than usual as he contemplated Leeza's idea. "You're saying they got us to go nuts, to wreck the town and put up that wall—just for PR? To help them gain sympathy from the rest of the skunks?"

"Yes. It is a very subtle move, but I wouldn't put it past these aliens for an instant."

"What the hell are you two talking about?" I demanded, not quite getting it.

"Just think about it," Harris said. "All of this—the whole thing—might be a PR stunt. What these skunks need to do first is unify their entire planet against us. So, what do they do? They announce an attack is coming. An attack so heinous that we overreact. Then, they shuffle things around on the board, making it look like they're coming at us hard—but it's all bullshit to get us to look overly aggressive toward peaceful civilians."

"Exactly," Leeza said.

I was dumbfounded. When you had a brain like mine, that happened a lot.

We all surveyed the quiet city from the wall top. Harris marveled at the supposed cleverness of the skunks. "They got Graves to blow up buildings right and left. They're probably filming all that stuff and sending it home to their brothers and aunties and cousins... building up true hatred—exactly what they need to get their scaredy-cat people ginned-up enough to fight."

We all stared at the smoldering scene. Here and there, tendrils of smoke and ash floated into the air. The ruined buildings we'd stomped flat to build our strange, instantaneously constructed walls looked like broken teeth.

I turned away from both of them, ignoring them, and summoned my techs. I ordered them to send out another flock of buzzers in every direction. We searched for the enemy—and for their next target.

We found nothing. The streets were quiet, the hills and verdant forests surrounding the capital city were quiet, too.

"It must be ten in the morning," I said, "they must not have gotten the memo about predawn attacks."

They both looked at me like I was crazy.

"Look, these skunks are nocturnal animals, right?" I said. "That means they're more awake at night."

"That's true," Harris admitted.

"So maybe, just maybe, they're thinking the right time to attack is dusk. Something like that, huh?"

They rubbed at their chins and muttered in confusion.

We waited for hours. We soon grew bored, parked up on the walls in the hot sun. We played dumb games on our tappers and bet on who would bag the first skunk.

Sometime after noon, they finally decided to show their wet, black noses. It all started when we heard a rumble from the distant jungle.

It was a strange sound. You felt it as much as heard it.

"My boots are buzzing," Harris exclaimed. "What the hell is that?"

"There—out to the east," Leeza pointed in the direction of the ocean. That was where the waters were closest. If you went farther in that direction, you would come to docks and eventually waves.

"What the hell?" Harris repeated, leaning out over the edge of the crenulated wall.

We were staring in the direction she'd indicated. Men moved, talked, shuffled about, and squinted in the sun.

Finally, I saw what they were looking at.

"The wall—it's moving!" Leeza said.

She was right. The thin, puff-crete wall was wavering. Thin though it might be, the wall was as strong as ten centimeters of tempered steel. But still, it was shivering, almost undulating, like a massive flag in a stiff breeze.

"What the hell is doing that?" Harris demanded. "Some kind of a vibration weapon, maybe?"

"That's it! Sonics!" Leeza said.

"Nah," I said, "you'd be hearing something, even this far away. If they were bouncing high-frequency vibration waves off the corner of this fortification, we'd know it."

"I can feel it in my boots," Harris insisted, and I thought about that.

I closed my eyes for just a second. Yes, I could feel something too, a slight, occasional vibration under the soles of my boots.

Then my eyes snapped open again. I knew what we were facing.

"That's coming from underneath us," I said. "They're digging down there."

Harris's and Leeza's eyes widened, and they glanced back from each other to me.

"They have sappers?" Leeza asked.

That's about when a crack appeared in the far eastern wall, starting at the bottom and working its way up. The crack split into three different fingers.

The ground underneath the puff-crete wall had opened up like a black wound.

"Might just be a sinkhole," Leeson said in our helmets. "This whole place is a jungle on top of a pile of quicksand, if you ask me. It's a natural phenomenon."

He could be right, but there was no way to be certain. I immediately directed my techs to send their buzzers to circle around the area. A half-dozen other unit commanders had already done the same. The place was soon swarming with drones.

"Fly them low," I told Natasha.

She was on the wall with me, directing her drones with twiddling fingers on her portable computer.

"See what's going on at the very base of that wall," I said

Legion Varus buzzers were more sophisticated these days than they'd been in the past. Instead of bearing simple radio communications and a camera, they held delicate, advanced sensory technology. Among these were a LiDAR array. She activated this now and began to scan the rubble all around the base of the puff-crete wall.

"There's something down there, all right..." she said. "Something large, long—and hot."

"What kind of shape?"

"Cylindrical, it seems like—but it's not straight. It curves." She looked up at me in alarm.

I frowned back at her. "How big is this thing?" I asked, because I already suspected what it might be.

"A meter thick. Probably more," she said.

"What's its temperature?" I asked.

"About twenty-eight degrees C."

I thought that over and nodded. "Not enough to be a mammal—and way, way less than it would take to be a machine, right?"

She thought it over. "It's definitely alive—and I think it's cold-blooded. Nothing else moves like that—kind of a sinewy, and undulating..."

"What the hell is a giant reptile doing burrowing under our wall?"

Natasha shook her head. "It's not burrowing. I think it's inside some kind of a sewer system. Maybe underground passages, that kind of thing."

I thought that over and squinted harder at the land, wondering what horrors the rubble was hiding. I recalled that when I first met up with the skunk King Vorhoos in his secret lair, he'd been hiding underground. I got the feeling that there were tunnels, or at least basements, underneath all these buildings. What if some of those chambers weren't completely filled in?

"Upload this information to Graves," I said.

"He probably already knows," Natasha pointed out.

"I don't care. Send it anyway."

She did so, but there was no immediate reply from headquarters.

That's when we heard another loud cracking sound. This time, it was closer to hand, on the opposite side of the compound we'd so hastily built upon the rubble.

The situation was very similar to the first bizarre event on the eastern side. Something was down there, undermining the integrity of the walls we'd erected so quickly just the day before. The troops that had been stationed up there on that wall streamed down, fearing they'd be knocked from the wall if the disruption grew worse.

Soon, the interior of the compound was full of soldiers. They were abuzz with excitement. We all knew an attack was incoming. We could feel it in our bones.

Everyone checked their rifles, aiming them down into the ruins of the town that lay flat around us.

But so far, there was nothing to shoot at. All the action—if there really was any action—was going on underground.

"Maybe we should advance," Leeza suggested. "Maybe we should go out there and help put them down when they come out."

"Like hell we're doing that," Harris exclaimed, glowering at her.

"Harris is right," I said. "We'll maintain our post here. The deck in this central structure is heavy brick. I don't think they can undermine these walls the way they're doing to those puff-crete sheets of molecular trickery out there."

Fifteen minutes after the strange vibrations began, one of the walls finally buckled. It was the one to the south of us that went down first—opposite from where we now stood.

It started with a big chunk of puff-crete that fell off the south wall and collapsed into the streets. It looked thin, especially from this distance. It seemed no thicker than an eggshell, although I knew it to be about ten centimeters thick.

At first, broken shards fell. They shattered and scattered everywhere. Then, a section of the wall collapsed, sinking into the earth. It had clearly been undermined.

I think, somehow, this single event signaled the waiting skunk armies all across the city. It was time to step up their attack.

The skunks finally made their appearance. They were not, however, massed infantry charging our damaged walls. No, not yet.

Instead of seeing skunks racing toward us in their thousands, we instead saw large theropods—dinosaurs with long legs that ran on their two hind feet.

These reptiles had short forelegs, big heads full of teeth, and long, sharp-pointed tails that stuck out behind them. They were not humanoid in nature at all.

On each of these theropods' backs rode a single skunk jockey. They whipped at the tough, scaly flesh of the dinosaurs that were their steeds, driving them to a wild, scrambling charge. They raced directly toward our cracked walls. Each of the four corners of our puff-crete structure had indeed cracked and ruptured open. Puff-crete chunks were falling.

"How in the hell did they manage to pull that off?" Harris demanded, pointing out in a couple of different directions.

"Skunk cavalry?" Leeson said, laughing. "They're going to get slaughtered if they charge our guns."

Leeson was right. Once they reached the breaches in our walls, they leapt through the gaping holes. Immediately, they encountered a swift death.

Ripping fire, mostly from morph-rifles held by heavy infantry, tore the theropods and their jockeys apart. Only a few of them made it in among the troops themselves and were able to create havoc.

Fighting with huge, snapping jaws, the dinosaurs plucked limbs—mostly from light troopers—and generally caused mayhem until they were brought down.

At each point of entry, humans outnumbered the skunks and their dinos. They were quickly surrounded and shot down.

But at that moment, when all looked to be lost for the skunk cavalry, the situation shifted. Violent explosions shook the ground.

"What in the hell...?" Leeson demanded. "Are those critters packed with explosives?"

Indeed, it seemed to be true. Once the theropods were in among our troops, and the riders could tell there was no hope of survival, bombs of some kind were fired off.

These tore through the troops that were at that time surrounding and gunning down the brave dinosaurs and their riders. A hundred human soldiers died in seconds.

But we'd rebuffed the attack, and for a time, everything was quiet.

"Uh-oh..." Harris said, looking at Natasha's LiDAR systems again.

She had her buzzers up and circling closer now to the inner wall. She tugged at my armor urgently. "Those things.... the underground reptiles that brought down the walls… they're heading for the compound now."

I squinted, thinking that over. I reported in to Graves with a direct call.

"What is it now, McGill? I'm busy."

"Sir, there are four things under our feet. Those digging creatures, whatever the hell they are, they're all converging on this central compound right now."

"I can see that, McGill. Don't you think I can see that?"

"Well, sir… we've got to do something."

"Like what, McGill?"

"There are passageways down there, sir. I know there must be openings—access points into the underworks of the city. Maybe we should send our troops down there to deal with them directly?"

Graves thought about that for a heartbeat. "Not a bad idea," he said.

"Mr. Primus, sir, I hereby volunteer for the mission of—"

"Forget it, McGill. Stay on top of the inner wall. I'll send Manfred and his team down."

Graves had already cut the signal. I grunted and went back to manning the walls.

I saw Manfred's team, the 7th, pull away from his location on the shattered outer wall and head for an access point to the skunk sewers that were underneath our feet. As he came close enough to the inner walls for me to wave at him, he waved back in return—but within his wave, his fingers made a prominent and vulgar display.

Perhaps he'd somehow learned of my suggestions to Graves, and he knew this idea was mine. He clearly wasn't grateful for this glorious assignment, however it had come to fall his way.

I took no heed of this, merely grinning, kissing my fingers, and waving at him even harder. He stopped at the entrance and began grabbing and shoving his heavy troopers down the hole, forcing them into the lead. Those that were reluctant, especially light troopers, he kicked in the ass. When it was their turn, they disappeared, swallowed into the earth.

I asked Natasha to arrange for a video feed from 7th Unit, and she obliged. "I know the tech over there. She'll let me have it. I'm not even going to have to hack in."

"Good," I said, and soon we were watching the action underneath the ground.

For a time, nothing much happened other than men crawling on their hands and knees. The skunk passageways were a tight fit for a full-grown male human.

But it didn't take long for them to meet up head-to-head with the nemesis that was coming the other way.

The thing that had taken down the walls was indeed startling in nature. It looked like a giant anaconda, or at least the head of one.

"A snake?" Harris shouted. "A fucking snake? You've got to be kidding me."

"Jungle snakes…" Carlos said. Somehow, he'd managed to get in on the feed as well. Possibly, everyone in my unit had it by now. "Even back on Earth, jungle snakes can grow to fantastic lengths. Here on this world, with perfect conditions, snakes can be something like thirty meters long and two meters thick."

"Yes…" Natasha said, agreeing.

The head of the snake, unfortunately for the beast, was not armored or shielded. Manfred and his men managed to blast it down to a bloody stump, losing only a couple of soldiers as it lunged at them and swallowed them whole.

At last, it ceased its thrashing and died. Oddly enough, when this happened, the groundbreaking effects that were going on above, at the street level, actually increased in intensity.

"It's got to be wearing some kind of harness," Natasha said. "I can't really see it, but it's the only thing that makes sense."

"What the hell are you talking about, girl?" I demanded, coming up and looking at her screen. "These snakes are obviously trained by the skunks, but how could they be causing so much damage up on the surface?"

"I think they wearing vibrational equipment—some kind of generator—probably tied on like a collar. It's so bizarre."

"What? That a snake would be wearing a collar?"

"Not just that," she said, "but the way these skunks and their technology works. We tend to go in entirely for machine-based technology. Some species out there prefer to create cyborgs like the Skay. Others are purely organic in their construction, like the Wur."

I thought about that, agreeing. The Wur from Death World and Green World were an alien species of plant-like creatures. Most of their kind were non-intelligent, but that didn't mean that their nexus plants were any less dangerous. They could command armies of less intelligent plant-creatures. It was only by the grace of God that they had never defeated us.

As we puzzled over the visuals coming from Manfred, who was down there fighting in the tunnels under the destroyed city streets, the battle seemed to shift again. The big skunk infantry-rush that we'd been expecting all along finally appeared. There were hundreds of them—then thousands.

The streets all over the city filled with white and black furred shapes. All bounding in our direction.

How many were there? Possibly… a million? I didn't know, but their numbers were startling. From a distance, they didn't even look like individuals, but rather like a flowing river. A single charging mass.

I realized then that they'd done well with their early assaults. They'd cracked all four of our puff-crete walls. They'd driven wedges into our lines, pushing us back from the battlements we'd so hastily built the night before.

Now our men were out of position, most of them being down in the open rubble areas between the outer puff-crete walls and the original fortress walls of Skunk Castle.

Was that the mission of the skunk cavalry we'd laughed at? To mount a suicidal charge to disrupt our lines?

They'd managed not only to shatter our outer walls but to force us to withdraw from them. Now, we were thrown into confusion the moment the real attack came.

I didn't know exactly what the enemy plan was, but I was certain they had the initiative. They were making the moves, calling the shots. It certainly wasn't Graves who was tactically performing maneuvers on this battlefield to force our enemy to react to us.

No, it was the skunks who were driving this battle to its final conclusion, whatever that might turn out to be.

## -35-

As anyone familiar with the skunks might have predicted, their approach to warfare could be described with a single term: tricky.

Many of the enemy didn't even have weapons. Instead of bothering to arm their troops with traditional things like uniforms, rifles, and the like, they were fortified by an almost maniacal fury to destroy humanity.

I was pretty sure this had been generated by passing around graphic videos of what had happened at their most sacred ziggurat out in the jungles at that tableau mountain in the distance. I had no idea what special significance that sacred place had for these people, but it had to be pretty significant, because they were blood-mad.

As most of our men were no longer standing on tall walls of puff-crete, we had to fight them at close range. This didn't allow our rifles to mow them down before they reached us.

I watched as individual combats played out all over the field. The skunks often charged directly at a given trooper. That man, seeing himself in danger, would naturally focus on a given skunk and gun him down.

This, of course, wasn't the only attack he faced. Instead, there was always another skunk coming in from a flanking direction. He would launch himself at the last moment, landing upon the back or the waist of the victim trooper.

Frequently, these flankers weren't alone. Instead of a single skunk, our men faced a team of them—or even a whole squad.

These threats came at us in a blur. They ran as fast as a fox might when racing on all fours. Troops would shoot one, but then when he turned his focus to the next to gun another down, two or three more would land upon him, always from a variety of directions.

They stabbed and slashed viciously with curved knives. They tried to work their blades into the softest spots they could find.

That was oftentimes nothing more than another distraction, but there was always at least one skunk going for a vital trick that would end the struggle decisively.

This was usually a plasma grenade. Most of our troops had them—hanging from our belts. Highly dexterous, small, probing, fuzzy hands manipulated these weapons. They activated the grenades, oftentimes without even alerting their victim—namely us.

One moment, a soldier was covered in a savage carpet of skunks. He was usually howling and stabbing wildly with his combat knife. He might grab one skunk at a time and throw it to the ground, dashing its brains out. But then, to this champion warrior's great shock and horror, he'd see the skunks all slip away. His grenade had been activated.

At that point, the soldier might try to escape his fate. Usually, the skunks got away, being much more agile and quick. The man was almost always doomed.

Frequently, in fact, neighboring soldiers were also doomed. They all went up in a glowing spherical ball of plasma and heat.

"Holy crap…" Sargon said, pointing here and there out on the battlefield.

The explosions were going on now so fast and so frequently, my eyes were getting after-visions. Burn-marks on my retina that didn't even have time to fade away before the next one flared in a new spot on my squinting eyeballs.

"They're wrecking our whole front line," Harris declared. "This is insane, absolutely insane!"

3rd Unit was, of course, manning the inner walls and using our rifles to great effect. We fired into the masses of skunks where they were pouring in through the cracks they'd created in all four of our puff-crete walls.

There were still four rivers of skunks flowing through, and I had to estimate that at least one in five of them didn't make it all the way through those breaches but were instead destroyed by our withering fire.

But the other units that had been deployed in the rubble area between the inner wall and the outer wall didn't have the kind of luxuries we did. They'd been chased down off of the walls because the skunks had shattered them.

They'd gathered between the puff-crete wall and the inner fortress walls. There, they'd fought against the skunk cavalry initially, and then the weird snake-like beasts underground. These side-missions had taken them out of position. They'd lost their height advantage and therefore they'd lost their greatest power—heavy ranged fire.

They couldn't shatter the ranks of the skunks that were flowing in from all parts of the city now, hell-bent on revenge. No, they were forced to fight in close-quarters, and there, due to their devious tactics, the skunks were able to wreak vengeance.

I estimated the skunks were dying two, three—maybe five to one versus the humans—but that hardly mattered, because I suspected they outnumbered us by at least a hundred to one.

Staring and firing at any knot of skunks I could without killing my own comrades, I was lost in the battle until I sensed a large, stinky presence nearby.

I turned, and as I suspected, I spotted Raash. He was up on the walls without permission, surveying the carnage surrounding the central compound.

I stomped over to him. I reached out, grabbing his thick shoulder with one of my large hands, and I gave him a shake. This had almost no effect on him, but he did turn to regard me.

"Is this your doing, Raash?" I demanded. "Is this what you wanted?"

"Precisely so, McGill," he said. "This is the demise of the plans of Sateekas. We will be overwhelmed. We will die here. But that is a small price to pay for the destruction of the Mogwa scheme."

"Are you nuts?" I demanded. "What's it to you if the Mogwa manage to build a Tier Three civilization out here in the Mid-Zone?"

"I have told you before—"

"Yes, yes, I know. Sateekas and Nox have this crazy scheme to put Nero on the Throne of the galaxy. That's probably never going to happen."

Raash made a sweeping gesture towards the absolute chaos and destruction that was all around us.

"Not now, it isn't," he said.

"So, what's in this for you?"

"The glory of a job well done, and a pleased master. This successful mission will be blazed permanently onto the history engraved upon my eggs."

"What are you thinking—that this will lengthen your tail? Just because you managed to make a human ruler back on Earth happy?"

He cocked his head slightly, as if considering my words seriously. "That is one way of viewing the realities of the situation," he admitted.

I let go of him and shook my head. I had no idea what to think of this lizard, so I stomped away angrily. My men were still plinking away, firing whenever they could at an open patch of skunks where no humans could be accidentally hit.

"Should we open up the gates, sir?" Sargon asked me.

"What?" I replied.

"The gates, the front gates. Some of our boys are down there, hammering to get in. They're all going to get slaughtered."

"Fuck," I said, and I immediately contacted Graves, asking if I should attempt to save as many as I could of the men struggling in the mass melee that now surrounded the central compound.

Every point of the compass was packed with skunks and struggling men. Hundreds of humans were dying, along with many thousands of skunks that lay curled up at their feet.

Graves answered, and he was in a red fury. "Why haven't you fired, McGill?" he said.

"We are firing, sir. I've got every snap-rifle, every morph-rifle—"

"No, you moron! Fire the 88s, wide sweeps!"

I blinked, stunned. I stared at my tapper. "But sir, we'll be hitting human troops. There's no way to avoid it."

"Of course there isn't, fool. Kill them, burn them—turn them all to ash. Do it now!"

The channel closed. My jaw wouldn't close with it, however.

With wide eyes and a feeling of disconnection from reality, I turned to my men, and I gave Leeson the signal to fire the 88s.

"It's about frigging time," he said, and the big artillery weapons began to sing. He'd wisely placed one at one corner of the compound and the other at the opposite corner. The weaponeers manning these systems, therefore, had a very wide field of fire.

The big weapons began to hum. Sickly green beams poured out with horrifying efficiency. Huge sickly green arcs of radiation swept over the battlefield, leaving lumps of ash behind the traveling beams.

After each sweeping arc, the gunners let the weapons cool down for a few seconds. Then they angled the nozzles a bit closer to our walls and swept back in the opposite direction.

By the second sweep, everyone down there—skunk, human or otherwise—realized they were utterly doomed.

A massive exodus began. The skunks that were anywhere near one of the four cracks in the puff-crete walls attempted to escape, pouring back out the way they had come in. More than a few human legionnaires followed, close on their tails.

"Should we shoot them down, sir?" Harris asked.

"No," I said. "Let the runners run."

How long did it take? Two minutes—or was it five? It's hard to say. But by the time Leeson's beamers were done, there was not a single living thing left squirming among the rocks and the shattered rubble at the base of our walls.

The revival machines would be busy tonight.

## -36-

As it turned out, Leeson and some of my weaponeers got a little overzealous. They ended up lighting the roofs of many buildings beyond our compound on fire.

Looking back on it, this seemed unavoidable. The skunks and their attack had broken through our walls, which meant that when the 88s swept their hot beams in a wide pattern, some of that radiation was bound to escape. The beams were so powerful that adobe bricks exploded when hit by them, and roofs naturally caught fire. By the end of the battle, when the skunk survivors retreated back the way they'd come, something like a quarter of the town was burning.

I stood on the battlements, surveying the situation—which was grim. Someone came up behind me, and I turned, expecting it to be Graves.

Instead, it was Sateekas and his son, Nero. They stood up there with me on the battlements, beaming with pride. It was like having a couple of six-legged roosters beside me, both ready to take credit for the sunrise.

"Such magnificent destruction!" Sateekas said to me. "Look at this, Son," he told Nero. "Their city burns. Could any other servant have caused such a vast wave of destruction in so short a time?"

"I doubt it, Father," Nero said, "especially not with only light artillery and small arms."

"Exactly. McGill here has provided us precisely the scenario that we were hoping for. First of all, his actions at the aliens' sacred site cause an amazing fervor among the populace—"

"Now, hold on a second," I said, finally interrupting. I couldn't contain myself. I was, if the truth be told, feeling a bit upset about the level of sheer chaos we'd just visited upon the Nebran people. "It was you guys who desecrated their temple. Raash ate their offerings right out of that sacrificial bowl. After that everything went sideways with *your* encouragement."

Sateekas waved one of his foot-hands at me dismissively. He added a loud, blatting noise with his mouth-parts.

"No, no, McGill," he said. "Don't even attempt to be humble. There's no need. I could not possibly take credit for this amazing level of debauchery. Look down there—see that wriggling form? The creature is turned half to ash but still, it suffers!"

"How did you *know*, Father?" Nero interrupted. He waved one of his limbs vaguely in my direction. "How could you have calculated that such a grotesque level of destructiveness was contained within this singular, oversized ape-creature?"

"It came to me in a bolt of insight during our previous campaign. This miscreant was able to, with only a small team of infantry, destroy a space cannon. The device was terrorizing literally hundreds of star systems by firing projectiles across interstellar space."

Nero turned and gazed at me with an expression I could only imagine was one of respect. "I had no idea," he said.

"Yes. So, you see, it wasn't sheer insight on my part, but rather an ingenious leap of logic. I reasoned that if the McGill-creature could cause a vast machine to explode with nothing more than primitive weapons of war, he could deal with these annoying rebels in an equally dramatic fashion."

"I understand now..." Nero said, and he sounded very serious about it.

"Well, sirs," I said, "I guess then that you're pleased with this result? I'm kind of surprised since there's not a whole lot of the colony left here to..."

"Oh, don't worry about them," he interrupted. "These creatures breed like the vermin they are. The key is they will now fear us and submit to our will. They have been broken, and it's all due to you. You have my thanks and my gratitude, Centurion McGill."

I was a little surprised right there because he'd actually used my rank. Normally, Sateekas only referred to me as a slave or an animal. I knew I should feel honored, but somehow I was still upset about the thousands of dead that were even now stinking up the entire region.

"Well, uh…" I said, "what exactly do you think we should do next, Grand Admiral?"

"I should think that would be obvious. You know exactly where that rebel king was last seen. Take a team, go out there, and dig him up before he can escape. Bring back that throne of his, too—the relic I saw in your videos. I think we'll have a good use for it."

I blinked a few times, surprised by this request. "But sir, most of the troops in my cohort died during the battle. All I've got left is my own unit."

"Yes, exactly. Your men will have to do. Hop to it! Chop, chop! Don't let the rebel leader escape—but even if he does, bring me back that throne."

I shrugged my shoulders, turned around, and gathered up a team. This consisted primarily of Harris and a platoon of heavy troopers. I left the lights and the weaponeers to man the walls—just in case.

We had to force the big front gates open. That took some serious effort due to there being so many bodies and so much debris. The courtyard outside was still hot, with spots that were glowing and flickering with dancing flames even now.

About then, Graves contacted me. "Where the hell do you think you're going, McGill?"

"Sorry, sir," I said, "I'm under orders from a higher authority."

I quickly explained what Sateekas had said. Graves gave up on attempting to coerce me back onto the walls and ended the conversation with a loud curse.

A few minutes later, with Harris grumbling at my side, we reached the wrecked outer walls. Behind us were thirty-odd heavily armed and armored men. We picked our way through the hot landscape and the broken walls.

Fortunately, our heavy armor had excellent air conditioners and thick insulation. This gear was rated for operation in deep space, and we were comfortable despite the flames and the radiation hot-spots. We ignored jagged debris and incinerated corpses. We only paused now and then to circumnavigate the hottest of the fires.

I led the group down rubble-strewn streets, climbing over mountains of debris that had recently been tall structures. I had some trouble navigating the ruined city, given how much the landscape had changed. Fortunately, my tapper was able to retrace my steps.

"All right, boys," I said, "this is it. Start digging."

Unable to locate anything that functioned as an entrance into the cellar area, my men had to dig their way down to the king's chamber. They used their exoskeletal strength to lift large chunks of stone and rubble, and at times had to cut through obstructions with their force blades.

Finally, a couple of men found a weak spot in the subflooring and disappeared, crashing through. Harris and I walked to the dusty hole and looked down. The men were down there cursing, but alive. We ordered them to move aside and hopped down into the hole after them.

"There it is…" Harris said. "Holy shit…"

His suit lights sent powerful stabbing beams of light around the chamber. There was floating dust and a fair number of terrified-looking skunks.

But there was also, at one end of the chamber, a large throne of bones.

"That's gotta be it," Harris said. "That's it, isn't it?"

"Yes, it is," I said.

"That's just crazy. I thought you were so full of shit about this throne-thing, McGill. I would never have believed it if I didn't have my eyes on it right now."

I nodded. I wasn't insulted or even surprised by his statement. After all, I was known throughout the cosmos as a man who oftentimes took liberties with the truth.

The skunks cowered back against the walls. Perhaps they were unable to escape, having been caught in this chamber when their buildings collapsed around them. I demanded to know if any of them were the King Vorhoos.

None of them confessed to this identity. In fact, none of them said much at all.

One of them, however, came creeping toward me very slowly with big eyes and fuzzy, furtive little hands. He was staring at me, making locked eye-contact. Slowly, he reached out with one of those weird, furry hands of his.

He was reaching for my belt area, and I knew in an instant what the plan was. I made a sweeping blow, knocking him aside.

"Forget it, skunk," I told him. "That's not going to happen. Not this time."

Hissing at me and showing me his teeth, he scampered away again into the dark.

"Well," Harris said, "if they're not going to tell us who Vorhoos is, at least we've got the throne. We can round them all up, put them in cages, and let the Mogwa sort out who's who."

I nodded. It was as good a plan as any. Sateekas had told me he wanted me to return the king. Quite possibly, one of these guys *was* the king. Hell, I couldn't tell one of them from the next.

But as I was a man who was only interested in completing the letter of my orders, not necessarily the spirit, I figured if I gave him thirty or so skunks and one of them was the right skunk—by damn, I'd completed my mission. That kind of success was inarguable.

Fortunately, King Vorhoos wasn't able to maintain his pretense for long. He looked like just one more skunk in the crowd until I dared to walk up to that bony throne.

This sacred artifact signified the legitimacy of the king's authority to every one of his subjects. When I laid a grimy gauntlet upon it, one skunk squawked and charged.

"You dare not touch our most sacred of relics!" he squalled at me.

I had, in fact, placed my hand upon one of the largest bones, which formed an armrest. The thing was as big as a mammoth's tusk and even thicker. To a skunk, I imagined it was the size of a tree trunk.

Smiling, I turned toward the complaining skunk—but I left my paw resting firmly upon the armrest.

"Oh, I don't know," I said. "I was thinking about sitting my big butt down on this here throne. I think it would look good on me. Don't you?"

I gave him a grin, and the skunk completely lost it. He charged at me, squabbling, squalling, all teeth and flying fur.

It was Harris who reached out and snatched him, plucking him straight from the air with fingers wrapped around the creature's throat. He pulled the skunk close, and he grinned into his face.

"You know what they say, Vorhoos?" he asked. "Back on Earth?"

"No," the skunk said, "and I could care less."

"What they say is that *pride goeth before the fall*—and buddy, you have just fallen."

## -37-

Several hours later, we had to bring a pig out from the central compound to do the digging for us. Using the big drone, we managed to root out all the skunks and, most importantly, Sateekas' new throne.

We did this last operation gently, using floater technology to get it out of the widened hole. Weightless and creaking, the throne glided up into the air and slowly drifted across the ruins of the city toward the Mogwa fortress.

As this was going on, I have to admit, I was having some misgivings. After all, these poor skunks had never really done anything to me—except for killing me a few times. But I could forgive them for that. We were invaders, and all the intruding soldiers who'd died on Nebra more than deserved it as far as the locals were concerned.

Now, don't get me wrong. These skunks were extremely unpleasant fellows. I would never want to visit this planet on a vacation, for instance. Hell, they'd probably steal your underwear and your kidneys during your first night's stay at one of their hotels. They were just that kind of an alien. Still, I couldn't help admiring their fighting spirit. They hadn't made this campaign an easy one for the Mogwa—or the Earthers.

Sometimes, a mission like this was distasteful to a man like me. I felt like the classic soldier of the past after atrocities had been discovered, claiming he'd just been following orders all along.

Once we reached the central compound, we found large work crews cleaning up the mess. Graves had sent another lifter over with several more pigs and some fresh troops. These individuals were clearing up the massive debris field that surrounded the fortress.

They used puff-crete along with heavy trowels to patch up the numerous holes in the outer wall, and painted over the divots and scorch marks.

Underneath the compound were sewers and dank tunnels that ran everywhere into the city. Legion Varus men had killed the large worms that had managed to rupture the walls. Recognizing our previous mistake, they dug deeper this time, pouring puff-crete into trenches. There weren't going to be any new underground attacks of that same nature.

The walls now extended ten meters below the ground and more than that above it. It was going to be much more difficult for them to rupture those walls again, should they possess the spirit to assault our fortress again. My suspicion was they didn't have the fuzzy balls to try it twice.

A full day and a night later, a humiliating ceremony was performed. Vorhoos, humbled and in chains, stood before his own throne—but he wasn't allowed to mount it.

Instead, this spectacle was being broadcast planet-wide. He woodenly performed a lengthy surrender-ceremony, which involved a series of humiliating steps.

I frowned, watching as Sateekas stood before him and accepted his unquestioning loyalty to the Galactic Empire.

"You realize, of course," Sateekas said, "that this province has always been owned by the Empire, that your state of independence has in fact been an affront to all Galactics for nearly a century now?"

I frowned to hear this. I didn't like to hear that planets in the Mid-Zone were declaring themselves independent. Anything about the weakening of the Empire was a negative in my mind.

For all of the destruction and horror we'd witnessed, I knew that it could be a lot worse. According to the darkest history books of the Galactics, before they'd exerted their influence across billions of star systems emanating from the central bulbous core of the Milky Way, the galaxy had essentially been a nightmarish, dog-eat-dog jungle.

Rulership between any two species was established entirely upon a predatory basis. Under the old ways, might made right and then some.

The Empire had originally brought order to this chaos. It ended the common practice of incinerating entire populations on worlds that had just been conquered. It added a certain level of civilization, perhaps just a thin veneer, but a welcome one.

The skunks had become citizens of the galaxy in those early times. They'd developed their singular trade good, which I learned about. Essentially, they'd traded large beasts of burden to other planets.

This made some level of sense to me. All of these dinosaurs had been carefully trained and bred them for labor. The skunks were a diminutive species race that appeared to detest physical work. They traded these beasts to other local star systems and had done good business.

Over time, however, the Empire had weakened. Out in the Frontier Zone where my own Province 921 was located, the borders had receded. The Imperial fleets had pulled back, unable to maintain order.

That was how a splinter colony like Segin had developed without being stopped and cowed by the Mogwa from Trantor. No, they'd been allowed to build their own society in the Mid-Zone—and so had the skunks.

All that had ended on Nebra and apparently several other nearby star systems as well. The Mogwa had again asserted their superiority and, in fact, had come to rule over all the most civilized and technologically advanced of the local worlds.

Earth had done exactly the same thing in our province. We were even farther out from the Galactic Core, so we'd been allowed to arm ourselves. We'd built our own fleets and enforced Galactic rule over dozens of inhabited star systems.

All this was disturbing. It was clear evidence that the Empire was in a severe state of decay—not just on the Frontier, but in the Mid-Zone as well.

Graves had always told me that I didn't want to know how bad things could get. He'd confessed to hating the Galactics just as much as any human did, but he felt that without their core stabilizing influence, billions of intelligent life forms would die every year.

There were thousands of disparate species sprinkled everywhere around the galaxy. Without central control, all of them would be at each other's throats. That level of destruction would be much worse what we'd witnessed today.

I wasn't sure about that. It made some logical sense, but I wished it could be something different. Plain common horse sense told me that if you allowed all these aliens to do whatever they wanted, the most aggressive ones would prey upon the weaker. The strife and war and conflict would be endless and infinite. The tragedies like we'd seen today would be played out across the galaxy over and over again, perhaps on a daily basis.

So, it was with a troubled heart that I watched the ceremony continue. Once the skunk king had read a very lengthy surrender document, Sateekas at last accepted his abdication from the throne of Nebra.

I fully expected to see Sateekas mount the throne and squat upon it. From the point of view of the millions of Nebrans watching, that would be an act of desecration.

But that's not what happened. In the end, Nero appeared. Lady Nox was walking with him, ushering him forward. The little spidery dude wore his finest. His outfit was embellished with a cape that shimmered. A blue nimbus of dancing light seemed to surround him.

About thirty skunks stood around in chains throughout the courtyard. They were the sad sacks we'd captured and brought back with us.

All of them stared in silence. None of them said a damned thing, but I could tell they were impressed. Their eyes were wide, and they didn't even blink as they gazed upon Nero.

Nero's shimmering cape was made of light. It was a trick, not a garment—but I didn't tell them, and none of them probably knew.

At first, I don't think any of the skunks, not even King Vorhoos himself, knew what was about to happen next—but I did.

Nero was ushered forward with great pomp and circumstance toward the dinosaur-bone throne. With as much dignity as he could summon, he crawled up upon those ancient bones and squatted on their sacred throne. He reared up, as tall as he could, to exceed the height of any skunk.

A great deal of hissing arose. The hisses weren't coming from the Mogwa, nor from the human guards. We legionnaires were all standing around dressed in our chrome armor with our rifles at our shoulders.

No, the hissing was coming from the skunks.

"Discipline these creatures!" Sateekas shouted toward me and my men. "They must learn decorum!"

Up and down the line, gauntlets were laid up against skulls. Some of the skunks fell senseless into the dirt.

Most of them skillfully ducked and then stopped their infernal hissing. Cowed, they stood looking resentful—but they kept their peace.

King Vorhoos was now kneeling before his own throne with Nero squatting upon it.

He didn't move. He didn't hiss. He didn't jeer. He didn't even raise his eyes.

"Say the words," Sateekas ordered.

Vorhoos slowly stood, rising from his knees. He began to speak words, words which I knew through my translator box were of supplication, of humility, with false claims of enlightenment and joy.

It was a long speech, just the sort of thing you might expect a Mogwa would've written about themselves. Vorhoos talked about how wonderful Nero was, how great Sateekas was, how happy he was that all this strife and killing had ended. He urged his people to submit to the rule of the Mogwa for the betterment of all.

Then slowly, very slowly, he approached the throne.

I frowned, becoming concerned. Beside me, Harris took his rifle down from his shoulder. He held it across his body, and I could see his gauntlets tightening upon it. We both knew these skunks very well by now, and we didn't trust them. Not one inch.

The Mogwa, however, seemed to believe that their victory was utter and complete. As Vorhoos slowly approached with those big, unblinking skunk eyes of his locked onto Nero's orbs, they didn't sound the alarm.

Vorhoos reached out with his fuzzy hands, and I wondered what his plan was. Was he going to grab Sateekas' son by the throat and throttle him? That seemed the most likely. Or would he perhaps set off an explosion of some kind? I wasn't sure, but I was ready for anything.

Then, in that intense moment—everything changed.

"There they are! Right on time!" Sateekas announced.

He craned his head back and directed his orbs up into the sky. It seemed to me that a cloud had come to squat above us. The bright, hot sun of Nebra had somehow been occluded.

A few seconds passed, during which others looked skyward and gasped. The gloom that had been suddenly cast over the courtyard deepened. The air even took on a faint chill.

But I wasn't fooled. I was certain this must all be part of some grand final skunk-trick. I refused to take my eyes from King Vorhoos. He had to be up to something—something evil.

But at last, hearing the growing chorus of gasps from humans and skunks alike, I finally glanced upward to see what all the fuss was about.

There, shining in the sky, was a massive starship—but it wasn't just a single vessel. No, there was an entire fleet up there, hanging in low orbit above us.

More ships were descending into view from the surface as everyone watched. One ship became dozens—then hundreds. While we all gaped and exclaimed over the following minute, perhaps a thousand, shining silver ships appeared.

My jaw sagged low. I was in utter astonishment.

"Is that... the Battle Fleet?" Harris asked in a hushed tone.

I gaped and I nodded because I knew in my heart that it could not be anything else. Had Sateekas somehow become a *real* grand admiral again? Had he somehow transformed Segin into a military powerhouse, capable of building a thousand starships? It didn't seem possible.

A Battle Fleet like the one we were witnessing in orbit above us had once annexed Earth. There were so many ships, layers of them with innumerable shining hulls, that the sky was dark.

That kind of power in the skies was terrifying. How much firepower was staring down at us? Those guns—even a tenth of them—could level every city on this planet within an hour.

The Battle Fleet. Yes, that's what it was.

In that instant, I knew how humanity had felt over a century and a half before. When Battle Fleet 921 had arrived to annex Earth. Just by hanging up there, they'd exerted their irresistible power over our home world.

It was humbling. It was awesome. It was like seeing the very gods themselves come to life in the skies and take shape as quiet, sleek warships.

## -38-

Harris walked close to me, and he gaped up at the sky at my side.

"That's a Battle Fleet," he said. "Don't even try to bullshit me on this one."

"Yeah," I said, "it's probably not the same one that used to patrol at Province 921—but it's definitely a Mogwa Battle Fleet."

"So…" Harris said. "If Sateekas had these ships up his sleeve all along, why in the fuck didn't he just roll them out in the first place?"

I squinted at him, realizing he was right. Why had we fought a desperate land campaign if the Mogwa Battle Fleet was parked nearby? I felt a burning urge to ask Sateekas this very question—but I wasn't able to, at least not immediately.

The coronation of Nero continued. For obvious reasons, Vorhoos was a reformed skunk. Whatever his plans had been for the moment he got his fuzzy hands on the young Mogwa—they'd now changed.

He truly looked like a supplicant, not like a slinking skunk planning a fast, vicious attack. Perhaps even he, the proud King Vorhoos, realized that it was hopeless.

The Mogwa had won. His people could never defeat these invaders—at least not until their fleet left Nebra's skies.

I watched Vorhoos. It seemed to me that cogs were moving inside that small angular skull…

Right then, I figured the rebel king had come to the same conclusions that Harris had. It was best to bide one's time in the face of overwhelming power. So he crowned Nero as the king of Nebra. There were some boos and hisses from the skunks in the area, but none charged forward. None risked their lives. They all seemed to accept their unhappy fate. And as the coronation was broadcast all over the planet, I knew that every skunk on this world was experiencing this humiliation with him, with their king.

After it was done, all the skunks were released, including King Vorhoos himself. His new mission was to urge his people to accept their new overlords and to run a local government responsible for the cleanup of the vast mess the war had caused in the capital.

Looking like a crestfallen, somewhat broken creature, he left the front gates of the central fortress and picked his way through the burning rubble with his followers trailing in his wake. Their tails, usually held high and proud, were dragging like dusters over the broken and exploded adobe bricks.

I watched them go, not listening to my own 3rd Unit troops, who were jubilant.

I knew why my men were so happy. Few of us had died in the battle. For once, the other nine units of 3rd Cohort had suffered most of the losses. They'd been burned to death in the final sweeps of Leeson's 88s, almost to a man.

But watching that sad group of skunks dragging their fuzzy asses over broken stones left me troubled. They now faced the monumental task of cleanup and rebuilding. I couldn't help but feel for them. This was their home, after all, and they'd lost their independence.

One by one, my adjuncts and noncoms came up to congratulate me. Most of them read my mood correctly and soon wandered off.

At last, however, a different presence came to stand nearby. This was a much smaller and somewhat stankier creature.

I turned toward him, tearing my eyes from the gaze of the burning city. I looked down upon the one Nairb in the cosmos I knew well: Seven.

"Hello, Seven," I said. "What do you think of all this?"

I waved vaguely at the horizon. My gesture was meant to include the jungle, the distant ocean, and all the smoke and haze in between.

"I think this is an occasion worthy of a beverage," he said.

I looked down at him, and, true to his word, I saw he was carrying a mug in each flipper. I took the one he was offering me and drained it.

My face twisted up as the brew was bitter—but it was strong, and it did hit the spot.

Seven watched me closely as I performed this act.

"You seem unchanged," he said. "I've never noticed before this particular assignment how little alcohol seems to affect you humans."

"Oh, I don't know," I said. "We've got plenty of drunks in our legion."

"Yes, but you don't fall prey to it as quickly as we do."

I shrugged again. "Probably because we're bigger. More mass, you know. Takes longer to get through our bloodstream and all that."

"Possibly..." Seven admitted. "But I think there are physiological differences between Nairbs and humans. We can hold a large volume of this substance due to our ability to store liquids on an indefinite basis."

"How's that, old friend?" I asked. I was draining my beverage, and it again had fired an explosion off in my gut. It was powerful stuff!

"Our bodies are an effective storage solution. We can store large quantities of liquids inside of safe bladders and digest them when we wish to."

I shuddered a little bit, disgusted by the whole conversation, but I decided not to let on. Seven, after all, hadn't even charged me for this latest beverage, which I so desperately needed.

"That's interesting," I lied.

"Yes, so although a small amount is needed for your average Nairb to become inebriated, we're able to store a lot of it. We can therefore leak it out into our bloodstreams whenever it is suitable."

"Huh," I said, thinking that over. "So… you're able to stay drunk for days? That's an interesting adaptation."

"It has to do with our aquatic background."

I did notice that for all his talk of alcohol affecting Nairbs more strongly, he seemed to be no more affected than I was by the single drink we'd both consumed. He was somewhat verbose, mind you, but he definitely wasn't slurring his words, or laying down his head, or otherwise acting highly intoxicated. I could only surmise that he'd built up a significant tolerance over the years since I first introduced him to Earth's favorite beverage.

Seven prattled on for a while, but I'd stopped listening. I made noncommittal grunts now and then, just to keep him happy.

"What are your thoughts, Centurion McGill?" he asked finally.

This startled me out of my reverie, and I turned to look at him. "Uh…My thoughts about what part?"

"About the ramifications of this campaign."

It was a surprising question, especially coming from a Nairb. Perhaps the alcohol *was* affecting him. He'd become slightly philosophical.

"Well… I think it's a damn shame these skunks had to suffer the way they did. I also don't understand," I said, pointing above at the silvery ships that still filled the sky, "why Sateekas put us through all this. Why did he kill so many of Nebra's finest? Why did he burn this city down? None of it was necessary if he had that fleet up there the whole damned time."

"Ah," Seven said, "I understand the nature of your confusion. You are ignorant of the circumstances of the political situation."

"How's that, exactly?"

"There is a secret reality in play. Sateekas does not have a long list of military successes on his record. This has been noticed by the officials of Trantor."

I laughed. "You're putting that mildly. What he's known for is a long string of expensive disasters."

"Precisely so. It has been my unpleasant duty to have accounted and totaled all of these tallies. I was asked to certify a precise balance sheet detailing every profit and loss during this campaign."

I turned to look at him, frowning. "So that's why you're here? You're a bean counter for Trantor?"

"Yes," he said.

"I was kind of wondering what your actual job was... So, you're not just along for the ride, playing the part of a camp follower who sells booze to whoever will buy it, huh?"

"No, that's merely a side hustle, as you humans term it."

"Okay... but you still haven't answered my question."

Seven looked furtive. "Did you realize that Battle Fleet 488 was in the star system the entire time? That we've never, for one instant, been alone here at Nebra?"

"No," I said, "I realized nothing of the kind until they showed themselves."

"Surprising. They were in high orbit. They lowered themselves during the ceremony. I would have thought your gravimetric sensors..."

"Well," I said, "maybe Merton knew. Maybe Imperator Galina Turov knew. Somebody like that. But nobody's telling a centurion running around down here on the ground that there's a thousand ships somewhere in the star system. Why the hell did they stay hidden for so long?"

"As you've been a benefactor to me in many cases in the past," Seven said, "I'll attempt to explain."

I nodded, hoping that his explanation wasn't going to take *too* long. Nairbs, like all bureaucrats throughout time, never seemed to know when a few words were better than an overly precise avalanche of them.

He started talking, and I listened for a bit—I swear it.

"...so you see," he continued, and right about then I realized I'd phased out for just a minute. I blamed the booze, even though I knew it was just my misfiring brain that'd caused me to miss most of the conversation.

I strained my ears and my mind, squinting my eyes at him so I could listen and absorb every word.

"Until the moment Sateekas managed to capture this planet, Segin was not a true Tier Three civilization. The Mogwa from Trantor, which he entreated with, were therefore unwilling to deploy or even to reveal the Battle Fleet you now see overhead."

"Ah…" I said, "I get it. They didn't believe he could pull it off. They wanted proof before they committed Battle Fleet 488 to this annexation ritual."

"Yes, precisely so."

"Huh... So even though they could have saved a lot of time and effort for Sateekas, they wanted him to prove to them that he could do it on his own."

"Correct. There's an unfortunate lack of trust among Core World officials for the achievements of Grand Admiral Sateekas."

"Right, right…"

I had another thought then, and I turned back toward the Nairb, but I found that he'd already left. He was humping his way back toward the safety of the inner sanctums beneath several layers of brick.

I'd thought to ask him if the battle fleet overhead right now was truly from the Core Worlds, from Trantor itself. I thought he'd indicated as much, but it just seemed so incredible…

Then again, it would be just as incredible if Segin had somehow managed to churn out so many ships from their single planet in such a short time.

No, that didn't seem reasonable. Not at all. It seemed much more likely to me that the magnificent fleet we'd all been gaping at had been built in the glowing, white-hot, radioactive core of our galaxy. A place where suns were so numerous and jam-packed together, they were rarely more than half a light-year apart.

Close enough, in fact, that they often affected each other with gravitational tides. Occasionally, those fat stars collapsed in upon themselves. Then they became black holes that swallowed their neighbors, becoming ever larger and more dangerous.

It occurred to me they were rather like the Galactics themselves.

## -39-

A few weeks after the Nebran King surrendered to Grand Admiral Sateekas, Nebra officially became part of the kingdom of Segin. With our primary mission complete, Legion Varus boarded *Scorpio* and left the stars of the Mid-Zone behind.

I, for one, wasn't sorry to see my last skunk-alien. I kind of hoped I'd never have to deal with them again. That said, I found myself still a bit troubled about the final results of the campaign on their home world. I couldn't help but wonder if things could have turned out better.

The journey home to Earth was a long one, even in a fast new ship like *Scorpio*. Built with the know-how of the Rigellians, *Scorpio* was actually a battlecruiser rather than a traditional transport. The ship had better technology than Earth-built vessels did in many ways.

Still, the trip required months to complete. Those dull days weren't happy times for one James McGill. Oh sure, I drank a lot, ate a lot, and shot up a lot of targets. Since we were on the way home, our exercises on Green Deck weren't of the deadly variety, and that part of life was kind of fun.

But still, I felt something was missing.

My natural response to boredom and malaise was to chase just about every skirt I could find aboard ship. That included Adjunct Leeza, Natasha, Evelyn Thompson—lots of ladies. Unfortunately, virtually every well I visited was bone dry.

Most of the girls who were on my permanent "maybe" list had found someone else—and the rest of them were wise to my tricks. They treated me roughly the way one might treat a skunk-alien from Nebra. In other words, like I was a furry, conniving leper.

I sent a few notes to Galina, attempting to cajole her into coming out to *Scorpio* to check up on things. She wasn't interested. I wasn't overly surprised by that, as high-level officers always had something better to do than travel through the interstellar void aboard a boring starship. She did, however, suggest that she hadn't forgotten about the cruise she'd promised to go on with me when I returned. At least I had that to look forward to.

Grumbling and somewhat frustrated, I eventually returned to Earth. Anyone who knows me well knows that once a mission in deep space has been completed, I want to demobilize and head home to old Georgia Sector as fast as a sky-train can fly me there. But alas, it was not to be today.

Before I could ride a lifter all the way down to Earth, I was already getting messages from various officers in Central. All kinds of irritants like Primus Bob were requiring my immediate presence at meetings.

Holy crap. Couldn't a man catch a break?

Cursing and bitching to myself, I gave into the reality of the matter. I was being summoned to report to the consul's office by none other than Wurtenberger himself.

Primus Bob was grinning about it when he informed me.

"That's right, McGill," he said. "I can't believe it either, but your presence is required today at the consul's offices by 0930."

"Ugh," I said. "Can you give me a hint as to what this might all be about, Primus, sir?"

"No can do," he said, grinning at me.

Primus Bob and I went a long way back, and virtually all of our interactions had been negative in nature. As was the case with most hogs, Primus Bob was a lifer—and I never got along well with such people. So, while I wouldn't say that Bob hated me, he certainly had no love in his heart for old McGill.

"I'll give you just one hint," he said. He was still grinning, so I knew it had to be something shitty. "Raash is already here, awaiting your arrival."

"What?"

But he'd signed off already, and his final words left me blinking and puzzled. I scratched at my head, and then my face, thinking hard.

Raash was there? What the hell was that lizard up to?

I thought it over, and I realized that I hadn't laid eyes on Raash aboard *Scorpio* during the long journey home.

Why not? Well, because he was an important lizard, of course. As a henchman of Alexander Turov, he was way more important than some run-of-the-mill human centurion such as myself.

He must have bought himself a ticket home, an immediate one-way trip through the gateways. He'd transported himself as a blip through the cosmos, probably the minute we'd wrapped things up on Throne World.

"Huh..." I said to myself.

If Raash had spent close to four months back at Hegemony Headquarters, with all that time to stir things up...

"Shit..."

I didn't know exactly what was coming my way, but I was already fairly certain it was nothing good.

A few short hours later, I found myself riding up the elevators to the pinnacle of Central's pyramid-like structure. The moment I arrived at the top floor lobby, I was ushered past a large number of unsmiling hog guards. Soon, I found myself standing in the glorious presence of Consul Wurtenberger himself. There were a few other simps in the room, but they didn't matter, so I didn't even look at them.

Wurtenberger seemed just as fat, sour, and euro-sounding as ever. He didn't greet me with anything like enthusiasm.

"Ah, at last!" he said. "McGill has finally decided to grace us with his presence."

"Insubordination from the start," another raspy voice spoke.

I turned and saw Raash, standing in one of the tall, slanted windows. No doubt he'd been lurking up here for a long time, spewing venom into Wurtenberger's ears for hours.

"This human is substandard, Consul," he said. "He's kept his masters waiting. Perhaps we should decide his punishment

321

for this additional act of insolence before we discuss the main charges against him."

I had already picked up the bad vibe in the room. I can be intuitive like that, no matter what my girlfriends say about me.

Charges? Insolence? Hell, I'd come here as fast as I could. Sure, I'd stopped for a beer and a sandwich at the station. But I wasn't even thirty minutes late yet. I'd just traveled thousands of lightyears to get here. Did these jokers really expect a man who was still shaking off the dust of the stars from his boots to arrive on time? That seemed highly unreasonable to this country boy.

I could have kicked off with a complaint about Raash, but I decided to take the high road. I shook off all my negativity, put on a big grin, and threw Wurtenberger a hearty salute. I didn't even look at Raash, but instead approached the grand conference table. Swirling and glowing just above the table was a large holographic display depicting our quadrant of the galaxy.

"Uh…" I said as I took a seat at the table. "To what exactly do I owe this honor, sirs? Don't tell me you're going to pin another medal on me."

As I said this, I flicked at the Dawn Star on my chest. I normally didn't wear my one and only medal. But today, due to having been forewarned of the negative nature of this gathering, I'd chosen to dust it off and pin it on. I wanted to remind my superiors I was actually a decorated member of Earth's legions. People like Wurtenberger were the only ones who seemed to be impressed by such things, and I wasn't above showing off a bit of bling if I thought it could get me out of something awful.

"Look at that," Raash said, rasping out the words from the window area. "This creature expects accolades and awards after having failed so utterly. This is an insult. At the very least, it should increase the penalty which is levied upon this nonconformant beast of a human."

Feeling driven to acknowledge him at last, I frowned and turned my gaze toward the lizard who was so clearly attempting to sabotage me. I pointed a big finger in his direction and waggled it.

"Can anyone tell me exactly what this alien is doing at a gathering of Earth's officers? At the very least, he's a security risk. You all know he's a spy for Steel World, don't you?"

Raash lit up, hissing and saying a few slurred things that were doubtlessly curses in his own language that didn't directly translate through his tapper.

I was glad to see he was discomforted. It'd long been my theory that the more aggressive and unpleasant an alien was, the more offended they were by any sort of criticism. In other words, those who could dish out the worst could never take it.

"That's a good question…" Wurtenberger said. "Before the debriefing continues, I have to ask that Raash be removed."

Oh, the hissing! Raash approached the conference table and drooled on the carpet. If he'd had hackles on his back, he would have raised them. But instead, he had only a tail. This had become rigid and curved upward behind him.

That signal told me he was in a high state of agitation. A stiff, erect tail was a clear marker of displeasure with any Saurian.

"Everyone here knows who I represent," he said. "It would be best for all that our true master is not displeased."

Wurtenberger scowled. He never liked to get reminded about the Ruling Council—and most especially the overbearing aura of Alexander Turov, who led that august body.

Technically, Wurtenberger was in charge of Earth and everything else. Sure, he'd been installed in that office by the Nine, but to his mind, that did not make him their servant.

"Out with you, alien!" he said.

"Bravo!" I said, clapping. "You know… if we just shoot him now and have him revived later, it will probably speed up the whole process of removal."

"There's no need for any further urging," Raash said. He left with poor grace, dragging his raspy tail behind him. It made extra-loud sand-papery sounds as he crossed the tile and sumptuous carpets.

At the exit, he turned to me and made one last cryptic comment. "You have been noticed, McGill," he hissed at me.

At last, the door slammed behind him.

"Damnation," I said. "I thought he'd never leave."

Wurtenberger and I faced one another. There were a couple of other primuses malingering, but they were only secretaries. Wurtenberger glanced at them.

"How do you feel about these officers, McGill?" he said. "Do you think you can speak plainly in front of them?"

I knew his comment was made in jest—but only partly. Once you're the consul of Earth, you really couldn't trust anyone.

I shook my head. "I do not."

"And why not?"

I shrugged. "Simple enough. I worked quite a bit with Drusus, you know, back before he made his final journey to… elsewhere."

Everyone there gasped slightly. They all looked down. It was as if I'd uttered a word that was on a sacred list of taboos—and that the was effect I'd been seeking.

I'd dared to name Drusus, the former consul of Earth. He was currently a non-person. Invoking his name was like discussing the devil at a church picnic.

"What's your point, McGill?" Wurtenberger demanded.

"My point is a matter of simple logic. Are you certain that no one on your staff is a spy? No one except for Raash, that is?"

Wurtenberger stared at me with his piggy eyes, and I stared back, meeting his gaze evenly. We communicated without words for several seconds.

Finally, Wurtenberger heaved a sigh. "I wish to speak to this witness alone."

The primus secretaries seemed startled. One of them was Primus Bob himself. I was impressed, because Bob had apparently moved up from being a lowly receptionist, operating as a desk jockey in the front staff room, to where he was actually allowed to sit in on meetings. I shuddered to think of the humiliations, the hazing rituals, and the sheer brown-nosery he must have committed to worm his way into Wurtenberger's inner sanctum.

"Consul," Bob said stiffly, "I must remind you that this particular man is dangerous and unreliable."

He began then to tick off a long series of negative adjectives. Wurtenberger soon grew tired of them, not too long after I did.

"Yes, yes, yes," he said. "Fine. If he shoots me, you can have him permed. Now, get out."

With great stiffness and many scowls cast in my direction, the little secretaries gathered their things and shuffled on out the door. They kept their tails tucked low over their buttholes as they did it, like freshly kicked dogs.

Wurtenberger then finally turned to me. "All right, enough theatrics. Speak."

"You know, sir, I've got to say that I'm pretty impressed that you value my opinion so highly as to meet with me in private like this."

"Make your report, McGill!"

"Well, sir, it would help if I knew what I was even being accused of."

Wurtenberger blinked in surprise. "How could you not know? Are you going to claim ignorance, or have you simply forgotten all your actions that occurred several months ago in the Mid-Zone?"

"Uh…" I said, "let me just say that my recollections may not match up perfectly with those relayed to you by Raash."

Wurtenberger nodded a bit, thinking that over. It hadn't occurred to him that he had been fed one version of events without the other side having a chance to say a damn thing. I knew, underneath, he was a fair man—at least in the broadest sense.

"Just so," he said. "This is about the rise of Segin to a Tier Three civilization."

"I'm with you so far, sir."

"You're aware then that their new status has now become official?"

"Yep."

Wurtenberger looked vindicated and scribbled a few notes on his vast desk. "An unexpected admission, but let us move on. Were you not informed by Raash, an agent of Earth, that the Ruling Council of your home planet did not wish for Sateekas to succeed in installing his son—?" Here, he paused and flipped through a few sweeps on the desk in front of him. "Oh yes. His name is Nero, a prophetic moniker, don't you think?"

"If you say so, Consul."

"Hmm," Wurtenberger said. "Nero was not to take the throne of Segin. There wasn't even supposed to *be* a throne of Segin. But now, that final technical obstruction for the Mogwa has been removed."

"Consul Wurtenberger," I said, putting on my most earnest and soul-searching expression. "Sir, I'm only a centurion from Earth's least reputable legion."

"I'm well aware of this, McGill. You're also infamous for meddling in matters above your station."

"You're right about that, sir. I get it. I get it. But in this particular case, I feel like I accomplished my mission and did absolutely no meddling of any kind."

"Explain yourself."

"Less than a year ago, we all sat right here in this room and hammered out the details of the contract with Sateekas. We accepted the contract, and I was hired along with my entire legion to perform a mission—and that mission has now been successfully concluded. Our client, who paid a lot of money, mind you, got the best possible service. He is one hundred percent satisfied. At no point during this campaign did I receive any orders to sabotage my client. As far as I knew, I was under the command of Grand Admiral Sateekas the entire time. Was I wrong about that?"

Wurtenberger nodded, shoving out a fat lower lip as he listened to my words. I knew that he was a rule-stickler. A rules-based argument was, generally speaking, something that would be effective with him.

"Normally, your statement would make a lot of sense," he said. "However, in this particular case, the individual known as Raash informed you of his intentions to derail Sateekas' plans."

He began speeching then. I thought about looking blank and ignorant as the storm of words washed over me. Maybe I could drop my jaw open and let my eyes go wide and stupid—but I decided to pass on that option. I didn't think it was going to work on Wurtenberger. Instead, I just nodded and kept quiet.

"...and finally," Wurtenberger said, "you know very well that Raash is in the employ of Public Servant Alexander Turov."

"I've heard such whispers, sir," I admitted.

Wurtenberger frowned at me. "Therefore, when he suggested that his mission was to prevent Grand Admiral Sateekas from achieving his strategic goals, you knew that was the will of the Hegemony at large. Therefore, when you helped Sateekas place his son on the throne, you failed Earth."

"Now, hold on a second," I said. "In what particular way did I fail Earth? What act did I commit, according to that crazy lizard you just kicked out of here, that could rise to the level of sedition as you so claim it to be?"

Wurtenberger revealed some anger in his fat fingers as they moved over the tabletop. He quickly flicked up some videos.

Certain highlights of the campaign played between us. The vids were short, showing key points, such as the day I'd been on hand to witness the defilement of the skunk's sacred site. After that, he skipped forward to another video. This one again depicted me on the upper battlements of the fortress in the capital of Nebra, defending the Mogwa heroically.

Here, Wurtenberger chose to play the long part where I fried all the troops and skunks with my 88s. After that came a few videos of my men laughing and high-fiving each other. They proudly survey the mounds of ash and the smoldering fires of the ruined city all around them.

"There, right there!" Wurtenberger said. "You knew the true goals of Earth, and yet you decided instead to ignore them. You personally defeated the Nebrans, which caused the annexation to be complete. This was the exact sequence of events that Earth did not want!"

"Now, hold on just a minute," I said. "Raash was not there that day. He was not on those battlements. He had no advice to give."

"Fair enough," he said. "What of the other time? What of when you defiled their most holy site?"

"First of all, I didn't defile anything. Here, let me show you some proof."

Figuring that Raash had heavily edited all these videos, I pulled out some videos of my own. I had carefully stored these, duplicating and even triplicating them. I'd taken precautions to keep them to myself, giving the files encrypted names, hidden locations—the works.

Surprisingly, as I swiped at my tapper, I found I was unable to locate the files at first. Everything that showed what had happened during the trip out to the Nebran's sacred site was gone.

Then I moved on to my secondary and then tertiary backups. In each case, I found the files deleted.

This was the sort of trick that all intelligence agencies excelled at, but I still wasn't deterred.

I sent out a quick request or two to some automated bots, which I'd had Natasha set up for me. Immediately, the files were relayed back to my tapper. They had names like "Christmas, two years ago" and "Etta's first birthday" written on their heavily disguised folders.

Triumphantly, I finally dug out a clean copy and threw it onto the desktop. I let it play.

Very soon, it was obvious that both Sateekas and Raash had participated in invoking the rage of the skunks.

Consul Wurtenberger knitted together his fat brows and pursed his fat lips. "I have not been shown these images before. Are you sure they're not AI-generated?"

"Very sure, sir," I said. "You may have your experts go over them. But think about it. It makes perfect sense. Raash was sent there to sabotage the efforts of the Mogwa. I understand that. But he used the same exact techniques as the Mogwa themselves. He figured that by enraging the skunks, he would cause the entire effort by Sateekas to fail—but he guessed wrong."

"Hmm…"

I leaned forward as the video played again. It was showing Raash eating out of the sacrificial bowls with blood running down his scaly neck. "It was that ugly-tailed lizard. The very alien you just kicked out of here, who caused all this to happen. He did it through miscalculation. Did I protect Sateekas? Sure I did. I followed the orders of my superiors."

"Are you sure about this, McGill?"

"Absolutely," I said. "At no time was I given a command to stand down or to change my behavior in any way. In fact, Graves was angry that I didn't fire those 88s from the wall top earlier than I did."

I had further evidence of this, which was easy to bring up. Apparently, Raash and his Intel butt-boys didn't consider those vids to be exculpatory.

Wurtenberger reviewed all the evidence carefully. At last, he sat back and heaved a sigh.

"What am I to do, then?" he said. "The Ruling Nine are very upset. They did not want Sateekas to succeed. Once they learned of this mad scheme of the Mogwa to attempt to place one of their own upon the Throne at the core of the galaxy, they've been trying to derail it."

"Excuse me, Mr. Consul," I said, daring to speak. "Why, exactly, is the Ruling Council so against the Mogwa gaining in prestige and power? So what if they retake the Empire and manage to put one of their own on the Imperial Throne? Would that be so bad? Earth would become a vassal of the most powerful galactic species. How could that be a bad thing?"

Wurtenberger gave me a bitter smile. He shook his head. "One wouldn't think it possible you could be so naive of mind, McGill," he said. "But as I sense you are being serious, I will indulge you. There are those who are in positions of great power here on Earth who don't want the Empire to be at peace. They do not want stable government at the center of our galaxy."

"But why not, sir?" I said. "It would bring peace to everyone. It would save a thousand planets a year from being scorched off. Species that we've never even heard of have become extinct. If you heard some of the stories—"

He stopped me, throwing up a fat hand. "I've heard them all, believe it or not, and many more horrors you will never become aware of. But think, McGill, if the Empire becomes whole again, if peace breaks out across the galaxy, what will happen to Earth? What will happen to our status as a reliable independent on the fringe of the galaxy?"

"Uh…"

"Right now, we're growing," he continued. "We're expanding our borders, gathering strength, learning new technologies. We're nowhere near as powerful as any of the Galactics... yet. But given a few more centuries..." he trailed off, and I stared at him, gob-smacked.

"What?" I said. "You think Earth can become one of the Galactics? That's sheer insanity. The Galactic Core races would never allow it."

"Maybe not," he said. "But perhaps they've never faced a species so ambitious and well-positioned as ours. Everything fades away into history, McGill, including every empire ever known."

I thought about that. I gritted my teeth, and I squinted.

I remembered that long ago, Graves said we didn't want to know what the universe was like before there was an Empire. That things were brutal, that life for any species was unfair, nasty, and short.

Did we really want to return to those predatory days? I, for one, didn't think it was for the betterment of all intellectual species that such times should return.

I shook my head, uncertain.

Wurtenberger talked on for a while, but essentially, he accepted my explanation that it was Raash's fault that things had gone awry and not mine.

Raash had helped Sateekas to enrage the skunks, not me. I'd simply followed my orders. It was now clear to the consul that Raash was attempting to deflect from his own guilt.

Those videos I'd so carefully hidden had given me the proof I'd needed. He planned to take those files, relay them to the Ruling Council, and quite probably get Raash executed a few times before the matter was concluded.

Being a long-winded man, he marched around his ridiculously outsized desk. He told me a lot of things I didn't care about. I nodded and pretended to listen, until eventually, he allowed me to leave.

Whistling, I marched out of the place as a free man.

Primus Bob was waiting in the lobby. He had lined up a large group of hogs—a full squad in fact—just outside the office door.

These portly gentlemen had guns raised. They were aiming at my chest as I exited the consul's chambers.

I feigned surprise, threw my hands high, and tried to look as stupid and guilty as possible.

With thirsty excitement, they swarmed me. I was arrested and cuffed. They were about to hustle me down to the detention levels for a brutal execution. Possibly, they intended permanent storage in the Vault of the Forgotten.

But then, at the last moment, Wurtenberger stepped out of his office.

"You were given no orders to perform this arrest, Primus," he said. "Release him."

"But, Consul…" Bob said, "sir, I thought we'd decided..."

"My decision has changed. Release him—and find that Saurian!"

Bob scrambled to obey.

The hogs melted away from me, taking only long enough to snap the cuffs off my wrists.

I thumbed my nose to all of them and marched out of the place before anyone could change their mind.

## -40-

Along with countless flaws, I do have a few gifts. One of them was an inborn awareness that told me when it was time to get out of town.

Accordingly, the moment that my demobilization orders came through, I stood up from my stool at a local bar and grill. I slammed down my beer, dropped a half-eaten sandwich, and paid the bill.

The bar was immediately adjacent to the sky-train station. As I'd already purchased a ticket, I boarded the first train down to Georgia Sector. I walked the aisles until I found an unassigned seat and squatted there. Within minutes, I was snoring all the way down the coast to home.

My folks were there when I reached the farm. They greeted me heartily.

To my mild disappointment, I found that Etta and her new husband, Derek, had long since fled the coop.

This wasn't really surprising. What newlyweds wanted to live with a couple of old farts on a farm in a swamp? Not these two, that's for certain.

After their honeymoon cruise, they'd gathered together all the money they'd gotten in cards at the wedding, packed up their stuff, and shipped out to Dust World. That had been something like six months ago.

I was mildly disappointed, but at least I was going to be allowed a certain amount of peace and comfort. Maybe Etta and Derek could tough it out on Dust World. It was a harsh, but viable option for kids with no cash and no record of serious accomplishments.

Hegemony wanted people to emigrate to her worst planets. Every colonist who decided to dare those grim deserts were allotted a small monthly stipend of credits. It was a homesteading program of sorts.

There'd never been a lot of takers, mind you. But Etta and Derek had decided to go for it.

I wasn't inclined to give any of that too much thought, but my mother certainly was. She went on and on about the decision, how foolhardy it was, and how terrible it would be if her own great-grandchildren were swallowed up by some vicious alien on a nasty planet.

I nursed a beer, making sympathetic noises every now and then. I pretended to listen for about an hour.

When I figured I'd done my duty as a thoughtful son, I excused myself and headed out to my shack. There, I fell asleep luxuriously on my somewhat moldy blankets. I made a mental note to wash all the sheets and blow all the dust out of the place in the morning.

Sometime before dawn, however, there was a tapping at my door. One would think that I had no cause for paranoia, but that might be because you haven't died several hundred times yet.

I came awake with a snort and a gun in my hand. I padded to the door, wearing nothing but underpants and a frown. I threw it open and peered outside into the purply, pre-dawn gloom.

It wasn't until I flipped on the light that I recognized the small form on my doorstep.

"Galina?"

"Yes," she said, "I hope you're not disappointed."

"No, not at all."

"Are you at least alone then…?" she asked.

"Of course, I'm alone girl!" I said. I was very glad I'd been a bit too tuckered out to go down to Waycross and pick anybody up the night before. That would have made an awkward reunion.

As she slipped inside, she wrinkled her nose at the state of my dusty and musty shack. She reminded me then of our agreement. She'd promised to accompany me and, in fact, pay for a cruise through the Caribbean.

"Oh, yeah," I said. "You do owe me one, don't you, girl?"

Galina smiled faintly, but she kept casting her eyes downward as she spoke. This set off certain alarm bells inside my thick skull. After all, I knew Galina extremely well. She wasn't the shy and demure type. She never had been.

If she was looking down and acting rather sheepish, that meant that she'd done something bad—or she was about to.

"Uh…" I said, "listen here, girl, have you bought the tickets yet? What's going to be our first port of call?"

I put my best "kid going to the candy store look" on my face.

She glanced up at me and then down again.

"Well…" she said, "there's going to be a slight delay."

"Oh, come on," I said. "I did my part! Hell, I did it like eight months ago. What's the holdup now?"

She dared to look up again. She gave me a little smile. "I need one more favor, James. An important one."

"Oh, geez. I found Drusus for you, right?"

"Yes. I confirmed that what you said was correct. My father did spirit him away. He is, in fact, imprisoned at my father's compound in Moldavia."

"Okay," I said, shrugging, "at least I know where he is. He's in good hands and—"

"No," she said firmly. "He's not. And I want to do something about it."

I stared at her, and she stared back.

Gone were those little downward glances. Gone was all the guilt in her eyes. She was flat-out scheming again.

"Can't we just go on the cruise? You can talk to me about it while we're having fun."

She shook her head. "I'll take you on that cruise—and it'll be better than I promised."

I wonder just how that could be possible. My mind began wandering off into different directions.

It'd been many weeks since I'd had a woman of any kind in my bed. Galina was one of the finest looking ladies of my entire lifetime.

I thought about reaching out a hand, putting it over hers. But I knew she'd only pull back. She hadn't yet committed to being my girlfriend again. Like most women, you had to kind of sneak up on these things before you could take all the sugar in the sugar bowl.

"What exactly do you have in mind?" I asked.

"I want to help Drusus," she said.

I blinked a couple of times. "Help him like… how? Like go over there and put some fresh water in his tank, or something?"

"He's not a goldfish, James."

"I know he's not," I admitted.

"Why do you care so little? I thought you'd be dying to go out there and break him out."

"Break him out? What do you mean break him out?"

"The way you did with Boudicca," she said.

"Yeah, well, that was in a bunker in my own backyard. And it took me months to do it even then."

She cast her eyes down again. Surprisingly, she was frowning. Her fingers entwined one another.

"Maybe this is useless," she said.

Galina moved as if to leave. My hand shot out and clasped both of hers.

"Hold on a minute, girl. Have you even got a plan for pulling this off?"

She paused and smiled at me. That was the first real smile I'd gotten this whole visit. It was a quiet thing, and it was a little bit evil. But I was willing to take it right now. After all, I was kind of thirsting.

"I *do* have a plan," she said. "But I need your help to pull it off."

"Ah, geez…" I said. "What are we going to do if we do break him out?"

"The same as we did last time."

"Uh…" I said. I gaped at her for several seconds, not comprehending. But then I got it.

"What? Are you serious? You want to take him back to Dust World and have the Investigator do a ghetto-revive on him?"

"Yes," she said. "That's exactly what I want."

"Damn, woman… you're crazy. Taking something out of a bunker on my back-forty, that's one thing. But going into Alexander Turov's castle and stealing one of his prisoners? That's just plumb crazy."

She pouted a little bit. "So, you don't want to do it?"

"Of course, I want to do it. I just don't think it's possible. I certainly don't want to pay the price that I'm going to have to pay when it's over."

"You won't," she said. "It'll be me. I'll be the one my father will blame for this."

I laughed. "I don't believe that for a second."

She pouted again. I'd called her bluff. We both knew that when any father had the opportunity to blame his own weaselly daughter, or a true buffoon of a man who he hated mildly to begin with, well, the choice was preordained.

"I think we have a moral obligation to free Drusus," she insisted.

"We sure as hell do," I said. "But since when did you care about any moral obligations?"

She pouted some more. "I did come back here to see you."

"You sure did. But now you're scamming me."

"What do you mean scamming you?"

"I was supposed to get a nice cruise and a bed warmed by the prettiest girl on planet Earth."

Galina gave me a tiny fluttering smile at this compliment.

"But instead, I'm getting an impossible mission with certain perming at the end. I didn't sign up for any of that."

She heaved a sigh and, still without raising her eyes, she pushed me lightly. I let her do it, and I sat upon my couch. She sat upon my lap.

This was a surprise. Even more surprising was when she began kissing on me. I was so surprised and so dumb that I just let her do it for a while. Finally, I responded and began to run my hands over her and kiss her more deeply. I was losing it when she pulled away.

"Let's spend the night together tonight," she said. "Then, we'll talk about Drusus more in the morning."

That was it. That was her trap—and I knew it, too. Don't think I didn't.

But I was a weak man, so I fell for it. I almost always did.

We had a glorious night together on those musty, crusty sheets—and we didn't do a whole lot of sleeping, I have to confess.

In the morning she showed me where she'd landed her aircar. It was out in the bog between some bald cypress trees.

She loaded my duffel in the trunk, then stuffed a big, half-retarded ape of a man into her passenger seat. When she lifted off, I felt like I was being abducted.

And perhaps, in a way, I was.

## -41-

By the time we arrived at her ancestral home in Moldavia, Galina had me wrapped firmly around her thumb. I would have said fingers, but her fingers were much too small and delicate for the likes of me.

She brought me to the castle-like Turov estate, and I soon learned all her family members were out of town. This couldn't have been a coincidence... it was probably well-timed by Galina.

Her father was off at some important off-world conference. Her crazy sister, who I'd kind of been looking forward to laying eyes upon again, wasn't even on the continent. As a full-fledged daughter of the house, she had the run of the place—especially when no one else of greater status was around to countermand anything she told the staff.

The first thing she did was give me a grand tour of the place. She brought with her a bulky purse—a bag so uncharacteristically huge she had to put two straps over her shoulder.

That purse had me frowning. Galina was the kind of woman who never had a purse large enough to even put a man's wallet inside of, much less anything useful.

Was she really going to try to stuff Drusus' brain in there? It just didn't seem possible. I shrugged, deciding I didn't really care what her harebrained scheme turned out to be.

The tour was deadly-dull. After going through something like seventeen boring-ass rooms full of original pieces of art from long-dead European guys, she showed me a collection of rugs. That's right, freaking rugs. Some poor saps back in the middle ages, or something like that, had spent lifetimes sewing these together with their bare hands like animals. It made me wince just to think about it.

At last, she led me to her father's study. I was pretty damned certain we weren't supposed to be in here, but I wasn't going to say anything about it.

Galina poured me some of her father's best hundred-year-old brandy. The stuff tasted smooth, but it didn't seem to be worth a thousand credits a sip to me.

I gulped rather than sipped, and I watched her as she did a little slinky walk around the room. The entire time she did so, she kept up a steady wall of prattle, talking about every artifact in the place as if I gave a shit—which of course I didn't.

But I'd long ago learned to let a woman talk as much as she wants to, as long as she's giving you sugar at night. I smiled, nodded, gulped her daddy's brandy, and watched her fine form as she moved from one place to another.

At last, I began to realize she must be searching the place.

"Uh... what are you looking for, exactly?"

"Shh," she said, hissing at me.

She gave me no answer, but instead continued to tell me about some kind of weird statue that looked like a flock of angels with intertwined wings and was apparently made of hammered gold. Why anyone would take the time to hammer a statue out of gold when you could just fire it right out of a replicator and spray-paint it in a jiffy? That kind of thinking was beyond me—but then again, I was no art connoisseur.

Finally, she began rattling around at her father's desk. She made a small exclamation and stopped prattling nonsense.

I walked over to where she was digging in the bottom drawer. She came up with something.

It was a key. Not your run-of-the-mill normal, earthly key, mind you. It was, in fact, a Galactic Key.

"Ooooh, look at that," I said. "I didn't know your daddy had one of those."

"He doesn't."

"But that just came out of his desk, didn't it?" I asked, befuddled.

"Yes, you idiot. He confiscated it last year."

"He did?"

"Yes. He was displeased about my... disappearance."

I thought about that, and I realized her dad probably was pissed at her. He'd wanted her to become the consul of Earth, not that fat-boy Wurtenberger. He'd probably taken the key to clip her wings.

Right then and there, I began to wonder a bit about Galina's motivations. Was she really in this adventure to help Drusus, or to help herself? My brain didn't spend much time puzzling on the topic, however... because the answer was obvious, even to me.

"So that's what you've been looking for..." I said.

"It's my property, James. Don't judge."

I shrugged, spread my hands wide, and shook my head. Who the hell was I to decide which of the Turovs had taken the Key from whom? After all, I'd been the original owner, and Claver before that. Who knew where he'd gotten it? Probably from a dead Mogwa somewhere.

Galina left the study then, and I followed in her wake. We began a long, circuitous route through the palatial residence. Every now and then, a guard spotted us. Galina did a little flirting, a little bit of hand-waving, and made up a few lies on each of these occasions.

The guards always seemed to fall for it, nodding and allowing her to pass. Maybe they didn't believe her, but they sure didn't have the balls to argue with a mistress of the house.

At last, we finally made it to a chamber which was full of illegal hardware.

"Wow, look at this junk!" I said, fondling a device. "You know what this thing is? It's a disintegrator. I haven't seen one of these since I booby-trapped the one Xlur had out at Trantor."

"Shut up," she said. "The walls might be listening."

I stopped and mumbled to myself a bit. I whistled as I admired and fondled the disintegrator.

It was a weapon of extreme effectiveness and, in fact, viciousness. It was designed to turn any physical body into a pile of ash, dismantling organic molecules by switching off whatever they called the force that held the atoms together.

The nasty part happened after the victim was a puddle on the floor. The disintegrator went further. It erased the victim from local datacores all across the galaxy, making sure that the individual who had been shot by it could never be reconstituted into a living being again.

I figured this sort of thing wouldn't work on a Claver, but it had once worked on a Mogwa named Xlur.

"Maybe we should take this with us?" I suggested.

"No, don't touch anything. Don't take anything. Come on, over here."

She opened some lockers, and she pulled out... Two teleport harnesses?

"Uh-oh," I said. "I don't even want to know what these are for."

"This is how we're going to escape the building," she said.

"Yeah... I kind of figured that much." I thumbed the two harnesses. "Do you know what these things are aimed at?"

"No," she said, "and I don't care."

She applied the Galactic Key to the harnesses, twiddled some of the coordinate values, and then handed me one. She put on the other.

I frowned. "Those coordinates don't seem to be quite the same."

"They aren't," she said. "Be glad."

I wasn't glad about it. I didn't want to be separated from her after this heinous action was done. Whatever it was she was planning, I was sure I was going to earn her attentions ten times over.

Growing increasingly reluctant, I followed her as we left the chamber with our stolen booty and headed down the hall to yet another secret location. This one, essentially, was a wall that didn't look like a wall. In fact, Galina simply walked into the wall and disappeared.

I couldn't believe it. I stood there, dumbfounded. "Where'd you go?"

"Come on," she said. "Just walk through it."

I stepped forward, stumbling and putting my hand into thin air. The wall seemed to swallow up my hand as it passed into it.

The experience was kind of freaky. Wincing a bit and feeling nothing, I followed her into the wall. I didn't even feel the soap bubbly push you felt when you went through a force field, or the bug-zapper sensation you felt when you walked through a pair of gateway posts.

Two steps later, I'd walked through the illusory wall and come out on the other side.

"What kind of sorcery is this?"

"I'm surprised you haven't thought of it before," she said. "It's simple. Two illusion boxes are set up in an opening. Remember the ones Claver used back on Tech World originally? Instead of clothing or faces, they project a field that looks exactly like the wall around them. Even though it's just a corridor, no one can see it."

I marveled at that idea. I'd never thought of it myself. Sure, you could put one of these illusion boxes on yourself, and you could change your outward appearance to be whatever you wanted. It was probably even easier to make a fake wall with the projection field.

"Huh…" I said. "That's pretty cool."

Galina yanked my hand, and I walked obediently after her, even though I could barely feel the tug of her small fingers. She led me down a twisted passageway that seemed to go down and down under the ground. We passed many stairways, all made of stone and increasingly ancient and dank in nature. I began to get the feeling we were going down into the dungeon that was underneath this castle—the place her father had long since called his home.

"How old is this place?" I said.

"Fourteen centuries," she replied. "At least the foundations are that old. It's been rebuilt, expanded upon, altered, refurbished… But down here, down at the very lowest levels, that's where it gets interesting."

Eventually, we found our way to a series of vaults. There was no one down here.

"No guards? No nothing?" I said.

"No one dares come down here. No one except for my father himself. Maybe he occasionally brings one of his most trustworthy guardsmen—but they sure as hell don't come down here when he's not home."

"Hmm..."

She opened a door with the Galactic Key. It sprang open and swung with a loud groaning creak. It was so loud that I wondered if they could hear it all the way back up in the castle above.

Inside, the dungeon cell was full of bubbling tanks. There were rows of them. Each had a brain floating within. None of them were labeled.

The brains were quiet, unlike those I'd met in the Vault of the Forgotten. Maybe these poor bastards weren't even hooked up to microphones and speakers.

Whatever the case, the place gave me the willies. The soft blue light shimmered with the bubbles in the tanks. The effect was haunting.

I'd been to places like this before—mostly underneath Central. I'd always found the light to be eerie and almost ghostly in nature.

"How can we figure out which one's Drusus?" I whispered loudly.

Galina shone a light from her tapper. She ran this bright beam over the various shelves. She drew her finger from each glass container to the edge of the shelf. Each time she did so, she made a visible line in the dust. It was like she was dragging her finger across a tram's dirty hood.

At last, she found a jar that wasn't surrounded by undisturbed dust. She dragged her finger around it completely, just to make sure.

"This one," she said, "it's the only one that's fresh."

I thought about that, and I figured it had to be true. The rest of them had probably been sitting down here for years.

What a lonely way to live—or rather, to *exist*. Because this was certainly not living.

"What are we going to do? Just grab the brain?"

Galina was already unscrewing hoses in the back. She unplugged the jar, and liquids gushed. Fluids ran over the floor, until she managed to seal off all the valves and stopped cursing. "So disgusting..."

Once she had disconnected the jar from the life support systems, she turned to me. "Pick it up."

I did as she asked, curling my lip. The jar was kind of... sticky. "Awww... nasty..."

Galina was already adjusting the fit on her teleport harness.

"Hey... That's it? Where are we going to meet up again?"

"Later. Don't worry about it."

But I was worried. I was worried plenty. "Where am I going?"

"You're going to go to Dust World. You're going to get Drusus a new body. That's all you've got to worry about. I'll catch up with you later."

"Ah, jeez..."

Before I got a sweet kiss goodbye or gave her tight butt a final squeeze, she began flashing blue and disappeared.

I gaped in the dark. Here I was, standing around alone at the bottom of a dungeon in Eastern Europe.

In my fool hands was a bubbling tank. Drusus was in there, looking like a gray lump of death to me.

I considered trying to return him to his shelf. I'm not proud of it, but there it was. I felt kind of cheated and my only urge was to get the hell out of there, pronto.

But Drusus' tank had already been disconnected. That, I realized right there, was sheer evil on her part. As it was, Drusus only had so long to live. His brain was floating, but off life support.

How long could the oxygenated fluids in that tank keep him alive? Surely, he would starve or drown or something if I didn't get him help soon.

If I connected him back up, it might not work. If I chose to simply teleport out without the tank... Well, I would probably kill poor Drusus.

Had all this been part of Galina's plan? I suspected that it had been.

I really had no choice. I had to take him to Dust World, just like she'd planned.

I cursed that woman's name, and I cursed my foolishness. Her delicate form, combined with my own dumbass, monkey-brained nature, had gotten me into this. I'd fallen for all of her wiles.

Here I was, doing her dirty work. Stealing something from the holiest of holies inside her own father's castle—and for what? All I'd gotten was a couple of nights of fun out of it.

What an idiot I was.

With a big sigh, I juggled the tank with one hand, and I pushed the button on my harness.

## -42-

Zeta Herculis was a double-star system. That meant Dust World had two suns in the sky, keeping the planet bright and hot most of the time. Due to the overwhelming heat, life could only exist in deep chasms in the surface.

When I teleported in, I found myself deep within one of those crater-like canyons. This one was a kilometer or more deep, and it was actually an ancient caldera of a volcano everyone dearly hoped was extinct.

In the center of the crater was a deep, cold lake. The water occasionally farted up foul fumes and was surrounded by swampy turf and strange waxy plants. Every time I came out here, I had to wonder why anyone had ever wanted to colonize this planet in the first place.

Normally, I used gateway posts to go to Dust World. These days, those posts were guarded by hogs, one of whom had managed to marry my daughter, Etta. But today was different. When I arrived via teleport harness, I didn't immediately recognize my surroundings.

For one panicky moment, I was concerned I was not in the right valley, the one where Etta's family had lived since the initial colony ship had arrived more than a century ago.

I was confused by the foliage. It was all wrong. Instead of large flowering plants with waxy leaves and even more waxy, skull-sized petals, there was a forest of sorts.

I blinked and gawked in surprise. These trees—and yes, they were trees. Even a xeno-botanist couldn't have denied it.

The trees had true leaves. They were gigantic, far bigger than anything I'd ever seen on Dust World before. If I hadn't known better, I'd have thought they were megaflora.

When the hell had I last seen such growths—out at Death World?

I stood there, staring all around myself, mouth agape.

These trees did look like those on Death World—but they were... *different*. Death World's giga-growths sometimes reached more than a kilometer in the air. That planet had trees so big they could pierce the clouds above.

If there had been such a growth so large in this secluded valley on Dust World, the crown would have reached all the way above the rim of the crater, probably burning it in the endless light of the two suns.

There was only one way such growths could have come here so fast, so unnoticed. The Wur must have come.

I hadn't yet wanted to put that label on this forest, but that's what I'd been thinking about as soon as I saw these trees.

Walking around, I examined the trunks and the leaves. Hmm...

I was no expert, but these growths weren't quite the same... they just didn't look right.

They were big, yes. They were green, sure. They didn't match the normal growth patterns of anything on Dust World. But I couldn't say they looked exactly like what I'd seen before on Death World and Storm World, either.

*What the hell were these things, and where had they come from?*

The answer struck through, assaulting my dull brain within moments of having all these disconnected thoughts.

There was only one reasonable solution to this mystery, and he had a name. They called him: the Investigator.

Who else on this distant, low population planet could have performed such an abomination of horticulture and probably altered botanical genetics to have created such massive growths?

I gave my head a shake, and I worked my tapper. It spun for a long time but eventually caught a signal that helped clue me into the direction of a village.

Marching through the forested area, I reached the tiny town before darkness fell.

I'd been here before, so I knew the place. I headed for their single tavern, and what I found there was beyond strange.

Instead of the usual pack of local, dusty inhabitants who were by no means either trustworthy or outgoing in their natures, I found a big pack of the clones.

Virtually everyone in the place, in fact, was a shirtless wonder clothed only in leather pants, and carrying nothing but a large dagger.

They all looked alike, and they were all looking at me when I walked into the place and set Drusus' brain-jar on the dirty tile floor.

The people serving the clones were normal Dust Worlders, at least. I'd seen some of them before. None of them said anything to me, but their eyes did widen in surprise at the sight of an outworlder.

"Hey," I said loudly, "did you people know there's... like... a big alien forest growing just a stone's throw away?"

No one answered me. That didn't surprise me much. The weirdos with the knives and the bare chests, they rarely spoke to anyone, and the people running the place looked afraid to speak.

That fearful look—that was unusual. Dust Worlders were tough people. They feared almost nothing.

But now, I sensed things were different out here. Things had become... strange.

"Uh..." I said when no one spoke, "I'm looking for the Investigator. Which one of you jokers will take me out there to talk to him?"

No one moved for several seconds. Then at last, one of the clones stood up. He walked near me and pointed at the knife on my belt.

I grinned at him. "I'm not buying an escort service with my knife, if that's what you're hinting about. You'd have to be a way lot prettier to get me to go for that bargain."

The Dust Worlder again pointed at my knife. I just shook my head and told him, "Uh-uh."

Frowning, he drew his own blade. I considered this to be the prelude to a possible attack.

As I was outnumbered something like twenty to one by clones, my mind told me it was best to act first and to act decisively.

I drew my blade in one smooth motion, almost as fast as he could lift his between us. As a matter of courtesy, just in case there was a misunderstanding going on here and he wasn't attempting to gut me, I didn't slash open his belly and spill his intestines all over the barroom floor. No, sir.

I slashed higher instead, cutting into his knife with mine. My weapon had a molecularly-aligned edge. It was as hard as diamond and sharper than glass. I sliced through the nice normal steel of his weapon.

His blade clattered on the stones between us, chopped off at the midpoint. He looked down at it, somewhat dumbfounded.

Without seeming to take offense, he turned and began to walk out of the place. So far, he hadn't spoken a word, and neither had any of the others. I saw among them, though, they were whispering, mumbling. It seemed to me when I'd dealt with these freaks in the past, they'd never spoke above a whisper, and they only talked to their own kind.

The man whose blade I'd cut in half beckoned with a finger. Giving a shrug, I picked up Drusus in his sloshing jar and followed him.

I took care to glance back now and then. I half-expected the rest to charge after me—but they didn't. So, I tucked my own blade back into its sheath and followed him.

Had I proven to him that I was an outworlder since I wielded such a blade? Or had I demonstrated I was a man worthy of keeping my fine weapon, and that he couldn't rob me of it?

I had no idea what this dude was thinking. But as no one was attacking me, and I was being offered an unarmed guide I knew I could defeat, I followed.

The sunshine was blinding, but it felt good to be outside in the bright sunlight again. Mind you, when I say sunlight, I'm not talking about the full blasting, double-barreled radiation of Dust World's twin suns. No, things weren't that bad.

Dust World's twin suns were bad enough to require some level of shade to be comfortable. We were down in a hole, essentially, more than a kilometer from the scorched surface. The reflected light that came down from the deserts above was more than enough. The two suns sent beams striking the cliff face to the north, which then bounced down to the depths of the valley.

Down here, it was relatively cool, but the light was still bright enough to make a man squint. An Earthman like myself wasn't used to the savagery of two hot stars in one sky.

I followed the clone, making sure to keep a pace or two back. That was partly because I was worried about an ambush, and partly because I didn't want to step anywhere his foot avoided. There were a lot of deadfalls and traps out here in the wilds of Dust World.

There was also the plain fact that he didn't smell too good. I was pretty sure nobody on Dust World had ever even heard of deodorant, and they didn't bathe too often, seeing as water was a rare and precious commodity in any desert clime.

I counted two thousand steps, then a thousand more. My tapper wasn't working again. It spun, not catching a signal—but that was pretty normal on Dust World. Lack of a proper grid was one of the reasons that so many desperados came here to hide.

The sloshing jar that held Drusus seemed to be intact and watertight, at least. I tried to be careful, to make sure he wasn't bouncing off the walls of the tank and bruising delicate tissues.

I had a few concerns that if and when I caught him a revive, Drusus would be reborn as a man plagued by strokes and aneurysms. I shrugged at that thought. What could I do? I was pretty much the only hope he had. I had to trust the luck.

After nearly four thousand steps—and yes, I was still counting—we reached a gloomy cave. This was a spot I recognized, but normally the area was blasted with sunshine.

The arched entrance was sandstone and granite. Deep within the gloom behind the archway were thousands of apartments. There were also galleries, meeting areas—an entire underground city long since abandoned.

What was different about the entrance was the new growth. It was now surrounded by vines and greenery. It was so bizarre to see that. Curious, I poked at a few waxy leaves of a large firm plant. The leaves seemed to squirm slightly at my touch.

Originally, this habitation had been drilled and blasted into the cliffside for the inhabitants of Dust World. The colonists had survived here for over a century on their own. Most of that time, they'd spent cut off from Earth. They'd found these walls comforting, I'm sure. They'd helped protect them from the squids and the brilliant beams of light above.

A brown hand, burnt by the sun, reached out and touched my wrist. I flinched, ready to grab my dagger again, but stopped myself. It was only my guide.

He caught my eyes and shook his head. The message was clear. I shouldn't be touching these plants. I shrugged and nodded to him reassuringly.

Maybe they were poisonous. Maybe I'd already infected myself with some alien toxin. Whatever. I wiped my hand on my pants and followed him into the tunnels.

He led me to the lab chambers that I'd known in the past. These were lonely spots deep within the stone walls of the valley.

No one came here anymore. No one except the Investigator and his followers.

And there he was: tall, lanky, and muscular. Ropey veins stood out on every limb.

"Ah," he said. His voice was strange and sonorous. "McGill, is it? How odd to receive a visitor at this time…"

"Well, hello, Mr. Investigator," I said, putting on a cheery tone.

"How is it that you have found me once again, McGill?" he asked.

I glanced over my shoulder, about to say that I'd followed the guidance of one knifeless local, but that man had already disappeared.

"Uh…" I said, "aren't you always down here, sir? In these labs?"

"Not always. I've been busy on the surface of late."

I blinked, thinking of the greenery. "Uh… I couldn't help but notice there were a few more plants outside…"

"Ah, you noticed that, did you?" He sounded amused.

"I could hardly see anything else. Are you engaged in some kind of grand terraforming effort?"

"In a manner of speaking, yes. However, I've noticed you're carrying a specimen. May I ask who it is in that jar?"

He pointed at Drusus, floating helplessly in his disconnected tank. At this point, the hanging ganglia and the drifting eyeballs were all drooping. He looked like a flower who had been cut from the stem a week ago. Drusus was beginning to wilt.

"Yeah," I said, "this is a friend of mine. Is there any chance you could hook him up and keep him alive?"

The Investigator approached. He took the jar from me. He fussed over it and muttered to himself. I heard the words "moron" and "arrogant fool" more than once.

Working with decisive movements, he connected the tubes up. Water flowed, then bubbled. There was even an under-light of faint blue.

"Will he live, sir?" I asked.

"He, is it? Yes, he should survive. But permanent damage is still a possibility. He had only a few hours left by the time you brought him here. Why did you take so long to reach me?"

"Well, there's this new jungle out front, see. I had to go get a guide."

"Ah yes, yes," said the Investigator, losing interest. He kept toying with the jar. "You still haven't answered my primary question, McGill."

"Uh…" I said, "and what was that again, Mr. Investigator, sir?"

"Who. Is. This?" He indicated the jar with a long knobby finger.

"Oh, right…"

I was beginning to scratch at my back. It occurred to me that the last time I'd been out here, I'd dealt with Boudicca. She wasn't overly fond of hogs. In fact, she was especially unfond of high-level members of Hegemony like Drusus, who'd previously been a consul. Although he'd been deposed, his rank was well-known.

I considered a half dozen lies over the next half dozen seconds. During this time, the Investigator watched me scratch at my collar, eye the ceiling, and generally appear dumbfounded. He crossed his arms. "You can't ask me to believe that you're uncertain as to the identity of this person in the jar? Who would steal such a thing from the Vault of the Forgotten and then transport it without such certain knowledge?"

"Whoa! I didn't steal the jar, sir—and I didn't get it from the Vault of the Forgotten, either." These were, of course, half-truths, but I spoke them with great conviction.

The Investigator squinted at me and blinked a couple of times. He, perhaps only second to my father, was an expert at deciphering my innumerable lies.

"All right," he said. "You've piqued my curiosity. I will accept this companion of yours. I will keep him—and we are correct in calling this specimen 'him', right?"

"Yes, that's right, sir."

"Very well... I will keep him alive. I may even grow him a new body from his DNA. Something suitable to house this brain..."

He tapped idly on the glass.

I grinned. "That would be mighty nice of you, sir."

"I'll do this service to solve the mystery you've posed today. Was that your intent?"

"Uh... not exactly. I just think he might do better if he was... incognito."

The Investigator gave me a sharp look. "I do hope this isn't Imperator Galina Turov..."

I shook my head vigorously. "No, sir! I wouldn't bring her back here. Not after last time!"

"Good," he said. "Boudicca doesn't get along with that woman."

"They're probably too much alike."

At this, the Investigator smiled, and there was even a faint laugh. That was a very rare sound to come out of his throat.

"Possibly you're right about that," he said. "But in any case, McGill, I accept this challenge, and I will ask you no more about it for now."

"Thank you, sir. I think that's for the best. Now, could I get a little help with my harness? It kind of needs a recharge... plus, maybe some new destination coordinates..."

"Where is it you'd like to go?"

"Earth, of course."

"Of course. For a man who's visited so many star systems, you are remarkably attached to that one squalid planet."

"That I am, sir. That I am."

He fooled around charging my harness and tinkered with the coordinates. Soon, he'd zeroed in on Earth.

"I'm surprised you've not asked me certain other questions," he said as he worked.

"Huh? Oh, right. I heard Etta and Derek came out here. Is that right?"

He nodded.

"Are they somewhere in this cave? I'd like to see them before I leave."

He shook his head. "No," he said, "they have moved on."

"Moved on to where?"

"To another valley."

"Uh... why?" I asked. "This is where Etta grew up."

"That's true. But most of the original colonists have... moved on."

I thought about that. My mouth fell open again, but I didn't speak. I realized then that I'd seen very few Dust Worlders so far on this visit. In fact, I was mostly seeing Boudicca's weirdo clone henchmen plus a lot of giant plants—and not much else.

"Has this place been taken over by Boudicca and her brood?"

"You could say that," he said.

"Why haven't you cleared out, then?"

He smiled at me.

Another smile? So odd.

"I am not so easy to dislodge from wherever it is I wish to be."

I knew that was for damned sure. This guy had withstood countless attacks from the squids with their Blood Worlder troops. Then, once Earth had arrived, all of Legion Varus couldn't pry him out of these cliffs. Since then, quite a number of others had tried, but all had failed.

"Okay," I said. "So, you figured it was too dangerous for Etta and her new hubby, is that right? And you sent them somewhere else—somewhere less weird?"

He nodded sagely.

"Can you tell me where that might be, sir?"

He pulled a map up on a table computer and gave me the coordinates. It was one of the other eleven major valleys that served as colonial outposts here on Dust World.

"One last thing, sir," I said. "This place is getting kind of freaky. What exactly is Boudicca planning to do with all these damn plants?"

"That is privileged information, McGill."

"Look," I said, reaching out a hand and touching him on the shoulder.

He looked at that hand, and he did not welcome my large fingers gripping his arm. He could have shook off most men, as he was a powerfully-built individual himself, but he knew from experience that he could never dislodge my grip from his body. So, he didn't try.

"I know what those plants are," I said. "I recognize them. They're from Death World. Something weird is going on out here... and you've got to be involved in it, sir."

"I'd rather not discuss it."

I nodded, but I didn't let go of him. "Somehow, you guys are involved in... What? The hybridization of alien plants? Something in-between the Wur and the local flora of Dust World?"

This statement made him eye me with surprise.

"As always, you confuse me, McGill," he said. "One moment you seem more ignorant and slow-witted than the lowest colonist on this planet—but the next you seem relatively quick of mind."

I let go of him, and I nodded.

"It's all a matter of priorities, Mr. Investigator, sir," I said. "Right now, I'm sensing severe danger to my daughter and her new husband—not to mention you and Floramel. You're all caught up in the middle of something I don't understand."

"That is correct," he said, nodding. "You don't understand it, and you're not going to. I would recommend, in fact, that you don't even try. All will become clear in time."

That was pretty much all I could get out of him.

While we were talking, he took my harness off the charger and handed it to me. As I put it on, he fluffed it a bit here and there.

It was important to have a good tight fit on a teleport harness before a man generated a field and flew many lightyears. Any exposed bits, anything that somehow strayed outside the field, was normally burned away to ash. It wouldn't do to return to Earth and arrive with a few toes missing.

"Should I come back in six weeks?" I asked him.

"Whatever for?" he replied.

I pointed at the jar, which was now bubbling, and the brain within it seemed to be floating a bit higher than before. "Because of my friend. I want to see how you've done with the revival process."

"Ah," he said. "No, McGill. Don't call us, we'll call you."

"What?"

I didn't really understand his reference, but the Investigator seemed to find it amusing.

Again, it was odd to me that he had a sense of humor at all. He'd never really had one before. But as I was puzzling over this, he reached out one of those long knobby fingers and stabbed the button in the middle of my harness.

I reached out to grip him, thinking about either dragging him with me or trying to rip the harness off.

In the end, I did neither. If I'd held onto the guy, I would have doomed him over the long jump. I was certain of that. On the other hand, if I attempted to get the harness off, it might only be *half* off, which would be very detrimental to me as I probably would arrive in a half-charred state. Even if I *did* manage to get it off before the effect took hold of my body and

I vanished, well, then I'd be stuck here without a teleport harness at all.

Then the few fleeting seconds during which I could have taken one of these choices passed by, and I disappeared from Dust World.

## -43-

Whatever else you might say about the Investigator, he was technically competent in just about any field you might imagine. He was a medical doctor, a scientist, a physicist, and God knew what else.

In any case, he'd landed me not just upon Earth, but in my own front yard. I found myself standing in front of my private shack in Georgia Sector.

That was alarming. How had he known the exact coordinates of this location on a planet so far away? How had he managed to get it to target this spot so precisely?

It seemed odd to me. It also worried me that anyone knew these coordinates. Hell, some joker could have sent a bomb right here, and you wouldn't even need to use a fusion warhead. Just about anything would do the trick. Everything from here all the way to Waycross would go up in a flash.

I gave my head a shake, trying to rid myself of such paranoid worries. In some ways, in modern society, we all lived at the sufferance of those around us.

At least I'd delivered Drusus, and as far as I knew, he was still alive. With any luck, the Investigator would grow him a new body to match that brain. Dust World was one of the few places that could pull off such a thing in secret. Drusus should be relatively safe until he crept out from under that rock and alerted someone in authority to his escape.

I had to wonder how life was going to go for old Drusus now. He'd fallen so far and so hard from grace. He'd been on top of the world—literally. Now, after having abdicated his position in front of the Ruling Council, he'd been immediately tried and executed. Worse, he'd been cast into purgatory.

I wondered if he'd even remember spending years as a brain floating in a tank. For his sake, I kind of hoped he didn't.

His fate gave me a little shudder, I don't mind telling you. As a Varus man who'd died hundreds of times, I didn't fear much—but spending years in one of those tanks... that wasn't on my bucket list. I hoped such a thing would never happen to me.

Right about then, I was jolted out of my reverie. I'd just stepped upon my creaking porch, my heavy tread causing it to groan in protest, when I noticed something was wrong.

I squinted at my dirty front windows. There was a faint light seeping out from under my ancient shades...

I normally never left a light burning in my shack—especially when I wasn't home. It would attract the bugs, and anyone who's lived in the swampy part of southern Georgia knows that you don't want that.

Staring at that sliver of yellow light, I froze. Had I already given myself away with these damned creaky boards? If someone was in there, someone possibly waiting inside with a gun, it was going to be very difficult to open the door and get the drop on them.

My tapper said the local time was 3:32 am. If someone was lying in wait for me, they'd probably been in there for a long time. I forced myself to breathe and took a moment to weigh my options.

I glanced over toward the main house where my parents slept. Their lights were all out, even the back porch light. Normally, they would keep that one light on at night if they knew I was out in my shack. If Etta or someone else had been out here, they would have kept it on for them, too, as a guiding light. They did that in case their guests came for help, or even just wanted to raid the fridge.

But the back porch light was out. That meant there were no guests out here—at least none my folks were aware of.

Still frowning, I turned my face back to my paint-peeled screen door. There was no way I could open that thing without causing a huge racket. I'd been meaning to oil the hinges and possibly replace the springs for years—but I'd never gotten around to it.

A few ideas came to mind. I could creep around to the back windows and peep inside. Or, I could make a loud noise and hope the intruder came out to investigate.

"Ah, fuck it," I said at last, discarding all these ideas. After all, it was three-thirty in the morning. If someone had been sitting here waiting for me—maybe for days—well, they probably weren't in a highly alert state. Therefore, I would rely upon speed and surprise rather than subtlety.

I stomped forward in a rush and threw back the screen door. With my other hand, almost at the same moment, I slammed a palm just above the doorknob, knocking it straight off the hinges.

The door crashed inward, and I heard a mechanical buzz and a rattling noise. It was a sound I'd heard before, so I froze.

"What the fuck?" said a small feminine voice from the dark interior.

Someone stirred on my couch, but I didn't dare move. I knew what I was facing. A small machine, no bigger than a stand-up sprinkler out in the yard, crouched at my feet. It squatted on my floor between the girl on my couch and my wide-open front door.

The machine in question was a small, automated gun turret—and I'd just pissed off its software something awful.

The thing clicked and whirred. It scanned me with infrared sensors.

I could see it, because the room wasn't entirely dark. If it had been, I probably would have marched inside and been shot to death.

The little robot had a tiny brain, which I knew was busy analyzing the situation. Right now, it was determining if I needed to die or not.

Fortunately, I hadn't dared to step all the way into the room. If I had, I would have been immediately showered by a spray of some fifty bullets.

I'd once seen Winslade get knocked to the floor and do a little dance of death when he'd set up one of these things in his office. It had mistaken him for an aggressor when he'd moved too quickly and decisively in its vicinity.

So, my eyes were moving, but not the rest of me. My hand was still frozen in the air, palm up, right where I'd knocked the door in. That meant it was intruding a few centimeters into the space of the shack.

This fact seemed to be intriguing the automated machine. It played a red light—a laser sight I'm sure—designed to help it aim with more accuracy. It hardly needed such a technical advantage, as it had the drop on me, and we were only about two meters apart. There was no way the frigging thing was going to miss if it decided to blast me.

"Who's there?" the girl said, and now I realized I knew her voice. I knew her lithe form, too, as she stood up from my couch and walked closer.

I didn't dare answer her. The tripod device on the floor was studying my hand, running its light over each of my fingers. It was deciding if it should blow any of them off. I thought about trying to back up and slip away off the porch, but I didn't think I would get away with it now.

The girl in my shack approached. She did so with a pistol in her hand—but then she recognized the oversized ape who was standing in the doorway, silhouetted by the stars outside. She straightened and put away her pistol. Her hands slid up to rest on her shapely hips.

"McGill?" she said. "Why are you breaking into your own house? Are you crazy?"

I didn't answer her. I didn't dare. My hands were still frozen in place in front of me. My eyes moved, but my head did not.

Galina stepped closer and flicked on another light. She was looking pretty good, I had to admit. She wasn't wearing much—a bra and panties, but nothing else.

I knew why she was in such a state of undress. It was summertime in Georgia, and my shack had never been the coolest place to sleep.

"Oh," she said. "I get it. You're standing there like a statue because of my little robot friend. Hmm. I almost like you like this. You're so quiet, so reasonable. For once, you're in complete control of yourself."

My face tightened in irritation, but I stayed where I was.

Galina smirked. "This is proof," she said, wagging a finger at me. She was turning into a Karen all of a sudden because she had me captive. "This is proof positive that you *can* control your impulses, James McGill. I will never again listen to excuses about your inner nature and your—"

"Turn it off," I said between clenched teeth like an amateur ventriloquist. I didn't dare do more than part my lips a tiny fraction.

Still, the machine between us reacted. She must have set its sensitivity slider to "highly vigilant." It's red aiming-laser was crawling around on my face. The laser shone on my mouth and reflected with a wet gleam off my tongue, which was pressing hard behind those clenched teeth.

"All right, all right," Galina said, "don't wet yourself." She stepped forward and pressed a single button on the top of the device.

It chattered, spun around once, and then collapsed upon the floor. It had put itself into sleep mode.

"I suppose that was the polite thing to do," she said. "After all, this is your house."

"Damn straight it is," I said. I walked in and picked up the device on the floor. I made sure it was completely switched off, then I flicked the safety on and rolled it under the couch.

"Don't do that," she said. "We might need it tonight."

I frowned at her. "Why's that?"

"I'm… I'm in a bit of trouble."

"What kind of trouble? And what the hell are you doing here at my place anyway, girl?"

"I'm meeting you like I said, remember?"

"Yes, yes, you did say you'd catch up with me later, but I don't think my parents even know you're staying back here, do they?"

Her eyes slid from side to side, avoiding mine.

"How long have you been hiding out here?" I asked.

"Not long, only since dark."

I pieced this all together and puzzled for a moment in my mind. "Did your daddy find out you ransacked his place?"

Galina pouted a bit, pushing out her lower lip and looking down at the floor. She gave me a tiny shrug. She looked for all the world like a kid who'd been caught with her hand in the cookie jar.

"He didn't buy all of your excuses, huh?" I asked.

"No, he was very mean. It's very unfair. It's disgusting, almost, that a father will not believe his own daughter."

"So... you're on the run?" I asked.

"Yes, I guess so."

"For how long?"

"Until he cools down and decides that something else is more important. At least until I become convinced that he's not sending assassins out here to get rid of me—or to put me in one of his brain jars."

It was my turn to frown at that idea. I really didn't like the thought of Galina's beautiful body being disposed of and keeping only the most evil part of her in a jar. That seemed like a crime beyond imagining. Talk about throwing away the good and keeping the bad...

I went over to my small fridge and opened it. I rummaged until I found two beers. I handed her one, but she rejected it.

Shrugging, I popped both open and began to guzzle. It'd been a long day, and I'd walked around Dust World for hours without revitalizing myself.

"Well," I said, "how's this going to work?"

"How's what going to work?"

"I'm talking about you hiding here at my place. Do you plan to stay for very long? Are you asking for my protection?"

Galina pouted a bit again. "You can't really protect me," she said. "If he sends one or two goons, sure, you could probably put them down. But really, my father, he's..."

"You can stay here, and you can hide," I said, "as long as you like. There's only one condition."

She pursed her lips and looked suspicious. "What condition? That we have to have sex?"

I laughed. "No, not that. I know you. We're going to be doing that, anyway."

She glared at me.

"I just want to make sure you're not going to snore or eat too much," I said.

She slapped me a good one. I laughed, caught her wrist, and pulled her down onto my lap.

She pouted a bit more, but she soon began to kiss on me. Not long after that, we became passionate.

By this time, I'd already figured out I wasn't getting my honeymoon cruise around the Caribbean. In fact, keeping her here and hiding her from her father might well get me brutally killed in the near future—but I'd always been a man who lived in the moment.

Right now, Galina was close and vital and wanting protection. How could I refuse her?

We made love until dawn, and then we slept till noon, when the growing heat drove us out of the place.

## THE END